THE BRINGER OF DEATH

A Thriller

MICHAEL MONAHAN

Copyright © 2017 by Michael Monahan
ISBN: 197641590X
ISBN 13: 9781976415906
Library of Congress Control Number: 2017914567
CreateSpace Independent Publishing Platform
North Charleston, South Carolina

PROLOGUE

FEDERALLY ADMINISTERED TRIBAL AREAS—PAKISTAN

Sadiq bin Aziz elegantly lowered himself into the spot designated for him on the threadbare rug that had been placed in the center of the windowless room and waited for his cue. At first glance, it would be easy to underestimate him. The wispy hair hastily retreating from a narrow and already elongated forehead only reinforced the fragility that his delicate frame suggested. A careful observer, however, would detect tenacity and unusual brilliance in the soft-brown eyes. But only one with access to the multiple numbered accounts he held around the world would appreciate the power of his darkness.

Aziz had arrived in the middling, remote mountain town with no intention of showing deference. The organization was failing, and these irresolute men arrayed before him had allowed it to happen despite his repeated warnings. After traveling at great personal danger to attend this meeting, he would leave with an answer. This time, either they would buy in to his plans or he would go it alone. As an impatient man, he preferred to move forward with them, if only initially. But, if there was any further dithering, he would use his considerable wealth and skills to pull together the necessary resources without them. A protracted process, if necessary, but one well within his means.

As soon as order was called, the wealthy Saudi slowly looked around the mud-walled room at the war-weary faces of the assembled group, finally settling on the bespectacled man with the distinct *zebibah* on his forehead.

Looking through the thick glass and directly into the principal leader's dark, conniving eyes, Aziz announced, "Your decision to abandon operations was a mistake. Because of it, our future is now very much in doubt."

In fairness, Aziz knew that the strategic decision to decentralize, made more than a decade earlier, had been considered necessary at the time. Al Qaeda and its leaders were under immense pressure that severely compromised their ability to govern effectively. Allowing subsidiaries to operate with nearly unqualified autonomy was supposed to deflect undue attention away from the core group while still allowing it to pursue its righteous objectives. Instead, the group's once-clear vision had been muddled by the parochial interests of those same subsidiaries. Although the resulting problems were serious, they were not unsolvable.

The much greater, perhaps fatal, problem was the existential threat posed by one particular former subsidiary. Given the current state of affairs, Aziz expected these men would appreciate that fact without the need for an historical accounting. The blank stares and lack of any response to his opening declaration told him they most likely did.

"Staying on the current path will only hasten our ruin," he continued. Time was running out, and definitive action was vital to ensuring the organization's future. He said there were three choices: undermine the rogue subsidiary with targeted attacks, merge with the former understudy, or reclaim prominence through the core group's own bold and decisive action plan. "The decision is simple. In order to restore our rightful position, we must resume jihad operations under our own banner. In a best-case scenario, the other two choices will leave us in a severely weakened state."

Without a moment's delay, Aziz explained his strategy for the terror group. The wide-eyed looks and forward leans were positive signs. When he finished with the broad strokes, he paused for effect and then told them the targets and the date for the first attacks under his proposed new scheme. This news drew different responses, and, for the first time, he sensed some pushback. He had expected it. He chose to ignore the doubts for the time being. He simply shifted back from the circle, indicating he was done with his presentation. Then he listened impassively as the council of leaders debated his plan with an apparent indifference to his presence in the cramped, shadowy room.

Aziz recognized that he was still considered an outsider. Up to this point, his life had been markedly different—in many respects, far easier than the lives these men had endured. Because of that, he suspected some, maybe even every one of them, resented his good fortune, not to mention his impudence. His royal lineage was another factor that didn't play well with this crowd.

Still, he remained confident that his views would not be easily dismissed. His credentials were undeniable, and he boasted an impressive track record in situations analogous to this. More importantly, he had redirected significant sums of his abundant wealth for the organization's benefit. If that weren't enough, he was a distant relative and former close associate of the organization's founder. In the end, their only choice was to go along with his plan; his money was the only thing keeping the organization alive.

The impassioned discussion went around and around for several iterations, with every man having the opportunity to debate the merits of and voice his position in favor of or against the new strategy and the bold plan to implement it. Aziz was only mildly concerned when the number-two man in the organization voiced his protest.

"This plan is too ambitious!" the man said. "We have heard ridiculous proposals like this before. Merely attempting this crazy plan will only put us back in the cross hairs of the Americans and their European pig allies." Several others seemed to be buying into the argument, adding to Aziz's growing impatience.

"For years, this organization has watched our affiliated groups carry out attacks in our name," Aziz said. "What has that done for us? Our affiliates conduct small operations in their home territories, none of which furthers our cause. As a result, recruits and money now flow to other organizations. We have been all but forgotten.

"Right now, we have an opportunity to act while our main competitor is under siege. That won't last forever, and neither will we, unless we do something. We have only one option if we are to survive—to prove that we can carry out a large-scale attack. Striking at the heart of America and two pillars of its sinful culture while the world watches will demonstrate that al Qaeda is, once again, the righteous and unquestioned leader of global jihad. The 'proposals' you mention were nothing more than ideas floated by feeble-minded and ill-equipped affiliates. Allah has blessed us with an opportunity to hit both of these targets as part of one masterful attack. You are fools to ignore our good fortune.

"If you believe you're advancing our cause by merely staying alive, hiding out in the mountains, tell me and I'll leave now. I do not wish to waste any more time or money on a hopeless situation. I will find other ways to proceed with my plans and bring about the caliphate our beloved sheikh envisioned."

Aziz pulled back and silently stewed as the others debated the issue. *These stupid deliberations are a perfect example of their incompetence,* he told himself. They ran the organization like some kind of social club, allowing its members to decide the rules and objectives. It needed the defined goals, structure, and discipline of a well-run business if the organization was to have any future, and he was determined to apply those principles one way or another. After a few minutes, he sensed things were once again moving in his favor. But getting approval for his masterstroke was only part of the equation. He had an ultimatum that was sure to draw more fiery dissent.

Eventually, a consensus was reached to generally approve the plan, subject to one condition. "We have a man in mind to lead this operation," the principal leader said, "and our approval will be conditioned on your accepting his appointment."

Aziz hid his satisfaction when he heard the name. In fact, Aziz was acquainted with the battle-tested warrior and had been prepared to insist on that man's inclusion anyway. He was tempted to push back for the sake of the leverage he would need later, but he realized it would appear contrived. He offered a quid pro quo instead. "That is acceptable, but I must have the privilege of personally sharing the details with him at the appropriate time."

There was no objection to his counter, and the group of elders assured him the man would remain out of harm's way until that time arrived. Now that all matters relating to the attack had been addressed, the council called for a vote.

"Before the vote is taken," Aziz said, "there is one additional item I wish to discuss. The world has changed since the organization was first formed. Competitors and adversaries are increasingly sophisticated and ruthless. In order to prosper in the future, we need to better anticipate and adapt to the rapid changes. We must also have the decisiveness and resolve to propel our plan forward. If I am to continue funding our cause, I must be confident that we have those capabilities. For that reason, I expect to be named coleader of the organization."

"That is unacceptable! It is not your place to make that kind of demand!" the number-three man shouted.

The principal leader raised his hands to silence the others. Succession planning had been on his mind for quite some time. On top of his increasingly fragile health and long-suffering fatigue, he recognized the need for a more dynamic leader if the cause and the organization were both to flourish again. It was time to either move forward or perish. "Your plan is hereby approved," he said, "and your demand will be accepted—if this operation proves successful."

Aziz feigned a polite smile, allowing his audience to infer that it was a sign of appreciation. It was not. He had no interest in sharing power with these pitiful men. Their contingent acceptance of his demand was merely the gateway to seizing power and imposing his own unrelenting vision to the cause. This first operation would be successful, and then he would use every one of his resources and abilities to finish what the sheikh had started many years ago.

CHAPTER 1

NINE MONTHS LATER
THE CARIBBEAN

The darkly dressed assassin sat down on a felled palm tree—likely a victim of the most recent hurricane to hit the island—and peeled off his mask before slipping out of his fins. The air was still and humid, yet he sensed through the thin three-millimeter wet suit clinging to his lean, sculpted body that it was several degrees cooler than the seventy-seven-degree inky-black water lapping at the shore just steps away. Although the hazards were potentially greater on land, he was relieved to have that first part of the assignment behind him.

He had hidden his anxiety when the new president and his boss laid out the mission. Despite years of extensive training and countless similar experiences, an aquatic insertion remained anathema to him. The water wasn't the problem; he loved to swim, just not in the open ocean. Especially in darkness. He was ten years old when he first saw *Jaws,* and, ever since, the film's powerful imagery had maintained a permanent residence in the recesses of his mind. Despite these anxieties, he would admit later that not all parts of the trip were objectionable.

They had started out from Georgetown aboard a *Benetti Veloce.* The $25 million, 140-foot yacht was one of the assets seized by the Drug Enforcement

Agency two years earlier from the former head of a middle-tier Mexican drug cartel. In a rare example of interagency fraternity, the Central Intelligence Agency was able to quietly purchase the luxury craft for situations just like this. The opulent craft maintained its moneyed aesthetics—essential camouflage in certain parts of the world—despite considerable functional modifications that included new communications and radar systems, weaponry, and a secret hold for amphibious assault equipment.

After leaving the Cayman capital early that morning, the ship sailed north on its stealthy journey, anchoring two miles into international waters just after 9:30 p.m. With some final words of encouragement from the crew, he and the pilot climbed into the smaller vessel perched above the ship's stern and were lowered into the black two-hundred-foot-deep water. The free-flooding vessel submerged to a depth of seventeen feet and began its northwesterly course toward the programmed coordinates. Cruising between seven and ten knots, the single, rear-propeller submersible delivered its passengers to the barrier reef in under two hours.

This was the only part of the mission he was dreading. Unable to proceed farther without potentially compromising the miniature submarine and revealing their presence, he would have to swim the remaining five hundred yards, the first hundred or so in heavy surf, up to and through the sharp coral reef. While he was treading water next to the sub and adjusting the demist shield of his Nivisys DVS-110 mask, he glimpsed the silhouette of something coming up out of the depths. Before he even had the chance to reach for the Colt M4 carbine slung over his shoulder, he watched as an eight-foot mako shark turned and retreated into the depths, apparently no longer interested in the commotion above. For the rest of the swim, he kept his head on a swivel, desperately searching for more menaces in the limited forty-degree field of view afforded by the high-tech underwater night-vision device. It wasn't until he was wading ashore that his heart rate finally settled back into the neighborhood of its customary forty-eight beats per minute.

Now, he carefully placed the mask on top of the fins and positioned the articles beneath some fronds of the fallen tree. Unfortunately, he'd need them again. He wicked the water from his close-cropped, textured hair before feeling for his six-inch Ontario MK3 knife and checking the assault rifle and the MK23 .45-caliber pistol strapped to his thigh. He hoped the assault rifle would prove superfluous. He carried it only for the worst-case scenario. He knew that if he needed it, he had bigger problems than man-eating sea creatures. With the tools of his trade properly in place, he gave one final tug on his waterproof rucksack and headed out, moving quietly down the beach.

His watch indicated a few minutes before midnight, leaving him just under an hour to reach his destination, complete the job, and get back over the reef to meet the sub. Before he departed for his swim, his colleague had informed him the sub could remain on site for no more than seventy-four minutes. Otherwise, it would have to return to the yacht to exchange the outsized battery, close to a four-hour round trip. If he was late, he'd be forced to hang out with the sharks while waiting for the sub to return—more than enough motivation to get his ass in gear.

On this occasion, his target was an American fugitive and accomplished bomb maker. In the early 1980s, Guillermo Sanchez had joined forces with a clandestine paramilitary group demanding Puerto Rican independence. Over the course of four years, Sanchez fashioned improvised explosive devices that were used in nearly sixty attacks in New York, Boston, and Miami. The casualties from those attacks included twenty-three dead and 159 injured.

While secretly living in Miami toward the end of his reign of terror, Sanchez had nearly committed a fatal error while assembling a bomb in his apartment. The police responding to the small explosion found Sanchez badly wounded and surrounded by four dozen sticks of dynamite and almost 150 pounds of other explosive materials. Sanchez was arrested and transferred to a local hospital for treatment of the extensive wounds to his hands and face. Later, with assistance from his attorney and a sympathetic physician working at the hospital, Sanchez managed to escape. He fled to Mexico and was arrested again, two years later, on charges of illegal weapons possession. But the Mexican government refused to extradite Sanchez to the United States to face trial. When he was later released from a Mexican penitentiary, Sanchez simply disappeared.

It was only very recently that Sanchez's location was learned. Early on during a routine interrogation, an Islamic State militant had divulged that the terror group had been purchasing bomb-making know-how from Sanchez. Over the course of the next several days, the skilled interrogators were able to elicit clues that ultimately pointed them to Sanchez's location here in the tropics. A surveillance team was immediately dispatched to the hostile locale, and, soon after, a plan was presented to the president of the United States.

The new president took office with a plain assurance to the American people that he would unapologetically do everything in his power to protect national security interests. Eliminating someone who had killed Americans and was now peddling his destructive expertise to a violent terrorist organization was an unequivocal means to that end. Just before he was dismissed, the president looked directly into his operative's eyes and said, with a matter-of-fact wink, "PJ, don't fuck this up."

Preston James Carpenter, PJ to his family and close friends, joined the Central Intelligence Agency nineteen years earlier, right after graduating with honors from Northwestern University. The agency's recruiters had been particularly drawn to his overseas experience and language skills. He majored in Middle East and North Africa studies and minored in linguistics. During a year at the American University of Beirut in fulfillment of a program requirement, Carpenter honed his fluency in Arabic, Farsi, and French. The ability to operate in various environments due to his biracial heritage was another compelling attribute. In many respects, he was the perfect recruit. But their concerns about potential behavioral problems had almost derailed Carpenter's chances.

His father was killed in a car accident when PJ was only four years old. He had few memories of his father but he still remembered the big smile and warm hugs he and his mother received every day when his father returned from work. Following his father's death, Carpenter feared losing his mother. He never wanted to leave her side. She was his entire world. When she decided to remarry eight years after his father's death, Carpenter put her happiness before his own, despite his misgivings about her new husband. It didn't take long before the courtship polish wore off, and his stepfather's true nature surfaced. Controlling, hotheaded, and quick with an insult were among his least despicable qualities. He and Carpenter were clashing almost from the start.

At first, the exchanges were strictly verbal. That changed one night when his stepfather decided that punching his mother in the stomach was just punishment for not having enough beer in the house. Two unpleasant years later, his beloved mother was dead, a victim of a long battle with diabetes. All Carpenter had left for family was his vile stepfather. Overcome with grief from losing the only person who mattered and hatred for her tormentor, Carpenter beat the shit out of the pathetic bastard the night of the funeral. By morning, he was gone, out on his own at fourteen years old. There were other incidents of violence to follow, but each time the authorities determined Carpenter's actions had been equally justified.

The agency shrinks ultimately decided to give him a pass, and his first assignment was as an operations officer in the Directorate of Operations, recruiting and running agents in Beirut. When he arrived in the late 1990s, the United States had a very limited presence in the progressively hostile region. Lebanon was still recovering from a long civil war, and Beirut and the Beqaa Valley remained fertile grounds for a plethora of increasingly anti-American terrorist groups. To compound the problem, the agency's human intelligence-collection efforts had been deteriorating ever since the United States withdrew its troops and reduced its diplomatic relations in response to the embassy and barracks bombings more than a decade earlier.

The slightly less-green Beirut chief of station instantly recognized a unique talent. He took notice as Carpenter quickly established himself as one of the few officers willing and able to recruit agents in the perilous region. Carpenter's combination of determination, intellect, and fearlessness greatly impressed the new COS, himself a former operations officer.

In the wake of the September 11, 2001 attacks, the COS endorsed Carpenter for inclusion in JAWBREAKER, the first CIA team to enter Afghanistan. In late September, Carpenter joined six teammates in Uzbekistan before flying in a patched-together helicopter over the Hindu Kush mountains into the Panjshir Valley north of Kabul. For the next seven weeks, he and his teammates lived in a stone house inside a walled compound at the base of a small mountain, subsisting on heavily chlorinated water, rice, and questionable sources of protein as they mapped frontline positions and worked to ensure the cooperation of the

Northern Alliance. Later, Carpenter was inserted with special-operations forces in the nearby Shomali Plain, where they fought their way through Taliban and al Qaeda forces while calling in precision-guided weapons from US warplanes. Living on the literal and figurative edge, exchanging fire with a determined enemy, besieged with violent gastrointestinal problems, and shitting in a hole in the ground for almost two months did nothing to deter his resolve to rid the world of those who had grievously harmed his country.

Citing a preference to remain in the field, Carpenter turned down an opportunity to move into a management position when he returned from Afghanistan. He said he was too restless to sit behind a desk. While that was true, the real reason was his primordial need for justice, and he knew from the limited covert operations experience he had under his belt that special operations could satisfy that need. Despite a lack of formal military training, he filed a request for a transfer. Those in his chain of command reluctantly yielded and approved his transfer to special operations.

Carpenter's move was atypical. Most CIA paramilitary officers are recruited from the most elite US military units and then made to undergo extensive clandestine intelligence training. Carpenter followed the opposite path. He spent the first two years after the transfer developing a high-level proficiency in the use and tactical employment of a wide range of weaponry, explosive devices, hand-to-hand combat, tactical driving, parachuting, extreme survival, and, his least favorite, scuba.

His trainers considered him to be one of the best all-around graduates from the program in many years, an accomplishment aided by Carpenter's exceptional critical-thinking skills and equally impressive athletic abilities. In addition to graduating with a 3.9 grade point average from Northwestern, he had earned all-state honors as both a wrestler and baseball player during the final two years of high school in his native Alabama.

Since the move, Carpenter had only gotten better, and he was considered the best of the highly select group of paramilitary officers in the agency's Counterterrorism Center, the interdisciplinary body made up of professionals from the Directorate of Analysis, the Directorate of Science and Technology, and the Directorate of Operations. The CTC was created specifically to destroy terrorist groups whose operations were not limited by geographical boundaries and, therefore, could not be sufficiently addressed by the CIA's traditional region-based divisions. Over the course of his career, Carpenter had operated in nearly forty countries. However, few of those countries were ever featured on the glossy pages of *Condé Nast*. Even the most adventurous who dared visit those countries avoided the places where Carpenter spent the vast majority of his time.

This was his first time in this country. Although this place had its charms, the risks could not have been higher. There really had been no need for the president to say "don't fuck this up."

As it turned out, Mr. Sanchez had purchased himself a nice seaside villa near Playa Maquina, at the northern edge of the Bay of Pigs in Matanzas Province, Cuba. At the location of an infamously failed covert operation decades earlier, the American fugitive enjoyed his stay as the exalted guest of the communist country's despotic leader.

When told of Sanchez's hideout, an incensed president remarked that the circumstances "are a middle finger to the United States." As testament to his commitment to his fellow citizens, the president insisted that his best operative be pulled out of an important mission in Syria to ensure the job got done. Although the United States would deny any involvement, the president wanted the world to know, unofficially, that there was no safe place for anyone who had inflicted, or intended to inflict, harm on the United States. Despite it being early in his presidency, he already trusted Carpenter, more than anyone else, to deliver that message. And Carpenter was more than happy to oblige.

As Carpenter snuck down the beach, he recalled the findings of the surveillance team. The team had reported that from roughly ten in the morning to seven in the evening, three locals provided various household services at the property, but none resided or remained on the grounds overnight. The surveillance team also reported that Sanchez, perhaps thinking he was immune from reprisal in the idyllic communist stronghold, did not have any dogs and had not installed a security system. Satellite reconnaissance for the last forty-eight hours confirmed the presence of only one person during the overnight hours. The pattern-of-life analysis also indicated that Sanchez liked to sit on his front porch, enjoying a cigar and a few glasses of rum late into the evening and early-morning hours.

As Carpenter moved closer, he caught his first glimpse of the modestly sized villa, set back less than twenty yards from the beach. The occasional break in the thick clouds and the lone light shining deep inside the house silhouetted its frame among the lush tropical vegetation. He set his eyes on several royal palms among neatly placed begonia bushes at the border of the wide sandy beach and the well-manicured yard. After taking a few more steps, he stopped momentarily to get a final sense of the surroundings. Satisfied everything was still clear, he rushed forward to the base of one of the palm trees before slowly raising his head over the flowering begonia bush and peering into the dimness. Even before he recognized the faint glow of the cigar, he could almost taste the rich, loamy earth through the smoke hanging in the thick air. He stayed only a few moments as he formulated his plan. On the difficulty scale of one to ten, this was shaping up to be close to zero.

Carpenter retreated down the beach and then carefully made his way through the flora and approached the house from the left side. He eschewed the night-vision goggles in his rucksack in favor of the full field of view offered by the modest ambient light. He nearly paid for that decision when he tripped slightly just before exiting the bushes. Fortunately, he caught himself without making any discernable noise. After pausing briefly to confirm the episode had not betrayed his presence, he took the few steps needed to cross the clearing and reach the side of the villa. As he slid down the wall, he pulled his MK23 with its built-in sound suppressor. He hesitated before soundlessly rounding the corner. He stood less than ten feet from his target, who was reclining in a chair holding a full glass of dark rum and clenching the butt of a cigar between his teeth. Slumped in the chair next to Sanchez was a naked woman—an unexpected complication.

As Carpenter stepped closer, Sanchez sensed his presence and swiveled his head. At first, the disfigured face revealed only modest surprise, but as fear quickly overcame the effects of the rum, Sanchez recoiled. "Who are you?" he asked in the bravest voice he could muster.

"I'm here to repay an old debt," Carpenter only said before putting two nine-millimeter rounds into the wretched man's head.

The woman didn't stir—at all—confirming Carpenter's suspicion that she was passed out from booze, drugs, or both rather than sleeping. He opened his small rucksack and used some flex-cuffs to bind the woman's hands and feet before hauling the man's corpse back into the house. He conducted a quick search of the home and then finished his plans for Sanchez. Back outside, he blindfolded and lightly gagged the woman before hoisting her over his right shoulder. He checked his watch. He still had thirty-two minutes to get back to the sub.

Three hours later and some twenty miles out to sea, Carpenter and the crew aboard the luxury yacht were enjoying some of Sanchez's cigars and rum when they spotted the fireball from the rear deck. In a "payback FU" gesture intended to clearly deliver the president's veiled message, Carpenter had placed a chunk of C-4, hooked to a timer, in Sanchez's lap. He blew out a ring of smoke and smiled, imagining what the confused Cubans would make of the woman when they eventually found her a quarter mile down the beach, propped against a tree, wrapped, blindfolded, and gagged with Sanchez's bedding.

Not a bad way to bring in the New Year and, hopefully, a sign of things to come, Carpenter thought. As the boat continued southward, his attentions—as they often did in rare moments of idleness—drifted to a particular terrorist for whom he had his own personal message. *Maybe this'll be the year I finally get that son of a bitch.*

CHAPTER 2

ARABIAN DESERT

A day later and half a world away, Hamid Fahkoury welcomed the cooling evening temperatures as he sat down on the fine sand and looked around. The gentle zephyr at his back would have been inaudible in this desolate and magnificent place were it not for the tent's sole obstruction of its easterly path. As he took it all in, Fahkoury appreciated the vastness of the place and the quiet solitude it afforded. It was an ideal place to collect his thoughts as well as a perfect sanctuary for a sensitive meeting, one he was increasingly eager to begin.

The breeze helped to refresh Fahkoury from his long journey to the Rub Al Khali—or Empty Quarter, as it is otherwise known—one of the most desolate places and harshest environments on the planet. Covering more than 225,000 square miles, the Empty Quarter spreads across parts of Saudi Arabia, Yemen, Oman, and the United Arab Emirates. Over the millennia, this vast desert of sand has been reshaped by prevailing northern winds, annual rainfall of less than two inches, and average daytime temperatures of 115 degrees Fahrenheit, resulting in a land that is inhospitable to all but the most resourceful humans.

Fahkoury took a moment to focus on the effect that the surrounding emptiness had on his senses, a practice that had contributed to his relatively long tenure as a member of al Qaeda's command structure. He noticed that in this expansive desert, there was no discernible smell, and even at this late hour, the gibbous moon in the cloudless sky overhead allowed him to see almost as well as during the middle of the day. As the hyperaware state overtook him, his attention was drawn to a scorpion scurrying about the desert floor a dozen or so feet away. Observing its apparent aimlessness, Fahkoury pondered whether the scorpion's meandering served a purpose or if, instead, it was a metaphor for his own uncertainty.

For some time now, Fahkoury had felt adrift. He had long been a loyal soldier of al Qaeda, and, despite his more recent reservations, his allegiance to jihad and the terror group remained steadfast. As a teenager, Fahkoury had left his comfortable station in Kuwait as the son of a deputy oil minister to help in the fight against the Soviets. His bravery, ruthlessness, and willingness to take on any task garnered the universal respect of his fellow mujahideen. A little more than a year after he arrived, the Soviets pulled out of Afghanistan, and a civil war broke out almost immediately. Struggling to find his calling in the battle between competing tribal factions, Fahkoury decided to return home to Kuwait.

He enrolled in university to study chemical engineering right before the first Gulf War started. Although his studies were temporarily interrupted by the conflict, he was largely indifferent to the war. It wasn't until Osama bin Laden later condemned the presence of US troops in the region that Fahkoury's animus for the West began to fester. Upon graduation, he accepted a job in the petroleum industry. He committed himself to his work and earned two promotions in his first three years. Yet he was unfulfilled.

Prompted by statements from bin Laden and others, Fahkoury had come to resent the Americans and Europeans who worked alongside him for exploiting Arab resources and bringing their filthy Western culture to Muslim lands. To feed his budding piety, Fahkoury dutifully studied Sayyid Qutb and read *Join the Caravan*, Abdullah Azzam's call for violent global jihad. He faithfully attended fiery sermons given by imams advocating the same views. He accepted the truth that the world had returned to the pre-Islamic barbarous state known as *Jahiliya* and that violent jihad was required to both defend the *ummah* and propagate Allah's immutable laws across the globe. He yearned to bring the fight to the United States and its Western allies—the most conspicuous representatives of *Jahiliya* and the leading oppressors of Islam.

The opportunity finally arrived in the form of bin Laden's 1998 fatwa for war against Jews and Crusaders. He immediately quit his job and returned to Afghanistan. When the Americans and their allies invaded Afghanistan in the fall of 2001, Fahkoury fought bravely and to the bitter end in the battle at Kandahar. Later, he commanded a small force at Tora Bora, unleashing a flurry of attacks and counterattacks against the Northern Alliance and the special forces of its Western benefactors. When all hope appeared lost, Fahkoury led a small party to negotiate a truce with the local Afghan militia commander. His wily plan served as the pretext for bin Laden and others—eventually including himself—to safely sneak away to the Federated Tribal Areas of Pakistan.

After al Qaeda regrouped in Pakistan, Fahkoury was pulled from the battlefield and sent to al Qaeda's officer school to learn how to plan and coordinate attacks, including skills to select and develop weapons to inflict maximum damage. By this time his commitment was well settled, but it was the creativity, adaptability, and resolve he repeatedly demonstrated that distinguished him from all others. He was marked as a special talent whose safety and longevity became priorities for the terror group. Even after the bloody battles in Afghanistan in 2001, al Qaeda did not lack militants, but attrition at the hands of the Americans and their allies had hit its leadership ranks hard. An intelligent true believer with leadership and planning skills had become a rare and extremely valuable asset.

Fahkoury rose to become the terror group's top attack planner as well as its preeminent bomb maker. In fact, the attacks orchestrated by Fahkoury in the al Qaeda strongholds of Afghanistan and Pakistan, including the Islamabad Marriott, were responsible for more than three hundred deaths and nearly $2 billion of property damage. In truth, the theater of his carnage was far broader.

Over time, the terror organization gradually ceded operations to its affiliated groups, and Fahkoury was no longer leading operations. Instead, he was relegated to sharing his bomb-making and planning expertise with al Qaeda's affiliates in Iraq and Yemen. The improvised explosive-device techniques Fahkoury provided were credited for thousands of coalition and Shiite casualties and for dramatically altering the course of the conflict in Iraq. His expertise helped al Qaeda in the Arabian Peninsula become al Qaeda's most prolific affiliate after al Qaeda in Iraq split with the parent organization. In short, Fahkoury was responsible, directly or indirectly, for far more deaths than any other jihadist.

He came to believe that his true purpose and service to Allah was to kill infidels. For that reason, the last several years had been particularly frustrating. The attacks conducted by core al Qaeda had been fewer in number each successive year and generally insignificant. He expected al Qaeda to do more to bring about an end to a world governed by secular regimes, but the senior leaders seemed uninterested in a return to violent jihad. Worse still, over the past nine months, it seemed as if a decision had been made to completely sideline him.

The reasons for his diminished role remained a mystery until just recently. Four days earlier, he had been summoned by the *shura*, the members of al Qaeda senior leadership who are responsible for discussion and approval of all large-scale attacks undertaken in the name of the terror group. He was initially confused and somewhat concerned when the news arrived.

In his role as an operational chief—a mastermind—Fahkoury had appeared before the shura on a number of occasions. In each of those instances, the appearance was at his request, to seek approval for a target he had selected and his proposed plan of attack. That was not the case this time, so he was worried the shura had somehow become aware of his growing irritation. In the hours before the meeting, he began to believe his presence had been demanded for the purpose of censuring or otherwise punishing him for perceived betrayal.

His concern quickly turned to exultation when the shura started the meeting by telling him that he had been chosen to lead an important overseas operation—a bold and critical mission to reinforce the terror group's claim as leader of the global jihad movement. Although the location and time of the attack had been approved, the council declined to share those details. He was told only that his role was to finalize the plan of attack based on his assessment of the targets and the capabilities of a team that had already been assembled. He was given an itinerary that would deliver him to the Rub Al

Khali. Along the way, he would be met by a trusted, yet unnamed, brother who would guide him to the meeting place. He would learn the specifics of the plan and more, he was promised, from a senior-level person who would meet them in the desert.

In closing, the shura advised Fahkoury that he was not to martyr himself but, rather, to plan for an escape. There were plans for him beyond this mission. The leaders stressed the importance of the operation and demanded that the strictest operational controls and "extraordinary precautions" be applied to ensure his and the operation's success. As its last item, the shura ordered Fahkoury to seek final approval just before executing the attack.

At that, Fahkoury was dismissed. Not counting the time allocated to social mores, the entire discussion had lasted less than fifteen minutes. He wasn't given the opportunity to ask any questions, and he knew better than to request one.

What the shura did not share with Fahkoury was that al Qaeda was about to embark on a new strategy, one that had been crafted over the better part of the past year. This operation was critical to the terror group's future. Without some level of success from this operation, al Qaeda would struggle to survive. Fahkoury was viewed as their best chance to pull it off, and the shura had essentially decommissioned him to ensure his availability. In addition to his being the terror group's most capable commander, the shura had selected Fahkoury for his relative anonymity.

Having marked him for what they hoped would be a long career, the shura went to great lengths to protect his true identity from the time he graduated officer school. Fahkoury was not allowed to be photographed, and he moved frequently, never staying in one location for more than three nights. Even when he was close to the battlefield, he had been ordered to operate in the shadows, always several steps removed from the actual attack.

Despite his gruesome record and the considerable efforts to identify him, Fahkoury's true name and identity remained unknown to Western intelligence services. He was known only by the nom de guerre his fellow jihadists used for him—Mumeet, the Bringer of Death.

CHAPTER 3

Now sitting outside the tent in the middle of the vast Empty Quarter, some-where, he reckoned, near the undefined border between Saudi Arabia and Yemen, Fahkoury struggled to keep his mind from racing. The wait was be-coming intolerable, and the lack of details necessitating his travels here con-tinued to gnaw at him. Fahkoury wondered whether, after all the secrecy and the long journey to this remote sanctuary, this meeting and the mission it concerned would live up to his growing expectations.

He pushed those uncertainties aside and forced himself to focus on the job at hand. There was work to do while he waited. Fahkoury undertook every operation rigorously, and he was determined to elevate that methodi-cal approach with this operation. The shura had admonished him about the slightest lapse in operational security. A careful review of every step of the journey he had taken to the Arabian Desert was required.

The itinerary had been unduly burdensome, but it was deemed neces-sary to guarantee that Fahkoury would arrive in the Rub Al Khali without notice. After being dismissed by the shura four days earlier, his journey ulti-mately covered more than two thousand miles over land and sea. The first leg was more tedious than dangerous. He traveled alone from Waziristan in the Pakistani tribal areas to Karachi, switching automobiles three times during the uneventful daylong trip. In Karachi that evening, he boarded a fishing vessel for the next stage of his trip and headed out to sea with a crew of three Yemenis.

The shura had assured him the Yemenis could be trusted; they had been recommended by al Qaeda in the Arabian Peninsula or AQAP. Fahkoury, however, trusted no one, especially someone with whom he had not been in battle. Until you proved yourself to be a true believer, you were not one, especially when the stakes were this high. He would defer to the shura, but he would ultimately decide whether the Yemenis could truly be trusted.

The trip was Fahkoury's first on a boat, and before it even ended, he hoped it would prove his last. As the ramshackle boat made its way westward through the Gulf of Oman, the first hours passed without incident. For the most part, Fahkoury stayed away from the Yemeni crew, but he saw and heard enough in those first hours to question their commitment. Over the bellows from the engine and the rhythmic slapping of the warm seas against the boat's wooden hull, he was able to hear laughter and bits of conversation. Apparently, the Yemenis had spent the night before departure drinking liquor and chasing women in Karachi. To a true believer like Fahkoury, even talking about those acts was *haram*.

A strong storm whipped up in the wee hours of the second day, creating fifteen-foot seas and torrential rains. For more than an hour, the forty-five-foot boat was thrust up and immediately back down by the relentless waves. By the time the storm ended, Fahkoury lay prone and soaking wet on the ship's deck, completely exhausted and nearly oblivious to the acidic aftertaste of bile in his mouth. The more-seasoned Yemenis were no worse for wear, and they found his condition a source of great comedic relief. After the storm subsided, and he regained his faculties, Fahkoury began to assemble a plan for the apostates.

Later that afternoon, after passing through the Strait of Hormuz into the Persian Gulf in calm seas under an azure sky, the boat approached the harbor at Khobar City, Saudi Arabia. With a population of nearly one million and being a popular tourist destination for people from neighboring Gulf States, Khobar offered an excellent opportunity for Fahkoury to enter the kingdom unnoticed.

Much to Fahkoury's surprise, those chances had been elevated. Somehow, the immoral Yemenis managed to haul in a decent load of shrimp after the storm passed. They claimed the catch would be sold in the Khobar city market to provide cover for the trip. Unspoken was the fact that the catch would also provide income beyond the money they were undoubtedly paid by al Qaeda. Normally, he wouldn't begrudge their good fortune, but Fahkoury suspected the Yemenis would use their newfound wealth in pursuit of more liquor and women if given the chance. The risks these heretics posed was not acceptable.

As soon as the boat was moored, the Yemenis immediately began haggling with the local merchants. Despite the shouted exchanges and flailing arms, terms were quickly agreed to, and the merchants, Fahkoury, and the Yemenis worked together to offload the catch. Shortly after the chaotic process started, Fahkoury melded into the crowded market. Slipping through the throng of people, he quickly distanced himself from the bustling market before eventually stopping at a café several blocks away. From its location at the edge of Half Moon Beach, the café afforded a panoramic view of the dock, the harbor, and the glistening sea beyond. He settled in with a cup of cardamom tea and watched as the remainder of the catch was unloaded.

Almost as soon as the process finished, the boat withdrew from the dock and began heading out to sea. Fahkoury could not know whether the Yemenis' unimpeded departure was the result of indifference to his whereabouts or his absence going unnoticed, at least by anyone who mattered. He didn't really care. Either way, he knew he had overcome the first genuine obstacle of his journey and was now safely in Saudi Arabia. He casually monitored the boat's progress from the café. When the boat cleared the harbor, he fixed his eyes on the vessel and watched as it gradually shrank on the horizon.

Once they were clear of the harbor, the Yemenis gradually built up speed. Approximately one mile out to sea, the engine caught fire, but it took several minutes for the Yemenis to realize the problem. The fatal delay allowed the fire to grow in intensity below decks and rapidly find its way to the severed fuel line. By the time they realized the problem, it was too late.

Upon seeing the explosion, Fahkoury hid a rare smile behind a nonchalant sip of the aromatic tea. Among his many talents, Fahkoury was a gifted mechanic, often performing work on the worn-down vehicles in the al Qaeda fleet. As the Yemenis increased speed, the boat's cooling system should have kicked in, but Fahkoury had made sure that wouldn't happen. He had triggered the fire and subsequent explosion by simply short-circuiting the cooling system and bridging the current to the severed gas line.

He had no regrets about the decision to eliminate the Yemenis. Their lack of piety could be exploited, presenting a security risk to both him and the operation. While savoring the last few sips of his favorite tea, he reflected that they deserved their fate and found it pleasantly ironic that fire would deliver them to the harshest depths of hell reserved for apostates.

CHAPTER 4

While the other patrons gawked at the fireball at sea, Fahkoury threw down five riyals for the two cups of the spicy beverage and then left, seamlessly joining the unknowing pedestrians as they rhythmically marched alongside slow-moving traffic toward the King Fahd Causeway connecting Saudi Arabia and Bahrain. A few blocks later, he stepped onto the manicured grounds of the SeaSide Towers and alighted the stairs to the third floor, where he used the access code provided by the shura to gain entry to unit 351, a residence purchased through a cutout by an al Qaeda sympathizer from Qatar. A wave of fetid, hot air greeted him when he opened the door. After flipping on the lights, he managed to find the control panel for the air conditioning and then went straight to the bed. Still recovering from his sea voyage, he was sleeping soundly within minutes, confidently secure in his anonymity to this point of his onerous journey.

Fahkoury had not been concerned on the short trip from the pier to the safe house. He was well practiced in the art of blending in, skills that were enhanced by a rather ordinary appearance. His trim, sinewy frame, measuring to just slightly below-average height, concealed the strength of someone who had lived the majority of his life without the efficiencies and comforts afforded by the modernized world. If he troubled with such matters, he would know that most women found him attractive, but none would be able to point to one particular feature as the reason. His face was indistinctive, the kind of face one tends to forget. It was forgettable for the almost perfectly proportional aquiline nose and thin lips residing on a symmetrical face that somehow maintained a relatively youthful and healthy appearance despite years of living in difficult conditions. Perhaps it was the dangerous allure of his dark, menacing eyes brooding underneath thick eyebrows that stoked the attraction. It might also be the combination of wavy, thick hair and smooth olive skin that thwarted attempts to define him as Mediterranean or North African or Arab on those rare occasions when he was clean shaven or maintained neatly trimmed facial hair.

But, in his mind, Fahkoury was defined by the only blemish to his otherwise unexceptional appearance—a disfigured left hand, the result of a premature bomb explosion. Fahkoury would carry shame for his carelessness for the rest of his days, a sentiment evidenced by both the subconscious and deliberate attempts he made to hide the stubs that had once been his pinkie, ring, and middle fingers.

A few minutes before 4:30 a.m., a soft knock at his door jolted him from his slumber. He had been asleep for nearly half a day. He cautiously opened the door and immediately recognized Fahd al-Rasheed, a Saudi who had fought alongside him during the Battle of Tora Bora in December 2001.

"As-Salaam-Alaikum!" whispered al-Rasheed.

"Wa-Alaikum-Salaam!" Fahkoury said as the veteran warriors embraced and exchanged traditional greetings. This time, Fahkoury agreed with the shura's assessment of al-Rasheed as a trusted brother.

After they separated and took a few moments to look at each other, al-Rasheed asked, "How are you feeling, brother?"

"Much better now, with a little rest. I arrived by boat yesterday and hope I never have to ride on one again. It's been a long time. How have you been? Where have you been all these years?"

Al-Rasheed related the story of how he escaped Afghanistan in early 2002 and returned to Saudi Arabia. Once home, he took on different jobs but continued to stay close to al Qaeda through local sympathizers. From time to time, he shared his experiences in Afghanistan as part of fundraising efforts but otherwise kept a low profile. After years of civilian life, al-Rasheed yearned for a return to the battlefield. His wishes were granted when he was sent to Syria ten months earlier to join the fight alongside Jabhat Fateh al-Sham, or JFS, the al Qaeda affiliate in that country.

In the wake of the Arab Spring, JFS had entered the battle to overthrow the Syrian government and the Assad regime. Later, the rise of the Islamic State—the latest iteration in a series of names, including AQI, ISIS, and ISIL, to which the terror group has been referred—threatened JFS's standing in the ungovernable country. So, for good measure, JFS included the Islamic State as a secondary target of its aggression.

Al-Rasheed served in Syria as an advisor to JFS and as a conduit for al Qaeda financing to the region, but the primary reasons he had been sent there were to recruit Westerners and develop resources for future attacks—more specifically, routes into Europe. Approximately two weeks ago, al-Rasheed was summoned home and given instructions to meet Fahkoury in Khobar City and accompany him to a meeting scheduled in the Empty Quarter.

Mujahideen and Bedouin himself, al-Rasheed was the ideal candidate to accompany Fahkoury to the Empty Quarter. Not only was he conversant with Bedouin customs, he was familiar with the territory. After he returned to Saudi Arabia in 2002, al-Rasheed worked for a few years as a frankincense export merchant, a job that required him to frequently travel into the Arabian Desert.

"Do you have any idea what this meeting is about?" asked al-Rasheed.

"Only that it involves an important overseas operation. I don't know the location or time of the attack, but I have a feeling it might be in America or Western Europe. At least that's my hope."

"*Inshallah*," said al-Rasheed. "My money is on Europe. After morning prayers, let's eat, and then we'll begin our journey."

Following morning prayers, the two partook in the dates, dried fruit, and *lebnah* that al-Rasheed had brought along. After they finished eating, they collected the remaining food, as well as the bedding and linens, and placed all the items in the building's incinerator. Still before sunrise, they quietly descended the concrete-and-steel ocean-blue-painted stairs to the parking lot and al-Rasheed's earlier-model Range Rover.

Once they were inside the well-traveled vehicle, al-Rasheed said, "We have more than three hundred miles ahead of us. Get some more rest while we are driving, as the last leg of our journey will not be so comfortable."

"How so?" asked Fahkoury.

"We will be traveling the Bedouin way—by camel."

Fahkoury muttered something indiscernible under his breath and stared mindlessly out the window.

CHAPTER 5

Once outside the SeaSide Towers neighborhood, al-Rasheed guided the truck southward onto the Abu Hadriyah Highway, a major new road in the Eastern Province. Al-Rasheed explained that although this new route eliminated the need to make two border crossings through the United Arab Emirates, there was still a chance of being stopped and questioned inside the kingdom. Just in case, he carried several bogus frankincense purchase orders from a perfume company loyal to al Qaeda. To anyone asking, they would be traveling to Oman and then on to Yemen to purchase the aromatic resin from local merchants.

They continued to follow the Abu Hadriyah Highway to a point just north of Shaybah, a major crude-oil production facility sitting twenty-five miles south of the Rub Al Khali's northern edge. As they passed by the endless range of ochre-colored sand dunes surrounding the facility, Fahkoury reflected that in other circumstances, Shaybah would make an attractive target. Destruction of this key petroleum facility, which sat on top of some fourteen billion barrels of light sweet crude and more than twenty-five trillion cubic feet of natural gas, would cause an oil-supply disruption and impact the economies of the infidel West and its apostate allies in the House of Saud. He made a mental note to broach the potential target with the shura.

A dozen or so miles beyond the oil field, al-Rasheed exited the highway and drove into the desert. "Get ready for your camel ride," al-Rasheed said, laughing. He told Fahkoury they would be stopping soon to meet a Bedouin who would guide them to the meeting location.

The Bedouin was new and unwelcome news. "How do we know this Bedouin can be trusted?" Fahkoury asked.

"Do not worry," al-Rasheed said. "I know his tribe. My ancestors have lived alongside that tribe for generations. Bedouin are fiercely protective of those in their good graces. Plus, I am Bedu. We will be fine."

After nearly six hours of monotonous driving through the faceless land-scape along the smooth Abu Hadriyah Highway, they were slowly bumping along the dusty desert, following a southwesterly path through a narrow val-ley created by *uruqin*, the somewhat orderly lines of sand dunes created by the relentless northern winds that had formed and reshaped the desert for thousands of years. A sense of calm replaced the anxiousness they had both felt on the highway, and Fahkoury momentarily allowed himself to appreciate the raw beauty of the Rub Al Khali. For a short time, he was consumed with following the distinct curling lines of the ephemeral ridges as they coursed from one dune to another in a never-ending chain.

An hour later, Fahkoury was startled from his reverie when an older man with three camels stepped out from between two dunes. Fahkoury initially thought the stooped, weathered man was the member of the local Bedouin tribe that al-Rasheed had mentioned. Dressed in a traditional white Arab *thawb* and wearing a *mashadah*, a customary red-and-white-checked head wrap, the man certainly looked the part. But as they moved closer, Fahkoury began to doubt his first inclination. The man was also carrying a Kalashnikov, and he was pointing it directly at their truck.

Al-Rasheed stopped the vehicle approximately fifty feet from the agitat-ed man. He slowly exited the vehicle and called out, "As-Salaam-Alaikum!" while rotating his right hand above his head, signaling that he was not armed. He then reached down and picked up some sand and tossed it into the air— the time-honored Bedouin sign for peace.

This did little to calm the windswept nomad. He immediately began shouting and pointing his rifle at Fahkoury.

"Slowly get out of the truck, and do what I just did," al-Rasheed said.

Fahkoury halfheartedly rotated his hand and tossed a handful of fine sand into the air, incensed to have to play along with this foolish charade. The performance was awkward, but it proved effective enough. The Bedouin lowered his rifle and smiled warmly at his visitors.

The Bedouin told al-Rasheed to leave the keys in the ignition, as someone would be arriving soon to retrieve the vehicle. He gave them each a thawb and mashadah and directed them to change quickly. When they were finished, the Bedu waved them over to the camels, who were now kneeling and ready for passengers.

Fahkoury's mood worsened when his beast of burden greeted him with a nasty burp that smelled like a pile of rotting compost. He spitefully jerked the reins to establish his dominion and climbed into the wooden saddle. Once everyone was mounted, the Bedouin called out an order for the camels to rise. The nomad turned his dromedary nearly 180 degrees and prodded the animal. The other camels, with Fahkoury and al-Rasheed securely aboard, followed suit.

It was early afternoon and approaching ninety degrees under a cloudless sky. Fahkoury was experiencing another mode of transportation for the first time. He couldn't decide what smelled worse: the camel or the decaying fish from the boat. He titled his head back in hopes of finding fresher air. All things considered, he decided he liked it better on land.

For the next two hours, the caravan proceeded south over rolling waves of sand that stood as foothills to adjacent towering dunes, some of which rose more than eight hundred feet from the desert floor. Other than them and their camels, there were no living creatures to be seen in the endless sea of sand, suddenly whipped up by an increasing wind. Fahkoury covered his face with the mashadah and tried to distract himself from the physical and odorous discomfort by imagining the difficulties of surviving in such a place. *How did one find food and water? What about shelter?* Even the severe Hindu Kush offered more amenities than this desert, he ultimately concluded.

An hour before sunset, the caravan arrived at the site, a relatively flat, acre-sized plot surrounded by dunes tall enough to veil the presence of three tents, one considerably larger than the others. The Bedouin called out an instruction, and each of the camels knelt on the ground.

"You may each choose from the outer tents," the Bedouin said. "There is food for you inside the leftmost tent." After that brief explanation, the ancient Bedouin gathered up the camels and left, quickly vanishing into the long shadows cast by the dunes and into the burnt-orange desert beyond.

Fahkoury and al-Rasheed moved to one of the smaller tents and prepared for the *maghrib*. Following sunset prayers, they partook in a meal of mutton, rice, nuts, and dried fruits. There was ample food for a few days, but since they did not know the length of their stay, the two ate sparingly. A short time later, they performed *Isha*—prayers at nightfall. And then they awaited the arrival of their host.

CHAPTER 6

C onfident there had been no unresolved security lapses on his journey, Fahkoury searched for the scorpion. He eventually found it ambling around when it abruptly changed course and scurried off in a straight line. He was reminded of Muslim folklore in which the scorpion is viewed as a protector against evils and bad luck. Fahkoury hoped that in this case its apotropaic virtues would prove true and that its apparent newfound purpose just might presage his own future.

He realized what had caused the arachnid to dart away when, a moment later, he heard the murmur of a single engine off in the distance. Al-Rasheed walked up next to him just before the pair was lit up by the bouncing head-lights of a slowly approaching vehicle. They watched as the SUV stopped in the center of the arranged tents, and three heavily armed men exited, tak-ing up positions equidistant from the truck. After scanning the area, one of the armed men signaled toward the vehicle. Another guard approached and opened the rear passenger door, allowing the last occupant to emerge. Fahkoury had been told nothing other than he was to meet with a prominent al Qaeda advisor. Squinting through the glare of the headlights, he recog-nized a man matching that very description.

Fahkoury had first become acquainted with Prince Sadiq bin Aziz in Pakistan in the late 1980s. Aziz had already established himself as a close bin

Laden associate by the time Fahkoury arrived. Much like bin Laden, Aziz was not a fighter. Operating alongside bin Laden from Peshawar, Aziz used his connections in the kingdom and elsewhere in the Gulf to secure much of the funding used to recruit and bring fighters to Afghanistan in the battle against the Soviets.

Aziz returned to Saudi Arabia following the defeat of the Soviets, but Fahkoury had heard that he continued to provide funding and support to al Qaeda. On at least a few occasions, he was present when members of the shura acknowledged gratitude for Aziz. He was also aware of rumors that Aziz played a pivotal role in the attacks of September 11.

What Fahkoury knew about Aziz certainly fit the shura's description of someone of high regard. Fahkoury would have been even more impressed had he known the whole truth about Aziz and his plans.

CHAPTER 7

In fact, the rumors about Aziz's role in the September 11 attacks were true. It was also true that Aziz had become much more active following bin Laden's death and the subsequent rise of the Islamic State. Aziz's personal ambitions included eventual leadership of al Qaeda—or, more likely, some facsimile of it. He saw himself as a leader of jihad in the image of bin Laden, and, like the former leader and his distant cousin, he had the power of the purse and an ego to match.

Having exercised his itch for youthful adventure during the Soviet conflict, Aziz enrolled in the London School of Economics shortly after leaving Peshawar. He stayed in London after graduation and started a private equity firm, seeding the first fund with his own money. The firm's initial focus was on high-growth companies across all segments of the consumer-products industry. After seven years, he had more than $500 million under management across three separate limited partnerships.

Leveraging the success and experience with those early-stage companies, Aziz began to take majority interests in better-established but stagnating brands. His turnaround approach was simple: return the brand to its original defining purpose. Aziz found that all too often, the original message was obscured by poor business decisions that ultimately led companies away from their core principles. Time after time, Aziz found success by simply modernizing the original vision of the brand.

His simple approach yielded impressive results and a dedicated following. When other firms were forced to reduce their management fees and carried interest in the wake of the Great Recession, Aziz was able to maintain his 2 percent management fee and 20 percent share of the profits. He emerged from that dark period of financial uncertainty with more than $1.5 billion under management in five different limited partnerships. He built a reputation as an astute and equally shrewd businessman, a man who ran his firm with the same efficiency as he did any of the consumer-brand companies in which he invested.

For the most part, the reputation was accurate except for one notable exception: he deliberately overpaid for legal services. Through an arrangement with the law firm's three partners, his private equity firm was overbilled by an average of 20 to 30 percent each month. Half of the overbillings stayed in the law firm, while the three law partners discretely channeled the other half to various charities that supported al Qaeda.

In 2012, after eighteen highly successful years, Aziz abruptly sold his interest in the firm to his junior partners. By the time he left, more than $48 million of his beneficence had been directed to al Qaeda. At the time, his personal wealth stood at more than $300 million. And, as a result of some savvy investing and discreet purchases of rare gems and art, that figure had grown considerably since.

Aziz made the decision to leave less than a year after the United States killed Osama bin Laden. Even before bin Laden's death, the al Qaeda brand was already deteriorating, a matter he had frequently addressed with the group's founder. The decline of al Qaeda's defining purpose as the unquestioned vanguard of global jihad only hastened following the sheikh's death. Never having lost his zeal for the cause, Aziz decided he needed to abandon his lavish lifestyle for the purpose of restoring al Qaeda to the forefront of global jihad. In order to do that, he knew al Qaeda would have to take that title from one of its former affiliates.

More than a decade earlier, before money and recruits started flowing to al Qaeda in Iraq, Aziz warned bin Laden and other senior leaders of the threat from the brash and ruthless acts of its former affiliate. At a time when al Qaeda was all but absent from the holy war, AQI's first leader, Abu Musab al-Zarqawi, pushed the parameters of violence against the infidels. And Zarqawi's uncompromising vision for a global caliphate governed by sharia served as a rallying cry for jihadists and financiers alike.

Later, when Zarqawi and his AQI jihadists were under intense pressure from a renewed effort by the Americans and their Iraqi allies, Aziz implored al Qaeda's leaders to use the opportunity to carry out attacks against American interests in other parts of the world. The attacks would bring followers and money back into the fold, he argued. His entreaties were ignored.

Another missed opportunity arrived several years later, as the Americans were about to leave Mesopotamia. Once again, al Qaeda stood by while Zarqawi's successor, Abu Bakr al-Baghdadi, seized the opportunity created by the power vacuum. As a result, the Islamic State, as AQI is now called, was widely viewed as the movement's undisputed leader, and al Qaeda and its brand were facing irrelevance.

After years of pressing his points, the shura finally acquiesced and invited Aziz to formally present his new strategy. Aziz challenged the apathetic stewards of the once-formidable organization, telling them right at the outset that they needed to change course or al Qaeda would fade further into obscurity. Definitive action had to be taken, he argued, in order to restore the al Qaeda brand. This could be accomplished only through the successful execution of large-scale attacks, preferably ones on US and European soil.

Aziz came prepared for the meeting, presenting the shura with the outline for such an attack. In exchange for his efforts and continued funding, he also demanded that he be named a coleader. Despite some misgivings, the shura council accepted his demand, provided the attack was successful. The senior leaders also approved his plan, again subject to a condition—the planning and execution would be masterminded by its best operator, the man known as Mumeet. Aziz had gladly accepted the condition—the Bringer of Death would have been his choice, anyway.

His wealth assured he could start his own organization, but as an impatient man and one who recognized opportunity, Aziz viewed al Qaeda as his best avenue. Despite its recent decline, al Qaeda remained a formidable force, and its diminished name still retained value. He was convinced his skills and wealth would turn the organization around and restore it to prominence. He would use what remained of the al Qaeda infrastructure to restore the group's reputation and, at the same time, build his own brand. In due order, he would attain his real objective. He had no desire to merely serve as a coleader of al Qaeda; Aziz viewed himself as *the* future leader of the jihad movement.

In order for his master plan to work, he would accumulate power by instigating continued attacks against the West. To do that, he needed multiple secure bases from which the organization could operate. And Afghanistan was a good option. After a lengthy war and an unsatisfactory conclusion, he knew the Americans would be reluctant to go back there, no matter how warranted. Just as important, the Taliban was once again in control of much of the country, and he had a way to gain their unqualified support.

Aziz had met Ahmad Ishaq when he was in Pakistan in the late 1980s, serving at bin Laden's side. Their paths crossed again years later. The former Afghan tribal leader was seeking ways to multiply the millions of dollars he had stolen from the Afghan government while serving in Hamid Karzai's transitional government. And his old friend Aziz was part of the solution. Ishaq funneled some of that money to Aziz, who put it to work in several of his private-equity limited partnerships. In three years, Ishaq had doubled the money he had with Aziz, and an enduring bond developed between the two men.

Ishaq still maintained close ties with the leaders of the hardline Islamic movement from his new home in Switzerland. When Aziz contacted him for support, Ishaq was more than happy to serve as his emissary to the Taliban. Aziz strengthened that support by promising Ishaq he would have a central role in al Qaeda's emerging enterprise in the poppy industry, a position that promised to net Ishaq millions of dollars each year.

As he exited his armored SUV and prepared to greet Fahkoury and al-Rasheed in the Rub Al Khali, Aziz had all the pieces in place to initiate his master plan. This operation would begin to restore the terror group's prominence and put him on the path to iconic status in the world of jihad. But this meeting was just the first step in this part of his plan. The most critical part of the operation would be getting its most essential component—Mumeet—onto the battlefield. As he had done throughout his successful career, Aziz had carefully planned and put the arrangements in place to make that happen.

CHAPTER 8

As Fahkoury and al-Rasheed approached the SUV shortly after midnight, Aziz spread his arms and proclaimed, "As-Salaam-Alaikum!"

Aziz warmly took Fahkoury's hand, and the two kissed cheeks, a sign of respect and familiarity. "Brother Hamid, how have you been?" Aziz asked. "It's been quite some time since we have seen each other, but I have followed your admirable pursuits to this day. I'm honored the shura chose you for this operation."

"Thank you, Prince Aziz. It is an honor to have been chosen for this important mission, whatever it proves to be."

Aziz smiled knowingly and then turned to al-Rasheed. "Brother Fahd, I am Sadiq bin Aziz," he said while shaking al-Rasheed's hand, an appropriate gesture for a first meeting. "It is my pleasure to finally meet you. My colleagues speak highly of you."

The pleasantries dispensed with, Aziz said, "There is much for us to discuss, and we will get to everything in due time, but first we must share some tea in accord with the local Bedouin custom. Please follow me into my tent."

The rectangular tent was nearly four times the size of those provided for Fahkoury and al-Rasheed and stood a hair under twelve feet at its peak. As the trio entered, one of the armed guards started a small generator located outside the rear of the tent, illuminating the interior. Large plush pillows were spread on top of an ornate rug that covered nearly the entire sand floor. There were no other objects inside the spacious nylon structure except a laptop computer positioned atop an opulent wooden desk opposite the entrance.

Aziz instructed his guests to join him on the rug while a pot of tea and a silver tray of cups were brought in and placed between them by one of the guards. The guard quickly left to take up his position outside with the others, leaving Aziz alone with his al Qaeda associates. For the next ten minutes, the men engaged in prosaic conversation, recounting glory days and discussing current regional events and politics. In between sips of the sweet and spicy tea and his limited contributions to the discussion, Fahkoury's mind raced to figure out what the operation would entail. He quickly lost interest in the trivial conversation and was contemplatively running his hand over the elaborate hand-knotted rug when Aziz finally moved the discussion to the issue at hand.

"This place of our meeting is symbolic," he began in an assured, deep voice that conflicted with his diminutive stature, "for these are the ancestral lands of the bin Laden clan and our beloved sheikh. His vision for a global caliphate defined al Qaeda, and he unified believers through momentous attacks against the Great Satan, culminating with the Planes Operation in 2001. In recent years, that vision has faded, and our support among believers has diminished.

"There is no longer a meaning synonymous with al Qaeda. We were once at the pinnacle of jihad, a title we claimed by leading the fight against the Crusaders and the Jews. Now, the original al Qaeda—core al Qaeda—no longer conducts operations. Instead of leading the fight, al Qaeda now simply approves operations that are conducted by our regional affiliates in Yemen, Syria, Tunisia, Libya, and elsewhere. Our affiliates have local interests and local goals and carry out local attacks to further them. These attacks do little to unify believers beyond the borders of the particular region in which they are conducted. Worse still, the affiliates are increasingly operating independently of our core group and no longer have compelling reasons to pledge loyalty to our leaders. Our system is falling apart because of a lack of bold leadership.

"In our absence, the Islamic State has seized our purpose and risen to the top. Followers and money flow to the Islamic State because it has a clear purpose—to establish a global caliphate. For the moment, it is the jihad leader, but it will not unify the believers. The disobedient Islamic State is more concerned with occupying worthless real estate and killing—including Muslims—than in truly establishing a global caliphate. It is not the answer, but if we do nothing, the Islamic State may be the only answer to our great cause.

"My friends, al Qaeda made a choice to retreat from the exposure at top of the mountain for what was believed to be a safer place out of view. Now, the mountainside is giving way underneath us. We must take actions to climb back to our rightful place at the top, or we will perish into the depths below."

Finally, someone with vision! Fahkoury could only watch helplessly as the one-time al Qaeda affiliate in Iraq rose to the top of the terror world. The success of the Islamic State had drastically stemmed the flow of money and recruits into al Qaeda and its affiliates. He had no reason to doubt reports that more than thirty-five thousand people had traveled to the Levant to fight alongside the Islamic State, including more than six thousand people from Western nations. He also knew firsthand of several formerly independent terror groups and one-time al Qaeda affiliates who had pledged allegiance to the Islamic State in recent years. In spite of its more recent losses in Iraq and Syria, the Islamic State still posed an existential threat to al Qaeda and its loose federation of regional terror groups.

"If al Qaeda is to regain its status as the undisputed leader of global jihad and unite all believers," Aziz continued, "we must reclaim our message. The only way we can do that is by once again conducting operations ourselves. And those operations must be levied against the Americans and their allies, preferably on their soil. But the world has changed, and so, too, must we change. We have to be smarter, and nimbler. The West has poured billions of dollars into new technologies and personnel to try to stop us, but their measures are far from perfect. They cannot see and know everything, and they cannot protect thousands of targets available to us. If one is careful and methodical, one can outwit them with simplicity. Allow me to explain how this new model will work.

"The militants for these operations will be drawn from our geographically dispersed affiliated groups. Not only will this feeder system streamline recruiting and provide a diverse talent pool, it will also scatter our resources. We will select candidates from that pool for attack-specific training conducted by members from our centralized Military Committee. The training locations will vary depending upon overall circumstances and those related to the specific attack. In exchange for the recruits and training locations, the affiliated groups will receive compensation from a pool of funds maintained by the Financing Committee for such purposes."

"What about the commanders?" Fahkoury asked. "How will the leaders be chosen and placed with the teams?"

"The leaders for these operations will be chosen from among our most seasoned veterans," Aziz said. "These men will also be scattered around the world and inserted into the battle arena only after the militants are in place and initial preparations are completed. Once in theater, the commanders will be responsible for making necessary revisions to the original plan, instituting final preparations and overseeing the attack. Absent special circumstances, the commanders will not be direct participants in the attacks. Rather, they will plan to escape for future assignments."

Fahkoury did not care that he was supposed to escape; he would gladly die for Allah. Doing his part to rid the world of nonbelievers was all that mattered, and this new model would put him back on the battlefield to fulfill his destiny. He was fully on board with the new strategy until Aziz mentioned timing.

"The ability to quickly assemble, train, and insert a team is to be the central principle of any approved attack," Aziz said. As further evidence of the velocity of operations under the new strategy, Aziz added, "No attack will be approved unless the commanders can infiltrate and execute the attack in less than one month."

"One month? What kind of attacks do you envision?" Fahkoury asked, believing Aziz must be talking about the same small, futile operations of recent years.

Aziz rose and motioned for the others to follow him to the wooden desk and laptop computer.

CHAPTER 9

On the short walk over to the desk, Aziz said, "This will be the first attack under a new strategy that will employ quick, devastating strikes under the leadership of our most capable operators. The attacks will be exclusively on Western targets and designed to inflict lasting psychological and economic damage. Since we will be operating right under the noses of the infidel, we must be able to strike quickly in order to evade detection."

When they arrived at the edge of the desk, the two men flanked Aziz as he opened the computer and pointed at the screen, which showed a map of the United States. "The attack will take place here. This city may not be well known to you, but it is, indeed, significant in America. And here," he said as the map on the screen was replaced, "is what you will attack."

Fahkoury's doubts about the meeting all but vanished upon hearing this news. He was vaguely familiar with the city and the principal target. Not long ago, an al Qaeda franchisee had publicly called for an attack there, but it didn't actually have the wherewithal to pull off such an operation. When he had first heard about it, Fahkoury had admired the idea. Now he would have the chance to pull it off.

Aziz started in with a high-level overview of the plans before pulling up a series of larger images on the computer and addressing the proposed weapons, methods of attack, and coordination. The more Aziz explained the plan, the more Fahkoury considered it achievable, at least at this high level. Yet, despite the limited information, he could see there were potential problems, as there are with any operation on this scale. That said, the potential impact outweighed the risk of a complete failure. The proposed attack was audacious, and it needed to be tried.

For the moment, Fahkoury's biggest concern regarded the quality of the team and its preparedness. "The shura explained that a team has already been assembled. What can you tell me about the team and the training and preparations that have been made so far?" he asked.

"The soldiers were selected from several different al Qaeda affiliates on the basis of ethnic diversity, language skills, and relative obscurity," Aziz said. He added that each recruit spoke at least passable English and had at least some formal education. Even more importantly, none were prominent militants, thereby reducing the chance they were on the radar of any Western intelligence agency. Once the selections were made, the fighters were trained in Afghanistan for what they were told would be an operation in the United States. Timing and target details were not provided. Their training consisted of essential weaponry, basic bomb-making, and tradecraft skills, all designed and imparted so as not to betray any operational details for this attack. If the fighters were captured, the attack plans would remain a secret and could be tried again.

When Aziz finished, Fahkoury asked, "I could imagine using dozens of men for this operation. How many will I have?"

For security reasons, Aziz explained, the identities and numbers of the militants could not be provided, but he assured the two men that a sufficient number of warriors had been carefully chosen by the Military Committee and approved by the shura.

"You said the team is in the United States. Can you tell me how they entered and how we will get into America?" Fahkoury asked.

"Once again, I cannot share the details of their travels. I can tell you that for some time now, we have been working with certain organizations that have well-developed travel routes into the United States and Europe. Those same organizations helped your team enter America and will assist you too. As for your journey, I will tell you only that it will continue from Cairo."

Up to this point, Fahkoury could accept the need for extreme caution, but he was starting to wonder whether this plan could work. He still didn't know a key detail—whether there was a proposed time for the attack. As much as anything, that detail would determine whether this mission was feasible or fantasy. Surely, he would have more than the month Aziz had mentioned earlier. "Has a date been selected for the attack?" he asked. "I will need sufficient time after I get to America to prepare. I will also need money."

"The attack must happen"—Aziz paused for effect—"on the first Sunday of February."

"That's basically only five weeks to get into America and prepare! We need to push the date back!" Fahkoury said.

"The date is absolutely critical," Aziz said. "The world will witness our awakening, as this city will be in the spotlight that day for most Americans and for millions more people around the world."

After Aziz further explained the significance, Fahkoury appreciated why the date had been selected, but he continued to express concern. "It will be very difficult to meet that deadline; it doesn't leave me much time. Even after we get to America, there will be much to do."

"The time is intentionally short," Aziz said. "Remember, our new strategy calls for swift yet momentous strikes that do not require a lot of time and planning while inside enemy lands. Across the West, the governments have greatly increased surveillance inside their countries, including spying on their own citizens. The risk of discovery is already high, so we must take careful measures to reduce that risk, including your travels to America. You will have more time than you think. Most of the things you will need will already be in place by the time you two arrive, and you should be able to acquire the rest without difficulty. The attack, however, must happen on that day. Do not delay it. If necessary, make adjustments to the plan. It would be better to execute a less robust attack than to miss this opportunity."

"How long will it take for us to get to America?" al-Rasheed asked, a question that took on increasing weight given the short window.

"That will depend on a number of factors, none of which I can disclose. Details about the travel routes are too valuable to risk in the unfortunate event you are caught along the way. Just know that much planning has gone into the route you two will take. Your security is paramount," Aziz said, looking directly at Fahkoury. "This operation cannot succeed unless you enter America cleanly. Your journey will take longer than you might expect, but the route will get you there with the least possible exposure. Let me explain what I can."

Aziz told them they must first get to Cairo. There would be some assistance along the way, but for the most part, they would have to improvise. He did not provide any details for the trip from Cairo onward, other than to say they would meet a contact in Houston, Texas, once inside the United States. Aziz handed Fahkoury a small sheet of paper that contained codes and contact information, including those for al Qaeda assets in Khartoum, Cairo, and Houston. Fahkoury took a few moments to memorize the items and then returned the paper to Aziz's waiting hand.

"Your flight from Cairo will leave in six days," Aziz said. "The travel from Cairo onward might not make sense, but know that it is for your and the operation's protection. If you have extra time, use it to rest and to plan for your time in America."

Fahkoury was losing confidence that this plan could work. There were still too many loose ends for his liking, but those decisions were out of his control. "Where will we meet the rest of the team, and where will we get money?" he asked, not wanting to waste any more time.

"The contact in Houston will have that information. Money in America will not be a concern; I have personally seen to that. I also have money for you to use on the journey to America. Use it for food and other incidental costs. Everything else has already been paid for." Aziz handed Fahkoury two rolls of banknotes of popular currencies in various denominations that amounted to a little more than $10,000.

After the exchange, Aziz asked, "Please, do you have any more questions about what we have discussed?"

Fahkoury now knew where the attack would take place, the proposed weapons and method of attack, and the date for the strike. He still harbored doubts about the team; he knew next to nothing about the men. It was clear he wouldn't get any more information from Aziz, so he would have to address those issues in America. His more immediate concern remained the schedule. No matter how long it took to get into the United States, he would be pressed to surveil the target, tweak the plan, and acquire the necessary weapons, not to mention have time to practice, before the attack was supposed to occur. Somehow, he'd have to make it all work. He wasn't going to miss his long-awaited opportunity to strike the belly of the beast and two significant representations of its sinful culture.

"No questions. We know the important matters; the rest we will figure out," Fahkoury said, answering for both men.

"Very good. In a few hours, the same Bedouin who brought you here will return and provide for your passage to Al Hudaydah, a Yemeni port city on the coast of the Red Sea. You will be met by a boat in Al Hudaydah. Once in Africa, you will be largely on your own, so you will have to improvise along the way. I know I need not say this, but use every precaution. This operation is too important. I wish you well and success, brothers. Inshallah."

With that, Aziz exited the tent, got into his armored SUV, and promptly left the remote camp.

As he and his security detail drove away, Aziz had no reason to suspect that his travels to the remote Rub Al Khali had been monitored by an experimental CIA satellite.

CHAPTER 10

HART SENATE OFFICE BUILDING WASHINGTON, DC

Two days later, Carpenter was striding into the secure room—oblivious to the desirous stares of the young staffers—and preparing for what he considered to be absolutely the most unappealing aspect of his job, worse even than being in the dark, open ocean. Fortunately, the obligation was one Carpenter was rarely called to fulfill. He had appeared a few times previously but never by himself and usually just as a showpiece. On this occasion, however, he would be alone, the victim of bad timing and, he suspected, a bit of managerial subterfuge.

His punishment, at least in his view, for the successful operation in Cuba was the opportunity to sit before the Senate Select Committee on Intelligence. While the president directs all covert actions, the SSCI is one of two legislative bodies responsible for oversight of the CIA and its Counterterrorism Center, the other being the House Permanent Select Committee on Intelligence. Although Carpenter appreciated that Congressional oversight of the agency was needed for effective governance, his tolerance for politicians had rapidly diminished over the years. He still harbored ill will for their shameful Monday-morning quarterbacking after the 9/11 attacks, and his cynicism stopped just short of contempt for the vainglorious overseers. It was too easy for these namby-pambies to criticize from the secure, comfy confines of the Capitol. It was altogether different to do it when operating downrange.

His immediate boss, Timothy Patrick, the current head of the CTC, had delivered the bad news about his impending testimony. After spending a couple of days snorkeling in the crystalline Cayman waters and lounging on the private beach, Carpenter had returned to DC to brief the president on the Sanchez operation. The idea of downtime was not Carpenter's but, rather, the president's. Since his own schedule was not going to be clear, the commander in chief more or less ordered Carpenter to remain in the Caymans after the mission was completed, even going so far as to personally make arrangements for him at the well-appointed condo on Seven Mile Beach. They were leaving the Oval Office the previous morning when Patrick delivered the news, putting a real damper on what had been a celebratory mood.

The hearing would be a continuation of regularly scheduled meetings held throughout the congressional calendar, an opportunity for the members to ask questions about highly classified operations and the most significant threats posed to the country. Every so often, the SSCI requested testimony from a field officer. It was an opportunity to hear directly from the front lines and assess the effectiveness of the government's antiterror policies and, by extension, the appropriateness of funding requests. Patrick assured him it was all routine, but Carpenter suspected there was an ulterior motive.

For the past two years, Patrick occasionally hinted—not so subtly—that someday Carpenter would be a terrific candidate to succeed him as head of the CTC. Patrick had been chief of station when Carpenter arrived in Beirut straight from the Farm, the CIA training center. Their careers had dovetailed almost ever since, the sole gap being the first few years after Carpenter joined the CTC. At nine years, Patrick was already the longest serving head of the CTC, and mandatory retirement was looming in a handful of years.

The intimations were both flattering and unsettling. Carpenter knew he'd have to leave the field one day, but he felt he had a number of good years left. Not long removed from his fortieth birthday, he had no plans to hang it up. If he was no longer the fittest member of the team, he wasn't far off. Anyway, his increasing cognitive scores more than offset any slippage at the hands of Father Time. What disturbed Carpenter most—in those moments he was truthful to himself—was his own mortality. Patrick had always been his principal mentor, a father figure even, and now he was being groomed to one day replace the man.

The night before, Patrick provided an overview of the testimony he and CIA Director Melissa Gonzalez had given earlier that day. Over the course of five hours, the two senior agency leaders dutifully answered questions on matters ranging from cyber warfare to Iranian and North Korean nuclear capabilities and, of course, terrorism. The Cuban affair came up, Patrick told him. Although there had been some feigned umbrage about killing an American, he and Gonzalez had put that to rest with the evidence against Guillermo Sanchez. No one disputed that it was just as heinous as the evidence used to justify the drone strike that had killed the American cleric Anwar al-Awlaki in Yemen a few years earlier. There would be no reason to plow the same earth during his testimony, Patrick assured him.

"Just relax; you'll be fine," the avuncular Patrick said as they wrapped up the preparations, all the while trying to hold back a laugh. "This will be great experience for you. Besides, the committee just wants the chance to be graced with the presence of a real-life 'secret agent,' and I thought since you're in town…"

Carpenter responded with a few choice words of his own.

As he settled into his chair in Room 219—the soundproof and heavily fortified hearing room inside the Hart Senate Office Building—Carpenter wasn't sure what to expect. Patrick's last words of advice had been to not allow himself to be caught up in any politics but to just answer as best he could and be truthful. Carpenter was resolved to follow that advice and remembered what Churchill had once said about truth: "Truth is incontrovertible; panic may resent it, ignorance may deride it, malice may destroy it, but there it is."

His absolute duty was to protect the citizens and interests of the United States, and he would not allow politics to influence his testimony. Carpenter planned to tell the self-important politicians the truth, whether or not they wanted to hear it.

CHAPTER 11

After he pledged to tell the truth, Carpenter sat down and exchanged glances with several members of the committee, who were arrayed in a horseshoe pattern on the platform above him. He discretely tugged at his collar and tried to hide the discomfort caused by the restrictive suit and tie he was forced to wear as suffered through the opening remarks of the Senate Select Committee on Intelligence chairman, Senator James McDermott.

"Mr. Carpenter, thank you for being here. We are here today to complete testimony from the intelligence community regarding this committee's regular interim update on existing and anticipated threats facing the United States. Since it's our first week back from the holiday recess, we won't hold you too long."

Sure, Carpenter thought. *Wouldn't want to work too hard the first week back from a three-week vacation.*

After about five more minutes of meaningless drivel, Chairman McDermott finally concluded his opening remarks. He then announced, "I now recognize Senator Wilson, who will begin the questioning."

Carpenter locked his piercing green eyes onto Wilson, seated two seats to McDermott's right, and steeled himself. He knew there wouldn't be any softballs coming from Senator Wilson. Her dislike of the agency was infamous.

Wilson shuffled some papers, and glared down at Carpenter condescendingly as she prepared to begin.

"Thank you, Mr. Chairman. Mr. Carpenter, your colleagues Ms. Gonzalez and Mr. Patrick testified earlier that the agency is not presently aware of any credible and specific threats against the country. Do you agree with those views?"

"Yes, I do, but I note the basis for my response is limited in relation to that of my colleagues."

"Very well," Wilson said. Not missing a beat, she then asked, "Based on your limited view, would you say the overall threats from what some refer to as 'radical Islamic terrorism' have generally increased or decreased over the past five years?"

"In my view, the threat has increased over that time period, and that trend started much earlier."

"Mr. Carpenter, do you agree that our aggressive actions in places like Iraq, Yemen, Libya, and Syria against what some refer to as 'radical Islamic terror' and 'Islamist terror' serve only to invite more of these threats, both here and elsewhere in the world?"

It appeared Senator Wilson intended to turn this hearing into the very political discussion he had hoped to avoid. Carpenter tried to stay above the fray, but he kept tabs on matters that affected his job and national security. He recognized the angle Wilson was playing. He knew that among the members of SSCI, Senators Elinore Wilson and Raymond Williams—the West Coast bookend to the East Coast Wilson—believed that national security policies *caused* every problem faced by the country. They pushed a false narrative that, but for what they called its "insensitive overseas aggression," the United States would be immune from the heinous ambitions of a few radicalized groups.

Carpenter's disdain was not limited to Wilson's thinking, however. It stretched to both sides of the ever-enlarging political spectrum. On the other end of that divide were people like Chairman McDermott and Senator Lawrence Grant. Their ilk seemed to argue that every problem faced by the United States, domestic or foreign, was a national security issue that required a military solution. To that point, the blinkered Grant dedicated the entire platform of his recent, ill-fated presidential run to national security. For his part, the servile McDermott was the poster boy for term limits. Now in his fourth decade in Washington and having adopted a preference for the tranquil shores of political correctness, McDermott was no longer willing to negotiate the turbulent waters where truth resides. Once an independent thinker, political winds and public approval now exclusively defined his positions.

To Carpenter, demagoguery and political correctness had no place in national security considerations. These critical issues required pragmatic dialogue and clear-eyed decisions to ensure the safety of the American people. Any political efforts to either modulate or inflate national security threats frustrated both diplomatic and military efforts to eliminate them.

"Senator Wilson, yours is more a policy matter, one outside my purview," he said, attempting to sidestep the political question.

"Mr. Carpenter," she said in a clipped, biting tone, "setting aside policy, I am asking your personal opinion as a United States government employee who is experienced in living and operating in countries outside the United States. Let me ask again: Do you believe there is a correlation between the hostile actions of the United States, including the use of those terms, and threats against this country?"

No way out of this one. Now that she asked for his opinion, he couldn't claim lack of insight. He had to answer the question.

"No, I wouldn't go that far, *Senator*," he said, sarcastically dragging out her title in his native Southern drawl. "As a means of promoting and justifying their acts, terrorist groups do claim that certain attacks are in retaliation for particular US actions. Those same groups also attempt to conflate the terms you mentioned and argue that the United States is engaged in war with all of Islam, but words have little bearing on their ideology.

"To further that point, I note that prior attempts to reclassify acts of terror as criminal activity and substituting the euphemism 'overseas contingency operations' for the 'global war on terror' did not at all stem the threat. In fact, the Islamic State emerged despite the softer language.

mply, Senator, even if it chose a policy of inaction and did not use those phrases, the United States would still be the prime target of certain terror groups due to its core—"

"Wouldn't it stop all the violence," she asked, "if our military and intelligence agencies weren't attacking Muslim people?"

Carpenter needed to compose himself. He wasn't going to play these bullshit games, but he couldn't lose his cool either. She knew the situation was far more complex than the picture she was painting. The problem was most certainly not Islam, but, rather, ideology. He had a uniquely informed perspective of Islam from studying the religion and his broad experiences with Muslims across the globe. Despite the nature of his work, he had encountered far more salt-of-the-earth, peaceful Muslim people than the evildoers he was tasked to defeat. At the same time, he recognized that the people perpetuating acts of terrorism claimed legitimacy under Islam. In their perverted interpretation, Islam authorized—demanded, even—violent jihad to rid the world of nonbelievers, and these people were not going away anytime soon.

Carpenter took a few deep breaths and said, "I believe that is highly unlikely. The goal of the Islamic State is to establish a global caliphate, a world governed exclusively by sharia law. Al Qaeda shares the same long-term objective. Secular governments have no place in their world, and the United States is seen as the foremost enemy that must be defeated in order to realize that goal.

"Let me try to conceptualize the problem. Picture three interlocking gears that fuel their extreme ideology: one gear represents radical teaching, another represents financing, and the third represents attacks. The output from these three gears is measured in terms of the number of true believers—the more believers, the closer they are to achieving their goal of a global caliphate. Each gear supports and helps move the others, but the largest and most influential gear of the three is the one representing attacks. That gear churns the others and is most productive when it is fueled by a successful attack on the West—the greatest impediment to their malignant ideology.

"For that reason, attacks against the West are and will remain priorities for groups such as the Islamic State and al Qaeda. In my opinion, political influence alone is not enough to stop these gears from moving. In fact, these gears will just chew up a policy exclusively comprised of political niceties. Aggressive countermeasures, including lethal force, are unquestionably needed to clog these gears."

"Mr. Carpenter," Wilson said, "we learned from Director Patrick that there are *no* current credible threats against the US homeland. Other than small attacks attributed to them by lone wolves, neither al Qaeda nor ISIS has been able to successfully conduct an attack on US soil since 2001. In light of the diminished threat to the US homeland, wouldn't you agree that now is the time to replace aggressive tactics in favor of a spirit of collaboration designed to soften any misguided views?"

"Are you in denial?" Carpenter almost said out loud. *These politicians only hear what they want to hear. She asked for my opinion. Maybe this will be crystal clear.*

"Senator, first, I emphatically do *not* agree with *any* view that reasons the United States homeland is no longer threatened by Islamist extremism. Anyone believing that is in for a rude awakening. Every day of every week, the groups I mentioned seek ways to attack us here and abroad, and once they find the opportunity, they won't hesitate to do so.

"Second, it is my professional opinion, based upon years of operational experience, that those preaching, financing, and levying this ideology will not 'soften' their views. They are not 'misguided,' as you suggest, and they do not seek to proselytize in the traditional sense. Instead, they will accept no form of appeasement other than absolute conversion to their radical Islamist views. They will simply kill anyone they deem to be a nonbeliever, and that especially includes the citizens of this country.

"So the choice is to either confront them now or allow them to grow into a bigger problem. For me, that's an easy decision. Right now, the number of people in these extremist groups is very small in terms of both the Muslim and broader global populations, but they continue to attract new followers all the time."

Second-term senator Elinore Wilson, minority leader on the Select Committee on Intelligence, was not accustomed to being addressed in this fashion. Her intolerance to fierce dissent could be traced to her background in academia. She had emerged from the ivory tower expecting that her views would be accepted with nothing more than minimal enlightenment from her patrician lips. Dissent from this jingoist was intolerable. Wilson's face flushed, and her nostrils flared as she glared down at Carpenter through her round designer spectacles, desperately searching for a worthy rebuke. A few audible huffs were all she could manage; she had been knocked from her soapbox and couldn't muster the words to reclaim it.

With no better comeback at her tongue, Senator Wilson muttered, "Mr. Carpenter, I object to your deplorable behavior and coarse language before this respected committee and will be sure to address it with your superiors. You are here to answer questions posed by this committee, not to lecture its members. Moreover, for the record, I believe you and people like you are why we have problems with certain groups around the world."

Carpenter wasn't about to back down now. He returned her stare with his own and said, "Senator, will all due respect, I am here to present the truth and my honest assessments based upon my experiences and knowledge. Today, I was also asked for my opinions, and I shared them, based on my experiences and truths as I know them. That you don't like my responses is of no concern to me."

Recognizing she could not save herself from further indignity, Wilson capitulated. "Mr. Chairman, I have no other questions for this witness."

"Thank you, Senator Wilson," a stunned McDermott slowly said. "Senator Williams, you now have the floor."

"Thank you, Mr. Chairman. I have only one question for Mr. Carpenter. Mr. Carpenter, doesn't the continued persecution of certain peoples only ensure that the United States will continue to be the target of attacks?"

"Senator Williams, I am unclear on what you mean by 'persecution.'"

"In this case, I am referring to the discriminatory travel restrictions placed on citizens of certain Muslim-majority countries from entering the United States."

"Senator, as I explained earlier," Carpenter said with more than a hint of exasperation, "al Qaeda, the Islamic State, and other terror groups are undeterred. They relentlessly seek ways to attack the United States on our soil as a means to further their objectives. The countries under the travel ban are either known sponsors of terrorism, failed states, or in the process of becoming failed states. I can tell you from firsthand experience, the security and intelligence in those countries are suspect at best. Quite simply, those countries are largely unable or unwilling to provide accurate background information for persons seeking to travel to this country. Moreover, terror groups enjoy considerable control and influence in those countries. These realities create a greater risk that groups like the Islamic State could more easily slip operatives into the United States to carry out an attack.

"Once again, the best recruitment tool for any terror group is the successful execution of a large-scale attack on US soil. Stricter travel policies and stronger border controls would seem a matter of sound common sense. I'm not sure why we would want to make it easier for a terrorist to enter this country."

"In light of the discriminatory nature of this policy, I'm a bit surprised at your answer, Mr. Carpenter."

"Because I'm black?" Carpenter asked incredulously. "Senator, this isn't a situation of discrimination like those faced by blacks, Irish, Italians, and Poles, among other racial and ethnic groups. In this situation, certain people—not all—who have moved into certain unstable countries are intent on killing us. Completely different circumstances."

"Very well, Mr. Carpenter. You indicated the policy is a matter of common sense. I am sure you would agree common sense is rooted in reality. In that regard, I note the fact that of the relatively few people from those countries who have visited this country, none has committed an act of terror in the United States. Aren't the chances extremely slim that any future visitors from those countries would be involved in a plot to commit an attack here in the United States?"

"Senator Williams, unless a person discloses it openly, intent is difficult to know. I don't believe there is anything controversial about that statement. The best way to determine a person's intent is to infer it from personal information and verifiable past behavior. As I stated, that kind of information in those countries is not reliable. Missing even just a few would-be terrorists presents tremendous risk. With that said, in my opinion, a greater threat exists from other more indirect routes into the United States."

"By indirect routes, do you mean illegally crossing the southern border?" Williams asked.

"I would not restrict my concerns solely to the southern border, Senator."

"Do you have, or are you aware the Central Intelligence Agency has, any proof that suspected terrorists are attempting to enter the United States through the 'indirect routes' that you are referring to?"

"Personally, I don't, but I strongly suspect they try. In the past twenty-four months, Customs and Border Protection has detained hundreds of special-interest aliens, or immigrants from countries known to support or suspected of supporting terrorism, including some from those countries on the list. To my knowledge, none of those detained are known or suspected terrorists. But that does not necessarily prove none of them had the intent, but for their capture, to do harm if they succeeded in getting here. More troubling is the fact that no one knows how many people, including potential terrorists, actually do enter the country illegally each year."

"Thank you, Mr. Carpenter. For what it's worth, I believe the concerns about terrorists crossing our borders are overblown. The soundness of our existing measures is evidenced by the fact that there has been no big attack here since 2001. I also believe the administration's aggressive immigration policies will only further incite our enemies. Mr. Chairman, I have no additional questions at this time."

"Thank you, Senator Williams. This has been quite a productive and *lively* discussion," the septuagenarian chairman said excitedly. "Senator Manning has also requested some time. When he is through with his questions, we will adjourn the meeting. Senator Manning, the floor is now yours."

Senator John Paul Manning was the newest member of the Committee, but from what Carpenter knew about him, the Tennessean appeared to be a straight shooter, interested only in protecting the interests of the country.

"Mr. Carpenter, you testified earlier that you do not agree that the threat of an attack here in the United States has diminished. Do you base that on the lone-wolf attacks of recent years, or do you believe another large-scale attack on the United States is possible?"

"The lone-wolf attacks represent a significant and continuing threat. Lone actors are difficult to detect and stop, and the Islamic State, in particular, has demonstrated an uncanny ability to radicalize people in Europe and here to wage attacks with common weapons, including vehicles. Worse still is that the 'flash-to-bang' time—the period beginning with the assimilation of online radicalization material and ending with the attack—is becoming increasingly shorter. As long as the terror groups inspiring the attacks remain strong and the radicalization materials they disseminate remain available, these lone-wolf threats will only continue to grow.

"Unfortunately, I also believe that another large-scale attack is possible. As a matter of fact, I believe one is inevitable. It is only a matter of time before another large-scale attack on US soil is attempted." Carpenter looked around and noticed that only Manning and McDermott seemed to be paying attention.

"Would the Islamic State be most likely to attempt a large-scale attack on the United States?" Manning asked.

"Probably. Despite progress against them in both Iraq and Syria, the Islamic State currently remains the best-organized and best-financed terror organization. Its intentions toward the United States and the West are well known, and it has shown an ability to carry out significant extraterritorial attacks, notably those in Paris and Nice. Up to this point, the Islamic State has only claimed to have 'inspired' attacks carried out here, but it has publicly expressed its intention to pull off a large-scale attack in the United States. For the foreseeable future, the Islamic State is the most likely group to attempt a large-scale attack here."

"Does al Qaeda no longer present a credible threat to the United States?"

"I would strongly caution against that assumption, Senator Manning. Core al Qaeda has not been particularly active the past few years, but its affiliated terror groups, in particular al Qaeda in the Arabian Peninsula—or AQAP—are very active and pose serious threats to US interests. However, these affiliated groups have, to date, largely limited their attacks to the regions where they operate. There have been some rumors that core al Qaeda wants to make a comeback. This could be wishful thinking, but a successful large-scale attack would certainly accomplish that goal, especially one here in the United States or in Europe."

"What do you make of the fact that core al Qaeda, as you call them, has been inactive in recent years?" Manning asked.

"Nothing positive, frankly. We know that al Qaeda is patient and methodical. It is playing the long game, and its intent to attack us here has not diminished one bit. It would be very dangerous to dismiss al Qaeda—it still presents a grave threat to our country."

"Thank you for your time, Mr. Carpenter. I hope your predictions about another large-scale attack never come to pass."

"I do, too, Senator."

CHAPTER 12

CENTRAL INTELLIGENCE AGENCY HEADQUARTERS LANGLEY, VIRGINIA

Carpenter was fit to be tied when he walked into CTC director Timothy Patrick's comfortable office on the sixth floor. He had been dismissed by the SSCI only forty-five minutes before and had spent the entire time simmering in rush-hour traffic.

"You look like you just ate a bag of lemons," said Patrick.

"Sometimes I really can't stand those fuckers," Carpenter said, using the salty language he used only in front of his closest associates and friends. "They don't give a shit about national security. They only care about gathering information they can use for their political agendas. I swear, sometimes they hear only what they want to hear."

Although he had already heard through the grapevine, Patrick played along. "What happened?"

"Things got a little testy with Wilson," Carpenter said. "I'm sure you'll hear about it. You can consider that my thanks for putting me in there."

"I wouldn't worry about it. It's about time somebody knocked her off her high horse, anyway. If Wilson tries to make a stink, Director Gonzalez will have your back. She's no fan of Senator Wilson, and neither is the president. Well, sorry about all that, but it will be good experience in the long run,"

Patrick said. "Switching gears, I'd like to get your thoughts on something else."

"If it involves politicians, I'll pass."

"No politicians. I read a recent report from one of our top al Qaeda analysts, and I think there might be something to her conclusion. I'd like you to read the report and meet with her tomorrow."

"If you're talking about Gabriella Rock's report, I already know about it. I read it on the flight from Syria, and I think she's spot-on. It might come as a surprise, but at least one of your Neanderthals can actually read."

Patrick giggled at the ribbing. He knew Carpenter had to be the most cerebral special-operations officer in the history of the CTC. A devoted reader of spy novels, Patrick often thought Carpenter would be an ideal protagonist. He was stupidly good looking and every bit the lethal ass kicker that any main character was portrayed to be, but the keen intellect that supported an uncanny ability to quickly process information placed Carpenter on a unique plane. That rare combination of mental and physical skills had borne tremendous results and made Patrick's job a lot easier than it should be.

"I told you weeks ago something's not right," Carpenter continued when Patrick stopped laughing, "and I'm pretty confident al-Zawahiri and his fellow al Qaeda scumbags haven't decided 'We're done here.' They're up to something."

Patrick had been hearing the same thing from Carpenter for several weeks—al Qaeda is up to something; they've been too quiet. He didn't necessarily buy into Carpenter's theory until the report started to change his thinking. His biggest issue remained the lack of any known evidence to support it. "I agree it's a bit odd," Patrick said, "but al Qaeda has real problems. This period of inactivity could just be natural decay."

"Come on, you don't honestly believe that. Those assholes will fight to the bitter end. What convinces me they're planning something is the fact there's been no recent mention of Mumeet for months. So either he's dead or they've pulled him for a major operation. My money is on the latter. If he were dead, we'd have heard about it."

Patrick now knew for sure why his friend was so invested in this theory. The man known as the Bringer of Death was a source of great angst for the agency and for Carpenter in particular. The name Mumeet had first popped up in intercepted communications during the Afghan invasion. Since then, the al Qaeda terrorist had been credited for multiple al Qaeda bombing attacks, including some of the most significant ones. By the time of the Basra bombings in 2004, forensic technicians were able to identify certain signatures in the powerful yet simply designed bombs attributed to Mumeet. Those signatures were again apparent in June 2008.

Late in 2007, Carpenter told Patrick he was numbering his days with the agency. Patrick knew Carpenter had fallen for a foreign-affairs officer assigned to the US embassy in Islamabad. He was getting married, Carpenter said to his boss, and the couple would be looking for work stateside. They wanted to start a family. The plan was for Carpenter to stay through the end of 2008, when Lizzie's tour of duty with the State Department would end. Patrick was thrilled for Carpenter and promised to do anything he could to help them settle back in the United States.

The news was bittersweet, however. Patrick had only recently assumed the top job at the CTC, and Carpenter had been a big factor in his decision to take the position. They first met in Beirut, where Patrick was serving as chief of station when Carpenter arrived. Since then, the two men had become very close friends and shared a deep level of mutual respect, a connection that was forged through common values, experiences, and perspectives.

Patrick himself had started out as an operations officer, beginning his career in Tehran twenty years before Carpenter showed up in Beirut. A brilliant recruiter and human-intelligence gatherer from the start, Patrick raised alarms of growing civil unrest many months before the first demonstrations began against the pro-Western Shah. Less than two years later, the swift revolution forced the Persian monarch into exile and ushered in an Islamic republic. Patrick's legendary status was cemented when he later tracked Ilyich Ramírez Sánchez, also known as Carlos the Jackal, to Khartoum, Sudan. At the time of his capture, the Jackal was the world's most wanted terrorist.

The events of an early June morning in 2008 tested but ultimately strengthened that relationship. That day, as Lizzie and several colleagues were walking into the Danish embassy to meet Denmark's new ambassador to Pakistan, a car bearing diplomatic registration plates swerved into the parking lot and sped past the unsuspecting guards. Before anyone could react, the car slammed to a halt and exploded an instant later. Lizzie was one of six lives lost.

In a statement released two days later, al Qaeda claimed responsibility for the attack, declaring it was in retaliation for both the publication of cartoons depicting the prophet Mohammed in Danish newspapers and the presence of Danish troops in Afghanistan. Forensic testing confirmed a short time later that the car bomb was the work of Mumeet.

Carpenter was beyond devastated. Before meeting Lizzie, he wasn't sure he was capable of loving anyone as deeply as he had his mother. Lizzie had changed him and shown him the joyous wonders of true love. And then she was ripped away by evil. But he wouldn't allow himself to grieve, insisting on returning to work just a few days after the incident. Patrick ultimately had to enforce a two-month bereavement period and called him back to the United States. After landing at Andrews Air Force Base, Carpenter jumped in a car and headed west, refusing to speak with Patrick or anyone else from the agency. He spent the entire time alone, traveling from one remote national park to the next, sleeping in the elements and avoiding all human contact.

When he came back, Carpenter was hardened and even more determined than he had been before Lizzie graced his life. It seemed he tried to push away his pain with a fervent application of his lethal skills. And as each year and every successful operation passed, Carpenter's torment appeared to lessen ever so slightly. But Patrick knew that grief would never release his friend from its insuperable grip. Killing Mumeet would be the only way for him to find some modicum of real peace, and the mysterious jihadist had become his undying obsession.

"You might be right," Patrick said in a consoling tone, "but we don't have anything at the moment to support a change from the status quo. And Mumeet has gone dark before, although maybe not for this long." Patrick knew that for certain, because there was an outstanding order that any piece of intelligence about Mumeet appear on his desk the moment it came in. For years, the name Mumeet popped up in intercepted communications every few months or so. That pattern had changed recently, something that Carpenter was also aware of because he asked Patrick about the terrorist every time they spoke.

"Anyway, I set the meeting for nine," Patrick said. "I have meetings starting at six thirty, so there's a slight chance I might be late. It's been a long day. Let's get out of here and go grab some dinner on me. I'll even buy you a couple of beers."

CHAPTER 13

Patrick was finishing off a doughnut when Carpenter arrived at his office just before nine o'clock the following morning. "You should lay off those things," said Carpenter, "or you won't be able to get your fat ass out of that chair."

The CTC chief flipped a good-natured, double-fisted New York salute to his insolent subordinate. Carpenter had a point. Too many hours behind the desk and too many hastily consumed meals had taken a toll. But Patrick ignored the constructive criticism. He was just happy to see there had been no regression in Carpenter's improved mood by the end of their dinner the previous evening. As the two men exchanged stories over steaks and more than a "couple of beers," Patrick sensed that Carpenter's unpleasant memories of the SSCI testimony were all but forgotten by the end of the night.

When Carpenter had phoned Patrick a few weeks before to say he had a "gut feeling" that something was up with al Qaeda, Patrick listened with a dose of skepticism, as was his nature. When he asked Carpenter what he had to support that feeling, Carpenter said, "You don't share any of that shit with me until you need me. You figure it out!" Patrick's thinking started to change right before Carpenter left for the Cuba operation. On Christmas Day, he read the analyst's report and began to believe there was more to his skilled operator's premise. He found the report compelling enough to schedule a meeting with the analyst and a senior intelligence officer. Patrick was slowly buying into the theory, but before he committed resources, he needed further convincing.

At precisely 9:00 a.m., Carpenter followed Patrick into the walk-in closet on the third floor that some bureaucrat had decided would make for a suitable conference room. When Patrick cleared the threshold of the door, Carpenter saw two very attractive women, one of whom he had worked with in the past, sitting on the edge of well-worn black-fabric office chairs around the nearer end of a rectangular conference table. As they moved into the small chamber, Carpenter took quick notice of the half-dead plant in the near corner, and a yellowed black and white picture of the Lincoln Memorial that hung askew on the left wall. *Nothing but the best.*

"PJ, I believe you know Samantha Lane, a senior intelligence analyst," Patrick said. "I asked Samantha here today to listen in. Depending on what we decide, she is the person I would like to spearhead any further analysis." Samantha's presence was a good sign. Carpenter knew Patrick regarded her highly. "Next to Samantha is Gabriella Rock," Patrick said, "a counterterrorism analyst who specializes in al Qaeda and its affiliates. Ella, of course, is also the author of the report and the reason we are here today."

Carpenter tried to read all relevant analyst reports, but ever since reading her first report a couple of years earlier, he made sure to read all of Ella's. They were a must-read resource for anyone wanting to understand the motivations, capabilities, and intentions of foreign terrorist groups, especially al Qaeda. He liked sharp, confident people, and, as he and Patrick settled into chairs opposite their colleagues, he looked forward to hearing more from the talented analyst.

After the introductions were completed, Patrick said, "OK, Ella, we're all ears."

"Yes, thank you, sir. Well, my thesis is that core AQ finds itself at a critical juncture and may not survive much longer unless it does something to change the paradigm," she said with a self-assuredness that further impressed Carpenter. "Before we get into how we believe al Qaeda intends to reestablish itself, let me first provide a bit of background.

"Leading up to the Afghan invasion, AQ operated under a centralized management structure. Al Qaeda senior leadership—the shura or

AQSL—maintained control of all operations, approving plans and overseeing the recruitment, training, and deployment of militants. This model was quickly upended with the Afghan invasion. Beginning in late 2001, the senior leaders were either killed or forced into hiding. Many al Qaeda fighters gradually returned to their home countries. With its senior leaders under constant pressure and its infrastructure destroyed, AQ evolved into a decentralized operating structure.

"Under the new framework, regional terror groups operate under the al Qaeda banner in exchange for a pledge of loyalty—*bay'at*—to the shura council. These affiliated groups operate autonomously for the most part; they need to seek AQSL approval only for major operations. Al Qaeda in Iraq—now known as the Islamic State—was, of course, a one-time AQ affiliate.

"As the affiliates gained more notoriety, al Qaeda more or less became a nominal leader and one with diminishing power. This trend accelerated following bin Laden's death. As the face of global jihad, bin Laden remained a strong draw for AQ, even as the core group began to pull back from actual operations. Although he arguably can match bin Laden's jihadist credentials, al-Zawahiri simply lacks the same charisma. That the affiliates would renew bay'at upon bin Laden's death was not a foregone conclusion.

"To add to al Qaeda's troubles, bin Laden's death came just six months after the start of the Arab Spring uprisings, and the repercussions were still playing out. In fact, many affiliates took their time pledging bay'at to al Qaeda under al-Zawahiri, the first signs of potential fractures in the coalition. At that time, AQSL must have appreciated that its uncontested grip on global jihad was dubious. If AQSL had any doubts, they were removed soon after, when AQI moved into Syria and became the Islamic State in Iraq and Syria—ISIS.

"Finding greater benefit from AQI's war against the US in Iraq, bin Laden had been tolerant of AQI's equally ruthless attacks against Shiite Muslims when the affiliate was commanded by Abu Musab al-Zarqawi. For his part, al-Zawahiri openly expressed his concerns about AQI's attacks against Shiites, believing they undermined the jihadi cause. When he later succeeded al-Zarqawi, Abu Bakr al-Baghdadi saw an opening for AQI to grab power after bin Laden was killed. When civil war later broke out in Syria, AQI moved in, quickly seizing territory and imposing its unyielding beliefs on everyone in its path. AQI renamed itself ISIS, and al-Baghdadi declared a caliphate in Iraq and Syria. That declaration and the ruthless tactics proved too much for al-Zawahiri and al Qaeda, resulting in an acrimonious divorce from its former affiliate.

"An emboldened al-Baghdadi steered ISIS to the forefront of Islamic terrorism. Using a cutting-edge marketing campaign, ISIS began attracting recruits in droves. In addition to the money it made from criminal enterprises, ISIS was also receiving funding from former al Qaeda benefactors. Finally, some terror groups that had formerly worked with al Qaeda switched allegiances to ISIS. By the end of 2014, the two terror groups were moving in opposite directions, and al Qaeda absolutely had to realize that its future was very much uncertain.

"Today, not much has changed for al Qaeda. It is increasingly cut off from funding, and potential recruits continue to favor ISIS, which is now known as the Islamic State. Moreover, there are increasing rumors of disenchantment among al Qaeda's affiliated groups. Any further deterioration in the alliance might have a domino effect, leaving core al Qaeda completely cut off from global jihad.

"For these reasons, al Qaeda is at a crossroads. If it does nothing to change course, it will cease to exist in any influential form. Its affiliates will simply proceed on their own or switch allegiance to the Islamic State. In order to remain relevant and regain its foothold at the head of global jihad, core al Qaeda has three choices.

"One option is to align with the Islamic State. That is unlikely for several reasons. First, the two groups have serious differences, and, as long as al-Baghdadi and al-Zawahiri are alive, they are likely irreconcilable. Second, there is no guarantee al Qaeda would emerge intact from such a merger. The Islamic State, despite its recent losses in Iraq and Syria, remains the stronger of the two. Al Qaeda really has nothing to offer in terms of money or men. It has only its diminishing cachet and its progressively loose federation of terror groups. Any combination will bear far more resemblance to the Islamic State than al Qaeda.

"The second option is to try to destroy the Islamic State. Once again, this is unlikely. For starters, al Qaeda cannot match the Islamic State's resources—fighters, weapons, and money. Furthermore, al Qaeda largely lacks a foothold in Iraq and Syria from which to launch a sustainable campaign against the Islamic State. Even if it is pushed out of the Levant, the Islamic State will metastasize elsewhere and remain a superior force to a status quo al Qaeda.

"That leaves the third and, in my opinion the most likely, option. The third option available to al Qaeda is to regain its former status by returning to operations, specifically with large-scale attacks. A successful large-scale attack would restore it to prominence at a time when its chief rival is under siege in Iraq and Syria. This option is also more feasible, because the resource needs for even a large-scale attack are much, much less than they are for the other two options. My conclusion is that, if al Qaeda has not already made its choice to pursue the third option, it will soon. I partially base that assumption on al Qaeda's surprisingly restored strength.

"You may recall that when we pulled out of Afghanistan at the end of 2014, the highest levels of our government pushed a narrative that al Qaeda had been 'decimated' and no longer posed a real threat to the United States. They claimed there were no more than one hundred fighters left in al Qaeda, hiding someplace in the tribal areas of Pakistan. At that time, our government was slowly recovering from having underestimated ISIS—you recall the infamous 'jayvee' comment a year earlier—and our focus was switching away from al Qaeda and onto what is now the Islamic State.

"While al Qaeda had indeed been diminished from the height of its powers, the falsity of that narrative and the claims supporting it were revealed a year later. In late 2015, we discovered two new al Qaeda training camps in Afghanistan—not in the tribal areas of Pakistan but, rather, in Afghanistan itself. It took four days and some seventy air strikes to destroy those camps. We killed nearly two hundred al Qaeda fighters—or twice as many as were claimed to be left in the entire terror group just a year earlier. Of course, many others were able to escape.

"Clearly, al Qaeda has been trying to reorganize in Afghanistan, and its advancements have been considerably underestimated. With the Taliban once again in control of more than half of the country, it is highly likely that al Qaeda is also gaining strength in Afghanistan.

"AQ may not have a better opportunity than the present to plan, prepare for, and execute an attack, and there are indications that is exactly what the group is doing. Until last spring, al-Zawahiri was consistently making representations that AQ would attack the United States everywhere in the world. In a complete change, he and other members of senior leadership have been noticeably quiet since.

"Finally, in the last few months, there haven't even been any significant local operations by AQ affiliates. We haven't even picked up anything about any planned attacks, small or large. This quiet period is consistent with AQ behavior leading up to other large-scale attacks such as the embassy bombings, the USS Cole, and nine eleven. If I had to bet, I'd bet that al Qaeda is planning one or more major operations, and, to ensure maximum impact, it will be an attack in the United States, Europe, or both. Thank you, sirs."

Carpenter had felt something was off before he read Ella's report. There was a certain tempo to the terror world that had been disrupted, but he couldn't put a finger on the reason. This presentation was far more detailed than the report and even more persuasive. Carpenter was all the more convinced al Qaeda was looking to make a comeback, but there was one aspect of his own theory she had not addressed.

"What do you know about Mumeet?" Carpenter asked.

"Only what is universally known: that he is a ruthless and extremely effective killer. Other than his bomb-making capabilities, almost nothing is known about the man. There are rumors he is Kuwaiti. The fact that we don't even have a picture for the file proves how little we know. That said, I have come across his name many times but not recently. I can't say for sure, but I don't believe I've seen his name in any intelligence reports for almost a year. There is some conjecture that he was killed years ago and that the bombs attributed to him in the last several years were made by protégés."

Carpenter didn't buy that Mumeet was dead. The guy had always proven elusive, and Carpenter was convinced Mumeet was somehow involved in whatever al Qaeda was cooking up. Carpenter's certainty on that matter would be irrelevant, however, unless they could figure out what AQ had planned.

"Ella's analysis and reasoning all make perfect sense to me, at least." Carpenter looked around the spartan room. "But, as has been pointed out to me, there is no actionable intelligence for us to pursue," he said while focusing directly on Patrick.

"At the moment, that's true," Patrick said. "But I think we can and should try to find out if there are any pieces of intel already out there that support our theory. I said 'our' because I now agree there might be something to it. If it is, in fact, a real problem, I don't want us to be blindsided." Patrick knew too well that key information was often overlooked. Despite an emphasis on intelligence sharing within the agency and the broader intelligence community, there was simply too much of it to analyze and comprehend. Sometimes, unless someone was specifically looking for it, there was a good chance the underlying meaning might be missed. After-the-fact analysis revealed this was too often the case.

Patrick turned to his senior analyst. "Sam, I'd like you to put together a team; shake the trees, and see what you can find. Tell me who and what you need, and you'll have it. I know I don't need to say this, but we're shooting in the dark at this point. Maybe there's nothing here, but don't overlook any detail, no matter how small or seemingly unrelated. I hate to do this, but based on what I've heard, I'm concerned it's also possible we might already be playing catch-up. We're going to have to work through the weekend on this. I'd like at least an initial report no later than next Friday, one week from today."

CHAPTER 14

CAIRO, EGYPT

For the better part of two days, Fahkoury and al-Rasheed had barely left the apartment in Zamalek, the affluent district on the northern end of densely populated Gezira Island. The cosmopolitan citizenry of the Nile River island delights in the many restaurants, museums, and nightlife that make the enclave the most exclusive neighborhood in Cairo as well as the home to numerous foreign embassies. However, the appeal of the posh area went unappreciated by Fahkoury and al-Rasheed while they holed up in the apartment after a leisurely, if not always luxurious, trip from the Rub Al Khali.

The Bedouin had arrived at their tent enclave shortly after dawn later that morning, just as Aziz had said. Once again, the Bedouin was accompanied by three camels. Redonning the thawb and mashadah the Bedu had provided the previous day, Fahkoury and al-Rasheed mounted their steeds and followed the man into the desert. They stopped a little less than two hours later at Wadi Hazar, a nearly deserted *markaz* in Yemen. The group was met at Wadi Hazar by another Bedouin and his battered Toyota Hilux truck. That man drove them to Sana'a, the sprawling Yemeni capital, where he zigged and zagged in countersurveillance measures. Outside the city, they picked up one of the few paved roads in Yemen and followed it down more than seven thousand feet in elevation to the seaside city of Al Hudaydah. There, much to Fahkoury's displeasure, they boarded a small boat that made the fishing vessel he had taken from Karachi seem like a cruise ship. Still, it was in much better shape than the other vessels clogging the crumbling wharf. Even though they left crowded port at dusk on a journey of just over two hundred miles, the trip across the Red Sea to the port city of Massawa, Eritrea, lasted until early the next morning. Fortunately for Fahkoury, the voyage was blessed with calm seas.

Although al Qaeda could have secured them Yemeni passports, documents from that country would have subjected Fahkoury and al-Rasheed to considerable and unwanted scrutiny nearly everywhere. Flying to Cairo had not been an option anyway, as the airports were closed due to the civil war in Yemen. The lack of proper documentation also meant they would have to improvise in Eritrea. In the end, Aziz and the shura had decided it would be less risky for the pair to travel without documentation and rely on porous borders and graft until they arrived in Cairo, where more reliable documentation could be obtained.

Once in the port city of Massawa, Fahkoury and al-Rasheed were on their own. Aziz had told them the trip through Eritrea to Khartoum would be the most uncertain part of their journey. Al Qaeda had no assets in Eritrea, but Aziz chose it as the entry point to Africa due to its loose border controls and its proximity to Yemen. Eritrea's poor transportation infrastructure would create some hardships and add considerable time to the journey, but ease and comfort were secondary to clandestineness.

As anticipated, there was no customs presence at the port, and they simply walked into the city and located the train station. Fahkoury used fifteen dollars from the money Aziz had given him to purchase two tickets to Asmara. The steam engine proceeded at a modest pace as it pulled three mostly empty windowless passenger cars through the arid landscape and up into the nine-thousand-foot jagged peaks of the Eritrean Highlands. At times, the train seemed to be on the very edge of thousand-foot drop-offs to the valleys below. Fahkoury found himself waving to the smiling villagers who rushed out of their makeshift stone huts to greet the train as it slowly passed through their small communities. As he drifted in and out of sleep while the train ambled along, Fahkoury found it difficult to harbor hatred for the impoverished Christian-majority Eritreans. They too were nonbelievers, but for some reason he seemed oddly at peace among them.

They arrived in Asmara in the early afternoon. Known for a history of rich religious diversity and wide boulevards that accommodate a beautiful and eclectic mix of Italian colonial, art deco, and futuristic architecture, the spectacular capital city sat at the edge of an escarpment separating the Eritrean Highlands from the Great Rift Valley in Ethiopia next door. But Fahkoury was not at all interested in taking in Asmara's stunning beauty. He was peeved that they had traveled only 350 miles in twenty-four hours from Sana'a down to and across the Red Sea before heading back up more than seven thousand feet to the Eritrean capital. And now he had to figure out how to get to Sudan.

He and al-Rasheed made their way to Al Khulafa Al Rashiudin mosque. The mosque, located on Peace Street—a street aptly named in a city where Sunni Muslims, Catholics, and Orthodox Christians have coexisted peaceably for centuries—was where Fahkoury and al-Rasheed hoped to find a means of transportation to Sudan. They arrived in time for Asr, the afternoon prayer. Following the modestly attended service, al-Rasheed approached the imam, explaining that he and Fahkoury were Yemenis fleeing the worsening conflict at home and traveling to Khartoum to look for work in the rapidly growing gold-mining industry. They didn't have enough money to fly to Sudan and needed other means of transportation. Could the imam help?

The imam, a truly kind man, introduced them to Basil Aswad, a fellow worshipper and the owner of a local transportation company, who regularly traveled between Asmara and Khartoum. Although Aswad was immediately suspicious of al-Rasheed's story, he eventually agreed to the imam's request. Al-Rasheed's offer of $150 certainly helped matters. Besides, he was heading to Khartoum later that day, and his only employee had called in sick.

Not long after the service, the two travelers arrived at Aswad's small wooden warehouse in the Sembel district on the outskirts of the city. After they helped load several crates of coffee bags onto the flatbed truck, Aswad provided his travel companions with company T-shirts. He hoped the Sudanese border agent at Kassala would just assume the scraggly nomads were his new employees. When the truck arrived at the border town a few hours later, this proved to be the case, but the border agent still demanded to see passports for the new guys. After Aswad accepted blame for not telling his new employees to bring their passports and offering the agent fifty dollars for his regrettable mistake, the truck was waved through and headed on to Khartoum.

Aswad left Fahkoury and al-Rasheed near a hospital on Mecca Street but only after he recovered the fifty-dollar bribe. From there, they proceeded on foot just a few blocks to an apartment located on a rutted, dusty thoroughfare called Khour Street in the al-Riyadh district, sandwiched between the Blue Nile and the international airport. Fahkoury felt especially privileged to be in this section of Khartoum, one rich in terrorist lore as the former home of both Osama bin Laden and Carlos the Jackal, the one-time PLO terrorist.

The door to the apartment was opened by a rail-thin man, whose dark, shabby beard and ebony skin contrasted starkly with his brand-new, oversized white Tommy Hilfiger polo shirt. Baggy jeans hung from his slender hips, and grimy sandals adorned narrow feet tipped with unnaturally long and ragged toenails. Fahkoury was not impressed. Without a word except to tell them his name was Fariq, the man showed them to the rickety table, on which he had placed *kisra*, a local bread made from sorghum flour, and *miris* stew. Famished from the long trip from Asmara, Fahkoury and al-Rasheed made quick work of the flavorful bread, dipping it into the peppery and heavily garlicked sheep's-fat stew and washing it down with cold *karkaday*, a popular Sudanese tea made from hibiscus flower.

After the meal, all three men sat on a springy couch and watched an English Premier League football match between West Bromwich Albion and Stoke City on satellite television. Other than the couch, wobbly table, and spanking-new fifty-five-inch flat-screen television, there were no other mentionable furnishings in the small apartment. Midway through the second half, sometime just before eleven in the evening, Fariq rose and told them it was time to leave.

They crossed the Shambat Bridge into Omdurman, at the confluence of the Blue Nile and White Nile Rivers, in what was once a new Nissan

Pathfinder and followed the world's second-longest river for thirty minutes as it meandered on its northeasterly path. Just outside Omdurman, they left the Nile and proceeded northwesterly through flat barren desert toward Egypt. After driving through the night, they linked back up with the Nile, crossing over to the east bank near Dongola in northern Sudan. Just before dawn, Fariq left the paved highway and entered the desert near Wadi Halfa, a small city on the Nile River close to the Egyptian border. Ten slow and bumpy miles later, Fariq discharged his passengers at a spot very close to the border but comfortably safe from any border control.

Fahkoury and al-Rasheed merely walked across the border and into the Egyptian town of Gabel Adda just as *adhan*, the call to worship, was sounding. Without much effort, they quickly encountered an entrepreneurial fishing boat captain willing to provide passage down Lake Nasser to Aswan for the tidy sum of twenty dollars.

They spent one night in the languorous city. A Nubian guesthouse not far from the Sharia as-Souq served their lodging requirements. Feeling secure enough in the mix of tourists from around the world, they spent part of the afternoon in the bustling twenty-eight-square-block market. There was a hint of sandalwood in the air as they slithered through the random maze of vividly colored stalls in search of nourishment. Al-Rasheed's childlike fascination with the merchandise—particularly the stuffed crocodiles, roughly carved copies of Pharaonic statues, and Sudanese swords—slowed their pace further, but Fahkoury tolerated the window-shopping, as it aided their obscurity. They eventually settled on a meal of falafels and peanuts before heading back to their room. Early the next morning, they purchased two ordinary—third-class—train tickets and left Aswan for Cairo, arriving in the bustling Egyptian capital sixteen monotonous hours later.

Now, for the past two days, they had been stuck in the high-rise Cairo apartment, barely speaking to their host, a reticent man calling himself Gamal Najjar. Earlier that day, Najjar set up a white background in the apartment and took their photographs. Najjar was now gone, having left to meet his cousin, a clerk with the Ministry of Foreign Affairs and a fellow al Qaeda sympathizer. The cousin would use the photos to complete the official Egyptian passports Fahkoury and al-Rasheed would use on their trip to Brazil the following evening.

After two days of mostly silent confinement, al-Rasheed was growing restless. "I can't sit in this apartment any longer," he said. "Let's use some of the money Aziz gave us and go to a restaurant for dinner. I'm hungry, and Najjar has only fruits and nuts. I remember seeing some restaurants close by."

Fahkoury was not at all comfortable in Cairo. Its busyness made him paranoid. Plus, he resented the fact that Egypt's secular government had allowed its society, despite being 90 percent Muslim, to be infused with infidel culture. Islamic dress was not enforced, and Western fashion was prevalent. To make matters worse, he and al-Rasheed were also wearing Western clothing, having been provided pressed slacks and polo shirts by Najjar to better blend in with the multiethnic crowds on the island. Najjar had also cut their hair and instructed them to shave before the passport photos were taken. As they sat in the apartment, they looked like two guys looking for a panacea of drinks and dancing to stem some midlife crisis. Fahkoury didn't like being in Cairo and wanted nothing to do with its wretched culture or people.

"It is better that we remain here. Aziz cautioned us about spies in Cairo," he said to al-Rasheed.

"I'm more concerned that three grown men confined to an apartment might create suspicion than I am about the chances of blending in with the crowd at a busy restaurant," al-Rasheed said. "If you do not hide it, your disdain for the infidel will give us away. We are deceiving the infidel in order to beat him. It is *taqiya* and permitted by Allah."

Fahkoury reflected on al-Rasheed's argument for a moment. Much to his displeasure, he had to concede that al-Rasheed was right; he needed to start getting comfortable among the Kafir. With any luck, he'd be operating in their midst for years to come. Eventually, he relented. "Fine. I'm hungry too, but we eat and come straight back."

While al-Rasheed was locking the apartment door, a short, stocky man approached them. Unbeknown to them, the man worked as an independent garbage collector, who maximized his earning power with hustle, prompt and reliable service, and the keen ability to recognize marketing opportunities.

Applying acute attention to detail and a prodigious memory, the man was able to recall the names, faces, and personal details of his four-hundred-plus customers as well as the faces and, oftentimes, the names of hundreds of other residents in this particular Zamalek neighborhood. He had never seen these two men and moved toward them in hopes of landing some new customers.

Wearing a big grin that exposed several missing teeth, the man walked right up to the two strangers and introduced himself. As Fahkoury slipped past him, the man asked al-Rasheed whether they had recently moved into the building and would like to retain his services. Al-Rasheed removed the key and started walking away, dismissively telling the man they were just visiting and would not require his services.

Once outside and thinking nothing of the encounter, Fahkoury and al-Rasheed found a restaurant just a short walk from Najjar's building and took one of the last available tables outside. A pleasant breeze had settled over the evening, and the location at the intersection of Mohammed Maraashly and Ahmed Heshmat Streets offered an ideal spot for people watching. A mix of Egyptians and Westerners occupied the tables nearby. That only a few women wore a *hijab* and none was wearing the *niqab* that he preferred did not sit well with Fahkoury, and he was already regretting his decision.

Al-Rasheed, on the other hand, noticed that most of the patrons were enjoying alcoholic beverages and that a considerable percentage of them were smoking, a passion of his. Although alcohol and smoking were considered *haram*, many al Qaeda fighters in places like Afghanistan smoked nonetheless. In Syria, however, the Islamic State did not tolerate any vices. To make sure the point was clear, IS decapitated a well-known sheikh who was caught smoking and placed a "No Smoking" sign on his headless body for all to see. Word quickly spread, persuading al-Rasheed to quit while he was there. He hadn't had a cigarette in weeks, and the sweet smell stirred his craving.

"I think I will buy some cigarettes," al-Rasheed said.

Fahkoury, who had never smoked or tasted alcohol, scowled his displeasure and abruptly shook his head no.

Al-Rasheed leaned in and said in a hushed tone, "We are likely to draw attention if we just sit here staring at each other waiting for our food. Everyone else around us is drinking alcohol or smoking or both. Remember what we just discussed? We must practice *muruna* and blend in by looking and acting like the Kafir if we are to be successful in this mission. You need to appear comfortable in these situations, or you risk exposing us."

Most of Fahkoury's operations had been in Muslim countries where Islamic law was largely followed. His piety didn't draw attention in places like Afghanistan and Pakistan, but it might seem unnatural, even to the casual observer, elsewhere. After a moment's deliberation, Fahkoury reluctantly nodded his assent. As soon as the waiter departed with their orders, al-Rasheed left the table to buy cigarettes at the bar. He returned a few minutes later with a pack of Cleopatra cigarettes, a leading Egyptian brand, and several boxes of matches that bore the restaurant's name and address.

Fahkoury enjoyed a sweetened tea and hid his displeasure as al-Rasheed joyfully smoked three cigarettes while they waited for their dinners to arrive. *Coming here was a mistake*, he thought. *The place is filled with infidels, like the woman who keeps looking over here.* Her furtive glances made him nervous, and he resisted the urge to examine her more closely. Once they had finished their meals, Fahkoury insisted they leave. Al-Rasheed paid for the dinners with the Egyptian pounds that Najjar had exchanged for them, and they made their way back to Najjar's apartment. Fahkoury was looking forward to leaving the following day. He didn't care to spend another moment in Cairo.

Early the next evening, as Fahkoury and al-Rasheed climbed into a taxi for a ride to the airport, they failed to notice the same short, stocky man loading bags of trash into a rusted-out pickup truck across Ahmed Heshmat Street. A few hours later, posing as Rasul and Umar Qureshi, brothers and businessmen from Alexandria bound for São Paulo and places beyond, they boarded Turkish Airlines flight 215.

CHAPTER 15

TRI-BORDER AREA OF BRAZIL, ARGENTINA, AND PARAGUAY

After a short layover in Istanbul, Fahkoury and al-Rasheed landed in São Paulo, Brazil, early Wednesday morning. As he cleared them through customs, the indifferent customs agent barely glanced at their newly forged passports and the ninety-day visas Najjar's cousin had also secured. Three hours later, they were aboard a one-hour, twenty-five-minute connection to the Brazilian city of Foz do Iguaçu in the state of Parana, at the junction of Brazil, Argentina, and Paraguay—an area known as the Triple Frontier or the Tri-Border Area.

Fahkoury stared out the window at the lush landscape as their plane approached the runway at Foz do Iguaçu International Airport. He had never before seen so many trees and so much green expanse. It was the complete opposite of the Rub Al Khali. In the distance, he could see mist rising from the Iguaçu Falls. Najjar had told them nothing about how they would actually enter the United States. He told them only that they would learn that information in Brazil. Fahkoury found it a strange place to be on their journey to America. But Aziz had very good reasons to send the jihadists through Foz do Iguaçu and the TBA.

For starters, the 165,000-acre Iguaçu National Park, which encompassed Iguaçu Falls, was a nature lover's paradise, making Foz do Iguaçu and the broader TBA one of the top tourist attractions in Brazil. Nearly a million people each year were drawn from around the world by the rich and diverse fauna and flora that thrive in the consistently warm temperatures and humidity that made the park seem like an oversized combination of zoo and greenhouse. The main attractions for most visitors were the breathtaking Iguaçu Falls, consisting of 257 individual falls that cascaded for two miles down the Iguaçu River, which served as the border between Brazil and Argentina. The region's cultural diversity further added to the magnetism. A citizenry that included Europeans, Chinese, and 50,000 Arab immigrants yielded a population of more than 260,000 in Foz do Iguaçu and nearly 900,000 in the greater TBA. That diversity lent to a collection of highly rated ethnic restaurants and notable museums, for which the region was known. Finally, the casual borders of the Triple Frontier region contribute to its renown as one of the world's foremost black markets and havens for drug smugglers, counterfeit goods traffickers, and other assorted criminals. Cash was king, and nearly anything was available for the right price.

These factors combined to provide much-needed cover and flexibility for Fahkoury and al-Rasheed, but the fruits of a budding al Qaeda presence in the region provided the more compelling reason for their presence in the TBA. Aware of the copious funding other terror groups—most notably Hezbollah—were securing in the TBA, al Qaeda sent a couple of representatives to the region two years before. The representatives were provided with $300,000 and told to parlay it in the black-market trade. They were also instructed to establish relationships with the transnational criminal organizations operating in the region.

The initial investment was now consistently contributing in excess of $50,000 every month to al Qaeda's treasury. More importantly, the representatives had also successfully formed ties with one of the foremost criminal organizations in the region, a group with well-established ratlines into the United States and Europe. And one such route started here in the TBA.

Fahkoury and al-Rasheed deplaned and made their way to ground transportation, pulling along nothing more than the few toiletries in their carry-on luggage. They were traveling in the same pressed pants and polo shirts they had worn in Cairo, supplemented by navy sports coats that Najjar had also provided. They exited the small terminal and were greeted by the oppressively humid air, which was powerfully laden with the scent of vegetation and rapidly moving water. They located the taxi stand a few steps away. Open windows did little to save them from a potent mixture of stale cigar smoke and the driver's body odor as they plodded along on a twenty-minute trip to the city center and its dozens of hotels.

Like several others in the TBA, the particular hotel they had chosen was but one cog in a complex money-laundering machine. Anyone attempting to secure a room online would find that the hotel was booked. In reality, only 23 of the 150 rooms were occupied. An opportunistic clerk greeted them at reception and regretfully informed them there was only a luxury suite available for $200 per night or twice the posted rate. Fahkoury glowered at the smarmy clerk and placed $300 on the desk without a word. The clerk beamed at the sight of three fresh banknotes, all too happy to accept the cash, no questions asked.

Their room was located on the fourth floor. Fahkoury had traveled with his father occasionally as a youth and stayed in some of the finest hotels in the Gulf, Europe, and North Africa. This "suite," adorned with cheap floral prints, faded photographs of the falls, and outdated and mildewy carpet was nothing more than a standard room with two thin-mattress double beds. It did, however, offer a panoramic view of the Parana River and Paraguay on the far side. This time, Fahkoury shut down any pleas to leave the room. As he drew the curtains, he told al-Rasheed they would stay in the room and rest until it was time to meet Najjar's contact at a café near the mosque in Ciudad del Este, Paraguay.

About an hour before the meeting, they were walking across the congested Friendship Bridge toward Paraguay, hidden among the cars, vans, motorcycles, and the even greater number of pedestrians, many of them with hand-drawn carts in tow. When they arrived at the café fifteen minutes later, only two of the dozen or more elegantly arranged Brazilian walnut tables were occupied. They selected one of the out-of-the way tables and sipped Yerba Mate, a flavorful bright-green tea, while the waited. It wasn't long before they were approached by a tall, lanky man wearing reflector sunglasses with slicked-back hair held in a ponytail.

"*Ahlan wa sahlan.* I am Adelin. Today was a beautiful day for bird watching, was it not, brothers?" he said as he took one of the two remaining chairs at the square table.

Fahkoury recognized Adelin's reference to "bird watching" as the code Najjar had provided. "Yes. We enjoyed a long walk and saw several golden parakeets."

Upon hearing "golden parakeets," Adelin switched to English and said to them sotto voce, "Be at the end of the walkway that overlooks Devil's Throat from the Brazilian side of the river tomorrow morning at ten o'clock. Bring a nice camera, and wear it around your neck," he said while looking at Fahkoury, assuming that since he had answered, he was in charge. "A man named Pablo will meet you there. He will be wearing an Argentinian soccer jersey, and he will ask if you would like him to take your picture in front of the falls. He does not speak Arabic, but he does speak English. You are to follow his instructions. He will be your guide all the way to America. If Pablo does not meet you tomorrow morning, return here to the mosque tomorrow for Maghrib, and we will formulate a new plan. Wait no more than thirty minutes for Pablo. Understood?"

Fahkoury indicated his understanding with a subtle nod.

Adelin returned the nod, stood, and simply said "As-Salaam-Alaikum" before leaving the café and disappearing into the throng moving toward the Friendship Bridge.

A few minutes later, they left some money on the table and went in search of a camera. Earlier, when they were making the elevated transverse over the Parana River into Paraguay, Fahkoury and al-Rasheed had both commented on the continuous stream of people coming toward them with multiple shopping bags and boxes of goods in tow. Now, standing outside the café and taking in their surroundings, they began to understand the flow of goods.

The café and nearby mosque were located in the middle of one of Ciudad del Este's many shopping districts. Every day, planes from Asia landed at the city's airport, attracted by Paraguay's very favorable sales and import taxes and carrying loads of electronics, perfume, jewelry, trinkets, and other sundries. Many of those same goods were openly smuggled across the Friendship Bridge and into Brazil, where they were sold in the black market for a comfortable margin. In an effort to curb what was estimated to be as much as $12 billion in illicit trade, Brazil had clamped down on trucks and vans entering the country from Ciudad del Este in recent years. The resourceful smugglers simply turned to another, albeit less efficient, mode of transport. Each day, nearly twenty-five thousand pedestrians crossed the Friendship Bridge hauling those same goods and, for the most part, were left alone by customs officials.

They had not asked Adelin what he meant by a "nice" camera, but Fahkoury understood it to mean a thirty-five-millimeter camera. From their vantage point on the sidewalk outside the café, they could see stores lining the curved street, advertising computers, clothing, luggage, leather goods, and electronics, among other items. Even in their limited field of view, they spotted no less than four stores offering cameras for sale. They walked over to the nearest one and found a beefy man sitting on a chair out front with a glass of *tereré*, a chilled herbal drink popular with Paraguayans. Fahkoury could see more than a dozen thirty-five-millimeter models in the front window as they approached the store. He became a bit unnerved when the shop owner spoke to him in Arabic as he was looking over the storefront models.

"*MarHarban*. Are you interested in a new camera? We offer the finest cameras money can buy."

"*Ahlan*. Yes, we are looking to buy a camera. How did you know I speak Arabic?" Fahkoury asked.

"Just a guess. I saw you approach from over by the mosque, and you look Arabic," said the shop owner. "Are you visiting our fine city?"

Fahkoury ignored the question and, instead, asked one of his own. "How much for this one?" he asked, pointing to one in the front window.

"Ah, you have excellent taste. That is the best camera we offer. It is a Nikon D7100, and it has a twenty-four-megapixel lens and a 1080p HD video camera. And it can take up to five photographs per second."

"Does it come with a strap?"

"Yes, of course. Would you like to see the camera?"

"How much?" asked Fahkoury, eager to be done with this busybody.

"Do you pay cash or something else? I do not accept credit."

"Yes, we'll pay cash."

"Nine hundred dollars."

"OK. We'll take it. We don't need the box. Just the camera and the strap."

The shop owner was accustomed to strange transactions. He had seen pretty much everything, but these two were different somehow. Two Arabs who appeared to be visiting the Triple Frontier, though they didn't say for sure. One was clearly agitated that the shop owner assumed they spoke Arabic. They rushed over to his store and bought a camera in just a few minutes. They didn't want to examine the camera and didn't ask any questions about the camera's features. They didn't seem to care. For some odd reason, they only cared that it came with a strap. Even more startling, they didn't even haggle over the price. *Everyone* negotiated in the TBA.

The shop owner found all this odd, even if they were just two clueless tourists bent on taking pictures of the mesmerizing falls. At the same time, he was convinced they were not smugglers. If they were, they would have negotiated price and purchased ten cameras. The shop owner knew they would be able to sell them elsewhere for closer to the $1,400 price tag in legitimate retail stores.

Their behavior was just too strange, even here in the TBA. After they left, the shop owner thought that it might be worthwhile to remember these two. He had a sense they were trouble. He had no intention of going to the authorities, but he would not be surprised if someone came around asking about these men. The shop owner went over the encounter again in his mind to better commit it to memory, information that might prove helpful the next time the customs agents came around to hassle him.

CHAPTER 16

CIA HEADQUARTERS

Samantha Lane and her team had worked nearly around the clock over the weekend and into the early part of the week. A few hours earlier, Samantha reached out to Patrick and Carpenter, saying her team had news to report. Without offering any details, she requested a meeting later that Wednesday afternoon, two days before Patrick's Friday deadline.

Four eager faces, including those of Samantha Lane and Ella Rock, greeted Patrick and Carpenter when they entered the same interior conference room where they had met with Ella and Samantha last Friday. The four analysts were dispersed around the laminated table, and a map of the Middle East and the Horn of Africa was projected on the screen at the far end of the room.

"Good afternoon," Patrick said. "All right, I understand we have a lot to cover, so let's get started with introductions first. Kevin, Matt, this is PJ Carpenter, head of CTC special operations."

Patrick then introduced the two new faces for Carpenter's benefit. "This is Kevin Lingel, a technical-development officer, who joined the CTC from the Directorate of Science and Technology; and Dalton Jones, a targeting analyst, formerly with the agency's Near East and South Asia Division. OK, Samantha, why don't we get started."

For lack of a better description, Samantha's job was to connect the dots and reveal the "big picture," not something within the capabilities of most people. In the intelligence world, information usually arrives incrementally, almost never simultaneously in a nice, comprehensible, and complete package. It's similar to putting together a puzzle whose pieces arrive at different times and are often mixed in with pieces from other puzzles. The skill rests in discerning a story from those incomplete and sometimes inconsistent bits and pieces of intelligence. A single new fact or piece of information can entirely change the trajectory of understanding.

In the typical process, the agency tackles this challenge by following an inductive reasoning process called pattern analysis. As it becomes known, information is aggregated and analyzed for correlations, eventually revealing a picture. However, because of the high degree of ambiguity arising from disparate pieces of partial information, the big picture can sometimes go unnoticed. September 11 was one unfortunate example.

To overcome this problem, creative analysts sometimes utilize deduction. In such an instance, the analysts start with a hypothesis and then determine whether what is known fits into a plausible story. From there, the field teams work to verify or debunk it. Carpenter had advocated a deductive-reasoning approach here, using Ella's well-reasoned hypothesis that al Qaeda would soon be forced into action. The danger, of course, was that bias framed by the hypothesis could result in seeing something that was not there—a false positive.

Patrick's decision to tap Samantha for this assignment showed his growing conviction for the theory that an attack in the near future was likely, if not already being planned. It was also a nod to the difficulty of the challenge they were facing. Samantha was one of the best in the entire agency and someone who also had proven herself to be an extremely effective leader and collaborator. Since she was known for her thoroughness, Carpenter figured that the fact they were meeting this soon indicated that Samantha felt the group had already uncovered some important clues. He leaned back in his chair and waited for her to begin.

"Thank you, Director Patrick. We moved this meeting up because we have gathered some potentially significant intelligence in the past forty-eight hours. The bottom line is that there are indications al Qaeda is in the operational phases of a large-scale attack. It is unclear at this time where that attack is planned to occur, but our best guess right now is Western Europe, followed by the United States. We note out front that there is currently insufficient intelligence to confirm our thinking, but we conclude the intelligence we have right now points to a terrorist attack as a very strong possibility."

Samantha's conviction was both disconcerting and remarkable. If al Qaeda was indeed in the operational phase, the problem was much more imminent than Carpenter had suspected. She had his complete attention, and Carpenter found himself edging up in his seat as he waited to hear how she and her team arrived at this conclusion.

"Our conclusion is based on several factors," Samantha said. "One, the apparent reemergence on the terror scene and recent suspicious behavior of a very successful businessman and member of the Saudi royal family. Two, potential links between the Saudi, two additional men, and Cairo, Egypt. Three, what we believe are related developments concerning certain al Qaeda affiliates. And, finally, four, the lack of any notable AQ activities in recent months, similar to the quiet period that often precedes major attacks."

Samantha switched over from the map and showed a picture on the white projection board. "Let me begin with the Saudi royal. Prince Sadiq bin Aziz, shown here," she said as his picture was projected, "is fifty-two years old and now maintains his primary residence in Riyadh. His title does not hold any particular distinction; he is merely one of the fifteen thousand plus members of the extended royal family. Instead, his accomplishments and wealth are almost entirely of his own doing. His personal net worth, all gained as a result of his successes as a financier, is estimated to be in the hundreds of millions. To clarify, that's dollars.

"Prior to 2012, Aziz ran a private equity firm based in London. By all accounts the firm was highly successful. In 2012 he sold his interest in the firm and returned to Saudi Arabia. Since then, he's had no known active business interests or any other official function. He has pretty much kept a low profile since his return to Saudi Arabia. His background would seem rather innocuous except that it includes previous links to terrorism, specifically to bin Laden.

"As you know, we gathered extensive intelligence about AQ and its re-formed structure as a result of Operation Neptune Spear. Aziz's name was found on two different documents in the trove removed from bin Laden's Abbottabad compound, but the documents didn't offer clues to explain why Aziz was mentioned in them. Notably, the latest one was created right before bin Laden's death.

"Before analysis of the Abbottabad intel was completed, our files on Aziz mostly contained unsubstantiated ties to terror. There are uncon-firmed reports that he is a distant relative of bin Laden. We knew that he helped secure funding for the mujahideen during the latter part of the Soviet conflict and that he was a known bin Laden associate during that time. There were also rumors he provided assistance to the nine-eleven operation in terms of recruitment and financing, but those claims have likewise not been verified.

"When we learned through the Abbottabad materials of his possible link to AQ and bin Laden, we approached the Saudi General Intelligence Directorate, Al Mukhabarat Al A'amah, for support. The agency made sev-eral direct requests for information on Aziz. Those requests were largely ig-nored, and the State Department later made it clear that Aziz is considered off limits to the agency, *intemerata hominem*—an untouchable person. At the conclusion of the briefing, we can discuss the appropriateness of renewing the approach to Saudi Mukhabarat.

"As I mentioned, Aziz keeps a very low profile. According to our limited file on him, since moving to Riyadh from London in 2012, he rarely travels outside the kingdom. Despite the pushback from the State Department and the Saudis, we kept him quietly on our radar after Abbottabad, checking on him periodically to mostly keep tabs on the people he meets and places he visits in Saudi Arabia. In light of current circumstances, one relationship we uncovered a couple of months ago may now be of particular interest. Dalton, would you pick it up from here, please."

As a targeting analyst, Dalton Jones developed a deep understanding of the target using a combination of human and signals intelligence, and satellite imagery as well as information in the public domain. Knowing each target's interests, habits, and idiosyncrasies allowed Jones to predict behavior that could be acted upon as necessary to eliminate threats to US interests. In fact, oftentimes the information used by Carpenter for kill or capture operations emanated from analysts such as Dalton Jones.

"Thank you, Samantha," Jones said as all eyes moved to him. "As Director Patrick indicated, I am responsible for targeting certain individuals, one of whom is Prince Aziz. Due to the issues Sam already mentioned, as well as Aziz's low profile, there was not much in his file when I started tracking him shortly after joining the CTC last year. At the time, we still considered him a pretty low-value target, anyway.

"Our interest was piqued back in October, when Aziz was spotted in Riyadh dining with Ahmad Ishaq, a former member of Karzai's government. From 2002 to 2014, Ishaq served as a provincial governor for Helmand Province, a former and recently reclaimed Taliban stronghold. The US had reservations about Ishaq and his seemingly close relationship with the Taliban when Karzai appointed him to the transitional government in 2002, but he was considered the best of a bunch of poor options. He said all the right things and had been mildly supportive of our forces in the early months of the invasion. Of course, that support came at a price.

"In 2001 and 2002, the agency dumped millions of dollars into the hands of influential tribal leaders and fighters, Ishaq among them. Our records are far from clear, but we estimate Ishaq's personal share of the largesse was close to a million dollars. That pales in comparison, however, to what we believe he stole from the Afghan government. Karzai deservedly gets all the attention for reportedly having stolen a billion dollars or more, but others in his government also made out pretty well, including Ishaq. The rumors in Afghanistan are that Ishaq secreted as much as fifty million more into Swiss bank accounts from 2002 to 2014.

"Beyond the money, Ishaq had a reputation for being soft on the Taliban and al Qaeda during his time in the Afghan government. He advocated for Taliban inclusion in the new Afghan government and encouraged focus on domestic-spending programs in former Taliban strongholds. It is suspected that his work on various infrastructure committees provided the opportunities for him to steal money. For the past couple of years, Ishaq has lived in Switzerland.

"In trying to understand the connection, if any, between them, I ran their photographs through facial-recognition software and discovered several photos of Aziz in France this past summer with Ishaq in the background. The photos were from a private party held on the patio of a hotel in Nice. At any given time, between twenty-seven and thirty-six people appear in the photos. No photos show Aziz and Ishaq speaking directly or even standing close together, but given the small number of people, we believe it is reasonable to conclude each was at least aware of the other's presence, and they very likely had an opportunity to talk.

"We are unable to determine how long they have known each other, or the reasons for the two meetings of which we are now aware, but we know each of them had ties to terrorism at one point. Although these meetings did not necessarily indicate any nefarious motives, they heightened our interest in Aziz. We decided we needed to pay more attention to Mr. Aziz. I'll turn the briefing over to Kevin Lingel to explain what we recently discovered."

"Thank you, Dalton," Kevin Lingel said while looking around the table. "As you've heard, our ability to surveil Aziz inside Saudi Arabia is restricted, but we were very recently able to take advantage of some evolving technology. For the past eighteen months, our government has been experimenting with the use of miniature satellites as a potential intelligence, surveillance, and reconnaissance platform. Each of these satellites weighs about a kilogram and, at approximately ten centimeters square, can fit in the palm of your hand. They are also pretty cheap, costing about a hundred thousand dollars apiece. Another benefit is the ability to tack them onto a launch of other more substantial payloads. The idea is that one day each of these microsatellites will be used to track specific targets for a specified duration. This will eliminate the difficulties of timely rerouting more expensive and sophisticated satellite technology in response to an urgent intelligence need.

"Last month, Special Ops Command launched several proof-of-concept prototypes on a SpaceX rocket. Through Director Patrick's assistance, CTC received permission to include three of our own prototypes that I developed here at CTC with the help of some of my former colleagues at the Directorate of Science and Technology. Given our surveillance difficulties, we decided to test one of the satellites on Aziz. In short, we felt we weren't risking much by using the experiment on Aziz. Now, we think the experiment has yielded some potentially valuable intelligence.

"Before I get into that intelligence, let me first explain a bit about the technologies utilized and the capabilities of the system. Each of our prototype satellites was programed to orbit earth from one hundred eighty miles, but the power system was designed to last only three weeks or less on these initial proof-of-concept tests. Later, I will explain how that limitation becomes important in this situation. The prototypes possessed relatively high imaging capacity that offered one-point-five-meter resolution. In other words, the imaging was able to differentiate objects, including humans, that are least one point five meters apart. In addition to tactical operation controls, we equipped the microsatellites with novel chemical-tracking technology.

"Over the past nine months, I have also been working with the Science and Technology Directorate to develop a more durable chemical taggant that can be used with the microsatellite. We've been working with undetectable chemical taggants for years, but tests confirmed the enhanced chemical taggant we recently developed will remain detectable for approximately forty-five days before decomposing—that's more than twice as long as earlier compounds. More importantly, until decomposition occurs, this improved chemical taggant is also able to withstand rain and washing. Ideally, the chemical is applied to the person, but in this case, we felt our best shot would be to apply the chemical agent to Aziz's principal vehicle, a late-model Chevrolet Suburban.

"As soon as the Spec Ops launched the rocket with our satellite aboard, our officers began eating meals at every restaurant Aziz was known to frequent. About a week later, Aziz finally showed up at one of them. The officer left shortly after Aziz arrived and was able to apply the chemical to the rear bumper of Aziz's SUV as he casually walked behind it toward his own car. The tagging marker allowed us to immediately locate the SUV from the microsatellite prototype, and we were in business.

"For the first seventeen days, Aziz's SUV remained in Greater Riyadh. We watched the vehicle as it traveled from Aziz's home to various office buildings and restaurants around the city. The person we believed to be Aziz always entered and exited the vehicle from the rear driver-side door. At all times, he was accompanied by a driver and, on some occasions, by one or two additional security men. It is not clear whether it was always the same men who accompanied Aziz.

"At approximately oh nine hundred on thirty-one December," Lingel continued, "the SUV left Riyadh city limits with who we believe were Aziz and three men. It was the first time the vehicle had left the city limits since we had been following it with the satellite. Aziz's vehicle was soon joined by two other SUVs, both Range Rovers. Later, we confirmed each of the other Range Rovers contained three occupants. The SUVs traveled south from Riyadh and eventually ventured into the Rub Al Khali. At approximately fifteen forty-five, almost seven hours later, the caravan stopped at a location in the desert where a large tent had been erected. For the next thirty-one hours, all eleven persons—again, we believe each to be a man—remained in the vicinity of the large tent and engaged in various unremarkable activities."

Carpenter reflected that all this had been going on while he was down in the Caribbean for the operation in Cuba.

"However, at approximately twenty-two thirty on January first, things started to get interesting. At that time, four men boarded Aziz's tagged Suburban and departed the camp. Our assumption is that those four men were Aziz and the three security men who had departed Riyadh together. The SUV headed almost due south and deeper into the Rub Al Khali, toward the Yemeni border. The SUV stopped at a second camp location at oh thirty hours on January second. There were three tents already standing at this second camp when Aziz arrived. The SUV remained there for just under three hours before departing with four people on board and moving in the direction of the original camp location. Let me show some video clips."

Lingel then pulled up the video on his laptop and projected it onto the conference-room screen. While he was doing this, Carpenter asked, "You keep saying 'we believe' the person on the video is Aziz. You can't discern faces from the images?"

"Unfortunately, we are not able to distinguish faces," Lingel said. "The quality is very good, but the imaging capabilities of a miniature satellite don't allow for resolution that refined. With these miniature satellites, target identification would have to be verified and achieved during the tagging process. Remember, the intended value is to be able to locate and continuously follow persons who have already been tagged with a marker. In this case, we were only able to tag and locate Aziz's SUV."

"Got it," Carpenter said somewhat dismissively. Right away, he knew he had fucked up. Patrick had pulled him aside many times, cautioning him about the need to temper his intensity in certain situations. It was impossible, Patrick said, to always expect everyone else to meet the nearly impossible standards he imposed upon himself. "Well, hey, this invisible chemical shit is right out of a Bond movie," Carpenter said, trying to cover his misstep with some humor, not his most developed skill. "Who do I see about a tricked-out Aston Martin?"

Amid some polite laughter, Lingel gathered himself and pointed to the video. "Ah, this first clip is a condensed version of the video at the second camp. Here you can see who we believe are two males walking toward Aziz's SUV as it arrives at this location. There are no other vehicles noted at this second camp at any time. After what appears to be a brief exchange between the two men from the camp and a person from the Suburban—again, we suspect that is Aziz—they enter the largest of the three tents erected at the camp. The tent is illuminated, presumably from generator power, as the three men enter. At oh three twenty-four, one person exits the tent, and four men, presumably Aziz and his guards, get into the Suburban and leave the camp.

"At this point, we had to make a decision. We figured we could pick up the SUV again later, so we all agreed to override the tracking program and stay on the second camp using the tactical control system. No movement was detected at the second camp until a few hours later. Let me pull up the second clip."

Lingel hastily closed the Apple QuickTime file for the first clip and opened a new one. "Here we see a person, who we assume is a man, arriving at the camp at oh six fifty-three hours on January second with three camels. Almost immediately, the two men from the camp and the third man mount the camels and head south, away from the camp. Later," Lingel said while fast-forwarding the video, "they arrive at an abandoned village in the desert. What appears to be a Toyota Hilux arrives there at approximately oh eight thirty-three. Two men get into the truck. Once again, we assume the two exchanging the camels for the truck are the two men from the second camp.

"We followed the truck to Sana'a," he said while continuing to breeze through unremarkable portions of the video, "and watched as it weaved through the city. Eventually, the truck headed out of Sana'a and traveled to the port city of Al Hudaydah on the Red Sea coast."

The image froze, and Lingel looked away from the screen and back to the room's occupants. "I referenced the operational time limitation earlier. At this point, the satellite had been in orbit for almost twenty full days of the maximum expected twenty-one-day planned orbit. As the truck wound through Al Hudaydah and entered the area near the harbor, the satellite's power system expired, and we lost coverage at sixteen forty-four local time."

"Do we have any guesses as to who the two men are?" Carpenter asked.

"Unfortunately, we do not," said Dalton Jones, the targeting analyst. "Because of the noted issues, our profile of Aziz's known associates is rather thin. We doubt they're anyone with whom Aziz associates inside the kingdom, anyway. That wouldn't fit with holding a meeting at a second location in the remote desert. Our assumption is that these two traveled from Yemen or some other place to meet with Aziz in the Empty Quarter."

"Makes sense," Patrick said, "but Aziz could've just as easily had these guys travel to Riyadh for a meeting. I can't think of a legitimate reason to hold a meeting under those weird circumstances."

"We agree," Samantha said, "and we believe the most logical conclusion is that Aziz chose the time and location to ensure he could have a confidential discussion with these two men. The obvious and unanswered question is, what were they discussing? In light of the circumstances and Aziz's previous ties to al Qaeda, terrorism is the one possibility on top of our minds."

"So," Carpenter said, "Aziz meets two guys in the middle of the night in the middle of the Arabian Desert for some unknown reason. Over the course of the next day or so, we track these two guys to the Yemeni coast. We don't know if that is the route back home or if they headed that way because of something Aziz told them, but I'm guessing that because of all the secrecy and Aziz's past, we're now assuming these two guys were sent off on some kind of mission. Do I have this right?"

"Yes—yes, you do," said Samantha, sensing Carpenter's skepticism and flinching for the first time.

"OK, we lose these two guys a little more than a week ago. Is that where things turn cold and the story ends?" Carpenter asked, hoping there was more than just this.

"We thought so at the time," Jones said. "However, some more interesting information came to light soon after. After his dinner with Ishaq, we received permission to have NSA monitor Aziz's communications. Aziz is not a frequent communicator, at least through media we're able to capture. We didn't turn up anything interesting until a few days ago. NSA intercepted two e-mail exchanges between Aziz and two separate Google accounts. Each time, Aziz accessed e-mail from his home computer in Riyadh.

"There are three interesting facts about the e-mails. One, the timing of the communications. Two, these accounts were accessed from two different Internet cafés in Cairo. And, three, each of those Google accounts appears to have been established for the very limited purpose of these specific communications. Before we get to the content of the two e-mails, let me first discuss the timing and the locations in Cairo.

"The first communication was intercepted on six January, four days after we lost the two men on the Yemeni coast. That e-mail originated from Aziz and was sent to a Google account that has thus far been utilized only that one time. A second e-mail was intercepted yesterday. This time the communication originated from the Google account user. Again, that account has only been used that one time to date."

Jones went over to the laptop and brought up a map of Cairo. "Here are the locations of the two Internet cafés I mentioned. As you can see, both cafés are located close to the Twenty-Sixth of July Corridor, a main thoroughfare that connects each side of the mainland to Gezira Island.

"I have marked a third location on the map, here in the Zamalek district. This is the Sedge and the Bee restaurant, also not far from the Corridor. An event there fits our timeline and may be relevant. We will further explain that potential relevance later, but I want you to note the proximity of these three establishments as we build this picture." Jones then passed out copies of the two subject e-mails before continuing.

"The first e-mail, dated January sixth, is from Aziz to the Google account and states, 'Our two dear friends who will be attending the big celebration will be in Cairo as expected. They are grateful for your assistance, as am I.'

"The second e-mail, dated yesterday, January ninth, was sent to Aziz. It simply states, 'I was honored to host our two friends. They send their regards.'

"The reference to 'big celebration' grabbed our attention. We are all familiar with the use of 'celebration' and 'wedding' as euphemisms for an attack. The reference to 'two friends' is consistent with the IMINT that the satellite captured from the Arabian Desert to the Yemeni coast. We are assuming the two men we lost on the Yemeni coast traveled to Cairo. The first e-mail is to tell the recipient that the men are on the way. The second e-mail is confirmation the person in Cairo met up with the two men. We know that the airports in Yemen are closed due to the civil war there, so it's possible it might have required several days to get to Cairo."

Carpenter mulled it over and conceded it was plausible that two people attempting to travel to Cairo without notice might take their time. Using less conventional routes to cover thirteen to fourteen hundred miles by boat or over land while trying to avoid border authorities could certainly require at least four or five days, putting the timetable in line with the e-mail communications.

"Our assumption that the two men from the Arabian Desert traveled to Cairo," Jones said, "is further supported by a report from an operations officer from Cairo station. I'll turn it back over to Samantha now to explain further."

"Before you do," Patrick said, "what is the significance of the name the Sedge and the Bee? For some reason, I think I've heard it before."

"The sedge represents Upper Egypt," Samantha said as she rose to resume the briefing, "and the bee represents Lower Egypt. The phrase was a title used by pharaoh and translated means 'King of the Upper and Lower Egypt.' The restaurant was also the site of the failed assassination attempt of Egypt's assistant prosecutor general four years ago."

Seeing that the reference to the assassination attempt had refreshed Patrick's recollection, Samantha continued the briefing. "We took several immediate steps when we lost coverage of the two men in Al Hudaydah. We first sent a request to Sana'a asking that an operations officer be sent there. After that, we sent alerts to all Near East and Africa stations. Without any sufficient level of detail, we simply requested notification of any observations of two unknown males traveling together, possibly without identification and who might seem misplaced or giving any indication of suspicious behavior. It was all we could offer in terms of details, and it was a real, real long shot.

"The officer dispatched from Sana'a didn't find anything in Al Hudaydah, and neither did any of our other offices in Near East and Africa stations. When we learned about the first e-mail from Aziz, we alerted Cairo station again. We heard nothing until earlier today. We have a possible hit.

"Kayla Bates is a first-year operations officer assigned to Cairo station. Monday evening, January eighth, two days after the first e-mail and one day prior to the second e-mail, she met a recruit for dinner at the Sedge and the Bee restaurant in the Zamalek district of Cairo. As Dalton noted, it is located at the highlighted dot on Gezira Island shown on the screen.

"Shortly after she sat down, Kayla noticed two men a few tables away. Apparently one of the men seemed highly discomfited. He continuously scanned the other patrons and the surrounding area, as if he were conducting countersurveillance or concerned he might be discovered. Because her focus is on developing sources on the diplomatic side, Kayla wasn't aware of our alert at the time, but she found the behavior suspicious and filled out a report the next day. Cairo COS read the report and contacted us earlier today."

Samantha passed copies of Ms. Bates's report to each attendee and then remained silent as each took time to read it. The report stated—

This report regards suspicious behavior of two unknown men observed by the author at the Sedge and the Bee restaurant, located at Ahmed Heshmat Street in the Zamalek district of Cairo on 8 January.

At 1830 on 8 January, I arrived at the Sedge and the Bee restaurant to meet Sven Johansen for dinner. Mr. Johansen is a foreign-service officer in the Swedish embassy in Cairo. This was my third meeting with Mr. Johansen, someone I am developing for possible recruitment.

Mr. Johansen was already seated at a patio table when I arrived. It was a pleasant evening, and nearly every table on the patio was occupied. Shortly after sitting down, I noticed two men seated three tables over, approximately ten to twelve feet from my seat. Their table was located at two o'clock from my position, affording me a side-on view of each man but a more head-on view of the shorter man of the two.

The two men left the restaurant approximately twenty-three minutes after my arrival. I did not follow the men after they departed and did not see the direction they took from the restaurant. However, during that time, I was able to make the following observations.

Appearance: Each man had dark hair of average length and olive skin, the latter attribute most likely indicating Arab or Mediterranean ethnicity. Neither man had facial hair. Ambient noise prevented me from hearing any conversation between the two men, but I was able to discern at least some spoken Arabic. Both men appeared to be in their forties to early fifties. The shorter of the two looked younger than the taller man. I would estimate his age to be forty-five years or younger. The taller man was perhaps fifty or even slightly older. Heights of both men were observed when they departed the restaurant. The shorter man was of less-than-average height, approximately five feet seven inches. The other man is six feet or slightly taller.

Behavior: I observed very different behavior in the two men. The shorter man clearly examined each person who entered and left the patio. He avoided eye contact with customers and the staff. He appeared to be intensely focused during the time I observed him. He was unanimated and kept his hands underneath the table much of the time, removing his right hand only to eat and drink what appeared to be tea. He held his left hand inside his right hand when he later exited the patio and restaurant. The taller man's behavior was in stark contrast to the shorter man's edginess and patent discomfort. The taller man smiled at several nearby patrons and the waiter serving them. He seemed to be enjoying the evening.

The two men spoke very little to each other; however, there was an occasion when the taller man leaned closer to the shorter man as he spoke. This was the only occasion that the men appeared to be in serious discussion. It appeared that the taller man was attempting to make a point or otherwise convince the shorter man. It was on this occasion that I heard what I believe was Arabic, although I cannot be sure due to the noisy atmosphere. A short time later, the taller man left the table alone. He returned a short time later with a pack of Cleopatra cigarettes, a leading Egyptian brand. He smoked several cigarettes while they were at the table. The shorter man did not smoke.

Other details: I came across the waiter who served the two men as I was leaving the restaurant. I suggested that one of the men looked familiar, like someone I had met overseas, and asked whether he knew the two men. He told me he recognized me (I have eaten at the restaurant several times in the past two months) but had never seen either man before.

Conclusion: The apparent furtiveness of the shorter man, together with what I would describe as unsocial and potentially paranoid behavior, suspiciously stood out among the many other joyous and gregarious customers at the restaurant that evening. The atmosphere was loud and festive. His conduct was markedly unfitting of the situation and setting. It appeared as if the shorter man was concerned he was being watched or about to be apprehended. For these reasons, I have authored this report.

s/Kayla Bates

9 January

Carpenter waited for Patrick to finish reading the report. He was less than convinced everything he had heard and seen added up to a terrorist plot. There were some potential pieces, but he was beginning to think they were grasping at straws to try to substantiate the working theory. He started in when Patrick looked up from the report.

"OK, let's summarize what we know or *believe we know* so far. Aziz supported the mujahideen with financing during the Soviet war but did not see combat in Afghanistan. He was a close associate of bin Laden during his time in Afghanistan. He might be a distant relative of bin Laden, and he might have had a hand in the nine-eleven attacks. He is a successful businessman with a boatload of dough. He has met at least twice with a former Afghan government official with suspected ties to the Taliban and a personal fortune of tens of millions of dollars stolen from the Afghan government. A little more than a week ago, Aziz traveled to the Empty Quarter and had a midnight tryst with two unknown men. The two unknown men hightailed it to the Yemeni coast, where we lost them. Since that time, Aziz had at least two suspicious e-mail communications."

Carpenter looked around the room to make sure everyone was with him before continuing. "Now, let's review what we *suspect*. We think Aziz is a bad guy. We assume the two men lost at the Yemeni coast are in cahoots with Aziz and also up to no good. We suspect those two men traveled undercover to Cairo to meet with the person or persons who controlled the two Google accounts. Let's just assume that is one person. We think the person who controls the Google accounts lives in Cairo, most likely in the Zamalek district.

We think one of our new operations officers spotted these same two men eating at a restaurant in the Zamalek district two days ago. Finally, given what we know about him and the weird meeting in the desert, we think Aziz and these two other men are plotting something, possibly some kind of terrorist operation. Do we agree that's everything that we know, we think we know, and we suspect right now?"

Everyone nodded in agreement.

Even though the information supported Carpenter's own gut instincts, this was a bridge too far. He needed to challenge himself as much as the team. The agency couldn't act on this information alone; they were still missing a lot of key pieces. There was a real risk they were ignoring other plausible explanations, something known as "target fixation" in the analytical world. He couldn't allow himself or the team to fall into any cognitive traps.

"We agree this is all pretty flimsy support for a conclusion that al Qaeda is planning a terrorist attack in Europe or possibly the United States, right?" he said. "Aziz probably has a lot of legitimate interests, including some in Cairo. Even if these two are involved with him, there could be a genuine reason for their meeting in the desert and trip to Cairo."

"I can see how you get here," Patrick said to the team, "but I agree with PJ. It seems a stretch to assume this all relates to a terrorist plot. Even if it does involve a terrorist attack, why al Qaeda? Why not ISIS or some other group?"

Ella Rock answered. "At the outset of this briefing, Samantha listed four factors leading to our conclusion. I will address the final two. I believe you will find further support for our conclusion that AQ, and not the Islamic State, is planning an attack.

"The first relates to human intelligence gathered from two al Qaeda affiliates. We have an asset inside al Qaeda in the Islamic Maghreb, a Tunisian named Malik Hasan. About a year ago, Hasan was unwittingly recruited by Franco Moscone, one of our operations officers in Tunisia. In short, Moscone flirts with the possibility of funding AQIM. Hasan pushes our officer for financing, but Moscone keeps putting him off, telling Hasan that he'd be wasting his money because AQ is finished.

"Two months ago, Hasan introduced Moscone to an AQIM lieutenant to try to close the deal. The lieutenant told Moscone he was wrong. He said AQ would soon show the world it is still the leader of global jihad. The lieutenant didn't go into details, but Moscone was able to tease out that back in June, the lieutenant sent two new AQIM operatives for training in Afghanistan. The lieutenant claimed the two recruits were being trained for an—I'm quoting here—'overseas operation against the filthy infidels.' Hasan later backed that up, telling Moscone that he knew one of the two men. But Hasan only provided the man's first name—Wasim.

"Standing alone, that intel could be written off as propaganda," the young analyst said, "but we learned some corroborative information from al Qaeda's affiliate in Syria, Jabhat Fateh al-Sham, or JFS, formerly known as al-Nusra Front. For the past couple of years, JFS has tried to distance itself from core AQ. Last year, it even announced a formal split, to which al-Zawahiri publicly gave his blessing. Make no mistake, however—we still consider and treat JFS and AQ as one and the same.

"As you know, the US government has been coordinating with the Kurdish People's Protective Units, or YPG, in Syria. This past spring, we learned that YPG and JFS were in the planning phases of a counterintelligence operation against their common enemy—the Islamic State. The plan was to infiltrate the Islamic State by having two new and unknown JFS operatives join up with IS in Tell Abyad, Syria. At the last minute, JFS said it was pulling its two men for another operation and scrapped the plan. Nobody from YPG met the operatives or knows who they are. YPG also doesn't know where or for when the operation is planned, but the JFS fighters were pulled in early July, right around the same time the AQIM recruits left for training in Afghanistan.

"So what we have are two separate AQ affiliates sending new recruits off for training in the same general time frame for some important, albeit unspecified, operation. This information dovetails with the second additional factor: the analysis I went over the other day with Mr. Carpenter and Director Patrick. To summarize, al Qaeda finds itself at a critical juncture and risks obsolescence unless it pulls off a major attack.

"When you step back and look at all this intelligence, you can see a picture coming together. Aziz popping up with Ishaq, a well-heeled and known al Qaeda sympathizer, is a significant piece of the puzzle. His secret meeting with two men in the middle of the desert is another. Add in the affiliates sending recruits off for training and the cryptic e-mails, and it's looking like some kind of big operation. On top of all that, the timing is right for an attack. With all the attention on the Islamic State, al Qaeda has had time to raise funds, strategize, plot, and plan."

"Thank you, Ella," Samantha said when her colleague finished. Looking over to Patrick and Carpenter, she said, "I'll admit, none of these pieces of intel on its own necessarily points to an attack, but when considered together, there is an emerging connection that supports the conclusion that al Qaeda is planning a terrorist attack. That said, we don't know when or where. Any thoughts or questions?"

CHAPTER 17

Quiet filled the room as Carpenter and Patrick continued to absorb the analysis and the conclusion put forward by the team. Carpenter still thought there were a lot of holes. Aziz was the only person who had been identified, and his ties to al Qaeda were stale and unclear. They had only the first name of another potential al Qaeda militant but no other names. There were vague descriptions of two men spotted in Cairo who might somehow be involved with Aziz. Most significantly, there was no information about possible targets or the proposed timing for the attack.

Yet, despite the lack of detailed information, the sum of what they knew and suspected supported Carpenter's own assumption that AQ was planning something. A few days earlier, Ella Rock had thoroughly and very convincingly taken him and Patrick through the reasons why al Qaeda needed to pull one off an attack and, in light of today's discussion, the possibility that they were actually in the process seemed even stronger. But for Carpenter, the frustrating problem was the lack of any actionable intelligence. "The question I have," he said, speaking directly to Patrick, "is with what little we have, is there a next step? And if so, what is it? Other than pinching Aziz, we still don't have anything we can act on."

Patrick didn't answer Carpenter's question right away but, instead, asked a different question. "What has Aziz been up to since the meeting in the Rub Al Khali?"

"As far as we know, he's in Riyadh," Dalton Jones said, "but we haven't seen him for the past thirty-six hours."

That piece of news was troubling. Still, Carpenter doubted the State Department would ever agree to ask the Saudis to bring Aziz in for questioning. The evidence was too scant. Aziz was probably a dead end for now.

"I think," Patrick said, "the only thing we can do—and it's something we should do, anyway—is to see what we can uncover in Cairo. Right now, that's our best shot. We don't have enough to approach the Saudis for help with Aziz, and if we poke AQIM or JFS too much, we could tip them off that we're onto the plot. Our best chance to stop this is to figure out who the two men from the desert are and where they are now," Patrick said.

"If they actually did go to Cairo in the first place, is there any reason to think they're still there?" asked Carpenter.

"I agree it's doubtful. Reading into the second e-mail, it's possible that they've moved on," Patrick said. "But if they and Aziz are part of a terrorist attack, Cairo is the best place to get some answers. Maybe the attack is planned for Cairo, and they're still there. The Islamic State has been targeting Coptic Christians there and elsewhere in Egypt. Maybe al Qaeda is planning to move in."

"It's also relatively close to Europe," Samantha said, "and a possible jumping-off point for an attack there."

"PJ, I want you to head over there and see what you can come up with," Patrick said. "We'll keep working things here on our end. OK, thank you, everyone. I have a feeling we're all going to be putting in some more long days."

Carpenter and Patrick left before the others and retreated to Patrick's office, three flights above the conference room. "You really think it's worth it for me to go to Cairo?" Carpenter asked once they were in the office. "At some point, I've got to get back to Syria. You can call me in when you've got something we can act on."

"I do think it's worth it. Let the other guys handle Syria," Patrick said as he slumped into his chair. "I don't like what I'm hearing, and I want to figure this out before it becomes a shit storm. You're closer to this than anyone in

Cairo. Even if they've moved on, you might be able to tease more information out of Kayla Bates or stumble onto something else."

"Maybe," Carpenter said, "but grabbing Aziz would be the easiest way to find out what's going on."

"Like I said to the team, that's not going to happen—at least not yet. All we can do is continue to quietly watch him while we try to find the two guys from the desert. I'll have a plane ready at Dulles. Grab what you need, and head over to the airport."

CHAPTER 18

TRI-BORDER AREA

Early Thursday morning, Fahkoury and al-Rasheed boarded a city bus a few blocks from their hotel. The bus delivered them to the entrance of Iguaçu National Park, where they queued up with the other tourists waiting for a different bus to the overlook for the Devil's Throat. The thunderstorms predicted for later in the day lengthened the line considerably. For the moment, the cloudless skies didn't portend any trouble, but the key ingredients of rapidly rising temperatures and humidity were unmistakable. Beads of sweat dripped down Fahkoury's back as they sluggishly moved up through the long line. Making matters worse, just ahead of them was a handful of older Americans camped under the shade of a large umbrella. As the line packed tighter, Fahkoury could hear the Americans prattling on about the beauty of the falls. One of the women turned to him and gleefully pointed to the perpetual rainbow cast above them. Fahkoury compliantly looked up and forced a return smile at the woman. *Soon, only one of us will be smiling,* he thought.

They were among the first to disembark the double-decker bus twenty minutes later and headed straight for the next line, one that would take them onto the walkway into the Iguaçu River for a close-up view of the Devil's Throat. As the highest and the deepest of the falls, the Devil's Throat was the most popular site in the park. On this day, the line just to enter the walkway snaked back and forth several times. A park ranger was telling people to expect a ten to fifteen-minute wait just to enter the walkway and up to forty-five minutes to reach the end overlooking the falls. As they proceeded through the lanes like cattle, they were enveloped in a cloud of malachite butterflies, one of the many colorful species inhabiting the park. The Lepidoptera were a source of wondrous fascination for the other tourists, but they served only to further Fahkoury's growing annoyance.

By 9:50 a.m., he and al-Rasheed were standing shoulder to sweaty shoulder on the crammed thirty-five-foot-wide walkway, making painstakingly slow progress toward the end of the pier. Fifteen minutes later, the crowd started to thin out as some tourists left to catch the next bus, which would take them deeper into the park. Fahkoury and al-Rasheed used the new space to squeeze their way down to the waist-high steel railing at the end of the walkway. To a casual observer, they were just two more tourists wrapped up in the beauty of the falls, but Fahkoury's mind was on something else. His panic that Pablo would not be able to find them was growing—that is, if he was even there. It was already past the meeting time, and Fahkoury had not seen anyone remotely fitting the description Adelin had supplied the night before.

They rooted themselves at the end of the pier and waited, ignoring the glares and comments from the visitors behind them who were waiting patiently for their own unobstructed views of the falls. Perhaps another fifteen minutes elapsed, and then someone behind them said, "Hola! Would you like me to take a picture of you two in front of the falls?"

Fahkoury turned to see a wiry brown man, shorter than himself, wearing an oversized Argentina national-club soccer jersey. He nodded and said thank you as he carefully slipped the camera from his neck.

As he took the camera from Fahkoury, the stranger said, "My name is Pablo. I believe we have a mutual friend, Adelin."

Fahkoury knew from Adelin that Pablo had been assigned to help them enter the United States. He didn't know and didn't care whom Pablo worked for; the fact that the arrangements had been made by Aziz and the shura was enough. Only later would he realize that Pablo was a member of a smuggling network and one of its best coyotes, a person who handled the primary crossing across the US-Mexican border.

In truth, Pablo's smuggling network was a part of a South American drug cartel that had a proven supply chain into the United States. Recognizing an opportunity to monetize that supply chain in the developing human smuggling business, the cartel established a selective yet lucrative subsidiary. The niche business did not solicit business. Rather, it selected customers solely based on referrals and recommendations from past customers or other trusted parties. It also operated at the upper end of the pay scale. The referring organizations were free to charge any fee they wanted, but the cartel's $35,000 per person fee was nonnegotiable and payable up front. The network offered a money-back guarantee after three unsuccessful attempts, a warranty it had never had to honor.

Although more and more people tried to enter the United States illegally each year, the number detained at US borders remained a mystery. The US government consistently issued conflicting reports on the number of detentions, ranging from several hundred thousand to several million each year. The most informed sources estimated that for every person detained at the border, another successfully entered the United States illegally. From practical experience, Pablo knew the one-for-one ratio was about right, but his rate of success was markedly higher. In the last four plus years, Pablo had personally escorted customers into the United States no fewer than a hundred times, and all of them had made it safely across the border.

Not surprisingly, the network had garnered acclaim for its specialized services in certain circles, notably those in countries with known or suspected terrorist ties—people referred to by US Customs and Border Protection as special-interest aliens or SIAs. Although most of his customers hailed from Asia, increasing percentages of his transports hailed from Africa and the Middle East, including SIAs from Pakistan, Iran, Syria, Somalia, Sudan, and Yemen. Word spread, and the reputation of his network eventually garnered the attention of al Qaeda.

Pablo's boutique network enjoyed the further distinction of reserving the right to refuse any customer, a privilege it had applied in the past when the customers were known criminals or persons with intent to commit crimes. Further scrutiny from South, Central, and North American immigration authorities for transporting and facilitating malefactors was not good for business. Of course, exceptions were sometimes made, but they came at a steep cost. Pablo had no way of knowing that al Qaeda had paid the network a premium total of $150,000 to ensure that Fahkoury and al-Rasheed would successfully enter the United States. Pablo had been told only that these two men were important customers.

Almost immediately, Pablo sensed his new customers were probably not simply trying to escape deplorable conditions in their home countries. The two Arab men looked at him with hardened and unforgiving eyes that didn't reveal the least bit of apprehension. Their steeliness was unnatural, and the professional smuggler suspected they might be criminals or even terrorists, but he couldn't risk caring. His superiors selected the customers, and he had been told to get these men across the US border without mishap. In not so many words, his bosses had made it clear that if he failed to deliver them undetected and safely onto American soil, he was not long for the world. Standing before them now, he wasn't liking his chances no matter the outcome.

Pablo placed the camera around his neck and then took several photographs. He put on a bit of a performance for anyone watching and then moved closer to Fahkoury and al-Rasheed, as if showing them his handiwork. As they were huddled closely over the camera, Pablo confirmed that it would be easiest to converse in English. Both Fahkoury and al-Rasheed held university degrees and spoke the language moderately well. With that piece of business out of the way, Pablo suggested they move to somewhere less crowded, gesturing for Fahkoury and al-Rasheed to follow him toward the shoreline. The trio casually retreated through the tightly packed crowd to the entrance for the walkway and then over to an unoccupied viewing post along the banks of the rapidly moving river.

"If possible, it would be best if we left today," said Pablo. "I had originally planned to leave tomorrow, but the pilot and the private aircraft that I have arranged now have to be in Cali, Colombia, tomorrow morning. I know it may seem rushed, but are you prepared to leave today?"

Fahkoury was instantly leery. They had just met this man, and he was already pushing them to leave. What would they do for clothing? Did they need identification? He didn't like not being in control. Nor did he like having to make hasty decisions. "We will leave when I decide it is appropriate," Fahkoury said.

"Yes, of course," replied Pablo. *Pendejo!*

Satisfied the pecking order had been established, Fahkoury asked, "How long will it take to get to the United States if we don't leave today?"

"That will depend on how we travel," said Pablo.

"Tell us the options."

"We have two options to get to the United States. One is to enter Mexico on foot with other migrants through Tapachula and then proceed to the border. That way is the customary way. The other option is to fly into Mexico on commercial airlines."

Pablo went on to explain that the best chance for anonymity all the way to the US border would be to enter Mexico on foot with the regular migrant flows through Central America. Under this route, they would mostly use buses and boats until they reached Guatemala. As they neared the Guatemalan border with Mexico, they would proceed by truck and then on foot, sometimes hacking through jungle, to a remote area on the Rio Suchiate, where they would pay one of the many boat operators for passage across the river and enter Mexico near Tapachula. Once safely inside Mexico, they would travel by car to the US border. Pablo told them that this overland path, in the best conditions, would require two weeks or more to reach the US border.

Had time not been a factor, Pablo might have tried to sell them on this route. It took a lot longer, but it offered the best chance for fulfilling his superiors' orders to get them to America anonymously. By traveling this route, he could all but eliminate the chance there would be an official record of their migration north. Even if they were detained, their true identities would likely remain concealed in the masses of other migrants. In this case, however, time was apparently a factor. Besides, he was already looking to be rid of them as quickly as possible.

Pablo told them the other option was to obtain proper documentation and fly into Mexico on a commercial airliner before ultimately proceeding to the US border by car. He explained that using private aircraft, like the plane they would use on the trip to Colombia, was not an option to enter Mexico. It was too risky. Private planes originating from South America were invitations for close inspection in Mexico as well as in any Central American country in which they chose to refuel. The commercial airline route would hasten the trip to the US border, Pablo said, only requiring a matter of days, but it was the riskier route because there would be an official record of their travel in both Colombia and Mexico.

After a brief pause to allow for questions, none of which were forthcoming, Pablo said, "Whichever option you choose, it will be safer if we remain completely anonymous until we reach Colombia. Flying commercial to Colombia would create a trail starting here in the TBA. The TBA has a reputation that is not good for our purposes. If you don't want to use the private plane today, we could travel by car or bus to Colombia, but the best route is more than four thousand miles on not-so-good roads. It would require many days just to reach Colombia."

Fahkoury was eager to get to the United States. He was short on time as it was. It had already been more than a week since they met Aziz in the Rub Al Khali. Losing precious days waiting for another plane, let alone days spent hacking through jungles, was not an option. He didn't consult al-Rasheed. They each understood who was calling the shots.

Fahkoury said to Pablo, "We will leave today on your plane, and we choose to fly into Mexico on the commercial airline. Will we have time to return to the hotel?"

"Our time is limited. The pilot must leave no later than three o'clock this afternoon in order to be in Cali by tomorrow morning. Is there anything there that you need?"

"We have a few clothes and toiletries in our hotel. We also each have small luggage."

"At some point, we will need to buy other clothes, anyway, clothes that will help us blend in with the other migrants, but we can do that when we are in Colombia. The clothes you are wearing are fine for now. We can get new luggage too."

"What about identification? We have Egyptian passports."

"You have them with you now?"

Both men nodded confirmation.

"Good, but your Egyptian passports are more trouble than they are worth where we are going. We will acquire new passports here in the TBA. My colleague can create the passports quickly, so that's not a problem."

Fahkoury had no affinity or purpose for the sport coat and the toiletries in the room. Al-Rasheed had left behind the same plus the cigarettes, but Fahkoury recalled him saying he preferred American brands to the Cleopatras. After thinking this over briefly, Fahkoury said, "We don't need to return to the hotel."

"Then it is all settled," Pablo said with a sense of relief. "We have a little more than four hours to secure the passports and get to the airport. If we can get out of the park quickly, that should be enough time to get our business done. Guarani Airport is only a few miles away in Minga Guazú. Let's get on the next bus back to Foz, and then we'll cross the bridge into Ciudad del Este."

Before they left, Fahkoury pointed and motioned for the camera. He glowered at the Latino as he pulled the memory card and snapped it in half between his right thumb and forefinger. After he tossed the pieces into the rapid current and dropped the camera into a nearby garbage receptacle, he said, "Let's go."

CHAPTER 19

CAIRO, EGYPT

Four hours after leaving Patrick's office late Wednesday afternoon, Carpenter was bound for Egypt in a chartered Gulfstream IV. After a brief refueling stop in the Canary Islands, he arrived in Cairo on Thursday just after 5:00 p.m. local time. By the time the agency driver dropped him at the embassy, it was nearing 7:00 p.m., and the place was nearly deserted. Carpenter was greeted at the front entrance by the Cairo chief of station, Douglas Root.

"Happy New Year! You look pretty refreshed for an old fart," the station chief teased.

"Nice to see you too, dough boy." The two had entered the agency at the same time and had known each other for years. "Yeah, Rooter, the timing worked out pretty well. Slept most of the way. Thanks for meeting me, by the way. Did Patrick bring you up to speed?"

"He did," Root said as he led Carpenter into the embassy toward his office.

They discussed the highlights, the plan of action, and the task before them as they walked to Root's office and waited for Kayla Bates to arrive. Root was an agency veteran and not easily rattled. He and Carpenter had crossed paths many times over the years. Carpenter could sense his skepticism as they discussed the intelligence and the working theory, but Carpenter welcomed his thoughts, nonetheless. This was an inexact science, and seeking more insightful analysis was always a smart move. After grabbing a couple of craft beers from the inventory that Root regularly replenished using diplomatic parcels from the States, they settled into comfortable leather chairs around a small circular table in Root's office.

"Ya know, this situation kind of reminds me of Nawaf Alhazmi and Khalid Almihdhar," Root said. He was referring to two of the nine-eleven hijackers who had been observed in Kuala Lumpur in January 2000 attending a gathering of suspected al Qaeda operatives. Despite the suspicious nature of the meeting, the two terrorists were allowed to enter the United States a few days later. Somehow, the agency lost track of the two men. Mild concern turned into true panic in June 2001 when Almihdhar was connected to one of the USS Cole bombers, and true panic became ignominy on September 11. Both men knew the potential consequences here.

"The similarity of the circumstances has crossed my mind," Carpenter said.

Root handed over sketches of the two men that had been made based on Bates's descriptions. They were better than nothing, but Carpenter could see the depictions didn't offer any particular distinctiveness about either man. "Any idea who they are?" Carpenter asked.

"No, and we've run them through our databases. I've had a team canvassing the Zamalek district over the past two days, and they haven't made any headway either," Root was saying just as Bates arrived.

Carpenter had reread her report on the plane. He was amazed that Bates had determined a report was even warranted. It demonstrated the strong intuition necessary to become an effective operations officer. The detail and confident reasoning impressed him even more. The same self-assuredness that jumped from the page was evident when she walked into Root's office and marched straight for Carpenter.

She was not quite what Carpenter had expected. While petite in stature, her efficient movement and lithe body indicated she had once been a competitive athlete, and her crystal-blue eyes and striking appearance were more apt to be featured on the cover of a Nordic fashion magazine than found in the rough-and-tumble world of espionage. More important to Carpenter, she was clearly undaunted and all business.

"PJ Carpenter, please meet Kayla Bates."

"It's a pleasure to meet you, sir."

"Likewise, and thank you for coming in. Please call me PJ."

"How can I help?"

As much as he respected Ms. Bates's report, Carpenter felt it was still possible that she might have overlooked some key detail. The smallest details could amount to key pieces of intelligence, but it oftentimes required a trained eye to spot them. "What drew your attention to these two men?" he asked, thinking it best to start the discussion with a general question.

"I try to always be situationally aware—a mind-set I first picked up in training—especially when entering a busy or crowed setting like the restaurant that night. So as I walked to my table and sat down, I casually scanned all the people at the restaurant. These two guys immediately stood out. They just seemed out of place. Everyone else appeared to be having a good time, and these two guys, by contrast, looked serious. Another thing is that they were dressed very similarly, almost like a uniform that business associates might wear."

Carpenter noted that the comment about the clothing was not included in the report—an oversight that might be relevant. Maybe she had missed something else, he considered as Bates described what the men were wearing. When she finished, he picked up the report and went over each sentence with Kayla, asking why she had included specific pieces of information and used certain adjectives, and he requested that she elaborate on certain descriptions. To test her recollection, he next asked her to describe the sounds, smells, and other patrons seated on the patio that evening. He asked whether there were any other unusual incidents or persons. He asked detailed questions about the Swedish emissary, who had chosen the restaurant and who had set the time for the dinner. He asked whether reservations were required. They discussed the interactions of the two men with the waiter, between each other, and with other customers. He asked her to explain the furtive behavior of the shorter man—how often he looked around, how long he looked in any direction, where he directed his attention. In sum, he took her diligently through every aspect of the evening in an effort to uncover any pertinent information not noted in her report.

Carpenter also employed these exercises to refresh Kayla's memory and to refocus her mind on the events of that evening. When he was satisfied she was fully engaged, he pulled out the drawings Root had provided and placed them on the table. "Are these pretty good representations of the two men you saw that night?"

"They are, from what I remember, but I didn't really study their faces. I was trying to be careful and not give away my interest in them."

"That's completely understandable," Carpenter said. He wouldn't have been as considerate with a more experienced officer, but the uncomfortable experience back at Langley was still fresh in his mind. "Did you notice any distinctive marks on either man's face or body?"

"No, other than what I wrote about the shorter man keeping his hands hidden."

"Did you notice anything particular about his hands?" Carpenter casually asked, not wanting to put too much emphasis on the piece of intelligence that had most interested him.

"Not really. It was just kind of weird that he was very calm, while the taller man was much more animated. The taller guy moved around in his seat and gestured with his hands, while the shorter man sat rigidly and kept his hands in his lap, except to eat. I only saw him use his right hand to eat and drink, but that is not uncommon in Egypt. I guess I just felt that the obvious contrast between the two was something to include."

"Yes, it was a good thing to note." Not exactly what he was looking for, but his suspicions had not been refuted. "You also mention that each man had average-length hair. How would you describe their hair? Was it well groomed? Did it look professionally styled?"

"Actually, it looked like they might have cut their hair themselves or had it done by an amateur. The hair was groomed in the sense that it was combed, but there was no style to either of their haircuts. Their haircuts reminded me of the time I got into trouble for giving a haircut to my little brother, when I was about ten years old."

"OK, maybe that's something. Now, I know that you speak Arabic. Why do you believe you heard the men speaking Arabic? Did you make out anything they were discussing?"

"There was a mix of languages, including Arabic, being spoken at the restaurant. That area of Cairo, in particular, is very multicultural. It was loud, and there was some traffic noise too. I didn't want to risk looking directly at them too often, but I'm almost positive these two were speaking Arabic. I couldn't make out the conversation, but I think I heard a couple of words from their table."

"What words?"

"I'm pretty sure I heard the taller guy say 'kafir,' and I might have heard him use 'muruna.'"

"I don't recall those words in your report." Another piece of information missing from the report, this one potentially more significant.

"That's because I wasn't sure I heard them, but I know I heard words sounding like 'kafir' and 'muruna.' Like I said, it was loud, and there were several languages being spoken in the immediate area, but those words grab your attention. Still, I didn't want to include something in the report I wasn't sure about."

This new information was particularly significant to Carpenter. "Kafir" was the Arabic word for infidel, meaning any nonbeliever, including those Muslims deemed apostates. It was a term commonly used by radicals. "Muruna" was a strategy that permitted believers to deceive and commit other prohibited acts in the interests of advancing a greater good. Essentially, it offered a dispensation from sharia law in certain circumstances. Smoking to blend in with the crowd would be one such situation.

"Were you able to detect a particular dialect?" Carpenter asked.

"No, I wasn't. My Arabic is good but not excellent. I'm not yet able to make distinctions among regions when I hear it spoken. Even if I had been right next to them and able to hear them more clearly, I probably wouldn't have been able to detect dialect."

Moving on, Carpenter said, "Tell me why you think the shorter guy was conducting countersurveillance."

"I remembered certain things from surveillance training that can give you away. One is to avoid looking suspicious. This guy didn't hide the fact very well that he was checking out everyone in the restaurant and the area around it. He wasn't very discreet or natural about it. It seemed like this guy was worried someone was watching them. I was taught this can be an indicator of burn syndrome. Another thing I noticed about him was eye contact. As I wrote in the report, this guy avoided eye contact with everyone except the guy who was with him."

After a few more questions, Carpenter decided to end the conversation and let Kayla go home for some rest. It was nearing midnight, and he still wanted time to reflect on their discussion before providing an update to Patrick. He made plans to meet Bates the next morning. He doubted the men were still in Cairo, but he wanted to go to the restaurant and look around its vicinity during the daylight.

Once Bates was gone, COS Root showed him to the room he had reserved for Carpenter in the embassy. Along the way, they talked about Bates and her report. Carpenter again said he was impressed with Bates and also gave kudos to his friend. Root deserved some of the credit. Carpenter knew his old friend stressed the critical importance of intelligence gathering and ran his office in a manner that encouraged reports like the one Bates had produced. Root showed him the room and then left for home with a promise that Carpenter would call if he needed anything.

There was a secure line in the room he could use to call Patrick, but Carpenter decided he had enough time to grab some food down the hall. Carpenter knew his boss would still be at HQS; Patrick was available 24-7 but pretty much maintained a 6:00 a.m. to 6:00 p.m. schedule at the office. An hour after Bates and Root had left, he called Patrick.

"How's Cairo?" asked Patrick as soon as he picked up the phone.

"Hasn't changed. Well, I just finished debriefing Kayla Bates. We were able to tease out some more information that might be helpful."

"Such as?"

"We went through an exhaustive review of the report and her recollections from that evening, and a couple of things popped out. For starters, she said the two men were similarly well dressed, but their hair looked as if they had cut it themselves or it had been done by an amateur. That might suggest it was recently and hastily cut, or it could simply mean neither one gives a shit about hairstyle. Either way, what are the chances they use the same crappy barber?"

"Probably pretty low," Patrick said.

"The more interesting element, however," Carpenter said, "involves the Arabic she thought she heard. She said she could detect several different languages on the restaurant patio, including Arabic. She thinks she may have heard the taller guy use the words 'kafir' and 'muruna.' She said she didn't include that in the report because she wasn't sure and didn't want to speculate."

"Those words would certainly be consistent with language used by two jihadists participating in an operation," the CTC chief said.

"For sure, but, again, she's not exactly sure she heard them."

"What is your thinking now?" Patrick asked.

"I look at it this way: it's more likely than not that the two guys from the desert traveled to Cairo. The timing and the e-mails support the conclusion that they came here. I think it's also likely that Kayla encountered the same two men, and I'm not holding much doubt they are part of some operation. The problem is that they haven't been seen since. Cairo is an odd place for them to hole up. I really doubt they're still here."

"Do you have a next step in mind?" the CTC chief asked.

"Yeah. We're going to meet in the morning and head over to the restaurant. As long as I'm here, I want to see it and the surrounding area. Maybe we can figure out where these guys were staying and have Rooter put a team on it twenty-four seven. Have you been able to uncover any known or suspected terror links to Zamalek?"

"No. To your earlier point, we don't have any record of any AQ or other terror-group safe houses in the area. It's a fairly high-rent district, and a lot of foreign nationals live there. Not exactly your typical asshole terrorist enclave. It would be a smart play, though; probably think that's the last place we'd be looking in Cairo."

Patrick shared that Aziz had been spotted once around Riyadh, but no further e-mails or other new information had come to light. He had also talked with CIA Director Melissa Gonzalez about approaching the Saudis, but she agreed there wasn't enough at this point to even ask for help. She said she would speak to the secretary of state to lay the groundwork in the event something changed. Gonzalez also planned to alert her European counterparts to the CIA's growing belief that AQ was planning a major attack.

Patrick then wrapped up the call by saying, "Let me know what you find in the morning. Get some rest."

CHAPTER 20

Bates arrived at the embassy promptly at 9:45 Friday morning. Carpenter didn't see the purpose of meeting any earlier, as he wanted to be in the area around the busier lunch hour. Even though government offices and many businesses would be closed on the day of rest, traffic was still bad and parking even worse. Those factors and the nice weather persuaded them to walk to the restaurant and surrounding area. Carpenter had no plans to visit either of the Internet cafés, but if that changed, they could always call for a car.

The US embassy was located about two miles from the Sedge and the Bee restaurant on Gezira Island. Encountering only the occasional fellow pedestrian on a partly cloudy, slightly-milder-than-average morning, Carpenter used the opportunity to ask Bates how she had come to work at the agency. Bates said she wasn't sure what she wanted to do with her psychology degree after graduating from the University of Massachusetts. Midway through her senior year, she decided on graduate school. One of her roommates suggested she should apply to the CIA. She dismissed the suggestion as inane but sent in an application anyway, confident she wouldn't hear back.

She didn't, until six months later. She was interested enough to delay the start of graduate school for a semester while the agency fast-tracked her application. She was offered a position as a case officer with the Directorate of Operations, partly due to her educational background and Spanish fluency.

After initial officer training, she was selected to attend the CIA's foreign-language immersion center, where, over the course of a year, she added Arabic to her foreign-language skills. Her first assignment after training was her current one—Cairo.

The conversation filled the time until they arrived at the restaurant just before 11:00 a.m. The staff was already preparing the tables for the lunch crowd. A three-foot-high decorative wrought-iron fence provided a barrier between the sidewalk and what Carpenter estimated to be a forty-by-forty-foot square concrete patio. He counted sixteen square tables made out of bronze synthetic resin woven in a wicker weave, each capable of seating up to four people in similarly fashioned chairs.

Bates pointed to the table she and her Swedish friend had occupied that night, as well as the one used by the two men. Carpenter saw that the tables were close enough that Bates could have heard parts of the conversation, notwithstanding the general din of a busy restaurant and the street traffic. This instilled more confidence in him for her report and recollections from that night.

Since Bates and Cairo station had already followed up with the staff at the restaurant, Carpenter saw no reason to spend any more time on that effort. Instead, he thought their time would be better spent first trying to find potential locations where the two men might be—or, more likely, had been—staying. They would first walk the surrounding area to try to pinpoint some promising locations for a terrorist safe house and then come up with a plan for a more concerted surveillance effort.

After Carpenter explained his plans for canvassing the two-block radius from the restaurant, they headed out walking east on Mohammed Maraashly. They passed several cafés, a supermarket, and numerous multilevel apartments as they made their way toward the Nile River. At Mohammed Mazhar, they turned right and headed south. Carpenter noticed the apartment buildings on Mohammed Mazhar were more upscale. Several large homes, posh hotels, and embassies, including the Apostolic Nunciature of the Holy See, occupied coveted spots on the banks of the river. Unlike the potential of the first block, Carpenter doubted the terrorists were or had been staying on this exclusive street.

They proceeded south to Ismail Mohammed and then headed back west on the busy and unattractive street. They passed as many businesses, including a Harley-Davidson store, as apartment buildings during their two-block stroll. Carpenter tabbed this as another low-probability area. When they reached Taha Hussein, they exited Ismail Mohammed and proceeded north. They immediately encountered several banks, a university, and plenty of businesses, but few residential dwellings on the early stretch along Taha Hussein. The first block was much more commercial than residential and also not the kind of neighborhood where two terrorists were likely to hole up.

However, as they continued north over the second block of Taha Hussein, they noticed more apartment buildings and several restaurants exquisitely positioned among towering sycamore trees. This area of Taha Hussein was more promising, but the presence of multiple restaurants convinced Carpenter this probably wasn't the right area either. With so many other choices nearby, there would be no need to risk exposure by walking to the Sedge and the Bee several blocks away.

They continued on, heading east again on Mohammed Anis. After a block, they turned south onto Ahmed Heshmat, the same street upon which the restaurant was located. *This*, Carpenter thought, *was more like it*. The quiet, leafy street was almost exclusively residential, offering a mix of large, high-rise, and smaller apartment buildings. Besides a small café, there were no eating establishments in the immediate vicinity.

Carpenter slowed the pace, and they engaged in idle conversation as they leisurely walked along the promising Ahmed Heshmat. Carpenter heard French, Spanish, Swedish, English, and what he thought might be Hungarian as they slowly moved south. This type of diverse, multicultural neighborhood would offer excellent cover to any operative, including their two suspected terrorists. The agency taught operatives to establish safe houses in pluralistic neighborhoods like this, because the impermanent residents tended to pay less attention to each other. The many different ethnicities tended to dull the sense of awareness that one needed to take notice of strangers. There was no secret to this logic, and, in Carpenter's experience, terrorists applied the same thinking.

There were literally thousands of different dwellings, but Carpenter's instincts told him that if there were any clues, they would find them on Ahmed Heshmat. They were half a block from the Sedge and the Bee and still had not seen another restaurant. This was the area where he would tell Patrick and COS Root to focus resources to look for the two men or clues relating to them. They were almost finished with their canvassing tour when Carpenter noticed a man pushing a cart filled with what appeared to be large canvas bags. "What's that guy doing?"

"That man is a *zabbaleen*, a garbage collector," said Kayla.

"He doesn't have a uniform. Does he work for the government or a private company?"

"Neither. The zabbaleen are independent contractors. They've materialized out of the government's inefficiency. The government can't keep up with trash collection in many areas of the city, so the zabbaleen move in and take over. They're more than trash collectors, however. In fact, they don't charge a set fee for trash collection. Instead, each customer is left to decide whether to pay them anything or nothing at all, but they make most of their money from recycling and in money saved by reusing things other people have discarded.

"I use the zabbaleen who covers my building. Any trash I put out is gone no later than the next day. These guys are hustlers. I think there is some kind of code whereby they don't poach customers from other zabbaleen, but any new person is fair game. My zabbaleen seems to know everyone in my building. Maybe we should go talk to this guy."

CHAPTER 21

Two hours later, Carpenter and Bates were back at the embassy. After speaking with Jabbar Sayeed, they had asked the zabbaleen to show them the apartment. Carpenter knocked on the door, but there was no answer. Jabbar told them he hadn't noticed anyone at the apartment other than the two guys he described. Bates gave Jabbar $200 for his help, and, in return, he gave them his mobile-phone number and promised to help further, if needed. Carpenter called Patrick as soon as he was inside the embassy's secure communication room.

"How'd your field trip go?" Patrick asked, without bothering to say hello.

"You know who the zabbaleen are?"

"Who?"

"Zabbaleen. It means 'garbage people' in the local Arabic dialect." Before he related what he and Bates had learned from Jabbar Sayeed, Carpenter first spent several minutes describing their canvassing activities earlier in the day, leading up to their chance encounter with the garbage collector. For further context, he then gave some background on the zabbaleen and their integral function in Cairo.

"So this zabbaleen's name is Jabbar Sayeed. We saw him as we were heading back toward the restaurant, about half a block from the Sedge and the Bee. At the time, he was loading a large canvas bag onto a rusted pickup truck parked in front one of the large apartment buildings. Apparently, that building is one of three in his territory. Anyway, at Bates's suggestion, we headed over to meet him. He's just a shade over five feet, probably in his forties, looks like he could knock out a young Mike Tyson, and, most importantly, we discovered he is a walking Rolodex of this area of Zamalek.

"Jabbar personally services more than four hundred customers, and he claims to know every one of them, including their family members, by name and appearance. He says this familiarity, together with his—I quote— 'excellent service,' engenders generosity from his customers. After a few minutes, I asked Jabbar whether he had noticed any strangers in the area, specifically two men, in recent weeks. He asked for descriptions, and Bates showed him the sketches and told him what she recalled about the men. Jabbar told us that earlier in the week—he thought it might have been Monday, the same day Bates was at the restaurant—he saw two men matching the sketches and Bates's description.

"The first time he saw the two men, they were leaving an apartment in the same building. He was collecting trash to bring down to the street as the two men exited an apartment on the sixth floor. Jabbar said this apartment had been unoccupied for some time. Ever on the alert for new customers, he asked if they were new in the building. He said the men were rude and pretty much walked right past him. The taller one mumbled something Jabbar couldn't hear.

"Anyway, remember, I told you this guy is very perceptive. He told us that he noticed the shorter man was hiding his left hand. Jabbar said the guy quickly turned his body to shield the hand and his face when he noticed Jabbar looking. Recall that Bates mentioned the shorter man left the restaurant holding his left hand inside his right hand. What scumbag do you know who supposedly has a fucked-up hand?"

Next to nothing was known about the man called Mumeet. The agency did not have a name or a picture of the man, and none of the US allies did either. The one piece of intelligence they had on the Bringer of Death came from a low-level al Qaeda fighter captured during a raid in Iraq a decade earlier. Almost immediately after his interrogation began, the Jordanian militant blurted out that he had been working with Mumeet when a bomb exploded in the makeshift laboratory. The Jordanian was unhurt, but he said Mumeet lost parts of fingers on his left hand. The intelligence was questionable, however. The jihadist couldn't offer any details to describe Mumeet other than he was about his same build and looked "ordinary." Some believed the militant simply fabricated the story; before he shared the intelligence, he had had the balls to ask if he'd be in line to collect a reward.

"We don't know if the story about his left hand is true. Plus, nobody has said this guy is missing any fingers—just that he hides his hand. But I take it you think Bates and the garbage collector might have seen Mumeet?" Patrick asked.

"Yeah, I do. It makes sense. We haven't heard his name in months. AQ has been quiet for months, maybe plotting an attack. Who better to command the attack than that bastard? Better still, I might know what name he's using."

"How's that?" Patrick asked eagerly.

"So Jabbar was in the same area the next evening, and he noticed the same two men getting into a cab. Each man was wearing the same clothes, plus a navy sport coat. Each also had a small suitcase; based on his description, I'd guess carry-on size. Jabbar didn't think much of it, other than he hoped they were leaving for good because they were such assholes, and he continued on his route.

"A few hours later, he was outside the same apartment where he had first seen them. He found two bags of trash and reluctantly picked them up, not wanting the garbage bags to untidy his building and thinking he might find something salvageable for his own use. Later still, as he was recycling the trash at his home, he came across a form from the Ministry of Interior's Travel Documents, Immigration and Nationality Administration—the TDINA issues passports for Egyptian nationals.

"The form listed a Rasul Qureshi at the same apartment address. Jabbar no longer has the document, but based on his description of the contents, it sounds like it was just travel tips, expiration reminders, typical bureaucratic follow-up."

Patrick let out a low whistle. "If it really is Mumeet, it's as close to him as we've ever been."

"The pieces are starting to come together. Even if it's not him, I'm now just about positive these two guys are part of some kind of operation. Check everything—the airlines, trains, boats—for the name Qureshi and see if we can find out where they went.

"Also, see what you can find out about the occupants of the apartment. I didn't have my kit and didn't want to bust in there in front of Jabbar. I'll have Bates send over the address and apartment number. Call me as soon as you find something."

CHAPTER 22

BOGOTÁ, COLOMBIA

A round the same time Carpenter and Bates were walking around Gezira Island in Cairo, Pablo and his clients were arriving in Cali, Colombia. After a brief refueling stopover in Riberalta, Bolivia, the previous evening, they arrived in Cali, Colombia, aboard the network's Cessna Skylane plane early Friday morning. They were met inside the private hangar by the customs agent, a drowsy woman on the network's payroll. She perfunctorily stamped their passports to authenticate their arrival in Colombia before Pablo led the men over to the modern commercial flight terminal, where he purchased one-way tickets to Bogotá on Avianca.

The one-hour flight put them into Bogotá before 2:00 p.m. A short time later, they entered one of the network's many safe houses in the Colombian capital. Nicely furnished with bright contemporary furniture atop dark hardwood floors, it was far nicer than the dump in Khartoum and Najjar's place in Cairo. Pablo pointed to two laptops positioned on a long dining-room table and told his clients the password for the secure Wi-Fi connection. Pablo grabbed one of the computers and immediately went to work on his cover story.

While they were flying to Cali, Pablo had shared some of the details about the itinerary. For security reasons, Pablo explained, they would be staying in Bogotá for two days before leaving for Mexico. He knew, courtesy of WikiLeaks, that US and other intelligence agencies, despite all their sophisticated technology, simply could not monitor the millions of airline transactions that occurred every day. Instead, the intelligence agencies focused their efforts on tickets that were purchased on the date of departure. The easy way around that problem was to purchase tickets at least a few days in advance. Before they left Ciudad del Este on Thursday, Pablo had purchased one-way tickets from Bogotá to Monterrey, Mexico, leaving Sunday at 12:30 p.m.

While it was true that spending a couple of days in Colombia would help with cover, Pablo didn't mention that he also needed the time to work out the remaining details of the plan he had begun formulating before they left Iguaçu Falls. Pablo's creativity, adaptability, and resourcefulness were essential skills for his business and were among the reasons his network could charge as much as it did to smuggle someone into the United States. Flying into Mexico required quality passports that would withstand scrutiny as well as a plausible cover story for the holders. Fortunately, Pablo had a solution to both issues.

Pablo's network had access to multiple passport options that would grant them access to Mexico without a visa—including Japanese, Portuguese, Venezuelan, and Australian passports—but his choice of Ecuadorian passports offered the greatest believability and the least risk. The long-standing Lebanese population in Ecuador, dating back to the nineteenth century, would allow his clients to pose as Lebanese immigrants whose primary language was their natural Arabic, a credible excuse for their lack of Spanish fluency. That they had no problems using them to book the flight to Bogotá gave him at least some confidence the passports would work in Mexico too.

As soon as he sat down with the computer, Pablo went to work on the finishing touches to his cover story. He would serve as the vice president of sales for a fictional banana plantation, and his two clients would pose as production managers. By the end of the day, he had a LinkedIn profile for himself and a basic website for the ersatz company. The following afternoon, Pablo picked up polo shirts and cheap sweaters, each article of clothing proudly displaying the Buena Fortuna Banana Company logo. In between these projects, he managed to find the time to acquire a box of new business cards for himself and items to fill three new carry-on suitcases. Each would pack a toiletry bag and a wardrobe consisting of underwear, socks, T-shirts, a black fleece jacket, and dark jeans to complement the new polo shirts and more stylish jeans they would wear on the plane.

While Pablo was preparing his cover story and acquiring supplies, Fahkoury used the other computer to do some online research. Though he wasn't happy about the time they were forced to spend in Bogotá, it provided his first opportunity to thoroughly examine each target and its vicinity, thereby limiting the amount of surveillance he would have to do in person—typically one of the riskiest parts of the operation. The first thing Fahkoury did was pull up a satellite image on Google Earth. He familiarized himself with the general area and then narrowed the view to the immediately surrounding buildings, roadways, and streets. He moved the satellite view in closer to focus on each target from above and then from street level. Deeper into his research, he found blueprints for his main target that showed details for all levels of the structure. He also found several articles about security measures employed at the site.

As he gathered more and more information, Fahkoury realized the success he expected would require a sophisticated and well-timed plan. This type of operation called for precision as much as raw manpower. He hoped the operatives Aziz was making available would prove up to the task on both counts. If they didn't, he'd simply have to improvise; he wasn't going to miss this opportunity to strike the heart of America.

Later that Saturday evening, Pablo called everyone together and shared his plan. "It's important that we go over our cover story. If we are questioned, we must tell the same story. Our cover story is that we are employees of the Buena Fortuna Banana Company traveling to Monterrey to attend the Fresh Fruit Summit. The conference is real, and although it does not officially start until Monday, some networking activities are planned for tomorrow night.

"Our purpose at the conference is to secure purchase orders from the supermarket chains that will be attending the meetings. I'm in charge of sales, and you two are production managers. The company has annual production of fifty thousand metric tons—a relatively insignificant amount—but we are considering options to expand if we can secure more business at the conference. You two would oversee any expansion and will be there to help me answer any production questions. Remember, too, that you are part of the Lebanese immigrant population in Ecuador. That will explain your preference for Arabic."

"We know nothing about growing bananas," al-Rasheed said.

"You won't have to. All you need to say is that you supervise the workers who take care of the plants and package the bananas for shipping," Pablo said.

Well after midnight and following several iterations, Pablo was satisfied each of them knew the cover story cold. He was tired and suggested that everyone get some sleep to prepare for their long day.

But Fahkoury was too wound up to sleep. He kept going over the attacks in his head, and he struggled to contain his anticipation. He was becoming more and more confident and was sensing the first tastes of victory. He wished he were already in America, but he would have to wait another eight hours before they even left Bogotá.

CHAPTER 23

CAIRO, EGYPT

Carpenter was chatting with COS Root at the embassy Saturday morning when Patrick called with the latest update. He had called late Friday night to report that the local team hadn't found anything at the apartment. There were some dirty dishes in the sink, and the three beds in the unit were all unmade. No personal effects had been left behind. At that time, there was no news on where the Qureshi boys might have gone. By Saturday morning, however, Patrick had some news about their probable destination.

"It looks like our boys on are the move. We pulled all the flight manifests for the past five days from the airlines that service Cairo and checked them for the name Qureshi. It turns out two men named Qureshi—Rasul and Umar—flew Turkish Airlines on Tuesday, January ninth, from Cairo and arrived in São Paolo Wednesday morning. You're a little more than three days behind them."

"Unless this is some kind of diversion, it's looking less like Europe is a target," said Carpenter.

"Maybe, but we still have no clue where these guys are headed or what they're up to. It's possible they could try to enter Europe from South America. They'd have less scrutiny, especially if they're able to pick up new passports from Brazil or another friendly country down there. We're checking São Paolo departures now to see if they stayed there or continued on to someplace else.

We're dealing with quite a few more airlines and passengers that go through São Paolo, so it'll probably take a little while.

"I was able to pull a favor from my counterpart in the Egyptian Mukhabarat. As expected, they don't have any information on the Qureshi boys, but he was able to send me copies of the passports issued four days ago by the Ministry of Interior's Travel Documents, Immigration, and Nationality Administration. I'll send over copies of the passport photos. Like any passport photo, they're not the best, but they're better than nothing. The sketches from Bates's descriptions are a reasonable match. In the meantime, I suggest you get wheels up and head toward Brazil. We can always divert the plane if necessary."

"Anything more on Aziz?" Carpenter asked.

"Still no sign of him, but Director Gonzalez spoke with the Brits. Apparently, MI6 also has Aziz on its radar, but they have no information that indicates he is in any way involved in an impending terrorist plot. I'll let you know as soon as we find anything more."

CHAPTER 24

39,000 Feet Over the Atlantic Ocean

The plane was ninety minutes from São Paulo, and Carpenter was lost in thought when he sensed the plane turning south. A moment later, one of the pilots opened the cockpit door and approached him. "Sir, you have a call from Mr. Patrick."

Carpenter went to the forward part of the cabin where the phone was located. "What ya got?" he asked simply.

"We just completed our review of the flight manifests out of São Paulo. It looks like they headed to the Tri-Border Area. Two hours after landing in São Paulo Wednesday morning, they boarded a flight for Foz do Iguaçu on Avianca. We've already started checking flights out of the regional airports in the TBA."

"Why would two terrorists head there? It's seems way off the beaten path for an operation in Europe or the States."

"That area has been on our radar for some time now. It's one of the largest black-market centers in the world. Some estimate the counterfeit goods trafficked through there generate twelve billion dollars a year. Terrorist groups have been quick to recognize the opportunities. Our analysts believe Hezbollah raises in excess of a hundred million each year, trafficking everything from cigarettes to DVDs. We've had reports that both ISIS and al Qaeda have looked to join the party over the past couple of years."

Carpenter thought about the possibilities for a moment. "Any chance these two guys are working with Hezbollah?"

"Doubtful if we're right that these two are AQ. Bin Laden made some overtures to Hezbollah in the early days, but AQ and Hezbollah really have no shared interests outside of the common enemy of ISIS in Syria. That'd be a long way to go to plan an operation against the Islamic State. Plus, it's not exactly difficult to cross the Syrian border and meet there."

"What about the financing angle?" asked Carpenter. "We know AQ is hurting for cash. If there's an opportunity to raise some serious money in the TBA, that could be their objective."

"It's possible, but at the same time, assuming we're still talking about the same two men, these guys are traveling long distances for that purpose. Why meet in the middle of the Arabian Desert to plan a financing trip and then take a circuitous route to South America? Wouldn't it be easier for Aziz to just send some other envoy directly from Riyadh?"

"Yeah, in theory it would, but maybe these guys are critical to that purpose," Carpenter said. "Maybe they're experienced money launderers or know the ins and outs of the black market. The meeting in the desert tells me these guys are either already on the hot list or they are really trying to protect their identities. Travel through Cairo to South America would make sense and be safer than going through Saudi Arabia, where security is tighter. That said, if they didn't go to Brazil to establish a funding pipeline, what other reasons are there?"

"At this point, we simply don't know. Like I said, I just got the flight information, and wanted to let you know you'd be heading to the TBA. Let me make some calls and see what more I can find out. They only arrived in the TBA three days ago, so there's a chance they're still there. I've already instructed the pilots. You should be on the ground in time for a late dinner. We have an officer assigned to DEA in Foz do Iguaçu. I'll brief him and have him meet you when you land."

CHAPTER 25

TRI-BORDER AREA

Carpenter was met by Joe Brzezinski, the agency man in Foz do Iguaçu, when he landed Saturday evening, a few minutes past seven thirty local time. Carpenter hadn't slept much after speaking with Patrick, but the short nap he had was enough to fuel him for a couple of days, if necessary.

"Hello, sir," he said as Carpenter neared the bottom of the air-stair steps, "I'm Joe Brzezinski."

Carpenter had chatted again briefly with Patrick before landing in Foz do Iguaçu and was expecting him. Brzezinski was assigned to CTC and had been in the TBA for the past sixteen months, charged with penetrating the terrorist organizations already established or seeking to establish there. After returning the greeting, Carpenter asked Brzezinski to bring him up to speed on what he had learned thus far.

"It's only been a few hours since the chief called me. I first started checking with my sources. I have an agent inside Hezbollah. He knows nothing about any recent visitors from Cairo, or anywhere else, for that matter. I've found him to be pretty reliable, so I think Hezbollah is a cold trail. We have a couple of guys we believe are affiliated with ISIS, but I haven't been able to recruit any agents with access to them. As far as I know, AQ doesn't have a presence here, but I've heard rumors. I asked DEA to check around with their assets. So far, nobody knows anything about our two guys.

"Shit. Any ideas?" Carpenter asked.

"Maybe. On a hunch, I started checking with local hotels earlier this morning and think I found something. That'll be our first stop."

Carpenter noticed some pretty nice homes inside gated neighborhoods as they wound through the lush city toward the setting sun in Brzezinski's car, a late model, white Fiat Mobi. Restaurants bearing Italian, Swedish, Chinese, French, and German names were doing brisk business as designer boutiques were beginning to wrap up their days. He said to Brzezinski, "This place looks pretty nice. Not what I expected."

As they continued west farther into the city, Brzezinski gave Carpenter the chamber of commerce summary. "Foz do Iguaçu—or Foz, as the locals call it—is a popular tourist destination and has one of the highest GDP per capita in Brazil. The actual GDP per capita is even higher because a lot of money is made in the black market. It is also a very cosmopolitan city for its size. There are some quarter-million residents, including notable numbers of Europeans, Asians, and Arabs in addition to native Brazilians. The wealthier Argentinians and Paraguayans in the TBA also tend to live in Foz."

They chatted more about Brzezinski and his time in the TBA for the rest of the short trip. Carpenter learned that Brzezinski's maternal grandparents were from the Algarve, Portugal's southernmost region. He was fluent in Portuguese and Spanish, ideal skills for this assignment. The CIA had only recently taken a keen interest in the TBA but had been slow to provide additional resources, Brzezinski explained. He pretty much operated alone despite requests for additional case officers. In spite of this, Brzezinski felt he had a pretty good pulse on the terrorist activities in the region. He also had a solid working relationship with DEA and had been working with its officers to explore potential relationships between the terror groups and the drug cartels. There was some evidence of coordinated money laundering and drug trafficking efforts but nothing solid.

"After checking with my agent and my contacts in DEA earlier this morning," Brzezinski said as he pulled the car onto Rua Osalvo Cruz and then into a hotel parking lot, "I had about an hour and half before I had to pick you up. As I mentioned, I have no intel of any AQ presence here, so I started checking hotels, figuring they need to stay someplace. Most of the trafficked goods are moved from the Paraguayan side of the Parana River, and that's where most of the illicit characters operate. So I started my search close to the bridge on the assumption these guys would want easy access to the full TBA offerings.

"I showed the passport photos to the manager of this hotel, the third one that I tried. He said he didn't recognize either man, but the Egyptian passports triggered a memory. The manager was on duty two days ago when housekeeping came to him with some items that had been left in one of the rooms. He said there was a pack of Egyptian-brand cigarettes and some matches from a restaurant in Cairo as well as two carry-on bags, two sport coats, and some toiletries. The manager said he thinks they tossed everything—that, or someone took the items.

"The housekeeper hadn't reported for work by the time I left to meet you," Brzezinski continued, "but the manager said she would be here this evening. He also said the other manager should be on duty by the time I came back. If he's here, we'll question him too. Could be a coincidence, but it might be our guys."

Carpenter was sure the two men he was tracking had stayed at the hotel. Any other conclusion would be highly improbable. Everything from the cigarettes to the carry-on bags matched up. That nothing important had been left behind was not surprising. Skilled operators wouldn't leave behind anything that was incriminating.

They walked into the lobby and approached the front desk. Brzezinski recognized that the manager was not the same person he had interviewed a few hours earlier, so he assumed that he must be the other one. He whispered the news to Carpenter just before they reached the desk. Without showing any identification or giving any indication of affiliation, Brzezinski explained they were looking for two Egyptian men believed to have stayed at the hotel recently. He showed the new manager copies of the passport photos.

After briefly studying the photos, the manager stated with some equivocation, "I'm not sure I remember these two."

Equating the man's reluctance with shiftiness—an impression he had before the manager even spoke—Carpenter got in the man's face and said,

"It will be in your best interests to recall everything you can about these two men. I don't have time to play games, and I'd prefer not to waste any bringing in the Departamento de Polícia Federal, but that can be arranged with one phone call."

"No—no, that won't be necessary," the manager stammered. "I am remembering these men more clearly now." Suddenly speaking with a certainty that belied a foggy memory, the manager said he was definitely on duty when the men checked into the hotel. Maybe it was Wednesday; he couldn't be sure. The two men said they didn't know how long they'd be in Foz do Iguaçu, so they paid for one night, in cash—that is not uncommon, he assured his inquisitors. The two men were nicely dressed and weren't particularly chatty, he added.

When the manager neglected to mention anything about their passports, Carpenter assumed the man had accepted a bribe in exchange for not asking to inspect or make copies of their identification. Carpenter didn't care; they already had photocopies. "Did you see them again, after they checked in?" he asked.

"I remember we only had a few guests in the hotel. It was pretty quiet. I noticed that they left the hotel a few hours after they arrived, and I was still here when they returned a few hours later. I remember thinking they must have gone to Ciudad del Este to do some shopping, because they came back with a nice camera. I didn't see the camera when they left. After that, I don't recall seeing them."

Carpenter had not noticed any security cameras in the hotel. If this place was as corrupt as Patrick had said, he didn't expect there to be any, but he asked the question, anyway. "Are there any security cameras?"

"No, sir. They are not something our customers would appreciate."

"Describe their physical appearances," Carpenter said, trying another approach.

"I don't remember much beyond what you can see in the photos, other than one was considerably taller than the other. The taller one was slightly taller than me." Carpenter, at a shade over six feet, was able to look the manager in the eyes. "They were both fairly thinner than they appear in these photos," the manager said.

"Any particular markings or abnormalities?"

"None that I noticed."

Once he got everything he could from the unctuous manager, Carpenter asked him to call for the housekeeper. A well-kempt middle-aged woman appeared a few minutes later. She told Carpenter and Brzezinski that she never saw the men when she cleaned their room the day after they checked in or when she entered to clean it again the next day. She confirmed the items the first manager had described to Brzezinski and mentioned that nothing had changed when she entered the room again on the evening of the second day. At the first manager's direction, she removed the items from the room but had no idea where they were now.

When they finished with the housekeeper, Carpenter and Brzezinski left the hotel and walked back to the car. It was pretty clear that the men they were pursuing had stayed at the hotel for one night; however, there was nothing to indicate where they might have gone since. Neither of them had any theories about the new camera. They couldn't put it into any context other than a possible connection to Ciudad del Este.

Brzezinski had earlier mentioned a mosque and a possible connection to suspected terrorists. Carpenter thought that was as good as any other place to nose around. "Let's go across the river," Carpenter said. "I want to check out the mosque and see what's around there."

"It'll be pretty quiet at this time. The shops all closed at nine p.m.," Brzezinski said.

"That's all right. I still want to check it out to see if we can come up with a game plan for tomorrow."

Since the hotel was just a few blocks from the Friendship Bridge and there was no sense in rushing over there, they set out on foot. As they neared Paraguay, the scrolling billboards and effervescent signs covering multiple stories of the densely packed buildings came into view, reminding Carpenter of Times Square or Piccadilly Circus. They worked their way through the shopping maze to the mosque, arriving there less than twenty minutes after leaving Brazil.

Carpenter had no intention of entering the mosque and asking questions. Even trying to enter would likely lead to unwanted problems. As they walked past, hidden among a decent number of people heading to the bars and restaurants in the area, he casually glanced at the few worshipers who were exiting following Isha prayers. He didn't really expect to see the two men, but one never knew. His focus remained primarily on the surrounding area as he tried to get a sense of where his quarry might have gone in this part of the TBA. After spending fifteen minutes canvassing the area, he saw nothing that particularly grabbed his attention except for several camera shops. He had a hunch that if there were any clues to the whereabouts of the two men from Cairo, they would find them at one of these camera shops. He told Brzezinski they would return here tomorrow, and then they walked back to Foz do Iguaçu.

CHAPTER 26

Carpenter and Brzezinski were back in Ciudad del Este shortly after it opened for business at 11:00 a.m. on Sunday, and they headed for the camera shop closest to the mosque. When they arrived, they were greeted by a hefty man with bushy hair and matching moustache, wearing board shorts and a Hawaiian shirt.

"Hello, my friends," the stout man said in flawless English from his stool in front of the store. "Are you looking to buy a camera?"

"Sorry, but we're wondering if you might help us anyway," Carpenter said. "We're looking for two Arab men who may have purchased a camera in this area recently. Do you recognize them?" Carpenter showed the man the passport photos.

The shop owner thought that he had been right to be suspicious of those men. He remembered how they had made a beeline from the direction of the mosque to his shop and, in the course of a few short minutes, purchased a camera without any deliberation or negotiation. "I'm not sure. My memory is a bit hazy," the man said.

Brzezinski recognized this play, and, before Carpenter had a chance to jump in, he handed over two crisp hundred-dollar bills. A smile instantaneously replaced the confused look on the man's face.

"I can't be sure. These photographs are not very good, but if we are talking about the same men, I sold them a nice Nikon camera. They were odd fellows," the man said.

"In what way?" Brzezinski asked.

"They didn't ask any questions about cameras. It seemed they didn't care about features. They picked out this model here," he said, pointing to the display in the front window, "and never asked any questions or to see any other models. For some reason, they only cared that the camera included a strap. In fact, they left the box, the camera case, and the instructions and took only the camera with the strap. I watched them walk here from over by the mosque. They were here no more than five minutes. Paid cash."

"Do you remember anything else about them?" Carpenter asked.

"They were wearing similar clothes. Both wore khaki pants and polo shirts. One shirt was white, and the other was blue."

Another consistency with Bates's recollection. "Anything else?" Carpenter asked.

"Yes. They seemed surprised when I spoke to them in Arabic. It was almost as if they didn't believe they looked Arabic, but they clearly did. Also, the shorter of the two men—the one who did all the talking, not that he said much—was missing parts of two or three fingers on his left hand. He tried to hide his hand when he pulled out the cash."

That clinched it! Carpenter was convinced that he was holding a photo of the man called Mumeet. "Have you seen them since they bought the camera?" Carpenter asked urgently.

"Yes. I saw them again on this street the next day," the man said. "They were with a Latino. I've seen him before; don't know his name."

"Did you happen to notice where the three men were headed when you saw them the next day?" Carpenter asked, sensing he might be closing in on Mumeet.

"No, I didn't. They took that street over there," he said, pointing.

"Have you seen them since?" Brzezinski asked.

"No, but as I say, I have seen the Latino before here in this area of Ciudad del Este. I have heard that he is a smuggler."

"Drugs?" Brzezinski asked.

"No, he is a coyote."

"What do you mean, 'coyote'?"

Carpenter knew the significance even before the man answered Brzezinski. He gave the man a card with just a phone number on it and asked him to call if he remembered anything else or saw either of the men. They thanked the camera shop owner, assured him again they were not interested in buying a camera, and walked quickly back to Brzezinski's car.

"These guys were definitely here in the TBA," Carpenter told Patrick when they arrived back at Brzezinski's small home office around two o'clock that afternoon. "Everything lines up, and there's no doubt that one of them is missing parts of fingers on his left hand. He's Mumeet; I know it." Carpenter told him the two men had stayed one night at the Hotel Nacionale in Foz do Iguaçu. For some reason, he explained, they made a hasty purchase of a camera in Ciudad del Este the same day they arrived. They were seen again the following day by the camera shop owner. This time they were with a Hispanic man. "This is the real problem," Carpenter said. "The Latino is rumored to be a coyote." He briefly allowed that to sink in before asking Patrick, "What do you know?"

"Still nothing on possible departures from the TBA. I spoke to US Customs and Border Protection not long before you called. I was going to share that there is a very real possibility these guys went to South America to get help entering the US or Western Europe. CBP says some drug cartels down there are now in the business of human smuggling. Their coyotes use the same pipelines the cartels use to smuggle drugs from South America into the US and Europe. Those pipelines would be worth a lot to a terror group.

"According to CBP," Patrick said, "the fees the cartels charge is twenty thousand or more per person and that the TBA has become a prime jumping-off point for immigrants—mostly from Asia but more recently CBP has apprehended people from Africa and the Middle East whose trip went through the TBA."

Carpenter recalled his SSCI testimony and Senator Williams telling him that concerns about terrorists sneaking across the borders were overblown. "For how long have we known the cartels are smuggling terrorists?" Carpenter asked.

"We don't know that for sure. None of the people apprehended by CBP had any terror connections that we know of or even any criminal backgrounds. CBP thinks the cartels are pretty choosy about who they will help; they don't want any more trouble than necessary."

"But you think the cartels might have made an exception here, and these assholes came to the TBA to hook up with a human smuggling ring?" Carpenter managed to say despite the pit forming in his stomach.

"That's certainly possible," his boss said flatly.

"This is looking worse by the minute. How long does it take to smuggle someone from the TBA into the States?" Carpenter asked.

"CBP says that on average, those they apprehended claimed it took several weeks to get from the TBA to the southern border."

"These guys might take a more direct and quicker route to the US," Carpenter said, increasingly concerned the two men might already be in the homeland.

"That's also possible, but you keep saying the US. Why not Europe?" Patrick asked.

"If Europe was the target, it just doesn't make sense to head to South America. They could just as easily jump off from Libya or a dozen of other countries closer to Europe."

"That's probably true, but we both know the extreme measures terrorists take to cover their trail."

"What about training?" Carpenter asked. "Not too long ago, I remember hearing about terrorist training camps in South America."

"That rumor does exist, but we have yet to find anything concrete to support it."

"So that brings me back to my assumption that they were or are down here to link up with someone to help them cross the US border."

"Right now, we can't say that for sure. Until we know more, Europe is still a possible destination. The TBA is place where they can probably get solid papers. They could use them to fly into Europe, the US, or anywhere else for that matter."

"I still find the European angle unlikely. Why add risk? Europe is nearly wide open right now. Border control is even more of a major issue there. AQ is certainly aware of that. I don't see how going from Egypt to South America substantially reduces the risk of getting caught trying to enter Europe," Carpenter said.

"Sound logic, but Director Gonzalez spoke with MI-6 again to ask what they know about the TBA. The Brits apprehended two Pakistanis at Heathrow ten days ago. They're not talking yet, but MI-6 tracked their origin to the TBA."

"Fuck me. These guys could be anywhere. So what do we do now?"

"If they've left the TBA, they did so sometime in the last four days. If your camera shop owner did see them Wednesday, they left sometime in the last three days. Either way, that still puts them well within the window CBP tells me it takes to get to the States. Gonzalez has alerted our friends in Europe, and she's reaching out for help in South and Central America. Everyone knows our thinking and has the Egyptian passport photos. CBP has the photos too. Right now, all we can do is hope we'll get lucky and find them somewhere during their travels."

Carpenter thought that was a long shot. "You want me back to DC?" he asked.

"No, I want you down there. If there's even a slim chance we can stop them before they get here or into Europe, we need to try. Let's see if anything breaks from the Americas, but until we know more, there's really no better place for you to be."

CHAPTER 27

MONTERREY, MEXICO

While Carpenter and Brzezinski were speaking to the shop owner in Ciudad del Este, Pablo and his customers were in Bogotá boarding a Copa Airlines flight bound for Monterrey, Mexico. After a brief layover in Panama City, they landed in the capital and largest city in the state of Nuevo León eight hours later and proceeded to customs. Three lines were established, including one for persons from South and Central America. As they approached the customs officials, they noticed there were two agents assigned to their line. When one of the officials motioned to them, Pablo went, believing the agent would notice that all three men were wearing the same shirts and that any tough questions would most likely be directed to the first person. Pablo quickly passed through customs, and Fahkoury advanced to the same agent.

As al-Rasheed awaited his turn, the other agent became free and waved him forward. "Hello. What is the purpose for your visit to Mexico?" the agent asked in Spanish as al-Rasheed arrived at the booth.

"Do you speak English?" Al-Rasheed asked in awkward Spanish.

Reconfirming the Ecuadorian cover on the passport, the agent gave al-Rasheed a quizzical look before repeating the same question in English.

"We're here to attend a fruit meeting," al-Rasheed replied in heavily accented English.

"Where's the meeting?"

"In Monterrey."

"Why are you attending the meeting?"

"We are banana growers. We want to sell our bananas to stores."

"Where are you staying in Monterrey?" the agent asked.

Al-Rasheed was not ready for this question and tried to hide his rising fear. He paused for a moment before saying, "I—I do not know. At a hotel, I think. My boss made those arrangements," he said, motioning toward Pablo.

His interest piqued, the agent asked al-Rasheed for his plane ticket. He examined it and asked, "How long will you be staying in Mexico?"

"Only for a few days."

"Your ticket is only for one way. How do you intend to leave Mexico?"

"We will fly back to Ecuador after our business here is done. We didn't know how long we would stay when we purchased the tickets."

The agent paused for a few moments to look at al-Rasheed and back again at his passport. He hesitated, trying to decide whether to pull this guy aside and add an unwanted problem to his day, one that was scheduled to end in less than an hour. After a moment's deliberation, he stamped al-Rasheed's passport and waved him through.

When they were together again, al-Rasheed told the others about his experience. Pablo tried to calm the man, but he was clearly shaken, the first real sign of emotion from either of them. He wasn't sure if the man was upset about the incident or if he feared his coldblooded companion. But Pablo needed to keep them moving, so he hurried them along toward the exits for ground transportation. There, the three men hopped on a Marriott bus from the airport to a Courtyard in Apodaca.

Pablo had arranged for his network to leave a car in the hotel parking lot, and he had no trouble identifying the beat-up Chevy Impala as one of many similar stolen and untraceable cars in the network's fleet. After locating the keys underneath the rear bumper, Pablo opened the trunk, and the luggage was placed inside. He asked for their Ecuadorian passports. He placed all three passports under the driver's seat, where he could get to them quickly if needed. He told Fahkoury and al-Rasheed that he would burn them later; they couldn't risk discarding them here in the city.

Following a quick stop on Carretela Miguel Aleman for *gorditas* and soft drinks, they headed out of the city. As they left the Monterrey metro area, they merged from Highway 100 onto Highway 85D, the Autopista Monterrey–Nuevo Laredo, for the 140-mile trip north. It was just after 9:30 p.m. Pablo hoped they would be at the border sometime around midnight. They needed to be at the pickup location no later than 3:30 a.m.

Pablo was careful to maintain his speed at the posted limit of sixty-five miles per hour as they drove in silence through the low hills of the scrubby landscape. That was likely all the dilapidated car could handle, anyway. Traffic was light, with very few cars traveling in either direction. By 11:45 p.m., they were just ten miles from the border town of Nuevo Laredo. Pablo maneuvered the car onto Route 2, and they headed southeasterly, paralleling the US border. They were entering the riskiest part of their journey, and United States Customs Border Patrol was not Pablo's only concern.

Contrary to the common belief of most Americans, the Mexican government had stepped up its efforts to curb illegal immigration. Although most of the measures were employed at Mexico's southern border, the United States had successfully lobbied for the Mexican federal police and military to begin patrolling the northern border as well. Pablo scanned the roadside and checked his mirrors religiously, looking for any signs of trouble.

Besides the authorities, one of his clients made Pablo anxious. Most of the people he worked with showed signs of nervousness, especially this close to the border, but the shorter guy sitting next to him in the front seat seemed completely detached. From the moment he met him, the shorter man had maintained an unyielding sense of purpose, yet he did so with an unnerving lack of emotion. His rigid demeanor and dark, menacing eyes only added to Pablo's unease. He could swear the sinister man had been watching and measuring him the entire time. Pablo tried to find comfort with the thought that he would be rid of them soon enough.

Pablo continued on Route 2 to a point just beyond the town of San Silvestre. They had not seen a single car for the last three miles when Pablo shut off the headlights and veered the car off the road into the desert, eventually stopping behind some bushes about three hundred yards from the road.

They were less than two miles from the US border when he removed the keys from the ignition.

Before getting out, he told his clients to change into the black T-shirts and fleece jackets he had purchased in Bogotá but to keep the same pants. Once they were across the river, they would change into fresh socks and the cheap jeans from the suitcases. The clothing he had purchased was more typical of migrants, and the dark colors would provide some camouflage. After everyone was changed and the old clothes and suitcases were back in the trunk, Pablo listened intently for a few moments to try to pick up any signs of patrols. The night was calm, and there was no moon. The stars peeking through some light cirrocumulus clouds offered the only illumination. A perfect night for crossing.

Comfortable they were alone, Pablo gave the initial instructions. "We will proceed very slowly from here. We'll use each opportunity to hide and pause behind the bushes to make sure we're still safe. Do not talk unless absolutely necessary, and even then, in nothing more than a whisper. After we have crossed the river, we will walk a couple of miles to the pickup point. Are you both ready?"

Fahkoury and al-Rasheed did not speak but, rather, nodded confirmation.

The group walked north, careful not to trip over any of the several cactus species, agave plants, and rocks littering the gravelly desert floor. At all times, their path kept them at least a hundred yards from the rutted roads used by the farm sitting a thousand feet or so to the east, the lone dwelling for a mile in any direction. Forty-five minutes later, they were hiding behind a compact-car-sized prickly-pear cactus within two hundred yards of the Rio Grande and the US border.

"We will go into the group of trees just ahead," Pablo said. "The river is on the other side of those trees. When we get into the trees, we will stop. I will go ahead to the river to listen and look for any patrols. Once I believe it is safe, I will come back to get you, and we will begin to head across. Understood?"

Both men nodded. Pablo said, "Let's go," and they sprinted the short distance to the edge of the trees. Pablo led them deeper into the scrubby forest and then motioned for everyone to get down. "Wait here like we discussed, OK?" Pablo whispered.

Fahkoury answered in a similarly soft tone, "Yes." And then Pablo was off.

"It looks clear," Pablo said when he returned five minutes later. "If there is a patrol hiding on the other side, the Americans will not wait for us to cross. Instead, they will shine a light on us and try to force us back into Mexico. They will call the Mexicans to pick us up. If we make it across, it means the Americans have not seen us. Once we are across, we will hide in the trees on the bank on the other side."

Pablo peered into the darkness at the two men, trying to get a sense of their readiness. The humorless, shorter man didn't flinch; he just stared ahead in anticipation. Pablo knew that guy wouldn't be a problem, but he was worried about the taller man. He had almost blown it back at the airport, and he was still shaken. Pablo hoped the taller man could remain calm and quiet. Although the river was sluggish and little more than two and a half feet deep at this location, it was not uncommon for people to lose composure during the crossing. The noise they would make, not the physical challenge, was his main concern.

"The river is not deep here," Pablo whispered. "At most, up to your waist. The current is not very strong, but the bottom is rocky. I'll warn you, the river is cold. Resist the urge to rush across; we must be careful not to make too much noise. It is better that you go slowly than slip on a rock and cause a splash. OK, ready?"

Each man nodded.

"Good. Stay close to me so that we don't have to try to find each other when we reach the other side. Remember, slow and quiet. Let's go."

Fahkoury followed Pablo into the icy river, with al-Rasheed right behind him. The river was just a little more than two hundred feet wide. Its width and freezing temperature reminded Fahkoury of a time he had crossed the Kunar River in Afghanistan. It had been during the summer, but the flows from melting snows and glaciers in the Hindu Kush ensured the water maintained a similarly frigid temperature. That crossing, too, had preceded an attack against the Americans, one that killed nine marines. As he made his way further into the river, he was emboldened by that previous success.

The three men shuffled with short strides, keeping their feet close to the bottom to ensure footing and minimize noise. At its deepest point, near the middle, the river soaked Fahkoury to his navel, temporarily leaving him short of breath. As numbness overcame his more sensitive areas, his breathing began to moderate. He looked over at al-Rasheed, but the water did not even approach the much taller man's waist. Ahead of him, Pablo nearly fell when he looked back to check on his customers, but he caught himself just in time.

It took them a little less than five minutes to cover the short distance through the frigid current. Pablo led them quietly ashore, and they headed into the thick woods and sat down. They waited there in silence and worked to control their labored breathing. After a few minutes, Pablo rose and moved into a crouch between Fahkoury and al-Rasheed.

"I am going to the edge of trees to take a look," he whispered. "We have to cross an open area of about one-quarter mile to reach a small creek bed. The creek bed is not a straight shot to the pickup point, but it offers good tree cover. Change into the black jeans and new socks while I'm gone. Hide the old clothes behind that tree," he said, pointing. "I'll be right back."

The woods where they were recovering contained mostly mesquite trees and extended about seventy-five feet from the river's edge. Pablo carefully made his way through the spiny forest and knelt down to listen at the edge of the clearing. He thought he could hear the faint sound of a vehicle off in the distance. He couldn't be sure whether it was traveling on Route 83 about a mile away or on one of the many dirt paths that crisscrossed the desert. The uneven noise could have also come from the farm, now about a half mile to the south. Pablo waited a bit longer. The sound, whatever it was, did not come any closer, and he no longer heard it. He returned to the spot where Fahkoury and al-Rasheed were hiding.

"OK, get ready to follow me. Stay low and be careful of the branches as we go through the woods. Once we are all on the edge of the trees, we will move quickly across the open area I told you about and into the trees bordering the creek. We should have good protection in the creek. The greatest chance of a patrol will be on the north side of the creek, where the ground is more open and there are some roads. It will be very dark underneath the trees, so we must go slowly to avoid tripping on the big rocks. We have a little more than an hour to reach the pickup point. Plenty of time."

Pablo pivoted away and led them deliberately through the branchy trees to the edge of the open field. Once they were ready, they ran as fast as they safely could in the semidarkness to the trees along the creek bed. They maneuvered the narrow band of trees and started following the middle of the dry creek on its serpentine route to the pickup location. They climbed over and through the large jagged rocks as they cautiously made their way north for about two-tenths of mile. At that point, the creek bed hairpinned and moved southeasterly for another thousand feet before it once again gradually turned north. After covering the last third of a mile, they arrived just south of a paved road. It was 3:10 a.m.

Across the road, about five hundred feet away, was one of several man-made lakes created from the flows of the intermittent creek. There was another smaller lake located just several hundred feet of raw, uninhabited land to the east. A few homes dotted the desert not far from these popular fishing spots, but none were within view of the pickup location—a point on the dirt bypass that veered from the paved road and ran along each lake's southern shore.

They had moved up about fifteen feet in elevation to the edge of the road when Pablo again heard the noise he had heard earlier. It was coming from the engine of a motorcycle or an all-terrain vehicle; he couldn't be sure. As the sound drew closer, he realized that there was more than one vehicle, and they were heading in their direction.

"Let's move back away from the road," Pablo said. "There are some vehicles approaching."

Less than a minute later, Pablo was able to get a glimpse of the ATVs as they passed by at around ten miles per hour. These were not US border agents. It was also unlikely that the riders were a couple of guys out for a cruise in the middle of the night. Rather, it was probable the riders were members of the many civilian border patrol groups that had formed along the border from

Texas to California. Most were former military or law-enforcement professionals, who carefully planned and executed coordinated operations. Pablo knew these civilian watchdogs would not hesitate to capture and detain anyone they saw sneaking across the border. They were likely armed too.

Pablo listened for a few moments as the ATVs continued to move farther away. He guessed the ATVs would continue westward another two miles to the Rio Grande and then turn around and proceed back toward them. If these two riders were alone, he should have enough time to get to them to the pickup location and out of there before the ATVs returned. It was risky, but he'd come too far with these dubious men to turn back now.

"We have to move now. Stay as low as you can," Pablo said as he inched up toward the road.

They crossed to the far side of the two-lane road and ran along the shoulder for the few hundred feet needed to reach the pickup location. Just as they ducked into the trees, Pablo saw headlights approaching from the east, the same direction from which the ATVs had come. As the vehicle moved closer to their location, its lights went off and on twice in rapid succession. This was the signal Pablo was expecting.

"This is your ride. When he stops, hurry into the back seat, and get low to the floor. We won't have much time."

The car turned off its lights as it pulled onto the dirt bypass several hundred feet away. Pablo waited until the vehicle was closer before stepping out from the bushes. He was pleased when he recognized Guillermo behind the wheel of an old red-and-white Ford Bronco.

The timing in these situations was never perfect. To compensate for the uncertainty, the network would have sent a different car down the road every twenty to thirty minutes during the anticipated window, in this case between 2:00 a.m. and 3:30 a.m. Getting Guillermo had been fortunate. He intimately knew every path and road in the area—valuable knowledge in the event they had to ditch the car and run on foot. It was looking as if Guillermo's expertise might be needed.

Pablo opened the rear door as soon as the SUV stopped. Fahkoury and al-Rasheed jumped in as Pablo spoke to Guillermo. "There are two ATVs patrolling the road," Pablo said. "I think they continued west to the river, but they will be coming back in a few minutes."

"I saw them turn around and head this way as I was driving on Route Eighty-Three. I should be able to outrun them, unless there are others."

"I didn't notice any others. Get out of here, and be careful."

Just as Guillermo was about to pull away, he and Pablo noticed lights through the trees as one of the ATVs crested the top of a small hill a few hundred yards to the west. After a few panicky seconds, the second ATV was still nowhere to be seen. Pablo figured the second ATV must be circling through the desert around the small lake. Pablo frantically mulled over the options. Even if Guillermo was able to outrun the ATVs, the one approaching on the dead-straight road would clearly see the SUV and call for help from his colleague and US Border Patrol. And running into the desert would lead them right to the second ATV. Hiding themselves and the SUV wasn't an option either. They were stuck.

While Pablo was trying to decide what to do, Fahkoury heard the approaching ATV from the floor of the back seat. He signaled for al-Rasheed to get out, and he moved to the driver's door, where Pablo was still standing.

"Do you have any weapons?" he asked the guides.

"No, we never travel with weapons," Pablo said.

Fahkoury focused on the approaching headlights, hoping the ATV would stay on the road, and continue past them. Through the low scrub, he noticed the ATV slowly turning left, as if it was about to enter the bypass less than two hundred yards to the west. He quickly decided on a plan. He sprinted toward the approaching ATV. Just before its lights would have exposed him, he darted into the vegetation and hid behind a short, gnarly tree.

Back at the SUV, Guillermo ducked down inside the vehicle, while Pablo and al-Rasheed hid behind it.

As the rider rounded the corner of the bypass, the SUV was exposed in the wash of the ATV's headlights. The rider abruptly stopped, no more than a hundred feet away from the seemingly abandoned truck, and contemplated his next move.

Fahkoury was in hiding no more than ten feet behind the ATV. He coiled as the rider put a hand on the pistol holstered on his right hip. As soon as the rider began to swing his leg over the back of the vehicle, Fahkoury sprang from his hideaway and slammed into him, knocking the man to the dirt road. Before the rider could roll onto to his front, Fahkoury was on top of him. He held the back of the rider's head, forcing his face into the gravel, while placing his knee on the rider's right elbow to immobilize the weapon.

The man was powerful, and Fahkoury struggled to maintain his advantage as the rider started to push off with his left forearm and knees in an attempt to roll to his right and throw Fahkoury off his back. Fahkoury was forced to let go of the man's head to keep his balance. The rider was beginning to make some progress when Fahkoury chopped his left hand into the side of the man's neck. Taking advantage of the man's momentary daze, Fahkoury grabbed one of several rocks nearby, raised it to his left shoulder, and smashed it into the back of the rider's skull.

Al-Rasheed and Pablo had left their hiding places to help Fahkoury and arrived on the scene just as Fahkoury was striking the rider with the rock for the first time. They watched in stunned silence as Fahkoury repeatedly slammed the softball-sized rock into the rider's head until he lay motionless on the dirt road. Pablo had looked away by the time Fahkoury grabbed the rider's head and twisted it violently, but the sound of the man's neck breaking was unmistakable. He turned back around in time to see Fahkoury, showing no emotion whatsoever, casually stand up and retrieve the pistol from the dead man's grasp.

The three men walked wordlessly back to Guillermo and the SUV. Fahkoury told Guillermo to get ready to leave as he and al-Rasheed climbed into the back seat. As Guillermo pulled away, Fahkoury leveled the pistol at Pablo's head.

Pablo thought he was dead, but Fahkoury only smiled devilishly as the Ford Bronco slowly moved away. His heart pounding, Pablo waited until Guillermo moved the vehicle around the short bypass and back onto the paved road before he collapsed to his hands and knees and vomited. He looked up in time to see Guillermo's SUV disappear on its easterly path. He gathered himself and moved apace toward the creek bed. Only an hour later, Pablo was back at the car on the other side of the border. He was sweating from panic as much as exertion. This was the first time anyone had been murdered on a crossing he had led. It would only be a matter of time before the body was discovered and a determined search was instigated on both sides of the border.

As he drove south toward Nueva Ciudad Guerrero, Pablo tried to figure out how he was going to explain this to his bosses. Murder was certain to draw heightened attention, a circumstance very bad for business. He also wondered what could be important enough to justify brutally killing someone just to get into the United States.

CHAPTER 28

HOUSTON, TEXAS

Guillermo managed to get them to the highway without any further harrowing episodes, but he knew the reaction would be swift once the civilian border agent's body was discovered. It wasn't until they were on US 59 North heading out of the Laredo city limits that Guillermo began to settle down, finding shadowy comfort in the regular flow of heavy traffic serving the largest inland trading hub in the United States and transfer station to nearly half of the international trade between the United States and Mexico.

As they made their way deeper into Texas, Guillermo was less concerned about the authorities, but his unease with the men in the back seat didn't waver. He had witnessed one of them brutally kill a man, and Guillermo feared the killer might have similar plans for him. He avoided eye contact with his taciturn passengers and sought solace from repetitions of the rosary. Finally, almost six stressful hours after leaving the reservoir, he stopped in front of the Museum of Natural Science in Houston. It was around nine thirty Monday morning when his passengers climbed out of the truck without a word. Guillermo was shaking as he started out on the ride back to Laredo.

Fahkoury spotted a public restroom, and the two men walked in to freshen up and shake the rest of the dust and thorny mesquite branches off their clothes. After consulting the map of downtown Houston displayed on the outside wall of the restroom, they hailed a cab to one of the shopping districts downtown. There, al-Rasheed purchased a prepaid mobile phone for thirty dollars at a T-Mobile store while Fahkoury waited outside on a park bench. Fahkoury used the phone to call the number Aziz had provided.

"May I speak with Hassam Abboud?"

"This is Hassam," the man said.

"Hello, this is Farooq. My partner and I have completed the due diligence you requested and are ready to present our findings at your convenience."

"That is excellent news! I have a meeting starting soon, but I could meet you afterward. Would you both be available to meet later this morning? Perhaps I can buy you an early lunch."

Plans were made to meet at a steak house on Capital Street at 11:45 a.m. With almost ninety minutes until the meeting, the two illegal immigrants used the available time to replace their migrant clothes. An hour after splitting up, they reunited at the same park bench. Fahkoury showed up in the new shoes, belt, button-down checkered shirt, and dress slacks that he had purchased at the Brooks Brothers store and toting a cheap canvas messenger bag, a notebook, and some pens secured from OfficeMax. When he arrived at the park bench, al-Rasheed was there reading a newspaper, looking very much the part of a casually-dressed businessman taking a late-morning break to catch up on the news.

Fahkoury joined him on the bench, and they feigned conversation while calmly searching for possible signs of surveillance. Finding no reason for alarm, they rose from the bench a few minutes later and headed for the restaurant, discarding their old clothes in a Salvation Army collection bin along the way. Fahkoury had been anticipating this meeting since leaving the Rub Al Khali. He was about to learn the whereabouts of his men.

"Hassam Abboud"—his real name, and the one used by everyone else was Abdullah Halabi—worked as a midlevel executive with a Saudi petroleum services company, a position he had secured three years earlier on the quiet recommendation of Prince Aziz. Abboud was earning a comfortable living and had the bounty of free time and disposable income enjoyed by a single man like him. That Abboud had decided to scratch an entrepreneurial itch was not at all remarkable to his local acquaintances. He was known to employ a diversification strategy for his accumulating wealth, using it to purchase several successful small businesses in the Houston area. In truth, the businesses—which included a portfolio of several duplex rental homes—were purchased with al Qaeda funds, and the earnings eventually made their way to its coffers.

Due to security concerns, Aziz had not provided Abboud with descriptions or the actual names of the various al Qaeda assets he had been asked to help. Aziz had told him only to lend assistance to any person who contacted him with one of several confirmation codes. Including "Farooq," Abboud had been contacted four times over the past several weeks. Farooq would be the most important contact, Aziz had told him.

The swarthy and nattily dressed thirty-eight-year-old Abboud arrived at the restaurant ten minutes early and, trapping a folded twenty-dollar bill in an open palm, politely asked the buxom concierge for a table near the back corner. The remote dining location would provide much-need privacy. It was also hidden from view of the front desk, a factor that would limit any awkwardness when two men he had never met arrived. They did, precisely at 11:45 a.m., and they followed the curvaceous woman as she sashayed to Mr. Abboud's table.

As Fahkoury and al-Rasheed approached with the concierge, Abboud rose from his chair and exclaimed, while not looking directly at either of them, "Farooq, it is good to see you."

Fahkoury stemmed the uneasiness by stepping forward and shaking Abboud's hand. He introduced his colleague as Robert Gomez. The concierge waited until they were all seated before giving Fahkoury and al-Rasheed menus. She smiled flirtatiously, told the men their waiter would be by momentarily, and then left the three of them all alone in the deserted rear corner of the dark, wood-paneled restaurant.

"I have been expecting you for several days," Abboud said quietly. "I received a letter from our friend in the kingdom that said to expect you sometime after the middle of the month. Did you have any difficulties on your trip?"

"No, the trip was fine," Fahkoury simply replied, downplaying the grueling quest and offering no additional details.

In fact, together he and al-Rasheed had traveled a circuitous route of over sixteen thousand miles by foot, camel, truck, boat, train, and plane, comprising more than twenty-one days to this point. Fahkoury had traveled even farther, with an additional four days from the remote Pakistani tribal areas. Despite all that, the journey was still not complete, and Fahkoury wanted to be on his way.

"There is a report on the news that a civilian border-patrol agent was killed a few miles from Laredo sometime last night or early this morning. Do you know anything about that?" Abboud asked in a conspiratorial tone.

Fahkoury fixed his eyes on the man and said, "We do not." After a short pause, he continued. "Our friend informed us that you have information and money for us."

Abboud smirked, understanding that Farooq did not wish to speak about such matters. It was of no concern to Abboud. In fact, he thought, it was probably better he didn't know. He pivoted to the outstanding question, and advised the two men that he did indeed have both. He handed Fahkoury a piece of paper with an address and the name of Fahkoury's contact written on it. The contact was a man named Abu Omar, and the address was in Dearborn, Michigan.

"Have you met this Abu Omar?" asked Fahkoury.

"Yes, I have."

"What can you tell us about him and your meetings with him?"

"This man, calling himself Abu Omar, contacted me here in Houston in late November. As with you, I was told to expect him. I met Omar only once. He's probably in his early thirties and is about your size and build," he said, looking at Fahkoury. "As instructed, I arranged for him to stay for several weeks in one of the homes I own here. I also provided Omar with twenty thousand dollars in cash. A few weeks ago, Omar contacted me by letter with this return address. I was expecting it. Before he left Houston, he told me to send any others who contacted me to the return address on the envelope."

Just as Abboud finished, the waiter arrived to take their orders. Abboud quickly ordered for each of them. Once the waiter was gone, Abboud handed Fahkoury a torn five-hundred-rial Yemeni banknote.

"Take this banknote with you," Abboud said. "I was told you will use it to get whatever additional money you need."

Aziz had never explained how he would get the money to Fahkoury in the United States, but Fahkoury assumed it would not be in the form of traceable credit cards or currency transfers. Fahkoury had used banknotes in the past for this purpose. It was a common token used in the *hawala* system, an ancient trust-based remittance system for moving money across borders. No physical money is exchanged between locations, and no legal contracts are utilized. Rather, recipients simply present a code or a token, such as a banknote, to a *hawaladar.* The code or token is proof that money is owed the recipient, and the hawaladar provides the stipulated amount.

In most cases, hawalas are used by overseas workers as a legitimate, efficient, and inexpensive means to transfer money to loved ones back home. However, because it operates outside the formal financial sector, transfers though the hawala system have also long been favored by terrorists and criminal enterprises. For that reason, al Qaeda's Finance Committee maintained connections with hawalas throughout the world, including several in the United States.

"Did you meet anyone else?" Fahkoury asked again.

"No, I didn't meet anyone other than Omar. In the weeks following my meeting with Omar, I was contacted by phone on separate occasions by two others. Each time, the caller provided a code over the phone. On those two occasions, I gave the callers instructions to the address to my rental home. The instructions were to a different address, four streets south and one building west of my home. The callers adjusted by using the prearranged code of 'forty-one.'"

The code was familiar to Fahkoury. It represented the number of times jihad was mentioned in the Quran, and al Qaeda often used forty-one as a code to provide directions. Sometimes it might mean passing through four towns in a certain direction and one town in another. In this case, it referred to streets.

Like many cities, Houston was set up in a grid pattern. The homes and buildings on each street contained the same numbers of those similarly situated on parallel streets. This numbering system hastened emergency response times and also made it easier for anyone else to find a particular location. The code was simple to follow—four blocks north and one home to the east of the address provided—and would keep any potential eavesdropper in the dark as to the true location.

"How many men are there in total?" Fahkoury asked.

"I am not sure I know, and even if I did, I am not at liberty to say," Abboud said. "As I am sure you have explicit instructions, I am sure you can respect that I have mine too. As I have said, I was contacted three times with a specific code and provided the assistance required. I met Omar and only spoke very briefly with two others. That is all I am permitted to tell you."

Fahkoury had to respect Abboud's discretion. He wasn't in the business of sharing information either, unless warranted. Abboud's shiftiness made him wonder, however, if there was more to Aziz's plans than he knew. "Is there anything more you can tell me about Omar and the others?" he asked, sensing Abboud had nothing else to provide.

"No, that is all," Abboud said. "Perhaps you will have the answers you seek when you arrive in Michigan."

They spent the rest of the meal discussing Abboud's time in the United States. He traveled frequently for his job and had been to Michigan a few times. Abboud shared what information he could about Dearborn and the other parts of the country he had visited. Fahkoury didn't flinch when Abboud mentioned the target city.

After they left the restaurant, Fahkoury was pleased with the controls that had been used thus far. Compartmentalizing information was the most effective means to ensure that no single person could jeopardize the operation. Abboud had only met Omar, al-Rasheed, and him; he hadn't met any of the others. And he apparently didn't know how many men had gotten into the United States. Abboud also didn't know the identity of the financier. Abboud did know the location in Dearborn, however, and that was a potential problem. Fahkoury had no choice but to trust the man, just as Aziz obviously did.

CHAPTER 29

TRI-BORDER AREA

On Monday morning, Carpenter waited in Brzezinski's modest apartment for news from Patrick. It was actually closer to a small fortress than a residence. Without an embassy or consulate in the region, the agency had been forced to outfit the dwelling with proper security measures and secure communications equipment. He had slept on the couch in the comfortable apartment on Saturday night but opted for a hotel last night. Crisscrossing the globe over the past two weeks was catching up to him, and he needed a solid night's sleep. Rest and a breakfast of freshly ground Brazilian coffee and *pão de queijo,* a baked cheese-flavored roll, helped to take the edge off as he waited to hear from Patrick.

"Any news?" Carpenter asked when Patrick called on the secure line midmorning.

"Nothing solid, but I believe they could already be in the States," Patrick said. "I checked with Customs and Border Protection myself. CBP told me a civilian border patrol was murdered along the border, just east of Laredo, early this morning. It's highly unusual. That was the first murder of a border agent, civilian or government, in the last five years."

"Not a good sign," Carpenter said.

"No, it's not, and the plot thickens. Our friends across the border report that two mutilated bodies were discovered a couple of hours ago in a national park, fifty miles south of Laredo. They haven't had any luck identifying the bodies, but they say the drug cartels are known for the practice and to use the park as a dumping ground for their victims. The Mexicans are under the assumption the two bodies belonged to smugglers and are somehow related to the murder of the civilian border agent here. They think some kind of transaction, either drugs or humans, went bad, and the cartel killed the men to limit future problems."

Carpenter did not believe in coincidences, especially when they were piling up. He had no doubts the events were related. "Obvious next question: if they're in the States, where are they going?" he asked.

"That is the sixty-four-thousand-dollar question, but there's more I have to tell you. CBP also said three Arab men were apprehended in New Mexico, back in late November. The men were caught in an area of New Mexico known to be used by human smuggling groups. Each of the three men claimed to be from Syria and asked for asylum. They were released with orders to appear before the immigration court. Their hearing was scheduled for just before the holidays. They didn't show, and CBP has no idea where they are now."

"Released? How is that even fucking possible?" Carpenter asked.

"Catch and release is a policy holdover from the prior administration. The new administration is making changes, but for now, it's still the law of the land. CBP had no other choice than to release those men."

Carpenter was dumbfounded. How could the government expect anyone who had entered the country illegally, been caught, and then released on their own recognizance to show up in court and risk deportation? It made no sense, and it just may have compounded their problem. "Obviously, if the three guys apprehended in New Mexico are involved, we're looking at an entire cell, not just these two guys," Carpenter said. "Do we have any clue where any of them might be?"

"Your guess is as good as mine," Patrick said. "Even worse, we still have no idea about the intended target or the timing for the attack. If we knew at least one of those, we could maybe home in on the terrorists."

"We've got to get word out across the agency to work assets, see if we can come up with anything to help," Carpenter said. "This is moving fast."

"Director Gonzalez has already moved on that," Patrick said. "We've also alerted the FBI and DHS that as many as five men, and possibly more, are probably in the country looking to do harm. Director Gonzalez wants us to brief the president again tomorrow morning. Get back to DC, and we'll go from there."

CHAPTER 30

OVAL OFFICE, WASHINGTON, DC

Including the meetings for the Cuba operation, this would be the fourth time that Carpenter had met with the new president during his short time in office. Based on those other experiences, it was clear to Carpenter that this president shared his own clear-eyed perspective of terrorism, and, unlike his predecessors, there would be no tepid or disorderly approach to combatting it under his administration. This new president only cared about results and thus far had shown he was not afraid to spill a little milk, if necessary, to get them.

President Daniel Madden had entered the White House a year earlier, following a highly contentious election season. He was an anomaly, having no government experience before taking the oath of office. His professed executive experience had been earned as an entrepreneur and venture capitalist. As a first-generation American, Madden epitomized the American dream. At the age of thirty-one, he had launched a tech start-up in Silicon Valley and, seven years later, sold the company at a multibillion-dollar valuation.

He furthered that financial success as an early active investor in several other tech companies, two of which were currently among the fifteen most valuable public companies in the United States. An uncanny ability to spot trends, coupled with archetypal management and leadership skills, expertly guided those companies and others on paths to commercial success.

Madden's business acumen was indisputable and, at the age of fifty-three, he was at number fifty-one on the Forbes 400 list.

His apparently gilded life was, on closer inspection, one marred by profound sadness. Three years earlier, Madden lost his wife of twelve years to a long, painful battle with cancer. With his two children grown, Madden found himself alone and looking for another way to better the world beyond his prodigious philanthropy. Frustrated with what he believed to be an inept federal government plagued by pervasive self-interest and divisiveness, Madden withdrew from his lucrative business interests and entered the presidential election campaign. He did so in the hopes of lending a new perspective to politics, one that embraced American values and the American dream rather than one that relied upon pitting one group of Americans against another. Much to the consternation of Washington's elite, Madden ultimately proved to be the proverbial dog who caught the car.

Few people had considered him seriously. Right out of the gate, the pundits dismissed his chances. Madden ignored them. He had overcome obstacles his entire life with hard work and determination. He campaigned relentlessly, espousing a platform of social liberty, fiscal conservatism, economic growth through deregulation, tax cuts, and national security anchored in unrepentant protection of the United States, including the enforcement of existing immigration laws.

First, during the primaries and again during the general election, he was pilloried for his lack of government experience and his bold stances on law and order and national security. In a bygone time of more decorous public discourse, he may have been viewed as a patriot, but in the current vitriolic period, he was labeled a naïve warmonger and, despite a long history of prodigious philanthropy, a greedy one-percenter. But most of the elitist disdain was aimed at Madden's views on illegal immigration.

None other than Senator Elinore Wilson had been his opponent in the general election. In every stump speech, she persistently hammered Madden's immigration policies, claiming they were immoral and contrary to American values. Despite a lavish lifestyle funded almost exclusively with the annual stipend she received from her trust fund, Senator Wilson disingenuously preached that Madden was just another rich guy and, worse, one who was indifferent to the plights of the less fortunate who were seeking a better life in the United States.

Madden loathed hypocrisy and intellectual dishonesty, but he largely ignored Wilson's rants. During an interview with CBS News, he was asked about the senator's criticisms. Madden said his accomplishments were largely influenced by his mother and grandparents. He told the story of how his family emigrated from Italy shortly after the conclusion of World War II. By the time they left Italy, his family had virtually nothing. Their home, located just outside Cassino in Frosinone Province on the principal road from Naples to Rome, was confiscated by the Nazis. In a last, spiteful act before Germany capitulated in May 1945, the Nazis burned the home to the ground and what little remained of their belongings with it. For six years, they took refuge in Canada before finally being accepted into the United States, a country, his grandparents believed, that would provide opportunities for their daughter and future generations. He concluded by stating that he was living proof of America's benevolence and opportunity for anyone willing to immigrate through proper channels.

The immigration issue was earmarked as the central theme for the second presidential debate, one hosted by another network and a moderator who did not bother with the pretense of impartiality. Amid great anticipation, the moderator teed up the question, attempting to lay the groundwork for Wilson to use Madden's own immigrant history to attack him for his current views. Madden, however, had done his homework and was ready. He first reminded the electorate that the United States had a demonstrated history of mercy to immigrants, including his own family. He readily conceded that changes to existing immigration law might be warranted but submitted that those issues were the purview of Congress. Until those laws were changed by Congress, as president he would enforce the existing laws in fulfillment of his sacrosanct duty under the Constitution to protect the economic and national-security interests of the United States.

His opponent pounced on the trap, declaring his statement was proof Madden lacked the compassion necessary to lead the country.

Madden looked over at his opponent and said, "Given your record, that's a richly ironic allegation."

Wilson's escalating discomfort was obvious as Madden recounted an incident from eleven years earlier. He told the story of a homeless, disabled army veteran who had broken into an unoccupied home in an affluent suburb seeking refuge from a brutal winter storm. Rather than show compassion for a fellow US citizen in need of help, the homeowner filed a complaint with the local police and demanded that the veteran be prosecuted.

"Where was your compassion then, Senator?" Madden asked. The awkward silence and the subsequent close-up of a disgraced Wilson combined for one of the key moments in the campaign, one that had put Madden into the White House with a landslide victory.

Madden's sobering views on terrorism and the necessary steps to counter it had also won favor with voters. He harbored no illusions about the threat facing the United States and the entire world from radical Islamic terrorism. He promised the American electorate that he would use all diplomatic and military options at his disposal to protect the country from the perverted ideology.

Early in his presidency, he began pursuing an aggressive agenda to build a coalition among leaders in the Islamic faith and governments in Muslim-majority countries to destroy the pernicious influence of Islamic extremists. President Madden repeatedly assured those leaders that the United States would be a steadfast ally in these efforts, a stark and welcome change from prior administrations. There were still many impediments to ultimate success, but cooperation and progress were forthcoming. But there was clearly more work to be done, as, now, that very same threat was rearing its head on the homeland.

CHAPTER 31

Carpenter was waiting with Patrick, CIA director Gonzalez, and FBI director Charles "Chip" Forti outside the Oval Office when Chief of Staff Bill Tackett opened the northwest door and summoned them inside. Homeland Security Secretary Elizabeth Wilcox and Secretary of State Julie Christensen were already seated opposite the president on one of the long sofas. The secretary of defense, retired general Michael Fitzgibbons, was participating by phone from an overseas location.

"Thank you, all, for coming," said President Madden as the latest arrivals moved into open seats. "Let's get right to it. Melissa, I'd appreciate it if you'd start the briefing."

Even though Director Gonzalez had earlier informed the White House of the agency's concern that a terrorist attack on the homeland was a real possibility, this was the first opportunity to present the intelligence and corresponding analysis to the president's full team of senior leaders. As she prepared to address the president and members of his cabinet, Director Gonzalez intended to leave no doubt as to the gravity of the threat facing the nation.

"Thank you, Mr. President. Over the course of the past week, the Central Intelligence Agency has been gathering intelligence that points to the strong likelihood of a terrorist attack on the homeland. At the present time, we know neither the time nor the location of the attack. In fact, it's not clear where we are in the attack cycle, but we believe we are in the operational planning stage. Weeks, if not months, of planning and preparations typically precede an attack. As such, our best guess is that it's far too soon for the deployment stage, but we can offer no assurances in that regard.

"As I mentioned, we have no intelligence to date that even intimates the intended target, but we believe the target has already been selected. Part of that conclusion is based on our opinion that a terrorist team has already infiltrated into the country. Tim Patrick and PJ Carpenter of the Counterterrorism Center have been spearheading the agency's efforts on this matter. I'll turn the briefing over to them to provide further details on this intelligence and our analysis of it."

"Mr. President, a man named Sadiq bin Aziz is at the center of this matter," Patrick said. "He is a member of the Saudi royal family and purportedly a distant relative of Osama bin Laden. During the nineteen eighties, he was working alongside bin Laden in Pakistan, helping to raise funds for the mujahideen in the battle against the Soviets. Our assessment of him at the time was that he was seeking privileged adventure; he had no real dog in the fight, if you will.

"There are unsubstantiated reports that Aziz was involved in providing assistance, financial or otherwise, to the nine-eleven hijackers, but that claim has been leveled against nearly every ultrawealthy person in the Gulf. It wasn't until his name appeared on several decoded documents found in Abbottabad that our interest in Aziz was elevated. Because of his royal position, our already limited ability to surveil individuals inside Saudi Arabia made surveillance of Aziz difficult. Despite several requests over the last half dozen years, we have received very limited assistance from Saudi intelligence regarding Aziz."

President Madden closed his eyes and grimaced. Saudi Arabia had been slow to increase its efforts against extremists with outside parties, including its close ally the United States. It was as if Saudi Arabia knew it had a problem but didn't want to admit it to anyone else.

Over the course of the next twenty-five minutes, Patrick continued to build the case against Aziz, chronicling everything from his financial success to his relationship with the shady former Afghan official Ahmad Ishaq and their luck in discovering the strange meeting Aziz had held in the Rub Al Khali with two unknown men. Patrick was explaining how the experimental microsatellite lost power after they used it to track the two men to the Yemeni coast when he was interrupted by DHS Secretary Wilcox.

"So where is Aziz now?"

"Aziz was last spotted in Saudi Arabia two days ago," Patrick said, "but we have not seen him since."

"What about the other two?" asked Secretary of State Julie Christensen.

"We're not sure," said Director Gonzalez, "but we believe they are now in this country."

The tension in the room spiked with that information. For a moment, no words were spoken; only some grave looks were exchanged. It was clear this was more than alarmist speculation. Everyone in the room was beginning to accept the seriousness of the situation.

"Following his meeting with Ahmed Ishaq in October," Patrick said, "we asked NSA to try to capture Aziz's communications. While we didn't find any smoking gun, we did discover some curious communications that led us first to Cairo and then to Brazil."

Patrick detailed the cryptic e-mails and explained how Carpenter had been able to track the two men from Cairo to the Tri-Border Area of South America. He told them the trail had gone cold in the TBA but mentioned how the recent murders near the southern border and an incident at an airport in Mexico might all be related to the two men. He told the attentive group that Mexican authorities believed there was a connection between the recent killing of a civilian border guard and two mutilated bodies discovered nearby on their side of the border. On top of these potential connections to the two men, he told them Mexican immigration authorities had reported a suspicious incident involving an Arab-looking man who had presented an Ecuadorian passport at the airport in Monterrey just hours before the murder of the civilian border guard. Patrick concluded his remarks by noting that the disappearance of three Syrian men—who had been detained by CBP and later released by the court—also fit within the overall timeframe, but he conceded there was no other information or reason to associate the Syrians with the two men.

"For these reasons, Mr. President," Patrick said, "we are now of the opinion that the two men Aziz met in the desert are inside the United States for the purpose of carrying out a terrorist attack." Patrick paused briefly to emphasize the significance of what he was about to say. "Based on eyewitnesses, we believe one of the men to be someone we know only as Mumeet, a long-time al Qaeda commander and extremely competent bomb-maker."

There was no reason for Patrick to expound further on Mumeet; the Bringer of Death was well known in intelligence circles. In fact, following the attack at the Danish embassy, the United States issued a still-standing offer of $5 million for assistance leading to his capture or death. Everyone in the room fully understood how his possible involvement greatly exacerbated the threat.

After allowing that to sink in, Patrick continued. "We just received this latest piece of information yesterday. NSA intercepted another e-mail to Aziz; this time it was sent from a public library in Houston. The sender wrote to Aziz:

"'As I know your keen interest, I thought I would share an update on my garden. The two fig trees are doing well. The same can be said for the three orange trees and three lemon trees; however, only four of my tomato plants have blossomed. Three of them apparently will not make it.'

"The NSA hasn't been able to determine whether Aziz accessed the e-mail. On top of that, there are ways he can conceal his location. Obviously, we were hoping the e-mail would lead us to Aziz. Even if NSA is able to figure out whether and from where he accessed the e-mail, it appears he's gone to ground."

"What do you think the e-mail means?" Secretary of Defense Fitzgibbons asked.

"It's our guess these references may be to operatives who are now inside the United States. If that's correct, there are at least twelve who made it in, including Mumeet and his travel companion," Patrick said.

"I think I already know the answer," said Secretary Christensen, "but what do you make of the three 'tomato plants' that didn't make it?"

"This is pure speculation," Gonzalez said, "but we now think the three men who claimed to be Syrians could be those 'three tomato plants.' One could conclude from the e-mail that they didn't hook up with the other cell members. Either way, we believe those three men are likely the 'tomato plants' referenced in the e-mail."

The picture was getting bleaker by the moment, and they all acknowledged the very distinct possibility that the United States was facing a major terrorist attack in the not-too-distant future. President Madden didn't waste any time. "Julie, I want you to work with Melissa to bring the Saudis up to speed," he said to his secretary of state and CIA director. "Maybe we'll get lucky and find out they know where Aziz is or can tell us something useful. The time for concern over bruised egos is now past. In the meantime, we've got to find these terrorists. What are we doing to make that happen?"

"We pulled the records for the Syrian men yesterday at Melissa's request," DHS Secretary Wilcox said. "CIA and FBI now have photographs of the three men and the names they gave to CBP. We have no expectation that the names are real. I fully agree we need to go ahead on the assumption these three supposed Syrians are bad guys, but I should note that we can't necessarily jump to conclusions about them not showing for the court hearing. Nearly half of those apprehended by CBP or other law enforcement don't show up for their hearings."

That fact was stunning, but nobody could do anything about it. The expression on his face left no doubt that President Madden was irritated. "Chip, what is the FBI doing?" he asked.

"We've distributed the passport photographs of the two men from Cairo as well as the three Syrian immigrants apprehended at the New Mexico border to all law-enforcement agencies. The five men have been identified as potentially dangerous and possibly in the company of others. We're asking for immediate notification of any actual or possible sightings. We have also asked for any and all reports regarding the usual list of preincident indicators," Director Forti said.

"That's a good step, but what are we proactively doing to try to find them?" Defense Secretary Fitzgibbons asked. "To a large extent, that strategy relies on the terrorists making a mistake."

"Even if we knew where to look for these guys, all we could do right now is grab them for being in the country illegally," the FBI director said. "Unless we catch them with bombs or guns, I haven't heard any evidence that is strong enough to support a search warrant, let alone an arrest warrant for a crime other than illegal entry. We need more evidence before we can charge them with more serious crimes."

"Chip, with all due respect, that's exactly why we're going to go about this differently," President Madden said. "Our first priority is to stop—and just so we're all clear, by that I mean eliminate—these terrorists. I'm not so much concerned with building a criminal case against them. These men didn't come here to commit crimes; they came here to commit war. In these circumstances, I don't see the law-and-order route as our best option. Here's what we're going to do."

Situations defined as incidents of national significance—a definition these circumstances increasingly appeared to meet—were subject to the federal government's National Response Framework. Under that framework, the Department of Homeland Security typically served as the principal agency for domestic-incident management while acting in consultation with various local and federal agencies, including the FBI and the CIA. But if this intelligence did indeed foretell an act of terror on the homeland, President Madden didn't want any bureaucratic entanglements to potentially frustrate a timely response. Before he laid out his revised framework, the president assured the assembled group he would coordinate any legal requirements with the attorney general and the Department of Justice.

"First off, the Interagency Incident Management Group will consist of the FBI, DHS, and CIA, represented by Chip, Elizabeth, and Melissa, respectively. You let me know what resources you need, and you'll get 'em. Information is to flow quickly and freely within the IIMG, and my office is to be kept current with any developments.

"Second, FBI and DHS will continue to be responsible for coordination with local law enforcement. For now, it seems all we can do is stress the need for awareness and vigilance in light of a potential terrorist attack. Chip and

Elizabeth, work out how best to do this on the local level while also mobilizing your respective teams to help.

"Third, I want the CIA working a parallel effort inside the country to locate these terrorists. I'll personally make sure we cross all the *t*'s with DOJ so that CIA can operate here. PJ, I want you prepared to lead that effort on the ground, with Tim organizing any support you need from the CIA, the IIMG, or my office.

"I know some of you might have some agita about empowering the CIA domestically, but the CIA and, in particular, PJ and Tim understand better than anyone how these people think and behave. We're apparently in a race against time, and they can help process any information that comes our way. If we even get a whiff of where these terrorists might be, I want PJ here and ready to deploy.

"My fourth and final point reflects my earlier comments about this being an act of war. I want everyone to know that lethal force is absolutely authorized on positive identification or suspicious circumstances. Don't take any chances to grab these terrorists unless they can be captured without *any* risk of losing *one* innocent life. Is everyone perfectly clear?"

"Understood, Mr. President," Director Forti said, recognizing the president's final point was particularly directed at him.

"What are the thoughts on sending the photos to the media?" DHS Secretary Wilcox asked.

Everyone deferred to Madden for a response, but he wanted to hear thoughts from the rest of the team first, without the influence of his own. "That's a tough call. Before I share my views, what does everyone else think?"

Over the course of fifteen to twenty minutes, the group debated vigorously. They had a theory, and a plausible one at that, but just a theory nonetheless. There was no credible and specific evidence yet pointing to an attack anywhere, let alone inside the United States. Rather, the support for the assumptions underpinning the theory, including the belief that at least a dozen men had illegally entered the country to carry out a terrorist attack, was all circumstantial. The decision whether to release the photos was a calculated risk.

"If we don't release the photos, and an attack does occur, the administration will be accused of withholding information that might have stopped a terrorist attack on US soil," said Secretary of State Christensen.

"I agree. There's too much risk in holding onto them," said FBI Director Forti.

"There's also risk if we do release them now," Carpenter said. "Right now, the terrorists still believe they hold the element of surprise. By not announcing we're onto the plot, the terrorists might let their guard down, if only a little. Under the circumstances, the best chance at catching them is through a mistake during the planning stage."

"But Director Gonzalez said we don't know if they're still in the planning stage. They could be in the deployment stage already," said Director Forti.

"No matter what stage they are in, releasing the photos could cause them to move up the attack before we ever have a chance to stop them," said Patrick.

"I'm not sure we get much further along releasing them, anyway," said President Madden. "If the e-mail interpretation is correct, there is a team of twelve terrorists in the country, including the two men with the Egyptian passports. The other photographs are of three Syrians who are apparently missing and not currently part of the terrorist group. Releasing the photos would simply allow the two Egyptian passport holders to remain hidden while as many as ten unphotographed men continue preparations for the attack."

"On top of that, we don't have any answers right now if we do release them," said General Fitzgibbons. "We have no definitive information about these men, where they are from, their true names, their relationships, and, most notably, even the slightest indication of their whereabouts."

"That's right. And the public and the press will rightfully demand more information. Without it, the administration will be accused of dysfunction, and our credibility with the public in the future could be eroded, especially if no attack eventually happens," said DHS Secretary Wilcox.

It was, everyone agreed, a tough call indeed. In the end, the group decided the current risk-reward calculus slightly favored holding on to the photographs for now. However, they also agreed that if no new information came to light, the photos had to be released and sometime fairly soon. Still, some degree of notice to the public was clearly warranted, and one of President Madden's cabinet members was thinking along that same line.

"I think we have to issue some kind of alert," DHS Secretary Wilcox said.

That recommendation engendered another round of discussion. The original Homeland Security Advisory System—which utilized a color-coded notification system—had been replaced by the National Terrorism Advisory System. Under the NTAS, bulletins and alerts provided timely information to the American public about terrorism threats. While a bulletin included current developments regarding broader or general trends, the two levels of alerts—"elevated" and "imminent"—provided notice based on more actionable intelligence. The decision of which notification level to use in this case was not black and white.

"Given these circumstances, I think the choice between an elevated alert and a bulletin is a distinction without difference," Secretary Wilcox said. "While we might agree the information before us points to an attack, there is no specific information about a target, method, or time for the attack. It is clear to me, however, that we have an obligation to summarize the issue—to wit, that intelligence indicates that terrorist organizations have renewed interest in an attack on the homeland."

"Done," President Madden said. "Please circulate a draft before you release the bulletin, Elizabeth, so that we're all on the same page."

"Mr. President, perhaps you could also remind the country during your weekly radio address about how the public can contribute to the counterterrorism effort—more specifically, asking the public to report any of the same preincident indicators the FBI has circulated to local law enforcement," Chief of Staff Bill Tackett said.

"That's an excellent idea too. Let's be sure to include that in my address this week."

With no further thoughts or comments forthcoming from the group, the president ended the meeting. "All right, everyone, let's get after it. And keep me posted on the progress. We'll revisit these issues as more information comes to light. Thank you."

⚔

As the group was leaving the Oval Office, Patrick slipped in alongside Carpenter. "On a lighter note, both of our teams are still alive in the playoffs. You want to try to win your money back from last year?"

"You're on," Carpenter said without hesitation; Patrick had been a mercilessly sore winner. "I hope you didn't spend that fifty bucks, because this year the Falcons are going deeper than your Steelers."

"Since you're feeling that confident, how about a kicker? Another fifty bucks if either team wins the Super Bowl?"

"Why not? Where is it this year?"

"In balmy Minneapolis."

"Wasn't it just there?"

"Yes, but the NFL had to move it from New Orleans after Hurricane Jerry hit."

"That was more than a year ago."

"There was some structural damage to the Superdome, and the area around it is still in rough shape. The NFL always keeps a secondary site as a contingency plan, and they liked how Minneapolis pulled it off last time."

"Doesn't matter where it is; you're on. And you had better start saving your hundred bucks."

CHAPTER 32

DEARBORN, MICHIGAN

After the meal with Abboud, Fahkoury and al-Rasheed went back to the shopping district to purchase some cold-weather clothes. Up to that point, their travels had taken them through warm and relatively mild climates. Fahkoury knew it would be much colder in Michigan at this time of year, and he didn't want them to show up wearing nothing more than long-sleeved shirts. They found a discount department store offering a selection of cold-weather gear. Not expecting to find heavy winter jackets this far south in the United States, they looked no further and purchased two midweight parkas and knit hats. With that task complete, they made their way to the downtown bus station on Harrisburg Boulevard, where Fahkoury purchased one-way tickets from Houston to Detroit for $204 apiece.

Thirty-six hours later, after connections in Dallas and Nashville, the Greyhound bus arrived in Detroit on Wednesday at 7:00 a.m. Unlike the other stops on their journey, Fahkoury expected they would stay an extended period of time in southeastern Michigan. Before they headed for the address Abboud had given him, Fahkoury wanted to assess the area for himself.

On the ten-mile cab ride from Detroit, Fahkoury recalled what Abboud had told them about the considerable Arab population in Dearborn. Abboud claimed that nearly 40 percent of the city's residents were of Arab descent. Most were Lebanese Christians, he said, but there was also a growing Muslim populace, principally made up of immigrants from Yemen, Iraq, and Palestine. Abboud pointed out that Dearborn was also home to the largest mosque in North America, a testament to this trend. Fahkoury appreciated that regular arrivals of new Arab immigrants would reduce the risk of exposure in Dearborn and help them and the other cell members blend into the general population. As the cab pulled into Dearborn, Fahkoury was comforted by the Arabic on the awnings and windows of many storefronts. From what he had seen, Dearborn was shaping up to be an ideal staging location for the operation.

Before he felt fully reassured, however, they needed to find Omar and the rest of the men. He asked the cabbie to recommend a restaurant near the center of the city. He explained they were meeting a friend later but wanted to eat first. The cabbie dropped them off in front of a Lebanese restaurant on Warren Avenue, telling his passengers this was the commercial center of the Arab section of the city.

The area was already busy with vehicles and pedestrians at just past seven thirty on a dark and blustery mid-January morning, giving Fahkoury assurance that he and al-Rasheed would be able to wander the area without being too conspicuous. They walked toward a convenience store a couple of blocks from where the cabbie let them out and purchased a street map of the city, some bottles of water, and weak coffee. They sipped the lukewarm coffee from the wax-coated paper cups at one of the small tables in the back of the dingy convenience store, while two Iraqi men played a game of backgammon at one of the adjacent tables. Fahkoury consulted the map and plotted a route to the address Abboud had provided. He assumed the address marked the place where Abu Omar and the others were living. He pointed out the location to al-Rasheed, about nine blocks south of their current location, situated in the center of the block on a wide boulevard.

A short while later, the two men exited the convenience store just as the sun was making its brief appearance above the horizon before it would once again disappear behind the leaden sky. Fahkoury steered al-Rasheed toward the intersection, telling him on the way that they would surveil the surrounding area and neighborhood before approaching Omar's residence. They crossed the potholed avenue, walking in the same purposeful manner as the other bundled-up pedestrians, and continued one block farther south from Warren Avenue. Once there, they diverted back to the west and started south, paralleling Omar's street.

The foot traffic lessened as they moved farther from Warren Avenue, but they still encountered at least a few pedestrians. None seemed to even notice them or give them a second thought. It was not the kind of day to delay one's arrival at a warm home or office. As they progressed through the area, Fahkoury noticed there were only residential dwellings on the boulevard, but the streets immediately adjacent to Omar's were made up of a mix of light commercial and residential properties. The mixed use suggested a steady rotation of customers, workers, and residents moving through the greater neighborhood.

Fahkoury was also pleased to see that several main arteries and parking areas served this section of the city. The available nearby parking and the lack of businesses on the boulevard meant that only residents were likely to park on the street. This would make it more difficult for the enemy to set up surveillance of Omar's residence, and the bustle of the general area would offer further concealment of their comings and goings.

They entered the boulevard two blocks north and walked it to Omar's address. The mostly neglected cookie-cutter homes were packed tightly together and set equidistantly back from the street, about twenty-five feet. There were only a few, mostly older, cars parked along either side of the boulevard. Before they approached the home, Fahkoury took a moment to look it over. The bungalow-style home had seen better days, but it still measured auspiciously to most of its neighbors. Overgrown shrubs left little more than a narrow gap to the crumbling concrete steps that bisected the similarly obscured porch spanning the front of the house. The peeling white paint adorning six window frames, the doorframe, and four porch columns had endured favorably compared to the faded gray paint on the decaying wooden siding. By all measures, it was an uninspiring home on a characterless street in the middle of an ethnically diverse but otherwise unremarkable city. Aziz and Omar had chosen well, Fahkoury thought as they approached the door to the home.

CHAPTER 33

A man fitting the general description Abboud had given them answered their second soft knock on the steel door. The slender, bespectacled man maintained a neatly trimmed goatee and stood eye to eye with al-Rasheed at the door's misaligned threshold, making him just about Fahkoury's height.

The man studied the callers for a moment before asking, "May I help you?"

"We have just arrived here in Michigan," Fahkoury said. "A friend of ours from Houston, Hassam Abboud, suggested we contact his cousin here in Dearborn—Abu Omar."

"I am Abu Omar. Please, please come inside," he said warmly while scanning the street for any onlookers before closing the door.

So far, everything checked out, but Fahkoury still needed to verify that the man was indeed Abu Omar. He said, "Mr. Abboud told us that you might know the name of someone who could help us find a place to stay."

"Yes, I do. A very good friend of mine. His name is Mohammad Hammoud," said Omar.

Mohammad Hammoud was the name of a fierce al Qaeda fighter who was killed in a battle with the Americans in Afghanistan in 2009. It was also the confirmation code that Abboud had given them in Houston. This man, Abu Omar, was their contact. After two weeks and thousands of miles,

Fahkoury had finally reached the United States. But with only eighteen days before the attack, Fahkoury needed to use every minute efficiently. His first priority was the team.

Aziz had designed a process where only Fahkoury and al-Rasheed knew the big picture—the target, the attack date, and the proposed method of attack. By the same measure, some information had been kept from Fahkoury, most notably the composition and capabilities of his team. Until Houston, he didn't even know where the rest of the team was located. Before he could put together his own plan, he needed to be sure the team was not already compromised. After that, he would find out what kind of soldiers he had and what they had been doing inside the United States the past several weeks.

"Where are the others?" he asked Abu Omar once they had settled into the mismatched recliners arrayed in a semicircle in the center of the long and narrow living room just off the front entrance.

"There are ten of us total. Three of us are living in this house. There are five others living in a house across the street. Two more are living in an apartment above a store about a mile from here."

His preliminary planning called for at least a dozen additional warriors, but Fahkoury would have to make do with the lesser number. Moving on with his agenda, he asked, "When and how did you get to the United States?"

"We traveled in separate groups and arrived in Houston at different times. My group of three was the first to arrive in Houston. We crossed the border near Brownsville, Texas, about six weeks ago. The last group arrived in Houston about two weeks later."

Omar went on to describe the route his group followed. It was similar to that taken by Fahkoury and al-Rasheed, except that Omar and his companions had traveled overland from Colombia through Mexico and into Texas near Brownsville. The second group of three had also traveled overland from Colombia into Mexico but had crossed the border into Arizona and then made their way to Houston by bus. The final group had followed a different path. Those four men had traveled aboard a Qatari-owned cargo ship to Montreal, where they slipped into Canada and later crossed the border near Massena, New York. They sat in a diner in Massena and studied the Walmart employees as they showed up for the midnight to 8:00 a.m. shift. They hot-wired an early model Ford Taurus that one of the employees had parked far from the front of the store and drove it to Houston. In an intentional ironic twist, they left the car in the parking lot of another Walmart store.

Omar also shared that he had been to the United States two other times. He held a degree in electrical engineering and traveled to the States for business while he was working in his native Iraq for a Swiss company. On those trips, in 2011 and 2014, he had been in New York and Chicago, respectively. The previous trips were of little interest to Fahkoury, but he reasoned that Omar's excellent English and experience in America were undoubtedly reasons al Qaeda leadership had selected him for this mission.

Reassured by Omar's telling of how everyone came to arrive in America, Fahkoury turned his attention to the next possible risk of exposure. "Tell me about your contact with Abboud," Fahkoury said. Abboud already knew too much for his liking, and Fahkoury wanted to make sure the middleman had accurately represented his interactions with the members of the team.

"Our trainers assigned one leader for each travel group. The trainers had us memorize his name and contact information and a code to confirm our identity. We were told to contact Abboud when we reached Houston. I spoke to Abboud on the phone once to set up my only meeting with him. The leaders of the other two groups, Hayder and Wasim, only called him. They never met him in person.

"When I met with Abboud, he gave me the address of a home in Houston and twenty thousand dollars cash. The house in Houston is a duplex. Eventually, we all stayed at the house before coming here. Abboud never came to the house, and none of us spoke with him while we were in Houston. After we arrived in Michigan, I sent him a letter with this address. That is all."

Pleased that explanation squared with Abboud's story, Fahkoury then guided the discussion to Michigan. Omar explained that he was given the name of a contact, a Yemeni named Zafir Bahar, at the end of training. Omar was told to travel alone to Michigan to meet with Bahar once all the cell members were established in America. He drove a 2002 GMC Yukon on that first trip as well as on his most recent trip to Michigan. He found the SUV on Craigslist and purchased it in Houston from the owner for $2,600, using the money Abboud had given him. During the first trip, Omar inspected two homes Bahar owned, the one they were currently in and the one across the street, and found them both acceptable. Omar stayed one night in the apartment above Bahar's mobile-phone repair shop and then drove back to Houston to get the others.

Before the group left Houston, Omar purchased two additional vehicles: a 2004 Chevy Astro van for $3,100 and a 2005 model of the same van for $3,600, each time purchasing it from the owner through Craigslist with the money from Abboud. On all three occasions, Omar had not been asked for, nor did he provide any identification when purchasing the vehicles. The men split up and drove the three vehicles on separate routes to Michigan. Omar said all the automobiles were now out of sight, parked in various municipal lots around the area. License plates that Omar and Bahar had stolen from a junkyard in Michigan now adorned all three automobiles.

Content with what he had heard so far, Fahkoury moved the discussion back to the team. "Did you know all the brothers before you assembled here?"

"I didn't know any of them before we were together in Afghanistan to train for this mission." Omar added that of the ten from the training who were now in the United States—there had been a total of thirteen in the training class, he said—he and two others were from the al Qaeda group in Iraq, two were from al Qaeda in the Arabian Peninsula in Yemen, three were from al Qaeda in the Islamic Maghreb in Tunisia, and two more were from Syria.

Fahkoury was troubled by the news that three men from the training class were unaccounted for. Omar claimed not to know if they were supposed to be part of the team in Michigan. He also mentioned that the three men largely kept to themselves during training. Fahkoury didn't know what to make of the three missing men. Aziz had not told him the number of warriors he would have or anything about possible problems. Fahkoury wondered if the others had been detained along the route to the United States or, for some reason, Aziz and leadership had other intentions for them. He pushed those thoughts aside and asked Omar, "What were you told about the operation?"

"Only that we had been chosen for an operation in America. Over time, we learned the attack would use bombs. Our instructions were to acquire large automobiles for use in getting here to Michigan as well as to scout areas to acquire the bomb-making materials we learned about in training. We were also told that a commander would meet us in America. Other than that, no details—the time and place—about the operation were ever given."

Fahkoury then asked about their training. Omar explained that each of them had gone through some prior training with their respective al Qaeda affiliates, but none had been involved in an operation before now. The training in Afghanistan taught them an array of practical skills, including basic tradecraft: how to avoid habitual behavior, how to conduct surveillance as well as how to spot and evade surveillance, and how to control communications to avoid detection. They also learned how to hotwire a car, disable various alarm systems, conduct reconnaissance, and break and enter buildings. They practiced using different firearms and were exposed to various bomb-making techniques and the types of common materials used to make them.

Omar explained that their ability to speak English was another commonality. During the four-plus months they trained together, that skill was honed. They spoke English exclusively and read American newspapers and watched American news every day. To help them better assimilate, they also received daily instruction on aspects of American culture—work habits, food, entertainment, sports, shopping, and politics.

The team was better equipped than Fahkoury had anticipated, at least based on Omar's recounting. As a last item, Fahkoury asked Omar to explain what he and the men had been doing in Michigan while they awaited his arrival. Time remained his most critical concern, and it was imperative that the men had been productive while they waited for his arrival. When the discussion ended more than four hours later, Fahkoury was satisfied with the precautions that had been taken as well as the preliminary work the team had completed.

At his instruction, Omar assembled the team in the dingy, low-ceilinged cement basement to pray and then to eat. During the meal, Fahkoury explained they would not meet as a full group again until he was prepared to share more details about the attack. It was too risky to meet in large groups, he told his team. Except for their participation in the preparations, Fahkoury told the men they were to remain inside the dwellings. He ordered the men not to communicate with anyone outside the group and received assurances no one had done so. He reviewed surveillance-detection methods and implored them to be vigilant and cautious at all times. Fahkoury closed the meeting by stressing the importance of this operation and the blessings they enjoyed for having been selected. By the time the meal was finished, he was certain that, to a man, each was fully committed to the mission.

Fahkoury silently commended Aziz. He was pleased with the men chosen for the operation, and Dearborn was an ideal location for the planning stage. Although he and his men could not expect any of the local Arab population to be sympathetic to their cause, if they were careful, they would not draw attention here. It was also far enough from the target city so as not to betray their plans if any of the men encountered any trouble, yet close enough to travel back and forth without much difficulty. The natural progression of these thoughts focused his attention on his next step in the critical preparations—target surveillance.

CHAPTER 34

MINNEAPOLIS, MINNESOTA

The next day, Fahkoury and al-Rasheed drove one of the Chevy vans to Minneapolis for a first look at the location for the main part of the attack. They had only arrived in Dearborn the previous day, but there was no time to catch up on rest. Despite leaving early that morning, an accident on I-90 in Chicago delayed their arrival in Minneapolis until almost 7:30 p.m. As Fahkoury worked the van through light post-rush-hour traffic, they caught their first glimpse of the main target. After taking the next exit, they circled back and drove around the entire building.

On the first circuit, al-Rasheed—concealed in the back of the van—took photographs with a digital camera they had purchased at a Best Buy in Janesville, Wisconsin. From the driver's seat, Fahkoury paid particular attention to the nearby parking ramps and the various entrances to the building.

They left the area and returned forty-five minutes later, making a second trip around the building, this time with al-Rasheed driving. Fahkoury was content with al-Rasheed's preliminary work but still snapped a few additional photos. For the most part, he directed his attention to the security presence. Each time around, Fahkoury had noticed a police car or two, as well as some private security vehicles. He was sure there were closed-circuit cameras all around the property, but they were difficult to detect in the surrounding darkness.

After the second pass, they drove about thirty miles south of Minneapolis and checked in to a small motel near one of the exits off I-35. Late the next morning, they returned to the main target area. Aziz had told them to expect between seventy and one hundred thousand people there on the day of the attack. Fahkoury had no idea how many were present this day, but there were, indeed, a lot of people.

They parked the van and got out. They were bundled up like the rest of the crowd, wearing heavy parkas and wool hats. They walked the perimeter of the building, chatting as if returning to their car. As they made their way around, Fahkoury nonchalantly followed the security patrols and snuck a few glimpses at the CCTV cameras mounted high up on the exterior walls. While he was confident their work the previous night had gone unnoticed, Fahkoury knew the risk of discovery was high during preoperational surveillance, so he kept this visit short. Slightly less than twenty minutes later, they were back in the van.

The more rigorous inspection did little to change Fahkoury's thinking; it more or less confirmed the plan he had devised from his extensive online research in Colombia. If nothing else, the surprising number of people there on a weekday boosted his confidence for the plan's success. Content to this point, he moved on to the next matter—finding a safe house.

Fahkoury called out directions as al-Rasheed steered the van through the southwest suburbs. Over the next several hours, they located more than a few possibilities that met his requirements. Each was isolated in a rural area, no more than twenty-five miles from the city, and large enough to accommodate their personnel and vehicles, but one in particular held Fahkoury's interest. But before settling on it, they would need to study the location more thoroughly, something they would do when they returned to Minneapolis later to study the second location for the multidimensional attack. In the meantime, there was much to do back in Dearborn.

CHAPTER 35

ALLENTOWN, PENNSYLVANIA

Carpenter had decided to take advantage of a rare opportunity. He couldn't remember that last time he had been in the United States for more than thirty-six hours. Now it looked like he might be here awhile. The day after the meeting in the Oval Office, he told Patrick about his plans. It would be another day or two before Patrick and the other leaders had set up a command center and teams to occupy it. Until then, unless they discovered some news about the terrorists and their plans, there was not much for Carpenter to do. Patrick not only approved, he insisted Carpenter use his personal car.

Once the president ordered Carpenter to stick around, Patrick had also insisted that he stay with him and his wife in their home in Bethesda. Carpenter didn't bother to protest; it would have been hollow, anyway. Patrick was the closest thing he had to family, and the prospect of holing up for an indeterminate period of time in one of the crappy hotels on the government's approved list offered zero appeal. After two nights of the Patrick's hospitality, Carpenter wasn't sure he ever wanted to leave.

That morning, Carpenter had set off on his trip in Patrick's Audi A4. He somehow managed to slip out of the house before Patrick awoke. A slushy snow started to fall as he headed north through Wilmington, Delaware, on the route that would put him in Allentown, Pennsylvania, sometime around sunrise. He sipped from a twenty-ounce cup of gas station coffee as his thoughts were consumed with memories of Lizzie.

Lizzie had been the youngest of three daughters to Paul and Mary Hewson. Married at the age of eighteen, Paul Hewson worked in the steel mills in Lehigh County until his death at the age of fifty-five. Lizzie was seventeen years old when her father suffered a fatal heart attack. Her mother and father sacrificed much to ensure that each of their daughters had opportunities neither of them had, including the chance to pursue a college degree. From an early age, Lizzie had demonstrated great promise, distinguishing herself in a household of highly motivated and principled people. She earned entrance and a scholarship to Princeton University, following in the footsteps of her older siblings as a college graduate and completing the fulfillment of her parents' dreams. While her sisters married and enjoyed successful careers near their hometown, Lizzie was gripped with wanderlust. She accepted a job with the State Department right out of school and met PJ Carpenter in Pakistan fifteen years later. She was all that mattered to him when she was ripped from Carpenter's life nineteen months later.

Three hours after leaving Maryland, as the faintest dimness appeared on the eastern horizon, Carpenter was standing at Lizzie's grave under an onslaught of large wet snowflakes. He softly spoke to her, something he had done every day since her passing. It was different and more powerful on those few occasions he was able to do so here. His mother had been a person of strong faith, something she passed along to her son, but Carpenter struggled to reconcile his faith with the losses of his mother and Lizzie. Forgiveness was another element of his faith that eluded him. He accepted his shortcoming, allowing it to fuel his commitment that no one else should suffer the loss of a loved one at the hands of evil. Before saying good-bye, Carpenter asked Lizzie for continued strength and help in his efforts. After taking a final silent moment to just be with her, he knelt down and kissed her headstone. Then he headed back to DC with a reinforced determination to find and stop the evildoers who were somewhere in their country.

CHAPTER 36

DEARBORN, MICHIGAN

The morning after they returned from Minnesota, Fahkoury and Omar walked into the mobile-phone repair shop on Warren Avenue to see Zafir Bahar. Fahkoury considered this meeting to be crucial. A lot rode on whether this one man could deliver. Aziz had not shared Bahar's identity with Fahkoury in the desert, but Aziz had told him the man was both trusted and well connected. Fahkoury was about to test those claims. Any shortcomings would severely impact his plans, not to mention the fact that Bahar could expose them all.

The Yemeni was engaged with a boisterous customer who was complaining about the screen on his phone. They moved around the cluttered store, pretending to look at the used phones on display. A few minutes later, the customer stormed out of the store, and Fahkoury approached Bahar.

"A mutual friend provided this to me," he said as he handed over the torn Yemeni banknote and got his first real look at the man. He measured a few inches taller than him and Omar. Baggy clothes concealed a thin frame, but their roominess was strained at the waist by a bulging stomach that flopped over a thick belt. His close-cropped hair was almost entirely gray, and his bulbous nose was a natural divider for the crescent-shaped collections of dark skin tags under each of his sleepy brown eyes. The man looked very much the part of the small-business owner and nothing like a committed supporter of al Qaeda.

In fact, Bahar had been an al Qaeda collaborator for nearly two decades, stretching back to his time in Aden managing finances for AQAP. For the last seven years, he had been secretly earning a comfortable living as a hawaladar in the United States. The extra income supplemented the meager profits from his store, which averaged little more than $18,000 a year. When he was contacted a few months earlier and asked for his assistance, Bahar quickly put two and two together and realized it was likely he would soon be forced to move on. The grim man now speaking to him all but confirmed it.

"Yes, I was expecting this," Bahar said evenly. "Some very good friends and generous benefactors stand behind this note. I respect them greatly."

Fahkoury acknowledged his appreciation with a slight nod and said, "I am told there is no limit on this transaction."

"That is true," said Bahar. "Of course, depending on the amount you desire, it may take some time for me to provide it you. I trust that you understand."

"Yes, I do. I would like twenty-five thousand dollars to start. Is that something you can arrange quickly?"

"I can deliver that amount to you right now if you wish."

"Thank you, but first I have some additional needs I hope you can help with."

Fahkoury didn't elaborate right away. Instead, he simply stared at Bahar, not bothering to hide the fact that he was sizing him up, deciding whether the man was reliable. Eventually willing to take a chance, he listed a number of items and told Bahar he needed everything inside ten days. As he continued to provide further details for the items on his list, Fahkoury saw that Bahar, to his credit, didn't seem at all overwhelmed by the requests.

Encouraged by this, Fahkoury said, "I am prepared to offer you twenty-five thousand dollars for all the items I requested."

Pausing for just a moment and never shifting his eyes from Fahkoury's cold stare, Bahar confidently said, "I believe I can arrange for everything on your list but the cost may be greater. Come back in a few days, and I will update you on my progress."

CHAPTER 37

Later that same day, Fahkoury and al-Rasheed shared certain details about the attack with Omar. Fahkoury realized he would have to delegate if he was to finalize the plan and complete all preparations for the attack, now just fifteen days away. Omar, among the others, stood out as the rare person Fahkoury could trust. In addition to his dependability, Omar was the most familiar with the area around Detroit, and that expertise would be needed.

Fahkoury instructed Omar to locate a facility in Detroit that could be used for practice before the team moved into position for the actual attack. He wanted printouts of satellite imagery for any buildings Omar proposed as well as photographs of all entrances and parking ramps. Before he dismissed Omar, Fahkoury told him to also secure two more vehicles of similar size, but different makes and models, to the ones the group already had.

After Omar left, Fahkoury shared with al-Rasheed an idea he had had while they were in Minnesota. In order to implement that idea, Fahkoury needed some additional equipment beyond what he had requested from Bahar. He gave instructions to al-Rasheed and tasked him with getting the necessary supplies.

While his most trusted lieutenants were off on other matters, Fahkoury would direct his efforts to acquiring the bomb-making materials.

CHAPTER 38

NORTHWESTERN OHIO

The cell members learned during their training in Afghanistan that certain fertilizers and fuels could be combined to assemble a powerful bomb. ANFO—ammonium nitrate mixed with fuel oil—bombs had been in use by terrorist organizations around the globe for decades. Al Qaeda had, in fact, used ANFO bombs as early as the 2002 attacks that killed more than two hundred in Bali, Indonesia. Fahkoury was also experienced with ANFO bombs, and, because of their simplicity, stability during transport, destructive power, and ready availability of materials, he had agreed with Aziz's decision to use fertilizer-based bombs in this attack.

As much as cultural diversity, its proximity to the American grain belt contributed to Aziz's decision to assemble the cell in Dearborn, Michigan. The farming industry utilized copious amounts of ammonium nitrate, a preferred fertilizer for bomb-making purposes. Omar had arrived in America with orders to scout large farms and farm-supply stores in the region while he and the rest of the team waited for their leader to arrive. Before the senior levels of the US government began to understand the likelihood of a terrorist attack inside their country, Fahkoury's team was well under way with the process of sourcing the materials they would use in that attack.

Over the previous several weeks, Omar, Wasim, and Hayder reconnoitered locations in the fertile regions of Michigan, Ohio, Indiana, and Illinois.

They identified more than three dozen large, isolated farms and several farm-supply stores as potential sources for the bomb-making materials. The locations of the farms and stores had been highlighted on a map, and each was comfortably within a four-hour drive. That map was supplemented with a digital file containing detailed notes and several photographs of each location.

Before leaving on their trip to Minneapolis, he and al-Rasheed had sat down with the scouts to review the intelligence. Fahkoury studied the map with the intention of aggregating the necessary materials from multiple locations over a broad geographic area. This would reduce the chance that anyone would be able to make a connection between the heists. After questioning the three men extensively about the individual locations, Fahkoury selected fourteen farms that he believed to be most suitable.

It being mid-January, the time of year worked in their favor. Lifestyle farming had largely given way to big business in the United States. Smaller farms were increasing rolled up into larger operations. These larger farms were small businesses, covering thousands of acres and generating revenues in the millions of dollars each year. Following the harvest period in the fall, the workers were laid off, and many of these business owners used the short rest period between seasons to visit friends and family or to head to winter homes in warmer climes.

Another benefit of this consolidation trend in American farming was the relative isolation of these large farms. There were often no other dwellings within miles of some of the largest farms. Two such farms were located off Route 127 in northwestern Ohio, and these would be the first tested by Fahkoury.

With no time to spare, Fahkoury planned the first missions for late Sunday evening, a day after he arrived back from Minneapolis. Despite having made progress with Bahar and sending Omar and al-Rasheed on separate assignments, rest was not an option. Just before midnight, he approached the first farm in one of the Astro vans with four of his better warriors: Hayder, Khalid, Marwan, and Wasim.

Wasim and had been by this farm twice before in the past two weeks and had not detected anyone or any activity either time. That night, the van made one pass before circling back. No lights appeared to be on inside the house or in the large steel barn looming behind it, but outside lights covered the front of both structures. At Fahkoury's instruction, Khalid stopped the van after they had passed the farm yet a third time in a little more than forty minutes. Fahkoury and the others spread out into the surrounding darkness, while Khalid remained with the van, approximately one-quarter mile from the house.

After a few minutes of their slow and cautious approach through the flat, fallow fields, Fahkoury spoke to the others using the two-way radios he had purchased through Zafir Bahar. "Wasim, proceed up to the house, and make sure there is nobody inside. After checking the house, move over to the barn."

Almost ten minutes later, Wasim said, "There are no lights on and no movement inside the house. The barn is also quiet."

Fahkoury signaled for the others to move forward and meet Wasim at the back of the barn, opposite Route 127 and out of the glare of the overhead light sitting high up on the front side of the building. When Fahkoury arrived, Wasim was standing at the door. It was a common house door, secured by a single-cylinder deadbolt and a regular knob-locking mechanism. Fahkoury had been able to obtain master keys for three leading lock manufacturers from the extremely resourceful Bahar. In this case, however, the door utilized locks made by a less popular brand.

Entry had to be covert, if at all possible. Simply smashing the door presented a problem. It would be readily noticeable by anyone looking after the property in the owners' apparent absence. Before taking that risky measure, Fahkoury commanded the others to start looking for spare keys.

Hayder shone a flashlight and felt along the outside of the doorframe but came up empty. Marwan starting moving several large rocks along the side of the building near the door. One of the rocks flipped over too easily. It was a fake rock, and inside it, Marwan found a key, which he gave to Fahkoury. They were inside the barn a few seconds later.

The building was large, approximately 120 by 60 feet. Taking care not to shine their lights near or toward any of the two sets of windows on the front side of the building, they set off in different directions on the smooth concrete floor in search of the supplies. It didn't take long before Hayder found what they were looking for along the far wall. There, neatly stacked, were probably more than a hundred, fifty-pound plastic bags of ammonium nitrate. Wasim located a hand truck adjacent to the fertilizer stash, and the men immediately began loading it with bags.

At this point, Khalid was scheduled to return with the van in just a few minutes. Fahkoury went out to the edge of the driveway to meet him, while the others stacked bags of fertilizer outside the barn. When the van arrived, Wasim, Hayder, and Marwan were ready with nineteen bags of fertilizer. All five men quickly loaded the supplies into the back of the van. When that was done, Fahkoury went back inside the barn to examine the stack. The shape of the overall stack of materials looked similar to how they had found it, albeit necessarily smaller. Satisfied with his men's work, Fahkoury locked the door and returned the key to its hiding place.

Since the van was nearly full, there was no need to visit the second farm. Two hours later, they were back in Dearborn. Fahkoury now had enough materials from that first heist to make one decent-sized bomb, but he still needed a lot more.

CHAPTER 39

SOUTHERN INDIANA

Given the success of the first attempt at the farm in Ohio, Fahkoury had dismissed farm-supply stores as an option for more materials. The risk was too high and unnecessary if the success of the first incursion could be repeated. However, with slightly less than two weeks before the attack date, time was running short. Once Omar and al-Rasheed had completed their assignments, Fahkoury was able to assemble two teams.

Over the succeeding days, Fahkoury and Omar captained one team, while al-Rasheed, Hayder, and Wasim led the other. Fahkoury's demand to emphasize diligence over haste guided the men in these pursuits. Each of the two teams attempted raids on different farms, none of them within seventy miles of another. On three occasions, the mission was aborted because either activity was detected at the farm or traffic in the immediate area spooked the team.

As it was collected, the fertilizer was stored in a fifteen-by-twenty-foot storage unit Bahar had rented at a mom-and-pop storage business in nearby Livonia, Michigan. When they finished, the cell had accumulated nearly five tons of ammonium nitrate, enough of the explosive material to make an equal number of significant bombs.

Fahkoury had a particular accelerant in mind. Most often, the fuel used in fertilizer bombs was either common kerosene or diesel fuel. A more powerful bomb could be created, however, by using racing fuel, properly referred to as nitromethane. Although nitromethane could be purchased from a number of different businesses, purchasing the seventy-five gallons Fahkoury estimated he would need was likely to create suspicions. As they crisscrossed the American heartland stealing ammonium nitrate, Fahkoury had identified a safer solution.

Drag racing strips are often located in remote areas due to the deafening noise created by the powerful eleven-thousand-horsepower engines, and one particular track on Route 52 in southern Indiana was no exception. Lights from the nearest town weren't even a speck on the dark, flat horizon, and there were no homes or businesses anywhere close to the track. Basically, the track was located in the middle of what otherwise would have been a very large corn or soybean field. Better still, because of the time of year, it had likely been dormant since the late fall and would remain so through the winter months.

Just after 11:00 p.m., two nights after first inspecting it, Fahkoury and his team returned to the track. An eight-foot-high chain link fence lined the perimeter of the property, and a second chain link fence separated the track and grandstand area from the parking lot. Inside the second fence, there were three buildings and two very straight 1.5-mile-long paved roads that were separated by twenty yards of dormant grass. A small cluster of wooden bleachers was positioned between the nearest drag strip and the building closest to the parking lot.

Using the bolt cutters that they carried in the van for these situations, Marwan was able to make quick work of the padlock before slipping the chain from the front gate. They pulled the van into the parking lot and parked it alongside the backside of the wooden bleachers. After Marwan cut the lock on the interior fence, they swiftly moved inside the track area. Once they were closer, they realized the nearest building was a combination of concession stand and restroom. They quickly turned their attention to the other two buildings. A tall pole with numerous lightbulbs mounted on it stood next to the second building, indicating the structure most likely contained the controls for the starting signal and timing mechanism. They continued around it and on to the third where they discovered two storage tanks on the backside of that building, each one fitted with a hand-operated pump secured by a padlock.

Once the padlock was cut, Marwan primed the pump several times. There was fuel inside. While Marwan manipulated the pump, Faheem guided the fuel into one of the five-gallon gas cans the team had purchased from local hardware and box do-it-yourself stores. As the cans were carefully filled with the highly combustible liquid, Fahkoury and Omar carried them to the parking lot and gently loaded them into the van.

Almost twenty minutes after they had cut the padlock on the entrance to the parking lot, they had managed to fill only three cans. Fahkoury realized the process could not really be pressed any faster. They had to guard against spilling a bunch of fuel that would betray the break-in on even a cursory examination. But Fahkoury was getting antsy. They had been there too long, and every additional minute exponentially increased the risk of discovery. He told the men to finish with the last can, that they would have to return another night or, better still, find another location.

After the loose chain was wrapped around the entrance gate, Fahkoury guided the van back toward the main road. They were almost to the intersection with Route 52 when a car pulled onto the two-lane road and headed toward them. As the car passed and the van slowed and prepared to stop, Fahkoury saw that it was a sheriff's vehicle. He glanced in the side mirror as he brought the van to a complete stop at the intersection before proceeding onto Route 52. The last thing he wanted to do was to give the cop a simple reason to pull them over.

As they started out on Route 52, Fahkoury looked across through the passenger window and watched as the patrol car continued down the road in the direction of the racetrack. For the next ten miles, he propelled the van eastward at the posted speed limit, constantly checking his mirrors for the flashing lights he was sure to come.

By the time they pulled into the storage facility early the following morning, Fahkoury had decided he wasn't going to take any further unnecessary risks. They had come within five minutes of being discovered, just ten days before the attack. He would simply substitute diesel fuel, as needed, to manufacture the bombs.

CHAPTER 40

TWIN CITIES AREA, MINNESOTA

As he and al-Rasheed neared Minneapolis, Fahkoury was not particularly troubled by the bulletin issued by the US government a week before. Essentially, the bulletin warned that there was an increased likelihood of a terrorist attack. The notice provided no details to indicate the Americans were even remotely close to uncovering his plans. If anything, the bulletin further strengthened his determination. Striking while they anticipated an attack would send a clear and daunting message to the Americans and the world that al Qaeda still possessed the capability to carry out a coordinated, large-scale attack.

He had two goals for the return trip to the Twin Cities. First, he wanted a further look at the primary target and an initial look at the secondary target. Knowing that additional security measures would be implemented in the days leading up to the day of the attack, he had seen no reason to risk inspecting the secondary target on the first trip. The bulletin certainly added a degree of danger but he had to chance the visits. He wanted a look inside the primary target, and this would be the only time he saw the second target in person. His other objective was to confirm his plans for the safe house.

This time, he and al-Rasheed entered the main target to further assess the wrinkle Fahkoury had added to his original plans. As they walked around inside, Fahkoury came to appreciate the building was even more immense in person than he had gleaned from his online research. He especially appreciated that a thoroughly devastating attack would require a team several times larger than what was available to him. With the resources he had, the building was simply too large to completely destroy, and there was simply too much ground to cover in a comprehensive assault. His small team wouldn't have the time or opportunity to cover all the means of escape and places the infidel could hide, but the attack could still convincingly deliver the message he had been sent to deliver.

As they moved deeper into the structure, Fahkoury considered how much his new idea would increase casualties. Several times during their stroll, he discreetly looked up at the large glass windows. He had read that the solar heat generated through the glass was sufficient to heat the building, even on the coldest days. He calculated the distance from the interior to the exits and the amount of time one would need for a hasty dash for the exit doors. By the time they left the building less than thirty minutes later, Fahkoury was convinced that his inspired twist, if correctly implemented, would greatly enhance the attack.

Once back in the van, they drove ten miles to the secondary target. Fahkoury marveled at the exacting clarity of the Google Earth technology as they drove around the area and along the specific routes he had selected during his research for this part of the attack. Although an examination now was riskier, his decision to wait had been the correct one. He saw that the newly emergent security measures would indeed impact his plans to a certain degree. Fahkoury had anticipated this and developed a more rudimentary plan to overcome the developing security measures he was now witnessing. Despite what he was seeing, he did not believe that any modifications to his original plan were needed.

An effective manager was the other key piece for this phase of the attack, and he would use his trusted senior lieutenant for this part of the mission. As they moved on to their next destination, Fahkoury reminded al-Rasheed of his responsibilities. He was confident his committed warrior would deliver. Besides casualties, Fahkoury anticipated treasure from a significant ancillary benefit—this part of the attack would be seen around the world in real time, dramatically ushering in al Qaeda's return to global jihad. Minutes later, another attack, where more casualties were expected, would decisively underscore that unmistakable proclamation.

The van entered the parking ramp and proceeded to the top floor. The uncovered level offered a head-on view of the secondary target several blocks away, as well as the main thoroughfare one of his men would use. It was from this location that al-Rasheed would initiate and manage this part of the overall plan. The position would expose al-Rasheed and complicate his escape, but it was ideal for his needs. Further reassured that his planning was sound, Fahkoury directed al-Rasheed to proceed out of the city.

The other, equally important reason for their second trip to Minneapolis was to settle on a base for deployment. The team would need a secure location to assemble the bombs and make final plans while remaining hidden in the final days leading up to the attack. When he and al-Rasheed were last in the Twin Cities, they had stayed on the fringes of the metropolitan area. Fahkoury had noticed several homes in the surrounding communities and determined that any one of them would make an ideal safe house. One in particular stood out.

The farmstead was located on rolling terrain about twenty-five miles southwest of Minneapolis, just east of the town of Farmshire, Minnesota. The secluded homestead was situated about a quarter of a mile from the nearest road, a lightly traveled two-lane country thoroughfare running east–west. The home and an accompanying wooden barn were surrounded by a small forest of trees and, farther out, acres of fallow cropland and empty fields. Despite being less than two miles from the main north–south highway leading into the city, the nearest home was slightly more than six-tenths of a mile to the west, and the nearest town center was yet another three miles from that. The home was almost perfectly isolated, and the barn appeared large enough for their needs.

To bide their time until well after dark, they drove south about an hour and stopped at a diner. When they returned to the farm homestead, it was nearing 9:00 p.m., and the sun had long ago set on the bitterly cold day. A full moon was forecasted for that evening, but its effect was muted by a covering of high, cirrostratus clouds that moved into the region late in the day. On their first pass, they noticed that Christmas lights still shone outside on the front of the house and, inside, only the first level was illuminated. They continued on a few miles before circling back. As nothing had changed, Fahkoury stopped the van to allow al-Rasheed to get out.

The halo phenomenon of the moon through the high clouds helped al-Rasheed see as he moved carefully through the small collection of mostly hardwood trees. He settled behind a large maple tree, offering him a concealed and largely unobstructed vantage point less than a hundred feet from the house. He squatted down and watched, comfortable that the lack of snow on the frozen ground would prevent anyone from later discovering his intrusion. He could see the flicker of a television through the side window but could not see anyone inside. Ten or so minutes later, the rear door opened, and an old dog loped down three steps into the frozen backyard. The dog ventured twenty feet from the house, lifted its leg next to a sickly bush, did its business, and then ambled back to the bottom of the steps.

When the door was opened this time, a man stepped out onto the small deck and offered encouragement to the decrepit beast. Gauging by his stooped posture and slow movements, al-Rasheed determined the man was in his sixties, if not older. The man was holding the door open as the dog slowly climbed the steps when al-Rasheed heard another voice from inside the house. It sounded like the voice of a woman, but al-Rasheed couldn't be sure.

A short time later, the television was shut off, followed by the lights on the first floor. Less than a minute later, a light was turned on in the upstairs front window. Perhaps another ten to fifteen minutes elapsed before the inside of the house went completely dark. The holiday lights remained lit outside. Al-Rasheed stayed put the entire time, only bouncing on the balls of his feet in an attempt to ward off the cold. To be sure he missed nothing more, al-Rasheed waited another fifteen minutes and then clicked his radio twice, the signal for Fahkoury to meet him alongside the road.

Al-Rasheed quietly closed the van door and immediately placed his hands in front of the heating vents. Fahkoury drove away from the area while al-Rasheed shivered and tried to warm himself. It was several minutes before his face thawed enough for him to speak clearly. He reported that an elderly couple and an old dog appeared to be the only occupants of the home; there were no signs to indicate there were any other inhabitants.

Fahkoury wasn't concerned with the present occupants, but it would still be a risk to seize the home. There was a chance that a neighbor or relative might stop by to check on the elderly couple while the cell was occupying it. Fahkoury reasoned if that happened, they knew how to deal with the situation. The farmstead was almost too perfect to pass up. It was sufficiently secluded, and it offered the barn to conceal the vehicles and provide a space to assemble the bombs. They were unlikely to find a better location. He decided the team would stay here for the last few days leading up to the attack.

Having completed this last critical piece of business, Fahkoury and al-Rasheed headed back to Dearborn. They would get back there with just more than a week remaining before the attack. And Fahkoury and his team were nearly ready.

CHAPTER 41

LANGLEY, VIRGINIA

The tension in the conference room on the ground floor of CIA headquarters late on Saturday afternoon was palpable. Following the briefing in the Oval Office ten days earlier, Director Patrick had set up a command center in the large conference room for the Interagency Incident Management Group task force. The command post, far removed from any exterior walls and windows, was occupied around the clock with representatives from the CIA, DHS, and FBI. The NSA had been added to the group originally convened on the president's orders, and its representatives rotated in and out with those from the rest of the alphabet agencies. Computers and phones cluttered the fifteen-foot-long table, and identical banks of flat-screen TVs nearly covered opposing walls. The already dirt-brown rug concealed spills of the mostly terrible food and a variety of beverages that were brought in regularly for six to ten people who typically occupied the space at any given time. The mood in the room was almost always serious, and as each day passed, banter was increasingly viewed as an unwelcomed guest. Despite doing everything possible, their efforts over the course of the past week and a half to locate the terrorists or uncover the plot had yet to bear any fruit.

Two days after the Oval Office meeting, DHS had issued the National Terrorism Advisory System bulletin indicating the increased likelihood of a terrorist attack on the homeland. The bulletin reminded citizens how to help the overall counterterrorism effort by reporting strange persons, behavior, thefts, and other activities. It also directed the public to the DHS website for a list of suspicious activity indicators. In order to further add to the state of awareness, the president had reminded listeners to "see something, say something" during his most recent weekly radio address.

The same day the DHS bulletin was issued, the FBI had alerted all state and local law-enforcement personnel to remain vigilant for common preincident indicators. Surveillance of airports and airplane hangars; thefts of delivery trucks, vans, or other large vehicles; and any modifications of vehicles to handle heavier loads or to increase storage space were among the listed items for which the FBI requested immediate notification. The bureau also asked for notice of all reports regarding the theft or odd purchases of firearms, certain agricultural and industrial chemicals, and explosive components. Finally, all law-enforcement personnel were also asked to be on the lookout for peculiar large vehicles operating in rural areas, particularly at night.

The Houston public library had been placed under constant surveillance in the hopes of identifying the person who had sent the latest e-mail to Aziz. All public computers in the library were being monitored around the clock by the NSA, and teams of FBI agents maintained a vigil outside and inside the three-level library. In addition to those efforts, warrants were secured from the Foreign Intelligence Surveillance Court to wiretap the communications of all non-US citizens from a handful of countries who were residing in the greater Houston area and not already under surveillance by the federal government.

While those efforts focused on activities inside the United States, others had been pursued vigorously outside the country. The IIMG team was particularly bewildered that the NSA, despite staggering signal-intelligence capabilities that captured billions of e-mails and phone calls every day, had not picked up any communications content relating to, or even remotely suggesting, an imminent terrorist attack. Human intelligence efforts had likewise failed to deliver any pertinent information. Case officers across the globe had been discreetly pressing their agents for any clues related to a possible attack without avail. As the days continued to pass, it was becoming clear al Qaeda had imposed a communications blackout. This type of "quiet period" was especially worri-some, as it was often employed immediately prior to a major attack.

Two days earlier, Carpenter and the rest of the principles on the IIMG team had agreed with the president that the short window to allow the ter-rorists to make a mistake had closed. An extra push was required. The presi-dent ordered that the five photographs, along with the names given to the authorities by the three supposedly Syrian men, be released to the press that same Thursday afternoon. Because it was true, the official statement from the government was that the bulletin, released a week earlier, and the men in the photographs were not necessarily related. This did not stop the press from speculating that the five men featured in the photographs were in the United States for the purpose of conducting an act of terror, a conjecture the govern-ment secretly hoped would further heighten public attentiveness.

The response to the photographs had been immediate, if not ultimate-ly helpful. On Thursday evening, there were news reports about a possible terrorist attack in Arizona. A car had careened onto the sidewalk during a biweekly art event in Scottsdale, injuring several pedestrians before finally coming to rest inside one of the many galleries lining the street. The lack of malicious intent was clear soon after the initial news reports, however. It turned out that the older gentleman driving the car had simply taken his eyes off the road and drifted toward the sidewalk. In trying to correct his error, he mistakenly pressed the accelerator instead of the brake. Slightly bloodied from the crash, the man and his wife wept through apologies given to the horde of reporters surrounding them as they were helped to a waiting ambu-lance. Less than a dozen hours later, reports came in about an explosion at a natural gas hub in southwestern Wyoming. A terrorist attack was immediately announced by the news services as a leading cause for the explosion. Among the gawkers who had assembled on the outskirts of the facility to view the raging fire was a resident of the nearby town. She told one of the reporters on the scene that she had recently seen one of the men in the photographs shown on the news. Within minutes, the woman was brought in for question-ing, initially by the local police and, later, the FBI. The small-town policeman knew the woman and her history of mental disorders. The two FBI agents, dispatched from the FBI office in Cheyenne, later confirmed the policeman's suspicion that, although an honest belief, there was no truth to the woman's claim. Calm was fully restored by midday on Friday when the explosion was deemed to have been caused by a ruptured pipe.

For the most part, Carpenter and other members of the task-force team members had kept busy over the last ten days trying to narrow the list of possible targets. Carpenter was convinced the attack would be on a high-profile target and likely on a soft one where security could be more easily breached. Patrick agreed with Carpenter, and they had had the team focus on upcoming notable events over the coming weeks. The task force's abridged list of possible targets included visits to Washington by two heads of state, a California trip for the duke and duchess of Cambridge, NFL playoff games, the NHL All-Star Game, different Hollywood awards ceremonies, a planned NASA launch, and the State of the Union address. All were legitimate targets, but there was no guarantee they were on the right track with any one of them.

Carpenter had been dispatched by the president to travel with the royal couple earlier in the week, and extra security measures were employed at every other event on the calendar. As those events passed without incident, the task-force team easily replaced them with new additions further out in time. Although they ultimately proved to be unrelated, the recent incidents in Arizona and Wyoming highlighted the nation's vulnerability, and the IIMG team's nearly impossible task of stopping various kinds of attacks on an almost endless list of targets.

Now Carpenter and other IIMG team members were assembled in the conference room that Saturday afternoon, waiting for a desperately needed break. A dozen or more terrorists were somewhere inside the country plotting an attack, and nobody on the task force had the slightest idea where, what, or when they intended to attack. There were literally thousands of soft targets, and the possible method of attacks, which included homemade bombs, chemical weapons, conventional guns and knives, and vehicle attacks such as those in Nice and Berlin were all plausible at nearly every identified potential target as well as those that didn't make it on to the list. Lacking more specific information, the task force was pretty much left with just playing the odds.

To make matters worse, the populace and more than a million law-enforcement personnel had thus far not been able to lend any assistance to the effort. It was also not helpful that the initial, nearly continuous coverage of the photographs was already beginning to wane. Despite the alarms from Arizona and Wyoming, the lack of new information over the past forty-eight hours deprived the story of oxygen, and other events were gradually replacing it at the top of the news cycle. The photographs did remain posted on most media-outlet websites, and the DHS bulletin continued to scroll regularly along the bottom of television screens tuned into the cable-news networks.

There was growing concern the terrorists might move up the attack in response to the release of the photographs. To add to this unease, there was still no sign of Aziz despite genuine assistance from the Saudi government. All the signs indicated they were nearing some kind of boiling point with no way to prevent it. Throughout the day, every time the phone rang or someone opened the door, those in the conference room at the time feared news of an attack in progress.

"If we're right that the terrorists are still in the planning stages of attack, there's a good chance they'll slip up and somebody will notice something," FBI special liaison Paul Dunleavy said. "The best thing we can do is to continue to push, looking for one or more of these preincident indicators. The fact that we don't have anything could mean the terrorists are not as close to attacking as we fear, or they might have called off the attack."

"That's probably wishful thinking," Carpenter said, "because they haven't slipped up yet, and they came here for a reason. They're not calling it off, and we better hope something breaks, because my gut tells me they're going to act soon."

The brief exchange offered a rare break to their solemn work, but everyone in the room knew Carpenter was right. It was just a matter of time before news of the attack consumed the stale room. A sense of foreboding ensued Carpenter's stark prediction, and the only sound came from the clicking of keyboards, as they desperately refreshed secure databases in the hopes of finding any updates that might be even remotely relevant.

CHAPTER 42

DETROIT, MICHIGAN, SUBURBS

ahkoury was satisfied with the team's progress, but he was beginning to feel
real alarm for the first time. His modest concern about the bulletin from
the American government was elevated when he returned from Minnesota
and saw his and al-Rasheed's faces on television with three other individuals.
Fahkoury had no idea who the other three men were, but before he could
ask, Omar and several others confirmed those three men had been part of
the training group in Afghanistan. Later during the report, Fahkoury became
even more disturbed when physical descriptions were provided for him and
al-Rasheed, particularly the description that he might be missing parts of his
left hand. *Who had given them that information, and how much more do they know?* he
wondered.

Fahkoury could see the angst on his fighters' faces, and he imagined
some were wondering if his and al-Rasheed's broadcasted images would spell
disaster for the mission. "We have all been very cautious to not be seen or
noticed, and the photographs of me and brother al-Rasheed are poor in quality and, more importantly, look nothing like us," Fahkoury said in an attempt
to calm the group and, he supposed, himself.

Fahkoury was right. Even the most astute person would have difficulty
matching them to the photographs. Ever cautious, Fahkoury had instructed
al-Rasheed on how to alter his appearance for the passport photo, including

how to appear heavier simply by subtly raising his shoulders while lowering his head and slightly puffing his cheeks. As a result, the images showing their formerly clean-shaven faces gave the impression each of them was fifteen to twenty pounds heavier. Now, with neatly trimmed beards and slicked-back hair, they looked almost entirely different.

Still, Fahkoury was disturbed that intelligence services now had a photograph of him, even if it wasn't of particularly good quality. There was no way around it. They needed passports for travel. He took some added comfort in the fact that the Egyptian-passport photograph on the television screen had to be the only one of him in circulation. Otherwise, he reasoned, they would be showing any others they had.

It was also true that they had been diligently keeping low profiles, mostly operating under cover of darkness while staying hidden indoors during the busier daytime hours. There was one recent exception. In hindsight, he probably should not have gone back to Minnesota. They especially should not have walked into the target building. Fahkoury tried to convince himself it wouldn't be a problem. The Americans didn't know where to look, and they had been very careful to avoid security cameras. Plus, the baseball hats they wore would have prevented any clear shots of their faces. He reasoned that if he and al-Rasheed were spotted in Minnesota, the Americans would have moved on them by now.

"Those other three men do not know anything about our operation," he said. "They cannot betray our plans. The Americans don't even know where we are. They don't even know for sure that we are in the country. As long as we remain cautious, they will have no idea where we are or where we are going." Just saying the words out loud helped to relax him. When everyone else had settled down, Fahkoury went off on his own to take a mental inventory of the materials and weapons he his team had assembled since he arrived in America.

There was enough nitromethane for one of the five bombs he would fashion from more than 9,600 pounds of ammonium nitrate. For the remaining vehicle bombs, he would use diesel fuel, an ingredient that could be easily acquired when the full team was in Minnesota. The black powder, purchased from an ammunition dealer in Illinois, would be more than sufficient for the smaller pipe bombs he needed for the new aspect of his plan.

Once the team had acquired enough ammonium nitrate, Fahkoury had turned his attention to the material they would use to detonate the bombs. Al Qaeda's long-standing proclivities with TNT was well known. Years earlier, several US media outlets published videocassettes of al Qaeda operatives manufacturing the explosive material. Wasim and Hayder were taught this skill during their training in Afghanistan, and, under his supervision, his two lieutenants manufactured all the TNT necessary to detonate the vehicle bombs.

Before even leaving the Arabian Desert, Fahkoury knew that guns would be more difficult to come by, but he had not been particularly worried. He knew that if he needed to, he could get them from the same cartel that had smuggled him, al-Rasheed, and the others into America. Aziz had given Fahkoury the cartel's contact in Chicago, a person Aziz assured him would be able to get all the munitions he needed.

Fahkoury kept his skepticism to himself and simply accepted the information from Aziz. He knew little about the cartel, other than it was driven by capitalistic greed rather than pure ideology. In his view, that meant its relentless pursuit of money detracted from the emphasis on discretion and security he demanded. He was also certain the cartel and its contact person in Chicago would quickly give him up to US authorities if and when the need arose. Following his experience crossing the border, he decided the cartel was more trouble than it was worth. In fact, he still regretted not killing both Pablo and Guillermo during the border crossing. Only Aziz's emphasis on the importance of the relationship with the cartel had prevented him from doing so.

After Fahkoury arrived in Michigan, he decided it would be safer to go through Zafir Bahar to acquire the guns he needed. The day he first met the Yemeni, Fahkoury had given him $25,000 and a list of items he wanted, including the weapons. Several days later, Bahar sent word to Fahkoury that he needed an additional $20,000 for the guns and ammunition. Fahkoury was doubtful, but he paid the extra sum anyway. It wasn't his money, he reasoned, and he needed the weapons. In the end, the Yemeni had, once again, demonstrated his resourcefulness, delivering AK-47s, FN 5.7-caliber pistols, and more ammunition than Fahkoury could ever hope his team would be able to use.

There was no place to practice with the guns, but that was not a problem either. He specifically asked for these weapons because they were common to al Qaeda and easy to use. All the men had extensive training with these guns, both before and during their time in Afghanistan. In order to ensure each weapon was in good working order, he and Omar had test-fired the guns while the team was traversing the far-flung countryside in search of bomb-making materials.

While Fahkoury was overseeing the efforts to acquire the bomb materials and weapons, al-Rasheed had been busy working on the new twist to Fahkoury's original plan. Fahkoury's primary objective was always to ensure a successful attack. A secondary yet equally important consideration was to inflict the maximum amount of terror and disruption possible, and the best way to do that was to inflict the maximum number of casualties.

Those two principles guided Fahkoury as he developed and refined his plan. He used information gathered from online mapping and satellite imagery, as well as both public and private enterprise websites containing target information to develop an attack plan that would serve that primary objective. However, when he viewed the main target in person, he recognized opportunities to further both his primary and secondary objectives.

Implementing the new twist would require impeccable timing; otherwise, it could compromise the element of surprise and, therefore, the entire mission. Based on his research, he was confident that the team could pull it off with the right equipment and only limited training. He learned that one of the leading drone manufacturers included an opt-out feature in its geo-fencing software that would allow the user to fly the drone in otherwise prohibited areas. The feature was controversial because it placed responsibility solely in the hands the operator.

In order to opt out, one needed only to file a credit card or mobile-phone number with the manufacturer. This information would enable authorities to identify and follow up with the user if circumstances warranted. Overcoming this requirement was easy. Al-Rasheed simply had three men purchase basic phones and no-credit phone plans from three different Verizon stores. They then registered those phone numbers with the drone manufacturer.

Fahkoury also learned that in addition to registering contact information with the manufacturer, the Federal Aviation Authority required all drone operators to register the machine with the agency and to clearly display an FAA-issued registration number on the device at all times. This created a potential problem during the practice the men would need, but there was a simple solution to this problem too.

While ensuring compliance with these requirements would be rather easy when the purchases were made from authorized retailers, Fahkoury realized it would be problematic in the secondary market. In order to impel subsequent owners to reregister the drones, the regulations required the previous owner to remove the registration number upon resale and cancel the registration with the FAA. All al-Rasheed had to do was find the right kind of sellers.

Although al-Rasheed did have to scrap two transactions when the sellers insisted on removing the FAA registration number, he was able to purchase three drones directly from sellers in Michigan and Ohio who were either ignorant of or indifferent to the rule. Each successful transaction was in cash for the full listed price and ended with al-Rasheed in possession of a drone bearing a valid FAA registration number.

Once they had the drones, they needed to find a place to practice using the machines. Al-Rasheed discovered that certain municipal parks were favored by several drone clubs in the area. Each of these municipal parks contained golf courses, nature areas, hiking and biking trails, small lakes for swimming and fishing, and copious amounts of additional open space over the thousands of acres within their borders. The vast parks were only sparsely used at this time of year, and they presented ideal training grounds for al-Rasheed and the two militants he and Fahkoury had selected for this assignment.

Fahkoury knew that the potential issue with this part of the plan resided in the timing. He had learned that a prompt from the drone manufacturer would appear once the drone was detected in a restricted area, requiring the registered user to verify the account and provide an explanation. The exact period of time to complete these requirements was not clear from the online information, but Fahkoury reasoned the manufacturer would need to allow at least two minutes to send the prompt and complete the verification process before sending a signal to disable the drone's operating software. Two minutes would be more than ample time, provided the drone was launched close to the target. Although this necessity might result in the operators becoming collateral damage in the attack, Fahkoury believed that the drones would greatly enhance success.

The other timing issue related to the deployment of the drones during the attack. Fahkoury intended to use the drones just prior to detonation of the principal bombs. This activity might alert authorities to a potential problem and provide them with time, albeit a very limited amount, to disrupt the attack. In the end, Fahkoury felt the timing risks could be limited, provided the men selected to operate the drones knew what they were doing.

The day before, Fahkoury had watched as the three operators conducted various moves with the drones. The operators demonstrated quick launches and rapid acceleration to mimic the plans Fahkoury had crafted for the machines. None of the multiple demonstration flights covered more than a few hundred feet. Two of the drones were loaded with small packages weighing approximately six pounds. Their performance did not appear compromised despite the payload.

As he wrapped up his mental inventory, Fahkoury concluded they now had everything they needed. If it were up to him, he would have moved up the date. He had an uneasy feeling the Americans were closing in. But Aziz had been adamant that the attacks must occur on the first Sunday of February. Since he had to wait, he would use that time for practice. And Abu Omar had found an ideal location for that purpose.

CHAPTER 43

PONTIAC, MICHIGAN

With just a week until the attack, Fahkoury was looking at the site Omar had chosen for the practice runs. It wasn't a perfect match, but the location was sufficiently similar and suitable for the purpose.

The previous evening, Fahkoury had gathered the entire team. He started by telling his fellow believers that it was nearing time to carry out the attack. He told the men the attacks on the Great Satan would be seen by the entire world and vault al Qaeda back into position as the undisputed leader in global jihad. Each of them would be revered as heroes. After the excitement quelled, Fahkoury outlined his plans.

Up to that point, only al-Rasheed knew when and where the attack would occur, but even he didn't know all the details. Fahkoury first told the men that the attack would be a martyr operation. None of the cell members showed surprise or concern at the news. Instead, it appeared that every man expected—hoped, even—to martyr himself, and each joyously welcomed the news.

He next told the men there would be two attacks on two separate locations. Al-Rasheed would lead two brothers in the first attack, he explained. Everyone else would be involved in the second attack, a more complex plan that required precise coordination. He then projected satellite images of the first attack location. As it did not require any special skills or timing, he spent only a few minutes on the straightforward plan. He knew al-Rasheed understood the scheme and was fully capable of ensuring its successful execution.

Fahkoury moved on to the second attack, showing images of the location for the more intricate operation and the principal target in his master plan. After he detailed the particular aspects, he walked the team through the sequence of the attack, explaining how and when the drones, vehicle bombs, and weapons would be used. Fahkoury repeated the process twice more and then randomly called on the men to describe what was to occur at specific times during the attack. By the time they were finished, each man had demonstrated his ability to accurately explain each and every aspect. Pleased with the results, Fahkoury opened the floor to questions.

The first question regarded assignments. Live operations are fluid, and there must be flexibility to switch assignments based on circumstances, Fahkoury counseled the men. That reality required that, for the most part, assignments not be given out until just before the attack. The men selected as drone operators were a possible exception. As such, every man must be prepared to assume any role at either location. However, given the simplicity of the first attack, only the second attack would be rehearsed. Each jihadist would practice each unique job during the trial runs for the second attack.

The next question concerned preparations for martyrdom. The men asked if there would be sufficient time for ritualistic final preparations, including last photographs, videos, and preparation of their bodies for the higher spiritual plane they expected to achieve. Fahkoury assured them there would be time for those preparations.

Someone asked whether they would be able to visit the locations beforehand. Fahkoury explained that due to the risk of discovery, heightened by the recent reports on television news, they would only see the target locations once in person before the attack, if at all. He was gratified when there were no further questions.

Before switching the display to the practice site, Fahkoury gave them a final opportunity to thoroughly examine the images of the second location. When the men were finished, Fahkoury pulled up the practice site and informed them there would be two trial runs conducted over the course of the next three or four days. The approaches and attack locations for the vehicles and drones were marked on the image of the practice site, but it was not possible to use the drones during the trials, Fahkoury advised them. For good measure, the sequence was reviewed yet again, this time with the men leading the discussion. When Fahkoury was convinced they were ready, he dismissed them with instructions to think about all the assignments until practice began the next evening.

Now, as he waited for the first practice run to begin, Fahkoury was at his observation post on the roof of a nearby building. The team went into the trial runs knowing that Fahkoury was expecting them to be choreographed exactly as they would be for the actual attack. As the team would not go through this same exercise at the actual target location, he instructed them to concentrate on their communication during these trials. During the actual attack, they would rely solely on the radios Bahar had provided, communicating only as necessary and always utilizing the prearranged code, he reminded them.

For the first practice run, Fahkoury split the militants among the three vehicles. Al-Rasheed rode along in one of the automobiles to observe from that perspective. Approximately fifteen minutes after starting, the three vehicles arrived on-site within twenty-five seconds of one another. It was far from perfect, but Fahkoury found it acceptable for a first attempt. Following a brief pause to mimic detonation once all the vehicles were in position, Fahkoury directed the team to retreat home. The second trial would be more thorough, encompassing additional aspects of the attack.

Two days later, the team ran through a second and more robust trial. It was midafternoon, a time selected to resemble the expected conditions at the time of the actual attack. This time, Fahkoury assumed a hidden position atop a nearby parking ramp that offered a view of three sides of the practice target. This didn't present a problem, as he knew he would have no better vantage point during the genuine attack.

For this practice session, two men occupied each of the three vehicles. The remainder of the men took up positions from which they would pretend to storm the building. Fahkoury watched and listened as the three vehicles approached the facility under a light mist. As the vehicles neared the designated spots, the men were in constant radio contact to ensure simultaneous arrival at the attack points. One of the vehicles ended up behind a municipal bus. As the bus stopped, the vehicle found itself out of position. One of the other two vehicles was able to compensate without drawing attention simply by adjusting its speed. The third vehicle feigned pulling over, as if to let out a passenger, before resuming its path at a slower rate of speed. Fahkoury welcomed the difficulty, as similar adjustments were to be expected during the actual attack.

A few minutes before the vehicles arrived on-site, Fahkoury gave the signal for the assault teams to move toward the building. The men entered the building at separate entrances and pushed into the interior and waited. This time, the men in the vehicles performed much better, arriving at their designated locations within eleven seconds of one another. Four minutes later, the assault team members exited the building and met the vans for the return trip to base.

The practice runs had gone well, and Fahkoury was confident the men were ready for the actual mission. Later, when everyone had gathered, he declared them ready and told them they would be leaving for Minneapolis in the next day or so. He allowed a moment of shared excitement, and then he dismissed them with instructions to meditate on their blessed opportunity. As the last euphoric member of the team left, Fahkoury hoped he was right about going to Minnesota. It really wasn't his decision to make. Two days earlier, following the initial dry run, Fahkoury had communicated the team's readiness and requested final approval from the shura.

CHAPTER 44

LANGLEY, VIRGINIA

As Fahkoury and his team were wrapping up their final practice, Samantha Lane called Carpenter and Patrick and told them to come down to the conference room; there might have been a breakthrough. It appeared that basic legwork had yielded some dividends, she said. A few minutes later, they convened in the task-force conference room to hear the latest.

Before everyone was even seated, Dunleavy blurted out that the FBI had two reports of thefts that could be related to the current threat. "The first involves a break-in at a racetrack near Rushville, Indiana. The track closes each year in October and reopens the following May. The track owner, Marc Budine, lives on the Mississippi coast during the off-season. Budine employs a local guy by the name of Doug Fraser to check on the track. Fraser works primarily as a cross-country truck driver and typically swings by the track every one to two weeks between hauls.

"Two days ago, Fraser discovered that the padlocks securing the chains on the front gate and the track entrance had been cut. He also discovered that the lock securing the manually operated fuel pump on one of the fuel-storage tanks had been cut. He reported his discoveries to Budine and the local police. Fraser had checked on the track ten days earlier, and everything was in order. He says the break-in had to happen sometime during that period.

"We're assuming whoever broke in stole some racing fuel," Dunleavy continued, "but we don't know how much, if any. Each tank has a capacity of a thousand gallons. There isn't a highly accurate gauge on the pump, and Budine isn't sure how much fuel remained in the tank after the season."

"Why is racing fuel relevant?" asked Ella Rock.

"It can be used to make a powerful fertilizer bomb. McVeigh used it for the Oklahoma City bomb," Carpenter said. "Typically, ammonium nitrate is mixed with kerosene or diesel fuel, but nitromethane—racing fuel—can be substituted. It's more complicated to make an ANNM bomb, but the destructive yield is considerably greater."

"This also could have been a couple of kids looking to give their own car a power boost," Patrick said. "They could've taken five or ten gallons. We don't know. You'd need a lot of nitromethane to build a bomb. I think McVeigh used more than one hundred fifty gallons."

"That's right, but that was a massive bomb," Carpenter said. "Someone could still put together a devastating bomb with less nitromethane. The fuel is only about six percent of the bomb's weight. The rest is ammonium nitrate. Even with just fifteen gallons of racing fuel, one-tenth of what McVeigh used, a decent-sized bomb could be constructed. Enough to kill a lot of people in a crowded location."

"It will come as no surprise," Dunleavey said, "that we also received a report about some potentially missing ammonium nitrate." Dunleavy explained that Jim Kietzman, a farmer from Holgate, Ohio, called the local police yesterday. The farmer had been in Saint Louis with his wife, visiting their daughter and her family for Christmas. They stayed in Saint Louis until January second, and then they drove down to Florida to visit some friends for three weeks.

"The day after they arrived back in Ohio, the couple started planning for the upcoming season. Kietzman and his wife place all their seed and fertilizer orders in January every year to ensure they won't be squeezed out in the rush right before planting season. The farmer says he keeps meticulous records of the inputs he uses every year. The previous season was particularly wet, so he wasn't able to use all his fields. So he had leftover seed and fertilizer from the order the previous January.

"Anyway, he went out to the barn to double-check his inventory records before they placed the order for the upcoming season. He said the stack of ammonium nitrate looked odd somehow, so he counted the bags. He counted only ninety-seven of the fifty-pound bags, while his records indicated he should have had a hundred sixteen.

"The police pressed him about how sure he was that some fertilizer had been stolen. He told the cops he's almost positive he's missing nineteen bags. He also said he didn't see any signs of a break-in, but he told the cops that he keeps a spare key hidden in a fake rock along the backside of the building. Not much the police could do, but they made a possible connection with our alert and notified our Toledo office," Dunleavy said.

"Did they check with the neighbors?" Patrick asked.

"They did. Nobody saw anything. The farm is on almost two thousand acres and in the middle of several even larger farms. The house and barn are pretty isolated. To someone conducting surveillance for a break-in, it would have presented an appealing target."

"How far is the farm from the racetrack?" Ella asked.

"Two hundred fifty-four miles," Dunleavy said.

The group debated the interconnectedness and potential meaning of the two reports. There was no disputing that the stolen materials could be used to assemble a powerful bomb capable of severely damaging a building and inflicting massive casualties in a congested area. The team's equivocation stemmed from the uncertainty of the people who had made the reports. Although the owners of the racetrack and farm suspected they had been victimized by break-ins, neither knew for certain that material had been stolen. On top of that, the locations of the suspected break-ins were separated by a considerable distance. Some quick research revealed several racetracks much closer to the Kietzman's farm in Holgate, Ohio, than the track in southern Indiana.

There was also confusion about the lack of relative proximity between the two locations and a potential target site. Detroit and Indianapolis were the nearest large cities to the two crime scenes. But Chicago, St. Louis, Louisville, Cincinnati, Columbus, and Cleveland were also within reasonable range of both locations. With the exception of the NHL All-Star Game in Chicago at the end of the month, there were no unordinary high-profile events planned in any of those cities over the next few months. As such, the prospect of an attack on one of the airports was elevated in the group's analysis, especially for Chicago and Detroit, each a significant airline hub. The stolen materials didn't match up with an attack on aircraft, but they could be used with devastating impact at the departures or arrivals areas, especially during a peak travel time.

Despite the uncertainty from the reports, they finally had some news. They had to acknowledge that these disturbing bits of information were more confirmation that an attack was imminent, but they needed more pieces of the puzzle if they were going to be able to identify a pattern that would lead to the terrorists.

"We have to see if there are any other similar situations," Carpenter said. "Let's ask all the state and local police forces to check in with farmers and racetracks located within at least two hundred miles of each location. It took some time for the farmer and the track owner to realize they might have been burglarized."

"We're already on it," Dunleavy said.

"Good," Carpenter said. "I'm assuming these guys are not hiding out in the country. Where are the most likely places for terrorists to hang out that are reasonably close to the two crime scenes?"

"Well, Chicago, certainly," Dunleavy said. "There is also a large Arab population in Dearborn, Michigan, but the diversity of any large city would offer some cover."

"Let's narrow that down and get some agents and police officers knocking on doors," Patrick said. "One last thing—are we all in agreement that this information changes the threat assessment?"

They were. This information, added to the circumstantial evidence they already had, rose to the level of a credible terrorist threat. Patrick retreated to his office and immediately called Director Gonzalez with this latest information and analysis. The alert should advise the public, Patrick suggested, that a near-term terrorist attack was highly likely and likely to employ one, if not more, vehicle-borne improvised explosive devices.

CHAPTER 45

DEARBORN, MICHIGAN

Fahkoury kept busy while he waited for word from the shura. While the rest of the men started the process of sterilizing the safe houses, Fahkoury paid a visit to Zafir Bahar for some cash and to further guarantee the hawaladar's fealty.

Fahkoury had five vehicles in his fleet, but he needed at least one more. He had been reluctant to secure the extra vehicle until now. Rotating the vehicles between several municipal lots and the small hidden parking lot behind Bahar's store was not without risk. Adding another vehicle to the fleet would have only compounded the problem and potentially drawn questions about their owners.

"I need your sedan," he said to Bahar upon entering the store, referring to the Yemeni's Ford Crown Victoria, "and forty thousand dollars."

Although Fahkoury had a genuine need, trustworthiness was the true motivation for demanding Bahar's car. Bahar presented a huge security risk for the operation and for Fahkoury himself. Although Bahar had repeatedly demonstrated his commitment to the operation, Fahkoury decided he would not leave anything to chance. The car was merely extra insurance.

More than a week earlier, Fahkoury had tasked Bahar to take an important trip. He authorized Bahar to purchase a round-trip flight to Washington, DC, and gave him instructions to spend two days in the city and return with several receipts and photographs of the US Capitol, the White House, and Union Station. When he returned, Fahkoury asked for his boarding pass, the memory card from the camera, and the receipts.

When he handed over the keys, Bahar knew the car, or at least parts of it, would someday be traced back to him as would the evidence from Washington, DC. The car was just the latest thread tying him to the fanatic standing before him. There had been no need to coerce his devotion, he silently protested; he had done everything asked of him. Fearing the madman was probably considering that he would be better dead, Bahar shared his intention to disappear that day. Fortunately, that news seemed to comfort the zealot.

It had. They both knew Bahar was in too deep to save himself. Plus, Fahkoury decided, killing Bahar was only likely to draw notice, perhaps even before they had a chance to leave Dearborn. He recalled, too, that Aziz had hinted that Bahar might be of use in the future. Keys in hand, Fahkoury approached Bahar with a steely stare. He embraced Bahar, not with warmness but, rather, in a ritualistic manner meant to convey his continued skepticism about the man. Then he left for the safe house to await approval from the shura.

Approval to proceed with the attack finally arrived the following afternoon. When it came, Fahkoury had just four full days before the attack, still enough time to get done what was needed as long as they got moving right away. Fahkoury put out word for the men to quickly assemble in the home on the Oakland Boulevard.

When they were assembled in the dank basement fifteen minutes later, Fahkoury announced with extremely rare enthusiasm, "Our momentous operation has been blessed by our senior leaders!"

After the cheering subsided, he assigned responsibilities for certain last-minute but critical matters that could not have been appropriately completed earlier. Before work began on the mundane matters, the men were first invited to make martyr videos and pose for photos. All the men accepted the offers. Out of respect, no other activities were permitted during the two-plus hours required to complete this process.

When that exercise was complete, teams were dispensed to the three residences in Dearborn to go over them a final time. He and al-Rasheed had maintained regular inspections of the dwellings throughout their time in Dearborn, and al-Rasheed had overseen the sterilization process when it began the previous day. Fahkoury was reasonably assured there was nothing to give them away, but he was taking no chances.

While al-Rasheed and Omar looked after the cleaning work at the two other residences, Fahkoury remained at the Oakland Boulevard home. After he completed his final inspection, he pulled out the evidence from Bahar's trip to DC. Leaving all of it behind, especially the photo memory card, was probably too much, he considered. If he left everything, the Americans would probably realize the evidence was a red herring. He decided he would leave only the receipts and some torn pieces from the map of the metro DC area. Since Bahar owned the home, his trip to DC would be easily discovered, and his disappearance would add to the intrigue. Fahkoury circled the US Capitol and Union Station on the pieces of map, and threw them in the trash with the receipts and the rest of the garbage. It was more than enough evidence to keep the Americans guessing in the event the Americans somehow discovered their safe houses before the attack.

By 11:15 p.m., the dwellings had been scrubbed and emptied of the men's belongings, the guns, and the three drones, all of which had been packed into the vehicles. The team reassembled to hear Fahkoury's instructions about picking up the bomb-making materials from the storage facility and traveling to Minnesota.

The materials would be retrieved from the storage facility in waves, Fahkoury directed. He announced he would drive alone in Bahar's car and then he assigned the men to the other vehicles. All six vehicles would follow the same route west until they reached the Illinois–Indiana border. There, the vehicles would split into groups of three and follow two different routes into Minnesota. The vehicles were to remain at least fifteen miles apart at all times, he ordered. He expected the spacing and alternative routes would provide protection for the others in case one of the vehicles was stopped by the Americans.

After Fahkoury explained the process, he provided the designated leader of each vehicle with a handheld GPS device and a burner phone. The two-way radios had a maximum range of ten miles, rendering them largely useless during the journey. Absent an emergency, each vehicle was to communicate only with the one in front of it and only to ensure proper spacing. Only he would remain in contact with all the vehicles.

In the event the police or other authorities tried to stop any of the vehicles, the men were instructed to "immediately alert the others and, if necessary, to fight to the death. Under no circumstances is the phone or GPS device to get into the hands of the authorities," Fahkoury said. There could be no record of their limited communications or destination. Various contingency plans, depending on the circumstances of any such apprehension, were provided for any unaffected vehicles.

Fahkoury told them he would transport the drones, al-Rasheed would carry all the nitromethane, and Omar would transport the TNT. Each vehicle, except his, was also to be loaded with as much ammonium nitrate as it could reasonably carry. He warned them about overweighting the vehicles. It was possible that some materials would have to be left behind, but that was preferred to exceeding the maximum capacity.

As his final instruction to the group, Fahkoury directed that each vehicle was to depart for the storage facility one-half hour after the preceding vehicle, giving each sufficient time to load up and leave before the next one arrived. The late hour presented enough problems, and having multiple vehicles at the storage facility would only increase the risk of being seen. Once he was assured everyone understood his instructions, Fahkoury indicated to al-Rasheed and his group that it was time to go.

He and Al-Rasheed drove into the storage facility at 12:10 a.m. They loaded al-Rasheed's black 2005 Ford Econoline van with the five-gallon cans of nitromethane and forty-one bags of ammonium nitrate, spread out evenly on the floor and covered with clothes belonging to the men. Eighteen minutes later, Fahkoury led al-Rasheed out of the storage facility toward the interstate.

Five minutes after Tariq and his partner left in the fully loaded 2008 Dodge Caravan, Hayder guided the fourth vehicle into the facility. But Hayder and his cohort had difficulty loading the van, and they were forced to unload nearly all the bags from the off-white 2003 Chevy Astro and start again. They finished reloading almost fifty bags just as Wasim and Fazal showed up in the fifth vehicle.

"Your van has too much," Wasim said as he pulled up. "I can see that it's sitting too low on the tires. You have to unload some bags."

The two groups worked together to remove several bags of ammonium nitrate, and then they redistributed the rest evenly between the van's two axles. This exercise put Hayder behind schedule and threatened to do the same to Wasim.

Thinking it was better to have only one vehicle running late, Wasim said to Hayder, "You need to help us load our van so I can at least get out of here on time."

Having learned from Hayder's troubles, the two groups were able to quickly load Wasim's slightly newer Astro van with the fifty-pound plastic bags. The two vehicles started to leave the storage facility just after 1:30 a.m., hoping to be gone before Omar appeared with the final vehicle.

The approach to the storage facility's outlet paralleled the lone road that passed by the facility. Just as both vehicles prepared to leave the property, they were forced to wait as a car approached and then passed the entrance. More interested in getting out of there before Omar arrived, none of the men in the two vans gave the passing car a second thought.

Omar and Faheem rode in the last vehicle. When they arrived at the facility, there were still more than fifty bags of fertilizer remaining, too many for them to carry in the well-worn 2002 GMC Yukon. They managed to load the TNT and all but fourteen bags of ammonium nitrate before Omar determined the SUV couldn't reasonably carry any more. Omar wondered why the other vehicles hadn't carried more bags, but there wasn't anything he could do about the excess. Fahkoury had given instructions to leave materials behind rather than overload the vehicles, so he left the bags behind, locked the unit, and left.

By 2:15 a.m., all six vehicles were headed westbound on Interstate 94, traveling at the posted speed limit as they maintained position in the convoy, no less than fifteen miles apart.

CHAPTER 46

LIVONIA, MICHIGAN

Aliya Ressam was in a near-zombie state as she drove home after another long twelve-hour shift at the restaurant. She noticed headlights out of the corner of her eye just as she was approaching the small storage facility she passed every day to and from work. She thought it was odd for two vans to be pulling out of the storage facility in the early-morning hours. It was probably nothing, but her president's call to "say something" resonated in her mind, and she determined she should call the police when she arrived home.

Aliya had dutifully listened to every weekly presidential radio address since becoming a United States citizen four year earlier. She was proud of her Iraqi heritage and, at the same time, grateful and fiercely proud to be a US citizen. Aliya had heard President Madden mention in his last two weekly addresses the importance of remaining vigilant and speaking up if strange behavior is witnessed. She had also seen the news reports warning about possible terrorist attacks, and someone from the FBI saying something about vans and large trucks. She decided she needed to "say something," but that would have to wait. Aliya made it an absolute rule not to use her phone while she was driving.

When she finally staggered into her apartment twenty minutes later, she fought off her desire to flop straight into bed and telephoned the local police.

She was sleeping soundly less than ten minutes later, getting much-needed rest for her next shift, which would start in less than seven hours.

Immediately after hanging up with Aliya, the telephone operator put a call out to Officer Louis Cosentino and asked him to check on the storage facility. It was 2:26 a.m. when Officer Cosentino pulled into the storage facility. Ten minutes later, he reported that after examining each unit and looking around the entire property, he couldn't find any signs of potential break-ins or any other trouble.

By this time, Cosentino still had ninety minutes before his shift ended. He needed some extra energy to carry him through. No matter how much sleep he had, it seemed like the overnight shifts wore him out every time. He thought about the hot new waitress at the diner, but then he realized he had only change in his pockets. Thinking he'd look stupid dumping a bunch of coins down, he decided he'd go back to the station for coffee. Besides, he'd be able to fill out the incident report. He was five minutes from the station when the dispatcher called again, this time with instructions to respond to an armed robbery in progress at a convenience store.

By the time he finished booking the heavily-intoxicated perpetrator, the caffeine-deprived Cosentino was already an hour into overtime, and the desk sergeant mercifully sent him home. The sergeant told Cosentino he could fill out the reports about the storage facility and convenience store on his next shift. Officer Cosentino didn't argue. He had the weekend off and didn't want to be sick and exhausted for the Super Bowl parties he planned on attending.

Cosentino would not complete his portion of the storage-facility incident report until he returned to work at noon later that day. When the lieutenant read Officer Cosentino's report, he immediately called the FBI's field office in Detroit, but the significance of what Aliya had seen wouldn't be realized until later that Thursday afternoon.

CHAPTER 47

THE OVAL OFFICE

Mid-Thursday morning, the principals gathered in the Oval Office for an update. The news was coming fast and furious, and none of it was good. The already-ominous mood in the ornate room darkened further when CIA Director Gonzalez announced that new intelligence from recently decrypted communications all but confirmed their fears that a terrorist attack was imminent.

"We have two pieces of SIGINT that we believe clearly indicate the attack is only days away," Gonzalez said. "The first piece regards two e-mails that were sent through *Inspire*, al Qaeda's online magazine. NSA completed decryption of those e-mails just a few hours ago."

The use of cryptography by terrorist organizations to secure their communications was an open secret. For that reason, Fahkoury was wary that intelligence agencies had back doors to widely available encryption tools like Telegram and WhatsApp. He persuaded the shura to communicate with him through *Inspire*, a method Fahkoury had used previously and deemed safer.

"The first e-mail was sent three days ago," Gonzalez said. "It states, 'The necessary props have been assembled, and the rehearsals have been satisfactory. Everything is now ready for the performance. It is our hope the invitation will be accepted.'

"The second e-mail was sent yesterday. It says, 'That is excellent news. We warmly accept the invitation and look forward to what will be a spectacular show.'

"In addition to these tidbits, NSA was also able to get some other interesting information, including the current location of Abdul Hussain, who happens to be in Zamakh, Yemen, by the way," said Gonzalez.

The meaning of the veiled language in the e-mails didn't require any explanation. It was plain that the first e-mail was a request to proceed with the attack and that the second e-mail was permission, most likely from al Qaeda brass, to do so. Given all that had transpired, the only other plausible conclusion was that the e-mails had been intentionally floated as a diversion.

"How did we get these e-mails?" Secretary of Defense Fitzgibbons asked, thinking along that same line.

"We know that al Qaeda uses various third-party apps for encrypted communications," Patrick said. "It also sometimes uses *Inspire* for secure communications. In fact, *Inspire* includes a twelve-page step-by-step guide on how to use encrypted communications. Al Qaeda uses the ubiquitous Pretty Good Privacy, or PGP, software for the encryption and makes the public-key available right on the website. The public-key is changed periodically, likely due to paranoia and an abundance of caution. The truth is, however, that the public-key doesn't matter. It's impossible to back-channel and crack the code through the public-key. The private-key is critical for decrypting the messages. In this type of setting, only the people at *Inspire* would know the private-key.

"NSA tries to get the private-key by bombarding the magazine with phishing messages in the hopes of tricking the people at *Inspire* into thinking the communication is from a fellow terrorist. The phishing message contains a link that, if clicked on by the recipient, allows the NSA to access the user's computer. On the rare occasions that happens, and we get inside, the NSA cryptologists still have to try to locate and break the private encryption key.

"Once in a while, like here, somebody screws up, and we get access to an *Inspire* computer. The encryption key was contained in a password-protected document. The techs hacked the password for the document by secretly installing and running software on the computer that identifies common keystroke strings."

Secretary Fitzgibbons and the others now understood that the possibility the e-mails were any kind of deception was highly remote. Carpenter himself had held the same suspicion before he heard the explanation earlier from Blake Palmer, the whiz kid from the NSA who had cracked the password.

Secretary Fitzgibbons asked, "Do we know from where the e-mails were sent or received?"

"On this issue, there were no mistakes," Patrick said. "Both parties at the ends of the encrypted e-mails used the Onion Router, or Tor. Once the service is enabled, Tor passes the communication through multiple proxy servers around the Internet that are controlled by various organizations and, oftentimes, private individuals. It's almost impossible to determine the source or location of either party, and, so far, we haven't had any luck."

"Who is Abdul Hussain? Is he involved in this plot?" asked Secretary Christensen.

"He's the number two for al Qaeda in the Arabian Peninsula," Carpenter said. "We've been trying to get him for a long time. His communications appear to have nothing to do with this operation. They all concern some money problems he's having in Yemen."

"There are few things I'd like more than nailing Abdul Hussain," said President Madden. "That son of a bitch is responsible for at least three marine deaths."

"I share those same sentiments, but we can't afford to go after him right away," Carpenter said. "Based on the difficulties we've had finding him, we know Hussain keeps his location very close to the vest. If *Inspire* is one of the few sources that know his location and we go after him now, AQ might realize we hacked their communications."

"Without that, can the user at *Inspire* still determine whether his computer has been breached?" DHS Secretary Wilcox asked.

"The NSA says it's possible, if the guy's any good, but he'd have to first look for a possible breach. Even if he did that, it would take him some time to realize it," Patrick said.

"If he does realize it, what are the chances the *Inspire* guy blows the whistle and they pull or at least delay the attack?" the DHS secretary asked.

"Madam Secretary, there is that chance, but it's pretty unlikely. We know of AQ guys who have been killed on the slightest suspicion that they were helping the enemy. In this case, this guy might have blown a major operation *and* given away the location of a high-ranking member of AQAP. Our guess is that if he finds out he's been breached, he keeps quiet," said Director Gonzalez.

"Why was there so much time between the two e-mails? Is it possible that someone had second thoughts?" Secretary of State Christensen asked.

"That's unlikely. If the 'invitation' was indeed meant for al Qaeda senior leadership, it would have been hand delivered using a chain of couriers. The location of senior leadership is even more closely guarded. AQ goes to great lengths to eliminate any clues that could lead to AQSL's location. If anything, the timing confirms AQSL involvement and the significance of this operation," Gonzalez said.

"You said there were two segments of SIGINT. What's the other?" President Madden asked.

Director Gonzalez first provided some necessary background. She explained that a significant gap in the NSA's SIGNIT coverage was revealed when the United States encountered the existential threat of radical Islamic terrorists who favored the use of remote regions as primary bases of operations. The NSA and the CIA responded by creating a specialized internal NSA unit, the Special Collection Service. SCS extended the NSA's capabilities into these remote, difficult-to-reach locations by clandestinely inserting communications interception devices.

"SCS reports there has been a spike in encrypted instant messaging in the last twenty-four hours. We are unable to decipher the communications, but the metadata tells us most have come from Afghanistan, Pakistan, Yemen, Tunisia, and Syria. AQ operates in all those locations. The patent increase in the number of messages in these locations, coming on the heels of the decrypted e-mails, indicates a pattern similar to the ones we've seen prior to significant attacks," Gonzalez said.

Carpenter took over and provided the intelligence team's latest analysis. The recent thefts of bomb-making materials, the notable increase in chatter, and the decrypted content of the e-mails were foreboding. The intelligence indicated the attack could be expected in a matter of days; how many could not be known. Depending on the locations of their safe haven and the target, it might take time—days, even—for the terrorists to get into position. If the two sites were not close, there might be a need for further target surveillance, offering more time before the attack. Carpenter cautioned the assembled group that he and the task-force team believed those chances were slim, however. It was far more likely the terrorists were now making their very final preparations.

The group sat silent for a moment. By all indications, their worst fears were about to be realized, and they still didn't know where to look. Time was rapidly running out to identify the target and find the terrorists before they could execute.

"The State of the Union address is next week, and the president will be welcoming the Chinese president the next day. Do you think they would be bold enough to try to hit the Capitol or the White House?" Secretary Wilcox asked.

"They would certainly be bold enough, and either would be a very appealing target," Carpenter said. "But terrorists know that a successful assault on the Capitol or the White House is highly improbable. If we have this right, our thinking is that a failed attempt would only underscore AQ's perceived limitations and undermine its plan to reassert itself on the global terror stage.

"We think it is far more likely—probable, even—that the attack will be on a soft target, something high profile with economic impact and a lot of people, where casualties can be optimized. The terrorists know the best chance for success is on a target where the security measures must be appropriately balanced so as not to unduly interfere with personal liberties and the free flow of commerce. That's why airports, especially outside the secured areas, are prime targets."

"I agree," Secretary Fitzgibbons said. "The problem is, we don't know where these guys are, and we can't very well cover all major airports and surrounding areas. What are the most probable cities for an attack?"

"Large cities, as always, are the most probable," Gonzalez said. "Besides the airports, large cities offer tons of other soft targets and greater anonymity. The thefts PJ noted were in the Midwest, but even if they are related, we cannot pinpoint any location. There are a number of large cities in the Midwest alone that we have to consider. But these guys could really be anywhere. We can't rule out New York or Washington, the two cities that are most targeted and are at the top of the list for symbolic significance."

"We are just guessing here," Carpenter said. "These people could attack anywhere in a number of different ways. And I want to make clear that we shouldn't limit our thinking to airports or big cities. But the best guess is a high-profile target that would yield economic repercussions and instill lasting fear. The recent attack at the airport in Brussels is one example, but so are the nightclub attacks in Paris and Orlando and the previous attempts to bomb Times Square. That's the problem; without more specific information, there are too many possibilities."

"What about the Super Bowl?" asked President Madden.

"It's an attractive target, for sure," Patrick said. "The event is broadcast all over the world. At the same time, it would be a difficult target. It's no secret that security at the Super Bowl is very strong, but the security plans are kept close to the vest. Al Qaeda most certainly knows this and understands that surveillance and planning would be very difficult, rendering execution a pretty low probability."

"I happen to think it's a leading possibility, given the timing of the most recent emails. There have been attacks at sporting events before, more recently in Europe, and the Super Bowl certainly checks all the boxes," Carpenter said.

"Well, it is the next big event on the calendar and only three days from now. Unless we learn something to change our thinking, I want PJ and a team on the ground in Minneapolis. PJ, I want you there to assess the security measures that have been put in place and to be prepared to help stop these bastards, just in case," the president said.

"I also want DOD and DHS to coordinate extra security inside and outside at all major airports. And Elizabeth," the president said to his DHS secretary, "I want an alert of an imminent threat of terrorist attack issued in the next two hours. All right, everyone, keep me posted, and let's hope we get some information in time to stop this."

CHAPTER 48

FARMSHIRE, MINNESOTA

ahkoury had accepted that pulling out of Dearborn was going to be tricky. There really was no way around it. Grabbing the materials during the daylight hours was not an option. Conversely, starting in the middle of the night as they had done meant that they would arrive in Minnesota during daylight hours. There was no way they could arrive in Minnesota with six vehicles loaded with weapons and accomplish what they needed to, so Fahkoury had been forced to improvise.

When the caravan was traveling through Indiana, Fahkoury, al-Rasheed, and Wasim directed their vehicles north along a route that took them through Illinois and Wisconsin and eventually into Minnesota. As those three took turns using rest areas and leapfrogging one another, hours were added to the typical travel time, putting Fahkoury at the Minnesota border a few minutes past 5:00 p.m., with al-Rasheed only a few miles behind. As al-Rasheed closed the gap with Fahkoury in western Wisconsin, Wasim slowed to create some additional distance. He entered Minnesota approximately forty miles behind Fahkoury.

Traffic was building for rush hour when Fahkoury neared the Twin Cities, but it was much lighter than normal. Many people had opted to work from home, get out of town, or partake in the week-long festivities leading up to the Super Bowl, now just three days away. Traffic lessened further as

Fahkoury and al-Rasheed eased the vehicles south of the metro area on a route that would take them to the suburb of Farmshire.

Just as the sun was setting, Fahkoury made the first pass of the farm he and al-Rasheed had scouted several days before. Much as it had been that day, only the first floor of the house was illuminated, and the same weathered pickup truck and late-model Honda Civic were parked between the house and the barn. Fahkoury swung the car around and made a second pass some twenty minutes later. Nothing had changed. The plan they had discussed was a go.

Al-Rasheed abandoned his diverted path when Fahkoury sent the signal that the plan was on. He pulled over a few hundred feet from the driveway and got out with Khalid, each man armed with a six-inch knife. Marwan jumped into the driver's seat and slowly headed away from the farm.

Keeping to the same interval, Fahkoury passed by the property again twenty minutes later and noticed the front-porch lights flicker, the all-clear signal from al-Rasheed. Fahkoury turned around and pulled into the long gravel driveway, parking the car along the side of the house and out of view from the road. He met Khalid at the barn, and they opened the door when Marwan pulled into the driveway a few minutes later.

The fifty-year-old wooden barn contained typical clutter as well as a medium-sized John Deere tractor and some accessories, but there was more than enough room right away for Marwan's van. The items could be rearranged later to accommodate all the vehicles and provide an adequate workspace. Despite the lack of heat, it would be an ideal place to assemble the bombs, Fahkoury decided. He sent Khalid back to help al-Rasheed while he and Marwan started rearranging the barn.

Al-Rasheed and Khalid had already begun the process of cleaning up the mess from their handiwork when Fahkoury arrived. The two killers stowed the bodies behind the barn, underneath a tarp that was also providing protection for various pieces of farm machinery. They had had little difficulty incapacitating the senior couple and their aged dog. The man was dead within seconds of responding to al-Rasheed's knock on the front door. Wasim wasted no time rushing through the door and ensuring that his wife joined him an instant later. Wasim supposed the infirm dog was not a necessary casualty, but he reasoned that even the beasts of infidels were unworthy of life.

Al-Rasheed was surprised to discover a third occupant during their sweep of the rest of the home. Before he was able to detect a faint rattle, he thought the woman, who appeared to be at least in her late eighties, might already be dead. As he suffocated her with one of the spare pillows, he assumed the frail woman to be the mother of one of the other two.

About a half hour after his own arrival, Fahkoury was guiding Wasim's van into the barn. He immediately tasked the two latest arrivals to hastily clear space for the remaining vehicles, the first of which was expected to arrive soon. Getting the vehicles out of sight was the top priority. A more organized setup would have to wait.

Less than a half hour after Hayder had guided his van into the barn, Omar was doing the same with the sixth and final vehicle. Fahkoury's plan had worked to perfection. While he, al-Rasheed, and Wasim had been heading north, Tariq, Hayder, and Omar continued west on Interstate 80 where it diverged from I-294 in southern Illinois. Their vehicles employed the same leapfrogging method along a longer route that took them through Illinois, into Iowa, and then eventually north into Minnesota. Staggering their arrivals was critical, and they had pulled it off.

Now that everyone was together again, the burner phones used during the trip were collected and immediately destroyed. The GPS devices were spared a similar fate, as they would be needed to the end. Then the terrorists got to work around the farmstead.

While four men assumed sentry duty, rotating strategic positions inside and outside the house, the remaining men directed their efforts to the house and the barn's interior. The shades were drawn, and the only lights that brightened the home were those on the first floor, continuing the practice of the former occupants. Dark blankets, removed from the house, were placed over the few windows in the barn, effectively eclipsing any light from inside. In less than an hour, a comfortable working space had been created, allowing the terrorists to unload the vehicles.

While the others were unloading, Fahkoury gave Omar and Wasim, his two best English speakers, cash and a list of nine big-box do-it-yourself retailers, all within a fifteen-mile radius of the farm. He told them to bring back fifty-five-gallon plastic containers but to limit the purchases from any particular store to no more than four of the vessels. He estimated he would need a total of eleven, but there were less than two hours before the stores were scheduled to close at 10:00 p.m. The rest of the containers they needed would have to be purchased the following day.

As soon as the first van had been emptied, Omar and Wasim left. An hour and a half remained before the stores closed, still enough time for them to visit two different stores, Fahkoury calculated. As long as they returned with some containers, he would be able to start assembling the first bombs that night.

CHAPTER 49

LANGLEY, VIRGINIA

At 6:00 p.m. Thursday, just as Carpenter and Patrick were finishing putting a team and arrangements together for Minneapolis, FBI Director Forti showed up at the task-force conference room with more troubling information. In the six hours since they had all left the White House, the FBI had found evidence that the terrorists had been holed up in Dearborn, Michigan, with bomb-making materials.

Forti started out by telling the team about Aliya Ressam, providing a summary of the account she gave to the Livonia Police Department and, later, to the FBI. He described how the FBI had contacted and ruled out each of the twenty-six storage-unit lessors with the exception of a man named Zafir Bahar. Bahar was in the wind, Forti said. His mobile-phone repair store in Dearborn had not been open for two days, according to several witnesses. TSA records revealed that ten days earlier, Bahar had flown to and then spent two days in Washington, DC.

A search warrant for the storage facility had been granted less than an hour before, and they already had something. Before getting into the details, Forti added that a request for a second search warrant, for Bahar's store and two other residential properties he owned, was being presented to a federal judge at that very moment. In the meantime, agents were canvassing the neighborhoods around Bahar's properties.

Forti then shared what he knew. "We found fourteen fifty-pound bags of ammonium nitrate in the storage facility."

Enough said, everyone thought. While this didn't exclude other possible methods of attack, there was no longer any doubt that a fertilizer bomb was part of the intended arsenal.

"Is there any way to determine if the ammonium nitrate found in the storage facility is, in fact, the same that was reported stolen from the farm in Ohio?" Carpenter asked.

"We don't know at this point."

"Any trace of the racing fuel stolen from Indiana in the chemical analysis?" Patrick asked.

"Again, we don't know," Forti said. "The team is still working the unit. They've been told to look for any evidence of any explosive materials."

"What's the model and make of the vans this woman saw?" Carpenter asked.

"She's not sure of the make or model," Forti said, "but based on pictures shown to her, she thinks they were both later-model Chevrolet Astro vans. Chevy stopped making these vans in 2005. She also says both are white or a light color, but we need to realize the paint color could have been changed a dozen times since 2005.

"Before anyone asks," Forti continued, "more than two million of these vans were sold from 1984 to 2005. We're still pulling data, but, based on the general rule for older cars, we expect that more than ten percent are still being driven. Better we have this information than we don't, but it doesn't tell us a whole lot to help us locate the vans."

Carpenter expected as much. Without very detailed descriptions, the information about the vans didn't do much to help the zero in on the terrorists. They didn't have time to track down close to two hundred thousand Chevy vans still on the road. In the Detroit area alone, the list was likely to contain thousands.

"What about descriptions of the men?" Carpenter asked, looking for another angle.

"Again, not much. It was dark, and this all happened in a matter of a few seconds. The ambient light from the facility did allow her to see two people—well, two heads, she says—in each van. All she can say is that none appeared to have dark skin, or at least very dark skin."

"Do we think these two vans will be used in an attack, or are they just transporting materials to a larger vehicle and, therefore, a larger bomb?" Samantha Lane asked.

"If this woman's right about the vans, each could easily hold fifteen hundred pounds or more—not a terribly large bomb but big enough to do damage to the immediate area," Patrick said. "If they do have that much ammonium nitrate, or more, and they bundle it into a box van or a semitrailer even, then we're talking massive, Oklahoma City–size bombs."

"We have to expect that either is possible," Carpenter said. "The type and size of the vehicle will ultimately be dictated by the intended target. A smaller van is more commonplace, providing better cover. It's also more versatile, which, obviously, opens more opportunities. There are fewer places a box van or semitrailer can go without looking suspicious."

The rapid-fire rate of questions, answers, and discussions continued as the task-force team tried to piece the information together in the form of actionable intelligence. At each turn, however, they found they were pretty much right where they had started. The group had already assumed the terrorists were in the country planning an attack, one that would likely use fertilizer bombs. Yet the all-important question of the target remained out of their grasp. Unless the nearly infinite list of targets could be adequately protected from a VBIED, they were not really any further along than before these latest discoveries. The team couldn't even realistically eliminate some key geographies.

It had been more than sixteen hours since Aliya Ressam noticed the vans, enough time to travel almost a thousand miles, by their most conservative estimates. Due to their proximity to the storage facility and the thefts in Ohio and Indiana, Detroit and Chicago took on increased meaning. Bahar's recent travels meant Washington was another strong possibility. All were well within the thousand-mile radius, as was New York, always a prime target and one that could not be eliminated. Minneapolis and the Super Bowl were also easily within range.

Using this new information, the group began analyzing methods and locations of attack, beginning with the Detroit metro area, since it was closest to the storage facility. The airport quickly rose to the top of the list, but Carpenter dismissed it as a potential target. "They would have struck by now. I don't see them driving around with a bomb for sixteen hours when the Detroit Metro Airport is less than ten miles away. It's got to be someplace else."

While Carpenter was speaking, Forti's phone rang. Everyone watched as the FBI director stoically listened and occasionally nodded his head, searching for potential clues about what Forti was being told.

"The second search warrant was issued and executed thirty minutes ago," Forti announced as soon as the call ended. "We had teams standing by at three different locations in Dearborn—the building containing Bahar's store and apartments upstairs and two residential homes located less than a mile away.

"They've found pieces of a torn map in a plastic garbage bag behind one of the homes. It's only a partial map, and it has food and soda stains on it, but it's clear that it's of DC. The Capitol and Union Station are circled on the map. They also found three receipts for taxis and restaurants—again, all from DC. The receipts are all dated within the past two weeks."

CHAPTER 50

FARMSHIRE, MINNESOTA

Almost forty-eight hours after arriving at the safe house, Fahkoury and his team remained secreted in their rural garrison under the mounting pressure of a nationwide search and alert about a terrorist attack. Every hour, beginning earlier that Saturday morning, the cable news channels were again broadcasting photos of five men, including Fahkoury and al-Rasheed, who, it was said, were now believed to be terrorists in the country and planning an attack. The Department of Homeland Security had raised the terror notice to an Imminent Alert, meaning the government had credible and specific intelligence regarding an impending terrorist attack.

The FBI director was asking for information relating to any of the men or any suspicious activity, especially anything involving box trucks, large passenger vans, and SUVs, and particularly in Washington, DC; Detroit; Chicago; New York; and Minneapolis. The television anchors reported that "sources inside the government claim there is no specific information" relating to a potential target, but these cities were currently the leading possibilities. That reporting was backed up by the talking heads who argued that if the United States intelligence community knew where to look, it would be sharing that information publicly.

As video of the extra security measures in the cities and airports of Chicago, Detroit, New York, and Washington, DC, was shown, the pundits speculated that the government was trying to cover all the usual targets, with the exception of Detroit. The experts surmised that there must be a connection to the Motor City but struggled to define likely targets there other than the airport. The consensus was that New York and DC, including the allure of the State of the Union address early next week, were the most likely targets.

On cue, the anchor pivoted the discussion to the Super Bowl as a potential target. Video of the festivities in downtown Minneapolis filled the screen as the coverage moved into interviews with representatives from the league and various security agencies working the event. Representatives from the NFL and state, local, and federal authorities all downplayed the threat to the major event, explaining that robust measures had been planned and put in place well before the alert was issued. As the video showed the security checkpoints and heavily armed personnel patrolling outside and inside the facility, various off-camera officials could be heard describing the screening measures and providing assurances for the safety of both fans and participants.

As he sat watching the broadcast, the closest thing to rest he had allowed himself in more than a day and a half, Fahkoury reflected that almost twenty-four hours remained before the attack—plenty of time for the infidels to figure out his plans. At this point, there was nothing he or anyone could do to change that reality. Except for finishing the last details, all they could do was wait.

Work had continued unwaveringly over the course of the past two days as Fahkoury and his men pressed on with the preparations. While al-Rasheed used the Honda Civic to shuttle small groups of men to both locations for the lone chance each would have to get eyes on the targets, Fahkoury personally oversaw every step in the assembly of five vehicle-borne bombs and three pipe bombs. Although the mixture of ammonium nitrate and fuel would remain relatively stable until the detonation devices were connected, he had insisted on a very hands-on approach to assembly. He need only look at his left hand for evidence of carelessness, something he would not allow so close to his most defining moment.

Shortly after Omar and Wasim had returned with the containers that first night, Fahkoury used most of the available nitromethane, combining it with thirty-eight bags of ammonium nitrate to assemble the first bomb. As the men added the bags of ammonium nitrate into the containers at his exacting instructions, Fahkoury carefully and slowly added the racing fuel, thoroughly mixing the materials to ensure saturation and maximum yield. When it was finished early Friday morning, the bomb—contained in two fifty-five-gallon drums—weighed just over 1,500 pounds. He estimated that the vehicle-borne improvised explosive device would deliver a two-hundred-foot lethal blast range, and its destructive properties would extend another thousand feet.

The remaining fifty-five-gallon plastic containers had been obtained by midday on Friday. Fahkoury used the rest of the nitromethane and diesel fuel in the second VBIED and diesel fuel as the exclusive accelerant in the final three bombs. Each of these four bombs weighed between 1,300 and 2,000 pounds. Fahkoury realized that only the largest of them would approximate the explosiveness of the first bomb, but he also knew that each one was still capable of causing significant damage and, if the circumstances were in their favor, substantial casualties.

CHAPTER 51

MINNEAPOLIS, MINNESOTA

At 12:25 p.m. on Saturday, the day before the big game, Carpenter and four other paramilitary officers from the Directorate of Intelligence arrived in Minneapolis. He knew the men well, having worked with each of them multiple times over the years. That he and Patrick had been able to pull together such a quality team on short notice was fortunate.

The evidence pointing to Washington, DC, as the potential target had not dissuaded Carpenter. He called it bullshit right away and explained his reasoning for why it was nothing more than subterfuge. Besides, the security measures in Washington and the other cities had been stepped up considerably, and none of those cities was promoting an event with the quantity of massed people that Minneapolis would have for the Super Bowl. President Madden had been convinced by Carpenter's argument and stuck with his original plan to send him to Minneapolis.

Carpenter and his team went straight from the airport to a meeting with the Super Bowl Security Coalition, a federation of delegates representing more than forty local, state, and private security agencies. As soon as he walked into the SBSC command center on the top floor of a three-story Georgian-architecture brick building two blocks from the stadium, Carpenter sensed that some feathers had been ruffled.

SBSC leadership had not responded enthusiastically to the unexpected call from DHS Secretary Wilcox. Earlier in the day, she had advised them that in response to intelligence indicating a likely terrorist attack on the homeland, President Madden was sending Carpenter to oversee security at the event. Disbelief with a tinge of defiance consumed the discussion, which began even before Secretary Wilcox finished her remarks. The secretary declined to address their shouted questions and simply told the group that Carpenter would brief the details when he arrived in a few hours.

A few minutes after Secretary Wilcox signed off, Chief of Staff Bill Tackett's voice emanated from the speaker at the SBSC command center. Seconds later, the recalcitrant attitude of SBSC leadership abruptly changed when President Madden spelled out, in forceful language, the new chain of command and his expectations that Mr. Carpenter was to be provided complete and forthright cooperation.

"Look, my team and I wouldn't be here if this weren't some serious shit," Carpenter said, instantly grabbing everyone's undivided attention. "You and your teams have a very difficult job to do, one that might have just gotten harder. Our presence is not a lack of confidence in you or your teams. We're here to help you make sure this game goes off without a hitch. I think when you hear what I have to tell you, you'll all be glad for the extra help."

He conceded, off the top, that there was no intelligence to indicate that the Super Bowl was, in fact, the target. Rather, the president and the federal government were simply trying to cover as many bases as possible in response to very disturbing intelligence. Carpenter provided a meticulous account of the people suspected to be involved, the relevant intelligence, and how it all fit into a preexisting analysis that a large-scale attack by al Qaeda on the United States was likely. Now, it appeared that such an attack was imminent. When Carpenter finished, questions and requests for clarifications poured from the SBSC team, any hurt feelings having been cast aside and replaced by a resolute cohesiveness to confront the credible threat.

Once those issues had been addressed, Carpenter turned the discussion to the security measures the SBSC had put in place. On the flight up to Minnesota, Carpenter had read the summary of recommendations from the red team simulations—exercises conducted by independent parties to test the SBSC's preparedness for a variety of attack scenarios, including several in which both the CIA and Department of Defense had participated. The report from the red-team simulations did not note any glaring failures; it only suggested areas of improvement. Before he made any decisions, Carpenter wanted a chance to hear for himself what the SBSC had in its playbook.

He and his team listened as the SBSC leader, Mark Zeman, outlined the security measures that had been in place all week and would remain in place through the end of the postgame festivities. In essence, Zeman explained, the strategy involved degrees of limiting and directing vehicle and pedestrian traffic in the areas surrounding the stadium. In order to execute that strategy, two security zones within the city had been created: the primary security zone—the area closest to the stadium—and a secondary security zone, extending farther out.

The two security zones were patrolled and monitored by a combined force of some six hundred security professionals and the latest secure communication and surveillance technology. Each uniformed security professional carried a helmet-mounted 24.1-megapixel video camera wirelessly linked to the command center. All six hundred members of the SBSC team could communicate with one another and the command center with wireless push-to-talk tactical headsets. Each of them was also assigned a personal geotag identifier that allowed the command center to speak directly with and reposition specific security-team members. Finally, high-resolution closed-circuit cameras, monitored by a team of seven video specialists inside the SBSC command center, were interspersed throughout both zones, offering 360-degree coverage with the latest video-content analysis and facial-recognition capabilities.

When he finished with the overview, Zeman pulled up a map and projected it on the screen. A rectangular area of downtown Minneapolis was highlighted on the map. "The security area," he said while outlining the area with a laser pointer, "is defined by Church Street on the north, River Street on the south, Eleventh Avenue on the east, and Third Avenue on the West. It encompasses twenty-four-square blocks."

"There are two zones within the secured area. Eighth Avenue, running north-south here," Zeman said while pointing with the laser, "serves as the boundary between the primary security zone and the secondary security zone. The primary zone is this area immediately around the stadium. The secondary security zone is this area here, which houses the hospitality tents. Traffic flows one way around the entire security zone in a clockwise manner. No unauthorized vehicles are allowed inside any of the secured areas.

"The primary security zone is continuously ringed with six-foot precast concrete barriers, preventing any unauthorized persons or vehicle traffic inside the zone. The only vehicle entrance to the primary security zone is here on Eleventh Avenue," he said while dotting the access point with the laser. "There are four security checkpoints, through which only ticket holders may pass into the primary zone. They are located at the four corners of the primary-zone perimeter," Zeman said, pointing to the northeast corner before continuing clockwise and finishing with the northwest checkpoint. "At each checkpoint, there are three-millimeter wave advanced imaging technology scanners, the same devices used at all US airports.

"The secondary security zone is designated as a pedestrian-only area for Super Bowl–related fan events. There are two drop-off locations designated on Third Avenue for public buses and private vehicles, here and here," he said, pointing to the locations on the western boundary of the security area. Circling the laser once again, he said, "Those are the only locations where vehicles are permitted to stop. In order to block vehicles but still facilitate pedestrian traffic into and out of the secondary security zone, we have spaced four-foot-high concrete barriers every eight feet along the perimeter. Everyone is allowed inside the secondary security zone; there are no screening measures.

"In addition to roughly eighty officers at the four security checkpoints, there will be approximately two hundred uniformed and undercover officers patrolling inside and around the perimeter of the primary security zone." Zeman added that approximately 250 men and women, made up of state and local police officers and private security personnel, were assigned to the secondary zone. State and local police would patrol the secondary security zone on foot and on horseback, while private security teams would serve at the numerous hospitality tents sponsored by the NFL, various corporations, and local businesses.

To finish his remarks, the SBSC chief added that two Blackhawk helicopters would patrol the skies above and around the stadium, providing surveillance and threat response from the air for the entire secured area and beyond. Emergent care needs would be offered through four temporary triage centers, two inside each zone, and a fleet of twenty-three ambulances scattered throughout the surrounding area.

As he listened to Zeman, Carpenter played out in his mind how an attack might go down. The choke points for pedestrians and vehicle traffic were his main concerns, but methods other than car bombs were also possible. An assault using handheld weapons—guns, knives, suicide vests—was his chief worry for the party atmosphere inside the secondary security zone, where there was no screening and anyone was allowed to roam. A car bomb or vehicle-ramming assault could be employed anywhere, but more likely around the perimeter of the primary security zone, where ticket holders would be converging to the four security checkpoints. For the most part, he was impressed with the tactical aspects of the plan, but he knew no plan was invincible.

When Zeman concluded his report, Carpenter and his team tried to poke holes in the SBSC security plans, but finding ways to improve them proved evasive. The suggestions all pretty much boiled down to extending the perimeter around the entire twenty-four-square-block secured area, but it was not feasible at this late hour to bring in more concrete barriers and further constrain already-limited parking options. Anyway, Carpenter noted, those changes would simply relocate the same problems.

There was one reasonable fix to reduce the potential threat to the stadium and those inside it, however. Carpenter ordered that an additional vehicle checkpoint be added on the lone vehicular approach to the primary security zone. Creating another checkpoint one block farther out could be done without much difficulty, and it would further reduce the risk of a vehicle getting through security and damaging the stadium.

"There's not much else that can be done at this time," Carpenter said. "The plan is pretty solid. These are not unexpected threats we are facing, and, under the circumstances of a major sporting event, the plan in place addresses them as well as any plan could. So let me talk instead about the response to any attack."

Reaction time would determine the full impact of any attack, he told the group. He knew the security teams had been extensively trained to look for and react to strange behavior. The recently shared news that a terrorist attack was possible would only heighten the state of awareness, but he thought it was still a good idea to provide a reminder with his concluding remarks. "No security plan can prevent every possible attack. The one you all have in place is technically sound. Our success will come down to awareness, reaction time, and discipline. Beyond the initial response, subsequent reactions have to be coordinated from the command center to ensure we don't abandon posts and outrun our coverage. If we all start racing toward one problem, we will create a greater or new vulnerability somewhere else. Your teams will handle the responsibilities on the ground, and my team will provide coverage support. Let's pray everything is quiet for the next twenty-four hours. Thank you, everyone."

After dismissing the rest of the SBSC leaders, Carpenter turned to the SBSC chief. "Mark, I think I know where I'd like to deploy my team, but first I would like to take a closer look at those areas."

CHAPTER 52

FARMSHIRE, MINNESOTA

The terrorists gathered on the first floor of the farmhouse early Sunday morning for the Fajr prayer. At Fahkoury's request, al-Rasheed led the men as they proceeded through the first of the five daily ritual prayers. Each of the warriors prayed not with anguish but, rather, with a serenity rooted in expectation of soon being in paradise. When the prayer was finished, the men rose and turned to Fahkoury, looking for further guidance.

"My brothers," Fahkoury began, opening his arms to the assembly, "today is the day we realize our great purpose and blessing from Allah—to bring jihad to the Great Satan. The United States of America, the tyrannical superpower, will again pay a heavy price for its history of violence and oppression against our people in all corners of the world. We mujahideen, by the grace of Allah, will deliver a victory for the righteous true believers, a triumph that will unify all Muslims against the Crusaders and lead to the realization of the caliphate envisioned by Sheikh Osama. As holy warriors, each of you is working in Allah's way. As witnesses, you will reside in God's presence in paradise and inspire others who follow in this great cause. Be confident that our training has prepared us for this great day, and do not let anything stop you from your destiny. May God's peace and blessings be upon each of you."

"Allahu Akbar!" the men shouted in unison.

Fahkoury shared his men's zeal, and he was proud to lead them. In less than three weeks, he had grown fond of them, inspired by their absolute commitment throughout the preparations. Aziz and the shura had done well selecting these fine men. The question that lingered in his mind, however, was how successful would they be?

Fahkoury accepted that execution of his plan did not necessarily need to be flawless for it to be considered a resounding success. Still, he strived for perfection, perhaps an unattainable standard in any operation, especially one on this scale. Despite it being the main objective, merely demonstrating the ability to carry out a coordinated large-scale attack inside America would not live up to his own measure of success. His passionate intention was for believers to revere this day just as they did that day in September 2001. And for that to happen, he needed to kill as many infidels as possible.

Fahkoury had handed out the assignments the night before. The first stage of the plan would set the tone for what would follow. Fahkoury would not be there to manage it, but he trusted his senior lieutenant would prove more than capable of making quick decisions and adapting to any changing circumstances. Wearing a football jersey and a knit cap bearing the local team's colors, al-Rasheed was the first to leave the farm, departing in the farmer's Honda Civic just after 9:30 a.m. on a very cold, dreary day with a chance of light snow in the forecast. An assault rifle, a pistol, and a drone armed with one of the three pipe bombs Fahkoury had assembled were hidden beneath blankets inside the trunk. In his pockets, al-Rasheed carried a burner phone and a few thousand dollars in cash as he headed north toward Minneapolis.

After fighting through traffic, al-Rasheed parked the car forty minutes later on the top floor of the parking ramp, a location he and Fahkoury had selected more than a week before. Arriving this early assured a parking spot near his point of attack. He left the compact sedan and went out to hide among the revelers for the next several hours.

A short time after al-Rasheed left, Fahkoury walked into the barn alone, leaving the men in the house to quietly contemplate their critical roles in what lay ahead. The bombs had already been carefully loaded into the four vans and the lone SUV the terrorists had used to travel from Michigan. The only task that remained was to place the homemade TNT on the bombs and wire it to the detonation devices. He had designed the bombs to be detonated either manually or, if necessary, through a burner phone that was modified and connected to the firing circuit, making the already-painstaking work even more laborious.

The temperature provided a further challenge. Outside the barn, it hovered just above zero, and it was not much warmer inside. The cold, damp air forced him to stop every ten minutes or so to warm his hands. This was the most dangerous aspect of the bomb-assembly process, and his fingers had to be nimble. He knew mistakes would not be forgiven. Fahkoury assiduously plied his trade until, finally, all five bombs were fully armed and linked with fresh burner phones. It was almost time to launch the first wave of VBIEDs.

CHAPTER 53

MINNEAPOLIS, MINNESOTA

Shortly before Fahkoury convened his team of terrorists for morning prayer, Carpenter arrived at his post inside the SBSC command center. Mark Zeman, the SBSC chief, was already there at 6:00 a.m., preparing for a long, tense day.

As the city gradually filled with the sixty-five thousand ticket holders— who were both fortunate and wealthy enough to have secured a pass for at least $425—and perhaps twice as many partygoers hoping to soak up the big-game atmosphere, Carpenter checked in regularly with the SBSC brass and his four CIA teammates, each strategically stationed around the stadium.

Zeman had stuck around after the meeting the previous evening to assist Carpenter and his team. Carpenter wanted his team in the best positions to help in case anything went down, and he considered the four pedestrian security checkpoints at the primary security-zone perimeter to be the most likely locations for any kind of attack. Unlike the secondary security zone, where pedestrians entered and exited at numerous locations, each of the four checkpoints at the primary-zone perimeter offered a shot at a densely packed group of people with a vehicle-borne improvised explosive device. A handheld-weapons assault was his main concern inside the secondary zone, but he would have to rely on the manpower of the SBSC teams there. Still, he felt he needed to place one man along Third Avenue, the main thoroughfare on the western boundary of the secured area, where people would be gathering for buses and private cars. Zeman offered his insights and answered any questions while George Murphy, one of the SBSC's technicians, took Carpenter and his team through a computer-generated 3D model of the areas around the stadium.

The sophisticated software allowed them to carefully analyze each potential location. Extraneous structures were redacted from the view, allowing each position to be assessed for its surveillance and tactical value. Toggling between 2D and 3D views, Murphy rendered both day and night-sky phenomena and revealed distances and vantage points from the positions selected by Carpenter and his paramilitary team. Distance was only marginally relevant to the highly skilled marksmen; each man was capable of hitting a baseball-sized target from over five hundred yards. Ultimately, the primary considerations were the long-range fields of view to the different hot spots and the all-around observation needed to assure mutual support.

The process continued until Carpenter identified close to a dozen posts for on-site review. By 12:45 a.m., he and his team settled on three locations around the primary security zone. Each of the three locations afforded clear views of two security checkpoints. Collectively, the three operators would have full coverage around the stadium. The fourth member of Carpenter's team had been assigned a position on Third Avenue, the western boundary of the secured area.

Now, as game time approached, Carpenter sipped his fourth cup of coffee and watched as the area continued to fill with revelers and ticket holders. Traffic was still flowing modestly around the secured area, either to pick up or drop off passengers or grab one of the few remaining parking spaces still available in the multiple parking lots and ramps in the area. Thus far, there had been no reports of suspicious activity from the SBSC staff, only a few incidents of drunken unruliness. His team also confirmed there was nothing to report since the last check-in ten minutes before.

It was 2:25 p.m., and the game would be starting in about three hours. The stadium gates were scheduled to open at the top of the hour. Outside the security checkpoints at the edge of the primary security zone, people were already queuing up to be among the first inside the stadium. Carpenter had Zeman send out a reminder to the entire security apparatus to remain especially vigilant. If an attack was planned, Carpenter believed it would most likely occur sometime between now and game time, when maximum casualties could be inflicted.

CHAPTER 54

MINNEAPOLIS AND FARMSHIRE, MINNESOTA

For no reason other than their relatively deficient aptitudes, Faheem and Mohammed were chosen for the most straightforward assignments. Their jobs were to simply detonate the bombs at the first target after reaching designated positions. At 1:45 p.m., in accord with Fahkoury's carefully orchestrated deployment schedule, Faheem left the farmhouse in the Econoline van. His only passenger was a 1,500-pound ANFO bomb, sealed inside two fifty-five-gallon containers.

Al-Rasheed had already returned to the Honda Civic when Fahkoury called with the coded message that Faheem had left on time. After the brief call, he exited the compact car to get a sense of when to expect Faheem. From his vantage point, he could see that traffic was still progressing, albeit very slowly, along the route Faheem would follow up Eleventh Avenue. He moved back into the compact car and waited for Faheem to contact him on the handheld radio, expecting it would be forty-five minutes or more, just as Fahkoury had envisioned. Until then, he would feign sleep while thinking about what was to come.

Mohammed, the third and last member of the attack team at the Super Bowl, left in the GMC Yukon exactly ten minutes after Faheem left the farmstead. Mohammed carried the smallest and least powerful of the five VBIEDs in the rickety SUV. Now that all the warriors in the first attack were in position or in route, Fahkoury's attention turned to the second attack and the main target.

Just as he had with the team for the first attack, he had doled out assignments for the second attack based upon his assessment of his fighters' capabilities. Omar, Hayder, and Wasim were responsible for leading the assault inside the principal target, and his most trusted warriors were scheduled to leave next. When Khalid radioed from his position outside in the trees that the road was clear, Fahkoury gestured to Omar. A moment later, his lieutenant and fellow fighters pulled Bahar's Crown Victoria around the house and proceeded down the gravel driveway.

Fahkoury moved over to the barn to check on the rest of his team. He watched in respectful silence as Marwan led Tariq, Hadi, and Fazal in prayer. The last three would drive the three remaining vans to the main target—simple yet the most critical tasks. Admiring the moment but needing to stay busy, Fahkoury used the opportunity to make a final cursory check of the bombs. As soon as the men finished with prayers, he walked over to the van drivers to go over their assignments one last time and provide some final words of encouragement.

As he and Marwan were closing the barn doors behind the last van, Fahkoury said his own silent prayer. *In our trust and faith in you, Almighty, we love death as much as they love life. Please bless these men in their own deaths and the death they will deliver to the nonbelievers.*

CHAPTER 55

MINNEAPOLIS, MINNESOTA

"Chief, it's Ese." It was Seth Anderson. The men called him Ese, a phonetic play on his initials as well as the Spanish word meaning "dude." Anderson was stationed on the roof of a six-story office building to the east of the stadium, affording him clear sight lines to the southeast and northeast security checkpoints.

"I have an early-model black Ford van approaching the stadium from the south on Eleventh Avenue," he said, referring to the eastern boundary and one of two northbound approaches to the secured area. Anderson was a little more than a quarter mile from the vehicle in question. "The vehicle is in a slow-moving line of cars. Right now, it's south of Pine Street, about three blocks shy of the checkpoint at River Street. I only see one person inside, and the van appears to be riding a bit low."

"Can you see the driver?" Carpenter asked urgently.

"The vehicle is now stopped behind six cars at the traffic signal," Anderson said. "I can confirm the driver is male; he's got a beard."

"Do you notice any tells?" Carpenter was asking Anderson whether the driver was exhibiting any nervousness, agitation, or other suspicious signs. Before Anderson could answer, Carpenter heard the voice of another of his paramilitary officers, Dan Hofstad.

"PJ, it's Hof," he called out from his rooftop position on a building close to the southwest corner of the stadium. "I've got a man on the top level of the parking ramp on the south side of Pine Street, a block and a half west of Eleventh Avenue. He just popped up from behind the half wall that surrounds the top level of the ramp. I noticed the same guy in the same spot about forty minutes ago. He's partially hidden by the parapet, but it appears he's monitoring the traffic on Eleventh Avenue moving north toward the stadium."

"Do you have eyes on, Ese?" Carpenter asked Anderson, who was to the east and slightly closer to the parking ramp.

"Negative" came the reply. "I'm blocked by the stairwell." Anderson was referring to the stairway penthouse on the top level of the ramp—in this case, a cinder-block enclosure.

"Does either man look like any of the men in the photos?" Carpenter hurriedly asked.

On the flight up from Virginia, Carpenter had had the men study the photographs from DHS, a predeployment identification practice each of the men had long since mastered. In case the expertly trained men needed a refresher, the photographs had been uploaded to the tablets they each now carried.

"From my vantage point, I can't really tell. My guy is partially obscured by the windshield," Anderson said. "Check that. He just ducked down and peered up. It's too tough to say for sure, but he looks younger than any of the guys in the photos."

"The one on the ramp might look like the taller guy from the Egyptian passports," Hofstad said. "But he's got a beard and a winter hat pulled down low on his forehead, so I can't be sure."

"Murphy," Carpenter called out to the SBSC video technician who was sitting next to him and listening to these reports, "pull up video from the cameras at those locations and link it to Hofstad and Anderson. Try to get a shot you can run through the facial-recognition software."

As Murphy quickly toggled through the list of CCTV cameras in that section and pulled up side-by-side views of both locations, Carpenter told his men, "I'm sending you guys video from the CCTV cameras."

The entire exchange between Carpenter and his men took only a few seconds. A moment later, Anderson was back on the line. "The light just changed, and now the driver is speaking into a two-way radio."

"The guy on the roof just ducked down behind the parapet wall," Hofstad said on the heels of Anderson's latest update.

Carpenter didn't like what he was hearing.

CHAPTER 56

MINNEAPOLIS–SOUTHWESTERN SUBURBS

Just as Fahkoury and the others were approaching the main target in the farmer's pickup, al-Rasheed phoned to report that he had Faheem in his sights. "I found my brother. He will be here soon," he simply said. The first attack would begin momentarily.

Although Fahkoury was expecting heavy casualties at the Super Bowl, the strategic purpose was to demonstrate to a worldwide audience that al-Qaeda had the ability to carry out a devastating strike on a secure target. The main tactical benefit of the first attack was to slow any response to the subsequent attack less than thirty minutes later on the softer principal target, an attack where he anticipated more casualties and enduring psychological terror. Due to distance and traffic, precise timing was not possible, but so far, things were going almost precisely as planned.

Minutes after the call from al-Rasheed, Fahkoury steered the ancient pickup into the parking ramp on the eastern side of the mammoth building. To his disappointment, there were fewer and fewer cars in the ramp as he made his way up to the fifth and highest level. Once there, he drove over to the southwest corner of the structure, a spot farthest from the entrances to the mall, located in the center of the ramp on the ground and third levels. With nothing more than a nod from Fahkoury, Marwan and Khalid jumped out and grabbed the drones and weapons from underneath the tarp in the bed of the pickup. As Fahkoury pulled away, the men were already moving into position.

Fahkoury exited the east ramp and circled around the building to the parking ramp on the western side of the building. He drove into the parking structure and turned toward the designated meeting spot on the ground level. In contrast to the higher levels of the east ramp, Fahkoury noticed there were very few vacant spaces here on the first level of the west ramp. It took him a few moments to spot Bahar's Crown Victoria, parked one row back from where he was expecting.

"Sorry; this was as close as I could find," Omar said as Fahkoury pulled up behind the car. "There was nothing available when we arrived. I had to wait until someone left to get this spot."

"It is fine," Fahkoury said as Wasim and Hayder joined him. "More cars mean more infidels. Are you prepared?"

"Yes," said Omar. "We were already on our way back to the car when I received your signal."

In order for the assault team to be able take up their initial positions quickly and without notice, Omar was instructed to park the car close to the ground-floor entrance. Fahkoury had sent them earlier than he might have preferred, but he had expected parking might be a problem. Rather than having them sit in the car looking dubious, Fahkoury told the men to separately venture into the mall to get a sense of the people and security. They had just returned to the car to gather their weapons when Fahkoury pulled up.

"It will not be long, brothers. With Allah's blessing, brothers al-Rasheed and Faheem will start the operation at the stadium any minute. Until our time arrives to enter the battle, pray for their success there and for ours here. All praise be to Allah," Fahkoury said before driving away.

After he exited the ramp, Fahkoury proceeded to a hotel across the street and parked the pickup at the rear of the parking lot. This placed him at a safe distance, but he was still close enough to witness at least some aspects of the impending carnage. Checking his watch, he expected everyone would be in position for the second attack in twenty minutes, more or less. He turned on the radio and waited for news from al-Rasheed's portion of the operation.

He would not have to wait long. Less than five minutes would pass before Fahkoury would hear the first reports on the radio about the bloodshed at the Super Bowl. His initial punishment to the infidel Americans and their blasphemous idolatry was under way.

CHAPTER 57

MINNEAPOLIS

"**G**ive me a sit-rep on the van," Carpenter said. "What's the guy doing?"

"He just put down the radio, and he's moving along with traffic," Anderson said evenly. "The van is now north of Pine Street, almost to Oak Street, two blocks from the primary-zone perimeter and the checkpoint at River Street. What are my orders?"

"Zeman, start moving people away from Eleventh Avenue and the security checkpoint at River Street!" Carpenter shouted to the SBSC chief.

Zeman immediately sent messages to all the officers whose geotags were within a block of the area.

"Ese, do you have positive ID on the driver?" Carpenter asked Anderson.

"Negative. I can see him pretty clearly; he's bent down looking up at the sky. He's definitely not one of the guys from the photos."

The rules of engagement were clear and had been given by the president himself. Once identification was made, the target was to be eliminated. Absent identification, any conduct indicating intent to harm was to be treated similarly. The ROE bordered on the extreme—despite the intelligence, there was still no certainty that the men from the photos were terrorists—but the president was not pulling any punches. He rationalized that these men had become a security risk to the country the second they entered illegally and under suspicious circumstances.

However, neither of those conditions presently existed. There would be hell to pay if Carpenter gave orders to shoot and an innocent person was killed. Less than twenty seconds had transpired since the van started moving again, but Anderson would have to stand down, at least a few seconds longer.

"Hof, what's the guy at the parking ramp doing?" he shouted to Hofstad.

"He's still down behind the parapet. I can only see the very top of his hat." And then, "I think...I think he just launched a drone. Yeah, it's definitely a drone, and it's carrying something underneath! It just cleared the parking structure and is moving toward the stadium!"

"Take the shots!" Carpenter shouted, no longer concerned about the possibility of mistaken identities.

Immediately turning to the SBSC chief, he said, "Zeman, jam all non-secure communications! Now!"

Hofstad fired twice at the drone's small surface area, hitting the cylinder underneath with the second shot, and then kept firing at the man squatting behind the parapet wall. At the same instant, Anderson was pumping four rounds into the chest of the driver and four more into the vehicle: one in each front tire and two more in the engine block.

The explosion dumbfounded the onlookers below, but the shrapnel raining down coupled with the crack of bullets flying into concrete and metal got them running west, away from the security checkpoint and the van as it proceeded on its slow drift through the intersection of Oak Street and Eleventh Avenue two blocks away.

Al-Rasheed didn't hear any gunshots, but he saw pieces of concrete fly as bullets slammed into the half wall. He quickly realized a gunshot must have caused the explosion—the fuse was set for thirty-five seconds, and the drone had been in the air for what could not have been even five. As bullets continued to rain down on his position, a swell of screaming floated up from below. He raised the assault rifle above the parapet and started firing, only to have it ripped from his hands by a barrage of bullets. He kicked the damaged weapon aside and started crawling along the parapet wall toward the stairway structure, expecting to hear a more thunderous sound any instant. But as he carefully made his way along the base of the wall, he didn't hear or feel the massive explosion he was expecting from Faheem's car bomb. Tucking into the corner where the half-wall intersected the cinder block penthouse, al-Rasheed reached into his pants pocket and pulled out the burner phone. He huddled into a ball for protection and then dialed the number.

"Zeman, what's the status on the jamming system?" Carpenter asked.

Before Zeman had a chance to respond, Faheem's van exploded, sending projectiles outward at more than ten thousand feet per second, and instantly killing anyone within two hundred feet from the spot where the van had once been. When the dust cleared, the bloodbath would be evident for hundreds of feet beyond that.

Shots continued to come in heavy on al-Rasheed as Hofstad emptied a second thirty-round STANAG magazine from his M4A1 carbine assault rifle. Al-Rasheed rocked into a sprinter's position and then sprang forward around the corner of the stairwell, out of the line of fire. Once inside the stairwell, he tossed his winter hat in favor of a baseball hat and stripped off his bulky jacket, revealing the football jersey he had worn on the drive in—an ensemble similar to thousands of others he had seen while walking around earlier. He rushed down five flights of stairs with only the phone in his pocket and the two-way radio in his hand. There wasn't time to grab the pistol from the front seat of the Civic.

When he reached the bottom of the stairs, he paused to punch in the number to the phone in Mohammed's van. It wasn't quite time for Mohammed to detonate his bomb, but he wanted the number ready in case he needed to send the call. He risked a peek through the glass door. Seeing only pure bedlam, he slipped outside into the mob of people running away from the stadium, holding the phone in his hand like so many others.

CHAPTER 58

arpenter ignored the pandemonium erupting inside the SBSC command center and kept barking orders right through the roar of the explosion.

"Zeman, get word to your group that this is a terrorist attack, and we've got at least one guy on the loose! Our first priorities are to get everyone away from the screening locations and away from any roads that are open to traffic! Tell everyone else on your team to help whomever they can until the emergency teams arrive, but make sure they coordinate to make sure their original positions remain covered!"

Giving Zeman a chance to comply, he turned immediately to the SBSC communications team. "Link me up with one of the helos!"

The dark Ford van was unexpected, fueling Carpenter's certainty that there was more to come. The intelligence included two light-colored Chevy vans, and thus far they had not been seen. "Murphy," he called out to the video specialist, "you and your team start scanning out from the primary security zone. You're first looking for any large vehicles within three blocks of the security checkpoints. That includes pickups, SUVS, box trucks, and vans, specifically light-colored Chevy vans. I want to know the location of each large vehicle within that three-block radius!"

A few seconds later, one of the communications technicians had Carpenter linked to Captain Brad Severson, who was piloting one of the helicopters. "Captain, what's your location?"

"I'm over the south side of the stadium," Severson said.

"We're looking for a tango on the top level of the parking ramp off Pine Street, about a block and a half due west of Eleventh Avenue. Do you see anyone there?"

"Negative. I am looking down on the parking ramp now, and I don't see a single person on the top level."

Shit! But Carpenter couldn't waste time looking for that guy. He was expecting a second wave of attacks, possibly handheld weapons or more car bombs—or both. If it came in the form of car bombs, the second wave would be designed to catch people as they fled toward safety or to strike the emergency responders to the first bomb. They had to get people away from the screening choke points and the streets along them.

"Tell me what you see around the security checkpoints on the south side of the stadium," Carpenter said.

"Sir, it's not good," Severson said. "The smoke and debris are still clearing on the southeast corner, but I see casualties around the bomb site, and they extend out a few hundred feet." He didn't bother to describe the crater in the street and the fire raging inside it. Having served in Iraq, he had witnessed powerful car bombs, and he was positive someone like Carpenter had too. "Emergency crews are moving in now. Everyone else is running away from the stadium, in almost every direction."

"Look for vehicles still moving toward the stadium and any large vehicles near the checkpoints."

"I don't see any vehicles of any kind moving toward the stadium. Everything is pretty much stopped. In terms of large vehicles, I see a minivan on Eighth Avenue, just south of Pine Street, but we just saw four people get out and start running south, away from the stadium with everyone else. Most of the traffic on the approaches from the south is over on Eleventh Avenue, and that's at a complete standstill. There are two SUVs in that pack; both of them are stopped south of Pine Street."

He told Zeman to send teams to check out the two SUVs and then went back to Severson. "What about the north side of the stadium?"

"There are no large vehicles within four-plus blocks of the perimeter on the approaches to the checkpoints."

"All right, what about the roads on the perimeter of the secondary security zone?"

"There are a few cars still moving away from the stadium on River Street," Severson said, referring to the one-way westbound street abutting the southern perimeter of the entire security area. "It's gridlocked eastbound on Church Street. I'm blocked out by some buildings, but it appears traffic is still slowly moving on Third Avenue," he said, looking at the main thoroughfare on the western edge of the secondary security zone. "Other than one large SUV and an open-bed pickup on Third Street, the rest of the vehicles on those streets are sedans and smaller cars."

Carpenter motioned for Zeman to have teams look into the large vehicles on Third Street. The fact that traffic had pretty much stopped, at least closer to the stadium, was a good thing. Looking at the monitors, he could see the SBSC personnel were doing quick work to get people away from the security screening checkpoints around the stadium. The SBSC team was also pushing people deeper into the secondary security zone and away from the perimeter streets.

Despite their efforts, Carpenter knew it would be a while before everyone was out of harm's way. A second wave of devastating car bombs remained a grave concern. A lesser yet still significant threat was an assault using hand-held weapons or suicide bombs in the ever-more densely packed secondary security zone. Unfortunately, in these circumstances, that was a preferable risk, one that would have to be accepted until they could clear the entire area. For the moment, his priority was Third Avenue, where traffic was still moving and people were fleeing.

"Can you take it up and get a better look at Third Avenue?" he asked Severson. "I want you to stay above your current position, if possible."

CHAPTER 59

SOUTHWESTERN SUBURBS AND DOWNTOWN MINNEAPOLIS

While he waited for the second attack to begin, Fahkoury heard the first news report on the pickup's radio at 2:44 p.m. There had been two explosions at the Super Bowl, a smaller explosion followed by one much, much larger. The larger explosion was said to be a car bomb. The number of casualties was unknown. People were fleeing the area around the stadium as emergency crews and security forces moved toward the scenes of the explosions. Fahkoury savored the joyful news, expecting that in a matter of minutes, there would be a report of a third explosion at the Super Bowl, this time five blocks west of the stadium.

Before Fahkoury heard the first radio report, Mohammed was approaching his designated spot, carrying the smallest VBIED in the less roomy and less sturdy Yukon. Its destructive potential was dependent on timing and location more than force. He had been instructed to get as close as possible to the transit stops on Third Avenue and wait to detonate his bomb until either al-Rasheed signaled him or exactly two minutes after he heard the first VBIED explosion, whichever came first.

The specific delay was intentional, the result of careful calculation. The designated traffic and pedestrian pathways had been published weeks earlier by the Super Bowl Committee, information that Fahkoury had used to plot the location for the second VBIED. Fahkoury knew that once the initial shock gave way to flight response, people would scurry away from the stadium toward every possible means of escape—including the transit stops on Third Avenue.

When Mohammed had heard the unmistakable sound of the first car bomb barely one minute earlier, he was still several blocks south of the nearest transit stop. Seconds later, traffic was forced to a stop by people fleeing across Third Avenue, trying to put distance between themselves and the stadium. Mohammed was frantically trying to figure out how to get to the bus stop where Emir Fahkoury had told him to detonate the bomb when he noticed a policeman pointing a rifle at him, screaming for him to get out of the car. He knew he had to make a split-second decision, or he might not realize his chance to enter paradise.

CHAPTER 60

"**T**-Dub," Carpenter called out to Terrance Wood over on Third Avenue, "we've got a black SUV a couple of blocks south of your location. Do you have eyes on?"

"Roger that" came the deep reply from the Kentuckian. "The guy looks spooked, but that may be because there's a cop pointing a gun at him."

Severson had taken the $23 million military attack craft up an additional six hundred feet to get a better view of Third Avenue. He had been the first to notice the black SUV and immediately alerted Carpenter. Now, he was hovering over Third Avenue listening to the exchange between Carpenter and Wood. He could see the cop and people desperately running away from the SUV.

"The SUV looks like it's trying to veer around the car in front and move onto the sidewalk!" Severson shouted.

Mohammed reasoned that if he was going to have any shot at eternal bliss, he needed to deploy his bomb where his commander instructed. He decided his only chance was to pull the vehicle up onto the sidewalk and race ahead to the bus stop. He cranked the wheel and depressed the accelerator.

An instant before Mohammed made his move, al-Rasheed hit Send on his burner phone. Not hearing an explosion, he placed the phone to his ear. Oddly, he heard nothing.

"Smoke him, T-Dub!" Carpenter yelled out to Wood.

Before Mohammed even cleared the fender of the stopped car in front of him, Wood buried a fusillade of bullets into his upper body and the engine block of the SUV, stopping the truck before it was even halfway onto the sidewalk. Barely clinging to life, Mohammed desperately tried to summon the strength to depress the detonator still resting in his skyward-facing right palm. As life poured out of him, Mohammed glanced at the detonator and in one last effort began to curl his hand around it.

With the dying terrorist still in his sights, Wood detected the subtle movement and pumped the rest of his clip into the man's right shoulder, nearly severing the arm from the torso.

Carpenter immediately dispatched the SBSC team of explosive ordinance device specialists to the scene and then considered his next move. With an increasingly fluid situation developing over a larger area, he needed to change his team's assignments. The sight lines they had used to select their positions were now obscured by the chaos below, but before he made any changes, he called out to his team for input.

"OK, boys, we've got a royal clusterfuck on our hands. We might've just dodged our third explosion. The two guys with the car bombs are toast, but there's a third guy somewhere in the city. Where are the rest of them? The intel indicates at least a dozen people in the terrorist cell. That leaves no fewer than ten, including the guy from the parking ramp, still on the loose. SBSC is trying to move everyone to secure locations. Are you guys any good where you are now?"

"Negative. All I can see from here is chaos," Ben Doran, the fourth member of the team, indicated from his position atop a four-story building on the north side of Church Street. "Traffic stopped moving, and people are abandoning their cars and running in every direction. With people darting all over, I wouldn't have a clear shot at any car or any one person. Conditions have completely changed."

The other three members of the team reported similar situations and frustrations, confirming Carpenter's revised plan. "All right, I want you guys on the ground in the middle of it. If the terrorists are spotted, it'll be too difficult to hit them from your current locations. I'll let Zeman and the SBSC know. Remember, ROEs are shoot to kill, and don't waste time checking in!"

CHAPTER 81

The worsening news about casualties was virtually impossible to ignore, but Carpenter was starting to feel better about the security situation, if only slightly. There had been no additional incidents since the second car-bomb attempt almost twenty minutes earlier. All four members of his team were now on the ground, standing ready to respond to a handheld-weapons assault, a threat that would continue until the evacuation was completed. Severson continued to call out suspicious vehicles from aloft, but so far all had been checked out and cleared. Yet, despite the improving circumstances, they were not out of the woods. Unless the intelligence was wrong, there were still more terrorists out there, and Carpenter knew that somehow, they would be hearing from them.

Suddenly, Severson's startled voice came over his earpiece. "Sir, I just saw a fireball south of here. I…I'm guessing close to ten miles away! It looked like an explosion down near the airport!" Only a few seconds later, the pilot shouted, "There were just two more explosions!"

CHAPTER 62

SOUTHWESTERN SUBURBS

The Great American Mall was the last place Tyler Kennedy expected to find himself on Super Bowl Sunday. Normally he'd be relaxing after a morning of hockey, but this week the usual shinny of ex-college and NHL players had been scrapped due to the Super Bowl. He had toyed with the idea of just going out and finding another game, but the six-below-zero wind chill and the prospect of playing with a bunch of choppers were reason enough to stay home with his aunt, uncle, and cousins.

After a two-year stint of professional hockey in Europe right after college, Tyler had accepted a job with a commodity trader in Minneapolis eighteen months earlier. Since he was just twenty-four and new to the area, his aunt and uncle, John and Jane Hogan, insisted that he live with them and his cousins in their spacious home in a tony southwest suburb.

His aunt had moved back from Hoboken, New Jersey, to the Twin Cities shortly after September 11, 2001. On that fateful Tuesday, *Good Morning America* was on in the background as Jane was preparing to leave for work at a boutique advertising firm on Madison Avenue. When she heard the anchor announce that a plane had hit the World Trade Center, Jane went to the balcony of the condominium. She was still looking across the Hudson River at the smoke billowing from the North Tower when she glimpsed a second plane slam into the South Tower. Her mind immediately went to her fiancé who had left two hours earlier to catch United Airlines Flight 93 to San Francisco to oversee an acquisition for his law firm's largest client. Jane continued to listen to the news reports and was watching the scene across the river in horror when the South Tower collapsed. Less than four minutes later, Flight 93 crashed in a field in southwestern Pennsylvania. She left New York a week later, returning home to Minnesota and her family. After three difficult years, when she was only starting to regain some sense of normalcy, she met John Hogan. They were married in 2006, and, at John's urging, Jane named their first child after her fiancé.

A few hours earlier, his aunt and uncle had returned from the grocery market with supplies for the Super Bowl party they were hosting for three other families. Alex, their oldest, was not yet home from a sleepover, but Max and Ava were home, bored and causing trouble. Knowing that the chaos was only likely to increase, his aunt pleaded, "Tyler, why don't you take the kids to the mall for a couple of hours? All the stores are offering big sales this weekend, and they each still have some Christmas gift cards to use. Your uncle and I could use some peace and quiet to get this house cleaned and to prepare the food and drinks for the party. I'll give you some money so the kids can go on some of the rides; they like that. Tire them out a little bit. Just be home no later than four o'clock. The party starts at four thirty."

While the mall would not have been his first choice, Tyler loved spending time with his cousins, and it would at least give them something to do. He also had some gift cards left over from Christmas, and that money would go a lot further with the significant sales at the Great American Mall. Shortly before 1:00 p.m., he started out with his highly excited preteen cousins on the short drive to the GAM.

The Great American Mall, sometimes referred to locally as the "Great American Sprawl," had achieved iconic status. As the largest retail center in the United States—occupying more than 8.3 million square feet—the mall attracted some fifty-seven million visitors each year, making it one of the largest tourist attractions in the country. Its strategic location right next to the airport and the lack of sales tax on clothing drew visitors from all over the globe to the more than six hundred stores and restaurants, twenty-seven movie theaters, indoor amusement park, aquarium, and the spacious rotunda that hosted more than five hundred live performances annually.

On any given day, as many as one hundred thousand people passed through its doors, among them the thousands of walkers who would descend on the mall each day to circumambulate one or more of the mall's four 1.15-mile-circumference levels. Even without shoppers, the mall had a population equal to that of a small city, boasting more than fifteen thousand year-round employees and up to eighteen thousand during peak times. In fact, there were so many visitors to the mall each day that despite the cold Minnesota winters, only the entrances were heated. The heat generated by visitors, lighting fixtures, and sunlight through fourteen acres of skylights allowed the operators to maintain an average temperature of seventy degrees during the brutally cold Minnesota winters.

Although Tyler was aware of the terrorist alert, he was somewhat surprised by the increased level of security when they had arrived at the mall. He had heard terrorism experts on cable news previously talk about the Great American Mall as a prime terror target due to its iconic status and economic impact. In fact, only a few years earlier, one terror group had publicly urged an attack on the mall. Despite that, the latest news reports seemed to indicate the warning—as it pertained locally—was directed only at the Super Bowl. There had been no mention of the mall as a potential target. Still, he took note of the increased security and determined to remain alert for any trouble.

On a day when most of the local community was consumed with the Super Bowl, the mall-wide discount promotion had been a magnet for shoppers. The discounts had started gradually and increased throughout the course of the week, culminating in a mall-wide 50 percent discount on Super Bowl Sunday. Although the crowd was starting to thin as game time approached, the number of people there was a testament to the marketing axiom that everyone loved a great deal.

As the clock approached 3:00 p.m., Tyler was exhausted, but he was not so sure Ava and Max were anywhere close to running out of gas. Keeping a constant eye on his energetic cousins in this horde had proved to be tiresome work. Between dodging shoppers, burdened like pack mules with overstuffed bags of heavily discounted items, and the chaotic buzz of the amusement park, he was ready to leave. In spite of his fatigue, he found himself laughing at his cousins' screams as they passed over him for the umpteenth time on the roller coaster. He yawned and rose from the bench to greet them as the ride slowed to a stop.

As his cousins came running toward him, he broke the news. "OK, guys, we should get going."

"No!" they shouted in unison.

Thinking quickly, Tyler came up with a compromise. "I'll buy you guys some cotton candy if we leave right now, but no more begging to stay. Do we have a deal?" Their beaming faces and clapping hands cemented the terms.

Ava and Max led the procession as they walked through the amusement park toward the alluring cotton-candy counter at its outer edge. After he plunked down twelve dollars, Tyler passed out the loose bundles of the colored sugary treat and guided his cousins toward the exit for the west parking ramp, one of the four main exits.

CHAPTER 63

THE GREAT AMERICAN MALL

While the vans were closing in, Fahkoury had directed Omar, Wasim, and Hayder to enter the mall just a few minutes before 3:00 p.m. Each man carried an assault rifle, several pistols, and as much ammunition as they could carry underneath their bulky winter coats. The short head start would provide Fahkoury's initial wave of warriors an opportunity to penetrate deeper inside the mall. There, they would wait for their opening in the well-choreographed attack.

Not long after he entered the mall, a security guard spotted Hayder. The determination in the man's gait and the intense look on his face, together with the bulky winter jacket, drew her scrutiny. She and her colleagues on the mall's security were not the same hapless characters portrayed in pop culture. These men and women received hundreds of hours of training from current and former intelligence professionals, including counterterrorism tactics and behavioral detection. In an effort to enhance counterterrorism capabilities, the mall had adopted a unique and sometimes controversial security program, one often criticized for overzealousness. As the security guard considered her next step, she fleetingly reflected on the last time she had stopped someone for questioning. That experience had not turned out so well.

Two years ago, the guard had noticed a disheveled man walking in circles and muttering to himself. As she moved toward him, the man started screaming at her and several nearby shoppers. Although the man was eventually found to be concealing a six-inch knife in his pants, the mall settled the baseless discrimination and wrongful detention lawsuit. For her efforts, the guard had been placed on mandatory administrative leave for three months and nearly lost her job.

Now she was looking at someone who had all the markings of a potential problem. She decided she needed to ask the scowling man in the bulky coat a few questions, but with the memory of her past trouble fresh in her mind, she settled on a careful and slow approach.

Despite his apparent tunnel vision, Hayder had noticed the guard soon after he entered the mall. As he moved closer, he veered slightly away from her position on the side of the capacious hallway. As he was about to pass her, he noticed the guard start to advance toward him, but it was a cautious, hesitant advance. The guard's moment of hesitation was all that Hayder needed. Before she took her second careful step toward him, he ripped open his coat, revealing a folding-stock Kalashnikov AK-47 assault rifle.

This time the guard did not hesitate. In the swift, singular motion of a well-trained officer, she pulled her nine-millimeter pistol from its holster and fired a round at Hayder, still some forty-five feet away. The shot just missed. Before the guard had an opportunity to level her aim for another shot, Hayder's AK-47 spat out a burst of bullets, one of which struck the guard in the head, instantly killing her.

Fahkoury's orders had been for the assault team to wait until the explosions before firing, but Hayder had had no choice. Although it was still too early, Hayder decided there was no reason to stop shooting, and he began spraying bullets into the befuddled onlookers.

Less than a minute later, at precisely 3:00 p.m., and unaware of Hayder's unfolding problems, Fahkoury signaled over the two-way radios for Marwan and Khalid to launch the two drones from the east parking ramp. Marwan, his hands shaking with anticipation of the slaughter to follow, had some difficulty lighting the fuse to his pipe bomb, but he managed to get it lit on his second attempt. Within seconds, each drone, armed with a metal pipe bomb packed with gunpowder and set to explode upon expiration of a thirty-five-second fuse, was hovering above the vast section of skylights covering the center portion of the mall and the amusement park below.

While the drones were still in the air, Tariq, Hadi, and Fazal were piloting their bomb-laden vans toward three of the four main entrances. Fahkoury listened over the radio as the three drivers updated one another on their progress. The drivers were now all on the road that encircled the mall. Not much more than one minute after the drones were launched, Hadi reported he was almost in position on the east side, between the mall and the adjacent parking ramp. Seconds later, Tariq and Fazal confirmed the same from their respective locations on the west and south sides. At exactly 3:02 p.m., the three bombers exchanged shouts of "Allahu Akbar" and then detonated the bombs, instantly immolating themselves and sending a concussive and destructive force deep inside the mall.

CHAPTER 64

Tyler and his cousins had taken only a few steps from the kiosk at the edge of the amusement park—enough time for Max and Ava to rip open the packages and smear cotton candy on their fingers and mouths—when he grabbed their slender arms and stopped. Over the screams and laughter from the amusement park, he was certain he heard the unmistakable sound of gunfire—first a single shot and then multiple automatic shots. The shots came from somewhere between them and the parking ramp, he believed. As he was trying to determine his next move, Tyler heard a very loud noise. Turning back quickly, he saw a large portion of the skylights above the amusement park shatter, causing shards of glass to rain down. Almost instantly, there was a second blast on another section of the glass ceiling.

Mayhem reigned as people from the amusement park starting running from the falling glass. Tyler and his cousins found themselves between an advancing herd and the gunshots. Thinking quickly, Tyler's instinct was to not run with the pack but, rather, to find a place to hide his young cousins. Not only did he fear losing them in the mad rush of humanity but he also quickly assessed a concerted effort to push people out toward the exits and into the sights of the gunman. He decided that until he could figure out what was happening, he'd skip the "Run" portion of the "Run, Hide, Fight" campaign for now. He grabbed his cousins and ran back toward the amusement park and the control room he had noticed when they left the area on the trip to the cotton-candy kiosk.

Holding onto his cousins, Tyler fought through the onslaught of people until they arrived at the partially concealed structure. He led them around its jungle-painted walls until they found the door on the backside of the small building, partially obscured by two potted palm trees and opposite an ersatz cliff face. The door was locked, but beyond it he discovered a small concealed area between the control-room exterior and the fake rocks. The small hiding place was large enough to hold his cousins. As he was ushering his cousins into the farthest recesses of the hideout, Tyler heard and felt several large explosions, one right after the other, coming from different sides of the mall. Separate walls of dust and debris soon began moving toward them from different directions. As the rumbling subsided and his hearing gradually returned, Tyler heard more automatic gunfire. This time, it sounded as if the gunfire was coming from out in the circular corridor that ran between the stores on each level of the mall. They were basically trapped in the amusement park in the mall's interior, separated from the exits by what he was sure to be encroaching gunfire. While there was still a chance, he had to find a way out before the gunmen systematically hunted them down.

"Ava, Max, listen to me," Tyler said, "I don't know what's happening right now, but you are safe here. I need to try to find out what's going on and see if there is a way we can all get out of here, but I need you guys to stay put and be quiet. Don't move until I come back to get you. Can you do that for me?"

Through red-and-blue tear-streaked faces, the tremulous kids reluctantly nodded their consent. Before he left, Tyler kissed each of them on the forehead and said, "Everything's going to be OK. I will be back, I promise. I love you."

After he slid one of the potted trees into the narrow opening, Tyler was overcome with rage. He knew exactly what this was and remembered how much his aunt Jane had gone through. He was not going to see her suffer again. *There's no fucking way anyone is hurting those kids,* he told himself. He would get them out of there, but he was also aware of the urge overcoming him to take the fight to whoever was responsible for this.

CHAPTER 65

Although he could not see the damage, Fahkoury saw and heard the car bombs detonate. He was reliant on radio communications for insights on the assault phase of the attack inside the mall. Despite his meticulous planning, Fahkoury sensed from what he was hearing that there were problems.

The plan he had designed had four rapidly sequential phases. In the first phase, the first three members of the assault team were to enter the mall, concealing their automatic weapons as they made their way to the interior corridor ring. Meanwhile, two other warriors were to launch the drones. In this second phase, the pipe bombs carried by the drones would explode on the large skylight section in the center of the building, creating chaos below and driving people toward the exits and the larger VBIEDs that awaited them in the third stage.

The VBIEDs were expected to incinerate those already in the area as well as those who most quickly reacted to the pipe bombs above the center of the mall. The car bombs would also close off most means of egress. The resulting confusion and fear was expected to cause the survivors to congregate in the massive unimpacted corridors inside. From their strategic locations in those same corridors, the full assault team would block the undamaged exits and use the guns and any means necessary to kill as many surviving infidels in the deadliest phase of the attack before they themselves were killed.

While waiting for the vehicles to get into position, he had listened as the first wave of the assault team—Omar, Wasim, and Hayder—entered from the ground level of the west parking ramp. Omar and Wasim successfully moved into their initial assigned position at the north entrance, but Hayder had apparently run into a problem. For some reason, he opened fire before the pipe bombs exploded. Now Hayder was out of position, potentially compromising Fahkoury's master plan. And that wasn't the only problem.

In addition to launching the drones from the uppermost level of the east parking ramp, Marwan and Khalid were to serve as the second wave of the assault team. However, due to the closeness in time between launching the drones and the car bombs, they were not able to enter the mall until after the VBIEDs exploded. They had been forced to take temporary shelter in the rear of the east parking ramp, the farthest point from the blast area of the VBIEDs. As the dust started to clear, they were expecting to be able to use the undamaged third-level walkway to get inside. Instead, they found that there was no way into the mall.

Based on their reconnaissance, Fahkoury had positioned the more powerful ANNM bomb on the busier, eastern side of the building. The force of the blast that Hadi initiated was, however, much greater than Fahkoury had anticipated. The mixture of ammonium nitrate and nitromethane nearly collapsed the entire eastern exterior, including extensive and unexpected damage the walkway connecting the third level of the east parking ramp to the mall that Khalid and Marwan were planning to use.

From his location across the street, Fahkoury was hearing Khalid inform the others that he and Marwan were still outside the mall, unable to break through the badly damaged exterior. They had been able to use the stairway at the back of the ramp, but when they arrived at the ground level, they were confronted with a pile of rubble. They were just now moving and climbing over the debris, a process that was causing them a delay of precious minutes. When they finally announced they were inside the mall, the news did little to quell Fahkoury's anger.

Besides killing anyone in their path, Marwan and Khalid were expected to provide rear support for Hayder as he moved deeper into the mall. Their delay left Hayder, already out of position, even more exposed to counterattack from the security guards already patrolling the mall and the additional ones sure to follow. More importantly, it was impairing the assault team's opportunity to quickly massacre the infidels trapped inside. Until Marwan and Khalid made their way to the north entrance, two of the others would have to stand guard there, leaving only one warrior to hunt and kill. Fahkoury knew the longer this went on, the more likely it would become that the Crusaders and Jews would be able to scatter and hide until help arrived.

Fahkoury had told his men to plan on having no more than fifteen minutes before the police and, possibly, the military arrived to reinforce the mall security personnel. Now, already half of that time was gone.

CHAPTER 66

THE SUPER BOWL AND THE GREAT AMERICAN MALL

Carpenter had to decide quickly. He knew instantly that the explosions off to the south were not accidents—they were related to the attack at the Super Bowl. The question was whether they were part of a larger attack elsewhere or they were meant as a diversion before the attack resumed in earnest at the Super Bowl. The improving situation at the stadium was still sketchy. Tens of thousands of people had yet to be evacuated, and at least one terrorist remained at large. The possibility of a second wave of attacks during the evacuation was high. His decision was made seconds later when reports started coming in about explosions at the Great American Mall.

"Severson, it's Carpenter. I need you to pick me up at the command-center helipad. Have the second bird assume your position over the security zone."

"Roger that," the pilot replied.

"Zeman," he barked to the SBSC chief on the opposite side of the room, "there's an attack at the mall, and I'm heading there. Terrance Wood will be your primary contact. Have comms link him up with you right now."

"Guys," he called out on his team's secure channel, "there have been multiple explosions south of here. Initial reports indicate it's the Great American Mall. My gut tells me this is the main attack. I'm heading there now."

"You taking anyone with you?" Doran asked. "I can probably get there in five or less."

"Not enough time to wait. Plus, I might be wrong; the explosions there might be a diversion for a second wave here. On top of that, we know at least one guy is still running around. We're not in the clear here by any stretch. I need you guys here in case anything else goes down. I'll let you know if we need to change plans. T-Dub, you coordinate with Zeman."

Severson was lowering the helicopter onto the pad just as Carpenter was signing off. Before Severson touched down, Carpenter heard the first report about gunfire inside the mall. As the chopper lifted and raced south, Carpenter called Patrick with an update and asked him to clear the way for his arrival. There would be no time for bullshit when he got there.

The SBSC team had linked up the chopper's communications with the mall's security unit. As they neared the massive dust cloud billowing high into the air, Carpenter and Severson listened to reports of significant casualties and heavy gunfire inside the mall. At least a few members of the security team were among the casualties. The other members were trying to get control of the escalating madness inside and outside the building. The mall security chief, Betsy Ford, told them there were five explosions: two smaller bombs on the skylight section at the center of the mall, followed by three larger ones outside the southern, eastern, and western exterior walls.

As they neared the building, the scene was worse than Carpenter had imagined. Through the haze of smoke and debris that hung menacingly over the area, he could see several fires burning among the rubble that had once been three sides of the mall. The eastern side had almost entirely collapsed, and the southern and western sides were not in much better shape. On the positive side, Carpenter didn't see any vehicles near the mall, other than those exposed in the crumpled parking ramps. The chief had done a good job of securing the perimeter from all nonemergency and nonpolice vehicles.

While the threat from additional VBIEDs had been reduced, he had no information about the threats that resided inside the mall. Security had yet to determine the number of shooters. He briefly considered lowering himself through the gaping hole in the skylights at the center of the roof but swiftly brushed that plan aside. He'd be a sitting duck on that route. Instead, he instructed Severson to land on the undamaged north side, where the mall security team had set up a temporary command center. He'd have to get in that way.

He grabbed his weapons and jumped out of the helicopter before Severson even had it on the ground. As Severson pulled the aircraft up, the mall security chief moved toward Carpenter.

"Sir, I'm Betsy Ford, head of security here."

"Preston Carpenter; call me PJ. What's the sit-rep, Chief?"

"I've got twenty-three members of my team inside the mall, and there are thirteen of us outside, including three of us who came from our headquarters across the street. The traffic ring around the mall has been cleared of all undamaged cars, and I've got six cars blocking the entrances to the mall roads. Communications are mostly down with the team inside the mall. It's likely that the communications center was damaged by the explosions. I'm using cell phones to communicate with my team inside."

"What are you hearing from inside?"

"In terms of shooters, I have reports of at least four or five gunmen, including at least one just inside the north entrance. Right now, I don't know the exact locations of the other shooters. As I said, our communications are limited to cell phones, so I don't have a full picture. My understanding is that gunfire erupted shortly after the large explosions. Gunmen moved through the mall, killing anyone they could on the ground floor. From what I'm hearing, my team is trying to shepherd people into larger stores on upper levels and placing other members at the entrances to repel the gunmen. My team is trained for an active shooter situation, though not one that also includes bombs on the outside of the building."

"What about access to the building?"

"There are entrances on each side of the building, six in total. There are only ground-floor entrances here at the north side and on the south side, each one serving as a public and private transportation drop-off and pickup. On the east and west sides, there are entrances at the ground floor and at the third level of the adjoining parking ramps, for a total of four. The entrance on the south side and the four entrances from the parking ramps are severely damaged, if not completely destroyed. The same is true for the smaller ground-floor entrances on those sides that are reserved for store and mall employees."

"Have you tried to enter here through the north entrance?"

"I have three people stationed outside the entrance, but as I mentioned, there's at least one shooter somewhere just inside. Two of my people were shot at when they tried to enter. One of them was hit in the shoulder. We can see people lying on the floor inside, either wounded or deceased. I was told not to try any further attempts at entry until you arrived."

Although barely ten minutes had passed since the first explosions, Chief Ford had done a remarkable job understanding and responding to the situation. Carpenter now had a pretty clear picture of how this attack had been planned and what the end game was. Getting people out of the line of fire into an area that could be secured, at least temporarily, was a good first step, but he knew the gunmen would systematically move to the upper levels after they had killed everyone they could on the ground floor. He had to assume the terrorists would move fast to kill as many as possible. The terrorists knew and expected they would be killed in the counteroffensive.

"What other resources do you have?" he asked.

"Local police forces are stretched pretty thin due to the Super Bowl. A lot of officers are helping out downtown as part of the security team there, so most forces are keeping their people close to home until we figure out what's going on. I asked them to send anyone they could. I'm promised there are two SWAT teams on the way from Saint Paul. The first SWAT team should be here within fifteen minutes. Ambulances are staging across the street where medical personnel are treating those who we have gotten out of the mall so far, and waiting for more."

They could not afford to wait for the relatively skilled SWAT teams. And Carpenter knew the mall security and local beat cops were no match for this situation. He said to the security chief, "Here's what we're going to do."

CHAPTER 67

THE GREAT AMERICAN MALL

Tyler stayed low and hidden as he edged out of the amusement park and closer to the corridor that bisected the ground floor. A cacophony of gunfire and intermittent screams rushed toward him from opposite directions. There must be more than one shooter, he concluded, and they were methodically hunting people down.

Before the shooters moved into the amusement park, he had to find a way out. Going back through the amusement park was not a good option; glass was still intermittently falling from the skylights, which covered most of the area. The only way to the outside was through the mall exterior, but the thunderous explosions he had heard had undoubtedly damaged large parts of the building. Until he knew the best way out, his cousins would be safest where they were.

As he made his way out into the corridor, he noticed the first bodies. At seven, including two young children close to his cousins' ages, he stopped counting. With blood pooling beneath their bodies, each appeared the victim of multiple gunshot wounds. The next body he saw belonged to a female. He recognized the mall security uniform. She held a pistol in her motionless hand. Tyler moved closer and noticed she had been hit three times, including once through the neck, a shot that had also pierced her communications equipment. He gently pried the gun from her hand, silently thankful it was a model he was familiar with.

As an avid hunter, Tyler had readily accepted a professor's challenge to a shooting contest when he was in college in Maine. The weapon of choice had been a Sig Sauer P239, a common firearm with the police. The shellacking from the professor in that first contest fueled him, and he narrowly beat the professor the second time. After the fourth match, the professor waved the white flag; Tyler's shots either hit the bull's-eye or inside the nine-point ring on every shot from twenty-five yards.

With the pistol now in his hands, he instantly felt better. He checked the ten-round clip. The single-stack magazine still contained nine nine-millimeter bullets. There was no spare clip on the guard. If he needed them, he'd have to make each shot count. His first priority was finding a safe way out. But he wasn't going to hesitate if he encountered trouble along the way.

Liking his improved chances, he started moving toward the main entrance on the west side of the building, but the cloud of smoke and dust obscuring his view only worsened as he crept closer. Leaving that way didn't appear a viable option. The next closest exit was at the mall's north side. Judging by the sound of the screams and automatic bursts of gunfire, he concluded at least one gunman was in that direction and not too far away.

He saw no signs of life as he moved farther north, carefully choosing shelter behind the kiosks selling hats, scarves, phone cases, and other assorted items that littered the hallway. He dipped into several storefront entrances as he closed the gap with the source of the gunfire. The body count continued to rise, but the screams seemed more distant. The gunfire, however, was drawing closer. He darted back into the hallway for a wider view. Peeking around the palm tree inside the large pot he was using for cover, he caught his first glimpse of the shooter. The gunman's back was to him, and he was firing an automatic weapon, one that looked eerily similar to the AK-47s Tyler had seen in so many films.

The gunman suddenly stopped shooting and reached for one of the several magazines that were hooked inside his belt. In the ensuing quiet, Tyler could hear sobs and desperate pleas for the man to stop, but he could not see the people behind those cries. He felt slightly ashamed for not shooting that instant and possibly saving lives, but he knew that if he didn't take this guy down, none of them were likely to survive. The man was more than fifty yards away. Tyler needed to get closer.

The man completed the exchange and was now shouting into a handheld radio. By the sound of his voice and the gestures he was making, the man was clearly agitated with the person on the other end. While the man was distracted on the radio, Tyler dashed forward to another kiosk, fifteen or more yards closer. He was now close enough to take a shot, but the man was partially blocked by a four-sided store directory. Either the man would have to move, or Tyler would have to risk getting into a better position.

As Tyler was deciding what to do, the man stuffed the radio into his pants pocket, moved away from the directory, and raised his assault rifle at the second level of the mall. With the gun on automatic fire, the shooter began firing off a 360-degree barrage of bullets at the partially exposed balcony above. Tyler had just enough warning to duck behind the kiosk before he was in the man's line of sight. When he calculated the shooter had moved past him, he chanced a quick peek. The man's back was once again to him. Using the loud staccato bursts to mask his approach, Tyler jumped up, ran several steps, sighted the man's head, and fired. The man's head exploded a millisecond later, an instant before his lifeless body crumpled to the ground.

Tyler sprinted forward and ripped the semiautomatic from underneath the corpse, forcefully kicking the stiff twice in the ribs for good measure. A measure of tranquility descended on the immediate area as he assessed his next move. He could still hear occasional gunfire off in the distance, possibly from one of the upper floors. He decided to head back to check on his cousins. As he took his first cautious steps, he heard a whimper. Dropping down to his knees, Tyler saw a middle-aged woman huddled underneath the couch a few feet to his left.

"Are you OK?" he whispered. The woman just stared vacantly as he moved closer. "Are you injured?" She shook her head. "We have to get you out of here. Come with me."

The woman reluctantly abandoned her hiding place. "Where are we going?" she muttered between silent sobs.

"Back to check on my cousins. They're hiding not far from here."

His cousins shrieked when they saw Tyler's head peer around the corner. "Sssh!" he said. "I want you to meet my friend Emily." He ushered the woman into view. "She has a son who's your age, Max. Emily is going to stay with you while I try to find a way out for all of us."

After his cousins had settled down, and Emily was in the small space with them, Tyler moved back into the corridor. He moved several hundred feet toward the north entrance and then stopped at a store entrance for a quick reconnaissance. Looking back, he noticed another figure through the dusty haze. The figure was moving cautiously, deliberately scanning side to side and holding a rifle in front of him. With nowhere to go without being noticed, Tyler ducked into the store and hid inside the closest rack of clothes.

CHAPTER 68

Almost immediately after the massive car bombs had exploded, people started rushing toward the north entrance. Omar and Wasim had been there waiting and ready, killing dozens of the charging infidels before the rest of them retreated into the mall. Now there was nobody left to shoot.

Their orders were to guard the north entrance until Hayder showed up. Then, one man would be left guarding the entrance, while the other two moved to the upper floors. This process was supposed to repeat later when Marwan and Khalid showed up. Only moments earlier, they finally heard from Hayder. He had been delayed and was, once again, moving toward them. Hayder also said Marwan and Khalid were finally inside the building and should get to the north entrance shortly after he did.

Thinking there was no reason for both of them to wait for Hayder, Omar decided to improvise. He told Wasim to guard the entrance until Hayder arrived; he was going to the upper floors. As Omar worked his way back into the mall, Wasim moved farther away from the doors and into better cover from any enemy forces that were sure to enter at some point. Omar had not been gone long when Wasim noticed two heads pop up inside a store. The store was less than a hundred feet away but farther from the entrance that he had been ordered to guard. After a moment's pause, the temptation to kill infidels proved too strong.

Carpenter's original plan had been for the security guards to provide cover while he slipped inside, but he called it off when he spotted movement from outside the entrance. He could see the man's head and upper torso, but the rest of him was partially hidden behind a large fountain at the center of the atrium. Since the guy wasn't running or hiding, Carpenter concluded he was one of the terrorists. After motioning for the guards to stand down, he snuck inside the entrance and slid in behind the fountain between him and the terrorist. He dropped down and crawled a few feet around the circular water display to where he expected a cleaner view. The terrorist was moving deeper into the mall, but the new vantage point offered Carpenter a full-on view from perhaps seventy-five yards. The AK-47 in the man's hands and the pistol tucked in his waist removed any doubt as to the man's intentions. The man was moving away and to Carpenter's right, purposefully creeping toward one of the stores. Just as the man started to lift his rifle into firing position, Carpenter squeezed off two silenced rounds into the man's skull.

Before the man's body even hit the floor, Carpenter heard a single gunshot close by and off to the west. That was almost immediately followed by the unmistakable staccato of automatic gunfire coming from on one of the upper levels, off toward the east side of the mall. He headed west, determined to eliminate the most immediate threat first.

CHAPTER 69

Tyler caught something out of the corner of his eye. He parted the clothes for a better look and noticed another gunman. This one was coming toward him from the north. "Shit!" he said to himself, realizing he was now stuck between two encroaching killers. He tried to calm his breathing as he watched the second shooter dart across the corridor toward the store's front entrance. Just outside, the man paused. Maintaining a narrow slit between the hanging clothes, Tyler saw the man was dressed in black tactical gear, expertly hovering his finger over the trigger of an assault rifle. Something in the way the man moved told him this guy was not part of the terrorist group. Still, he couldn't be sure. He was trying to decide whether to shoot him or chance a whispered call when the man swiftly sidestepped into the store and hid behind a display table, slightly in front of and less than five feet away from Tyler.

"Don't move one muscle or you're dead," Tyler warned the man. The man didn't flinch.

"You'd be dead already if I wanted to kill you," the man calmly said as he remained focused on the corridor.

"Who are you?" Tyler asked between gritted teeth.

"I'm one of the good guys. If you were a terrorist, you would have tried to shoot me before I even entered the store. Since you didn't, I didn't shoot you first. I assume you're either a security guard or just some guy in the wrong place at the wrong time."

"My name is Tyler Kennedy," he said after thinking it over, "and yeah, I'm in the wrong place. I'm here with my two young cousins. They're hiding back at the amusement park with a woman I helped." He gestured in the opposite direction from which the man had arrived. "I left them to try to find a way out. The closest exit was clouded by dust and didn't seem any good, so I headed toward the north exit to check it out. I picked up a gun from a dead security guard and followed the gunshots. I killed one of the motherfuckers."

When he made his way into the mall, Carpenter had stepped over the dead terrorist, giving him a good indication there was at least one friendly inside. That comforting thought caused him to move even slower and more cautiously, however. Sometimes even well-trained officers succumbed to high-stress situations like this. The last thing he needed was to surprise a friendly with an itchy trigger finger. Things became even more dicey when he noticed two terrorists coming toward him.

Carpenter had assumed that whoever had killed the terrorist had also seen the two approaching terrorists and found a spot to hide. While he was keeping one eye on the distant terrorists, Carpenter looked for the potential ally and a place to launch his counterattack. His attention had been drawn to the dimly lit entrance of the clothing store on the far side of the corridor. He would launch his attack from there, he quickly decided. As he made his way toward the wide front entrance, he looked through the floor-to-ceiling glass window and noticed some movement among the clothes hanging on a circular rack, just steps inside the store. He had found his potential ally. The decision to enter without lethal force had been a calculated one, but it had paid off.

"I'm Preston Carpenter; friends call me PJ. There's more help on the way, but in the meantime, I'm it. Listen, there are two guys coming this way. After I take them out, we'll go get your cousins and the lady."

"I only saw one guy," Tyler said.

"Well, now there are at least two," Carpenter said. "Move back into the store, and stay put until the all clear. I'll come back as soon as I take care of these two. Got it?" Carpenter didn't wait for an answer.

Carpenter stooped low and edged out into the mall, taking refuge behind one of two large sofas arranged in the center of the hallway. He raised his head and saw that the terrorists were still on opposite sides of the sixty-foot-wide corridor, one about five paces in front of the other. He would wait a bit to make sure nobody was behind them. He dropped back down and was turning his head to check on Tyler when the kid dove in next to him. He gave Tyler a pissed-off look and whispered, "I still see only two guys, but they're coming toward us from opposite sides of the corridor, checking out each store as they pass by. They're about seventy yards out."

"Which one do you want me to take?"

Who the fuck is this guy? "Can you use that thing?"

"You saw my proof. I popped that asshole from thirty-plus yards, one shot."

Like it or not, Carpenter thought, he was stuck with him, but once he popped these two guys, Tyler was going back to his cousins. The police SWAT teams should be on the scene any minute. He would call for officers to come in and escort Tyler and his crew to safety outside while he hunted the rest of the killers. That would have to wait, however, because the immediate threat was now only three stores from their location. The first terrorist was no more than a hundred feet away, and the second not far behind, still on the opposite side of the hallway.

"All right, on my call, you take the guy on the left while I take the guy on the right," Carpenter said, figuring since the shot on the left was slightly closer, it would be a bit easier. It wouldn't matter, anyway; he would have enough time to shoot both of them. His guy would be down before the hot-shot kid even pulled the trigger.

As the two men edged closer, Carpenter nodded to Tyler to get ready. He held up three fingers and shook his hand, letting Tyler know they'd be using a countdown. Tyler nodded his understanding and gripped the pistol in his left hand. Just as Carpenter folded his third finger, he and Tyler simultaneously rose from behind the couch. In one smooth, continuous motion, Carpenter sighted his target, spat out a quick double-tap with his assault rifle, and then swung it around to where Tyler's target should have been.

Carpenter looked down and then over at Tyler, who was scanning the area, alertly looking for other terrorists. He had heard Tyler's gun fire twice and assumed he'd missed the target, but the terrorist was slumped on his side, exposing distinctive gunshots wounds to the chest and jaw. Tyler hadn't missed; two shots, two direct hits.

"Nice job" was all Carpenter said.

With these two terrorists no longer a concern, he and Tyler listened and searched the area, making sure there were no upright terrorists in range. For the moment, everything was quiet. Carpenter used the solitude to check in with Chief Ford. He reported there were four terrorists down; the number of others was unknown. Based upon gunfire heard earlier, he believed there was at least one terrorist still at large, somewhere on a higher level. When he finished his side of the update, he asked expectantly, "Do we have any backup yet?"

"The first SWAT unit just arrived," Chief Ford said, "and the second SWAT team is pulling in now. Police officers from two different forces are now helping to secure the outside. Should I send the first SWAT team inside?"

"No! Let me speak to the commander first," Carpenter said.

"Sir, this is Commander Brian Liesch," the man said an instant later.

"Commander, I want you and the other SWAT team now arriving to enter the building and secure the ground floor. There are four tangos down. We don't know how many more are inside. Gunshots on one of the upper levels indicate at least one. Work to clear the ground floor, and get as many people out as possible. You will find a young man, two children, and a woman behind a small control-room building on the western edge of the amusement park. Get to them as quickly as possible."

"Yes, sir. Where will you be?"

"I'm going to the upper levels. Tell your men I'm the guy dressed all in black and to expect to hear some gunfire up there."

Carpenter signed off and looked at Tyler. "Let's go get your cousins."

CHAPTER 70

Right after he left Wasim, Omar spotted a group of people on the second floor, but since pumping two forty-round magazines into the fleeing crowd, he had found targets hard to come by. He pursued some of the survivors into a large department store, but he'd been forced to retreat when his attempt to go in after them drew heavy fire. He was hesitant to force his way into that store or any other until reinforcements arrived.

But as he waited for a response from his brothers, Omar was coming to the realization that he was left alone to hunt the infidels. Wasim wasn't responding, and neither was Hayder. Marwan and Khalid had checked in just a few minutes before but hadn't responded to his latest call. Omar had to assume the few random gunshots he had heard most recently were probably from the enemy. It didn't matter; he welcomed death, but first he intended to bring more of it to the immoral Americans.

The realization he was alone only stirred his wrath more. It was also liberating. No longer did he have to worry about assigned positions and teamwork; he could just hunt and kill. He decided he would work his way back toward the north entrance. If Wasim was dead, he knew it would only be a matter of time before the pigs realized they could get out through the only undamaged exit. He might also run into Khalid and Marwan, if they were still alive.

Omar determinedly slammed in a fresh magazine and started out. When he was almost to the expansive atrium at the north entrance, a band of people came around the curve of the hallway, heading toward the elevator. They saw him at the same time and started running back to the west. He fired a quick burst, ripping through three of them before the rest disappeared around the corner. Omar gave chase, determined to close the considerable gap and slaughter every last one of them.

CHAPTER 71

PJ and Tyler were making their way toward the amusement park and Tyler's cousins when they heard a burst of automatic gunfire above and behind them, back toward the north entrance. Another quick burst, followed by on-rushing screams, confirmed the gunman was coming their way, by the sound of it, on the partially exposed second level.

This time Carpenter did not even bother to tell Tyler to stay put. "Come on, follow me over to that escalator! We don't have much time!" he said over his shoulder.

The gunshots were becoming louder and the torrents longer. Between the barrages, harrowing shrieks and shouts of "Allahu Akbar!" echoed down from the balcony. Carpenter had encountered this behavior before and knew this guy beckoned martyrdom and was planning on going to paradise in a glorious rage. As a group of terror-stricken people ran past on the balcony above, Carpenter smashed the Mollyguards—the protective plastic coverings for the escalator control switches—hit the emergency shutoff buttons for both the up and down escalators, and then quickly explained his plan.

Tyler scampered up the escalator closest to Carpenter's position below. As he approached the top, he looked over to Carpenter, hidden behind a store corner, and waited for further instructions. Carpenter pointed two fingers at his eyes and then pointed above toward the second-level balcony, indicating he would soon have the terrorist in his sights. He motioned Tyler to move higher up on the disabled escalator. With both Carpenter's fully loaded MK23 and the security guard's P239 in his hands, Tyler inched up the last few steps until his head was less than two feet from the surface.

Tyler looked back at Carpenter, who was holding up the familiar sign of three fingers. Tyler nodded, and Carpenter began the countdown. Before Carpenter ran out of fingers, a torrent of bullets pinged off the escalator guards—their destination, a middle-aged woman who looked fleetingly into Tyler's eyes before falling facedown on the top steps of the adjacent escalator. Carpenter wasted no time bombarding the terrorist with his own salvo. As expected, the terrorist immediately moved to the edge of the balcony and began firing at Carpenter's location—Tyler's cue. Tyler pushed himself up, swiftly set his feet, and, from less than five yards away, emptied the ten-round magazine from Carpenter's semiautomatic pistol into the terrorist's left side.

Carpenter came up as Tyler was staring down at the bullet-ridden jihadist. "Are you OK?" he asked.

"Yeah, I'm fine." Tyler paused a moment. "But that woman looked at me just before she died. I'm not sure I'll ever forget it."

CHAPTER 72

SECURE SITE NEAR THE GREAT AMERICAN MALL

Two hours later, Carpenter emerged from the communications center, which was located in the temporary holding station that had been established at a big-box retail center a half mile from the Great American Mall. A light snow had begun to gently fall, offering a semblance of serenity after the horrors of the past few hours. He had just briefed Patrick and the president on the worst terrorist attack on US soil since September 2001.

The mall and the immediately surrounding area remained on lockdown, but the entire building had been cleared. Not long after Tyler shot the terrorist at the top of the escalator, Brian Liesch, the SWAT-team commander, confirmed that the ground floor was secure, before he and his team moved to the upper floors with the assistance of three late-arriving tactical units. Twenty minutes later, the all clear was sounded, and the evacuation and triage processes began in earnest. The number of casualties would not be known for hours, if not longer.

Over at the Super Bowl, Terrance Wood had reported there was no sign of the terrorist from the parking ramp. A Honda Civic parked nearby was found with a pistol on the front seat and five hundred rounds of ammunition in the trunk. An assault rifle was found not far away, next to the parapet wall. Otherwise, the situation was similar. Buses continued to evacuate the rapidly diminishing number of people downtown. As the emergency crews continued to attend to victims, missing persons reports were mounting. The casualties at the Super Bowl were rising rapidly and were estimated to be in the hundreds.

After he hung up with the president, Carpenter went looking for Tyler. When he found him, Tyler's aunt and uncle had just arrived at the holding station, and Emily had already been reunited with her family. Upon seeing Carpenter, Tyler broke away from the tight familial embrace that typified profound gratefulness for having endured tragedy. Carpenter put his left arm around Tyler's shoulder and extended his right hand to Jane and John Hogan, telling them the country was indebted to their nephew for his heroism.

"Young man," he said after he and Tyler had stepped away, "what you did in there was pretty special. Your calmness and clear thinking helped save a lot of lives. You should be proud of yourself. I want you to know how much I appreciate what you did."

"Thank you, PJ, for everything, especially making sure my cousins made it out safely. I won't ever forget that."

"Like I said, I'm the one who should be thanking you. I know you want to get home, but a very important person would like to thank and speak to you about what you did in there. OK?"

"Whatever you need, PJ."

CHAPTER 73

WESTERN WISCONSIN

Fahkoury fumed as he traveled east on I-94 in the 1993 Toyota Camry he had hotwired in the hotel parking lot. He had stuck around long enough to hear Omar futilely trying to summon his fellow warriors. Yes, the attacks had been successful as most would use the term, but his plans had not measured up to his expectations. Most of his ire was directed at the mall operation. The early reports were short on details, but he knew the casualties wouldn't be nearly to the thousands he had projected. He had seen the helicopter descend from his position opposite the north entrance. He watched the man jump from the airship and move confidently toward the mall, showing no trace of fear. The man must be especially skilled, he decided, for not long after that man's arrival, his plan quickly deteriorated.

Although his expectations for the attack at the Super Bowl had not been as high, that too had not gone as planned. One of the car bombs failed to detonate, and from what he was hearing on the radio, some quick countermeasures spared too many infidels. He wondered if the man from the helicopter had had a hand in that too. Maybe he had underestimated the Americans.

Yet, he reminded himself, America had still been dealt a crushing blow. The news reports estimated the death toll could reach the hundreds, with many more wounded. His attacks demonstrated that al Qaeda was still a force in global jihad, a position bolstered by the fact it remained the only group to have successfully carried out a large-scale attack on American soil. The Americans would soon learn this war was not over; there was more misery to come. He actually managed to laugh when he heard a caller to a radio program complain that the Super Bowl might be canceled.

He had designed a plan to take advantage of congestion, chaos, and confusion. Perhaps his planning had proved too difficult for his men to execute, although a lesser plan, he reasoned, would have lacked the dramatic and everlasting effects these attacks would have, no matter how successful they were deemed. Despite the problems, his men had performed bravely, and they were now *shahid*, to be celebrated by all true believers. In a way he envied them, but Aziz and the shura had other plans for him.

He would stop at the pickup location, only briefly, to see if al-Rasheed was there. Together, they had pulled off the largest attacks inside the United States since 2001. He hoped his fellow warrior would be by his side again when he orchestrated the next crushing blow to the infidels. He also hoped he would somehow cross paths with the man from the helicopter again. He had a feeling another encounter with the American was in his future. *The next time, there will be no mistakes*, he promised himself.

EPILOGUE

THE WHITE HOUSE

The Super Bowl had just concluded, played before a full-capacity crowd that was brave enough to stare down the harrowing events three weeks earlier and enticed by heavily discounted tickets. The game itself was an intensely dull affair, won by Carpenter's Falcons by a score of 9–7 over Patrick's Steelers. The hundred dollars Carpenter won did little to salve the dishonor he felt for having let the nation down.

Over the past three weeks, he had rebuffed Patrick's attempts to impress upon him that the attacks would have been much worse but for his quick analysis and reactions. The president repeatedly told him the same thing and did so again before they all settled in to watch the game. At a certain level, Carpenter knew they were right. But he saw things differently. For him, mitigating an attack was not a victory; only stopping the bastards beforehand was. And he and the rest of the intelligence community had failed to piece things together in time to stop these attacks. On top of that, he felt he should have reacted quicker at the Super Bowl, and, when only three terrorists had been accounted for, been quicker to realize the possibility of another attack elsewhere. President Madden and Patrick both properly dismissed those sentiments as absurd. Deep down, Carpenter supposed they were right. Nothing in the intelligence pointed to an attack at either location. In many ways, it was a miracle he had been there to limit the damage. Still, he held himself responsible for the deaths of at least 179 innocent victims and the 468 others who had been wounded, a good many of them seriously.

Nearly everyone else saw it the same way Patrick and the president did. For the past three weeks, and again following a pregame tribute, the media and the pundits on cable news effused praise on Super Bowl security chief Mark Zeman and the mall's Betsy Ford for their quick thinking and decisive actions, moves that had certainly saved hundreds, if not thousands, of lives. Zeman and Ford unwillingly accepted their new status as celebrities, prohibited by the highest authority from disclosing Carpenter's involvement.

That he had been so close to the terrorist they still only knew as Mumeet pissed Carpenter off even more. Not long after the attacks, the Honda Civic was traced to the farmstead, and a search for the old pickup truck began immediately. A local policeman found it three hours later in the hotel parking lot. Carpenter imagined Mumeet sitting directly across the street, watching as he arrived in the helicopter at the mall's north entrance. He had been no more than three hundred yards from the terrorist and had not known it.

Six days after the attack, al Qaeda officially claimed responsibility. By then, forensics had already matched the car bombs to Mumeet's prior work. In a statement released to Al Jazeera, Aziz praised "Mumeet and his brave warriors for the crushing blow they delivered to the heart of the Great Satan." In calling for all Muslims to join the fight, Aziz promised the attack was just the first of its kind that the terror organization would strike in a renewed battle against the Crusaders. Aziz's involvement in the terror organization was no longer a question.

Social media was abuzz with praise for al Qaeda, and there were reports that the core group and its affiliates were garnering new recruits and funding in degrees not even seen by the Islamic State at its peak. There was much speculation as to Mumeet's true identity and when he and Aziz—who was being fondly referred to as sheikh—would strike again. One thing was clear, however: al Qaeda was, once again, the undisputed leader of global jihad and one that had reinvented itself with a renewed focus to commit acts of terror on a grand scale.

The attacks had served as a wake-up call to the country and, unlike terrorist attacks against military bases, gay nightclubs, and romantic European cities, Carpenter expected these attacks would not be so easily forgotten. Almost every American shopped at malls, and a great number attended the occasional high-profile professional or college sporting event. Although the attacks had been centered on a large metropolitan area, the terrorists had also killed and operated in rural America. Terrorism was no longer just a big-city problem. *Maybe*, he thought, *the entire country and civilized world would finally unite with the courage and stiff resolve needed to defeat this enemy.* But somehow, he doubted it.

"PJ," Patrick said, sensing Carpenter was again replaying the horrific events in his head, "enough of this bullshit. This would have been much worse if you and your team weren't there; that's a pure and simple fact. The truth of the matter is that we were lucky. Now we need to focus on finally putting al Qaeda out of business. Sometime soon, you're gonna get Mumeet, Aziz, and the rest of these bastards."

About that, Carpenter had absolutely no doubt.

Made in the USA
Lexington, KY
21 December 2017